continued . . .

Ace Books by Erin Lindsey

THE BLOODBOUND
THE BLOODFORGED
THE BLOODSWORN

THE
BLOODSWORN

Erin Lindsey

ACE
New York

ACE
Published by Berkley
An imprint of Penguin Random House LLC
375 Hudson Street, New York, New York 10014

Copyright © 2016 by Erin Lindsey

ISBN: 9780425276303

First Edition: October 2016

Printed in the United States of America
1 3 5 7 9 10 8 6 4 2

Cover illustration by Lindsey Look
Book design by Kelly Lipovich
Map by Cortney Skinner

This is a work of fiction. Names, characters, places, and incidents either are the product
of the author's imagination or are used fictitiously, and any resemblance to actual persons,
living or dead, business establishments, events, or locales is entirely coincidental.

For Nora, Edith, and Bill, in loving memory

ACKNOWLEDGEMENTS

There are certain things you only get to experience once in life. A first kiss, say, or a first novel. Moments you'll always remember and look back on with a certain bittersweet nostalgia. Finishing your first trilogy definitely belongs in that category. It's something I've always wanted to do, and I'll try to savour the moment—but already I feel that inevitable hint of sadness, knowing it's a milestone that's forever behind me. It's also a milestone that would never have been reached without the guidance and support of some truly wonderful and patient people. Writing novels is a team sport. Joshua Bilmes and Lisa Rodgers coached me through some pretty shaky drafts before the manuscripts were game-ready. Danielle Stockley and Rebecca Brewer kept me focused on the goal. My husband, Don, and my parents, Billie and David, cheered me on tirelessly, making sure my spirits never flagged. Leslie and Owain, Jordan, Pippa and Selwyn, Matt and Manda, and many others too numerous to mention—you've all helped and supported me throughout this adventure. I'm enormously grateful to all of you, and I hope you're as proud of the result as I am.

As bittersweet as it is leaving Alix, Erik, Liam, and Rig behind, I have no doubt they'll get on perfectly well without me. And who knows—maybe I'll run into them again somewhere down the road.

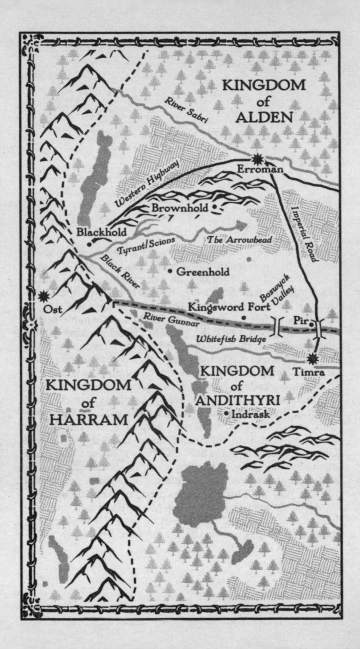

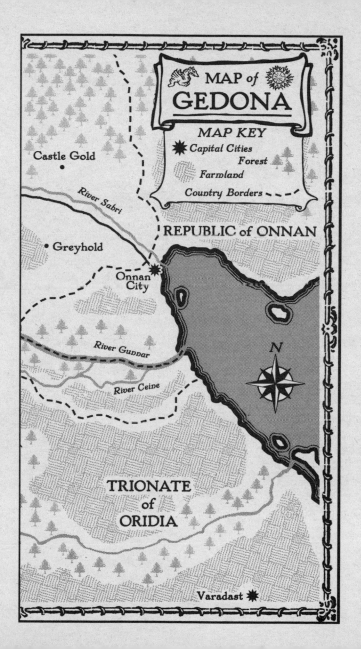

ONE

† "We're ready, Captain."

The anxiety in Pollard's eyes belied his words. A sheen of sweat glistened under the edges of his helm, and he clutched his spear in a white-knuckled grip. He might have been marching into battle against a horde of blood-bound thralls instead of preparing to walk down the burnished hall of the royal apartments. Behind him, the rest of the royal guardsmen fared no better, shifting on their feet and trading uneasy glances, a restless herd smelling a storm. One of them, a bull of a fellow called Notcher, looked like he might actually throw up.

Alix might have pitied them if she weren't too busy fighting down her own queasiness. "Remember," she told her new second-in-command, "this needs to be handled quickly and quietly. I'm counting on you, Pollard."

A convulsive, thin-lipped nod was the guardsman's only reply.

Feeling a hand on her arm, Alix glanced at Liam. Her husband was as pale as the rest of them, grey eyes haunted with guilt. "Are you sure you don't want me to come? Maybe I could talk to him, try to—"

"Nothing we do will make this all right. It's better you stay out of this. No point in the prince getting his hands dirty too."

"My hands are already dirty," he snapped. "They're never going to come clean, either, not after this." His voice dropped to a hiss. "It's *treason*."

Alix scowled. "You think you need to tell me that? I'm the king's bodyguard, Liam. I'm supposed to protect him."

"And I'm his brother. I'm supposed to support him."

Behind them, someone cleared his throat. Alix turned to find Albern Highmount levelling a reproving stare at both of them. Somehow, the chancellor managed to look both grave and impatient at the same time. "Your Highnesses. We have discussed this to exhaustion. We have no choice in the matter. The king is bewitched. We are at war. There is not a priest in the world who would condemn us for what we are about to do."

Alix wasn't sure about that, but she wouldn't argue with the chancellor—not now, in front of her guardsmen. "We've lingered here long enough. The last thing we need is a servant running to Erik and telling him we're about to stage a coup. Let's just get this over with." She marvelled at the steadiness of her own voice. She was about to lead her guardsmen into the royal apartments to arrest the king. Her brother-in-law. The best man she'd ever known—until the enemy poisoned his mind. Her insides were thrashing about like a fish on a barbed hook, but her expression remained firm, a mask of resolve. *Maybe you've finally learned a thing or two from Erik about controlling your emotions.* What a bitter irony that would be.

"With me," she said, starting down the corridor.

Sunlight slanted through the arched windows on the east side of the hall. It glared off the marble tiles, harsh in Alix's eyes, as though Rahl himself rebuked her for what she was about to do. Unwittingly, her gaze fell to the sunburst emblazoned on her breastplate. Rahl, the sun, first among the Holy Virtues and patron of the royal family. Patron of King Erik White, whose crown was about to be usurped by the people he loved most.

Stop it, she commanded herself. *This must be done. We have no choice.*

So why did it feel like a cold hand clutched at her throat?

Her mind snagged on a memory from their days at Greenhold: Erik sitting across from her in the solar, clasping her hand in gratitude. *You are a true friend, Alix.* A golden smile, blue eyes filled with trust and warmth and something more, something Alix hadn't recognised until later. He'd been hurting then, rolling the bitter taste of Prince Tomald's betrayal on his tongue. *I may have been deceived in my brother, but there are others I know I can rely on.* They'd stayed up all night, the two of them, drinking and laughing, Alix basking in the sunshine that had once been Erik White.

A true friend.

The memories flashed mercilessly through her mind now, one after another, each more painful than the last: Erik's arms around her, comforting her as she wept; shoulder to shoulder in battle, defending each other's flank; his laughter when he'd stumbled across her in her wedding dress, that cheeky wink . . .

She rounded the corner and there he was, on his way to his study. She froze.

Erik cocked his head. "Alix, whatever is the matter?" At first, she thought he meant the guardsmen, but he didn't even seem to have noticed them; his gaze, filled with concern, belonged only to her. "Are you crying?"

She touched her cheek; her fingers came away wet.

His glance flicked over her shoulder, taking in the guardsmen now. "What's happened?"

"I . . ." Though she'd rehearsed the words a hundred times, they died on her lips.

Erik gazed at her expectantly. He was immaculate as always, dressed in a blue doublet and leather breeches, red-gold hair tied back in a short, tidy tail. His posture was straight, eyes keen and focused. The enemy's dark magic left no visible mark upon him, and for a fleeting moment, a worm of doubt wriggled in Alix's belly.

But no. She knew him too well, and she'd seen too much. Erik was certainly bewitched.

"Alix?"

Pollard, bless him, stepped into the breach. "With regret, sire, we must seal off this wing of the palace."

"Seal it off? Why would we do that?" There was no suspicion in Erik's voice. He trusted Alix too much, even with the bloodbond gnawing at his mind. The enchantment wasn't yet at full strength. The bloodbinder, whoever he was, must still be too far away for his cursed magic to command Erik completely. Which only made Alix's task all the more painful.

She swallowed, tried to master herself. "Your Majesty," she began, before faltering again. Gods, it was so hard . . .

Now he *did* look wary.

"Sire," she said. "Erik. I'm afraid you're not well."

"Not well," he repeated blankly.

"There's a bloodbinder. An Oridian, one who knows how to warp men's minds. We thought the secret died with the Priest, but we were wrong. The magic is still out there, and the enemy is working it against you."

Erik's eyebrows flew up. "I beg your pardon?"

"It sounds strange, I know. I need you to trust me."

"Of course I trust you. More than anyone, but . . . ?"

The words cut her to the bone. Alix forced herself to press on. "Then you have to believe me now. The enemy has you in his sway, just as the Priest controlled his thralls on the battlefield. But I promise you we'll fix it. We'll—"

"What did you say?" He spoke the words in a cold, horrified whisper.

"The bloodbond. The Priest's dark magic. The Oridians are working it against you, manipulating you."

He stared at her, the blood draining from his face. "Why would you say something like that?"

"I know how it sounds . . ."

"How it *sounds*? Have you taken leave of your senses?" Still in that horrified whisper, as though he willed the conversation to be private, just the two of them, so she could take it all back and they could pretend it never happened.

"You have to trust me," she said again, pleadingly.

He took a step toward her, hands raised as if he were approaching a madwoman. "I don't know what in the gods has got into you, but you're not thinking clearly. The Priest is dead. We destroyed him. You were *there*, Alix. His magic died with him, and even if it hadn't, the enemy cannot simply snap his fingers and turn someone into a thrall. They would need my blood, a great deal of it. You *know* that."

Your blood, or your twin's. She couldn't explain it to him, not like this. Whatever happened, they needed to keep the existence of Erik's twin an absolute secret, even from her guardsmen. Besides, in his current state, he probably wouldn't believe her anyway.

"I'm sorry, Erik." At her signal, the guardsmen moved, heaving on the great panelled doors.

"What are you doing?" Erik cried. "Stop that at once!"

One of the guardsmen wavered, gaze darting between his captain and his king.

"Pollard, get him out of here!"

Her second obeyed, shepherding the reluctant guardsman away. The others resumed closing the doors, all except the four who had been chosen to stay behind to guard the king from within.

Alix began to back away through the narrowing gap.

"Wait!" Erik started toward her, but a pair of guardsmen grabbed his arms. He looked from one to other in stunned disbelief. "Alix?"

Tears splashed cold down her face. She continued to back through the doors.

"Alix, look at me, for gods' sake! Do I look like a thrall to you? *Alix!*"

"I'm sorry, Erik. I'm so sorry . . ."

"You can't do this!" Then, with quiet intensity, "Please, don't do this."

The doors were almost closed now. Through the gap, Alix could only stare at him, heartsick.

She saw it the exact moment he broke: his eyes, so painfully blue, went dull, and he wilted in his captors' grip. Alix's vision swam with tears, blurring out everything but his sagging form.

The doors came to with a cavernous *boom*. Alix slumped to the floor, hand over her mouth to stifle the gasps of grief. Above her, the guards hammered makeshift bars in place before withdrawing, leaving their captain alone with her misery and betrayal.

A soft rustle sounded against the far side of the door, as of someone sliding to the floor.

"Are you there?" In spite of the thick wood, it sounded as if he were right beside her, as though they leaned against each other instead of the barrier between them.

She laid her hand against the door. "I'm here." The words came out in a strangled whisper; she doubted he even heard.

"It's Liam, isn't it? He's poisoned you against me."

Alix squeezed her eyes shut, sending another flood of tears over her cheeks.

"Whatever he's told you, it's not true. He wants my crown. Can't you see? Just like Tom."

Her gaze strayed to the window, into the glaring sun. "I'm going to fix this. I swear to you, Erik." *I swear on my blood, and the blood of my family. I swear on the Nine Virtues and anyone else listening.*

A long silence. Then: "I never thought it would come to this. Liam . . . I believed he might betray me one day. Highmount too. But you . . ." When he spoke again, the ache in his voice was more than she could bear. "I tell you truly, Alix, I would rather have died than see this day."

She curled into a ball, arms over her head, shaking with silent sobs.

"It's done," Alix said dully, dropping into a chair across from Highmount. Beside her, Liam took her hand and gave it a reassuring squeeze.

Even the ever-stoic Highmount looked sympathetic. "I know this has not been easy, Your Highness."

She laughed bitterly and swiped at her eyes. "You have a gift for understatement, Chancellor."

"You did what you had to," Liam said. "We had no choice."

"Can we not do this, please?" Her voice wavered precariously. "I can't . . . I'd rather focus on where we go from here."

"Quite right," Highmount said with a brisk nod. "Your men are deployed, then?"

She drew a deep, shuddering breath. *Forward. Erik needs you to move forward.* "Four inside," she said, sounding steadier now. "Though Pollard thinks we should increase it to six when we bring the first meal."

Highmount grunted sceptically. "I do not think it wise to bring additional men into our confidence."

"Agreed," Alix said. "If we did augment the detail inside, it would have to come from the existing dozen."

"Meaning only six outside," Liam said. "Is that enough?"

"We don't dare have too many," Alix said. "People will notice, and our story won't hold up. There's no reason to post extra guards at the doors if the king is sick with fever."

"What do you intend, then?" Highmount asked.

"We'll keep to four inside for now. Two on the doors. The rest will patrol outside, keeping an eye on the windows. They're less likely to be noticed that way."

"And the bars on the doors?" Liam asked. "How do we explain that?"

"Those were only temporary, so we could get it done quickly. Pollard will replace them with something more discreet. We'll just say that the locks on the other side are broken. Those doors are ancient; no one will question it. Besides, I don't want anyone getting close enough to take a look. From now on, the corridor to the royal apartments is off-limits."

"Due to the risk of contagion, of course," Highmount said.

"Of course."

The old man nodded, satisfied. "Everything would seem to be in place, then. And what of your journey—whom will you take with you?"

"Three White Wolves, as agreed. Rona Brown, Dain Cooper, and Ide. I haven't told them where we're going yet, or why, but I'll have to explain once we're on the road."

Highmount grunted, but if he had any misgivings, he kept them to himself. "When will you depart?"

"Tomorrow morning. That should put me at the front in about five days. I'll spend a day or so with Rig, explain the situation."

"How do you anticipate he will react? Your brother and the king are close. If there is any chance he will not support us in this . . ."

"Rig will support us," Alix said firmly. "He'll support me.

And he needs to know. He's commander general of the king's armies. If we should fail, or if Erik were somehow to get word to him, my brother would obey whatever orders the king gave."

"Which orders would very likely have been fed to His Majesty by the enemy through the bloodbond. I do understand your concerns, and I share them. But you must ensure that General Black fully grasps what is at stake here. It is imperative that he guard this secret with his life."

As though Alix needed to be told. "My brother will do what is necessary," she said coolly. "You can rely upon it."

Highmount nodded again. "And then?"

"And then," Liam said, "it's off to Andithyri, smuggling herself into enemy territory." A scowl and crossed arms accompanied this interjection, in case either of them had missed the tone.

Highmount fetched a scroll case down from the bookshelf and rolled out a map of Andithyri. It had been updated recently, the borders redrawn in red ink along with a note in the chancellor's tidy hand: *Occupied by the Trionate of Oridia.* "Rodrik was raised here," he said, "in a village called Indrask."

Alix leaned over the map. Liam, she noticed, did not; instead he looked away, mouth pressed into a thin line. Alix didn't blame him for being unhappy—she'd feel the same if the situation were reversed and he was the one infiltrating occupied territory in search of Erik's captured twin—but sulking about it surely didn't help.

"As you can see," Highmount said, "Indrask is in the middle of nowhere. That was by design; we needed the boy kept out of sight, living in anonymity in a place no one would recognise him as King Erik's twin. That should work to your advantage, Your Highness. Enemy soldiers will be fewer and farther between, and I doubt the Warlord has troubled to garrison the smaller towns, let alone villages. If you stay off the main roads, you may well travel unmolested."

Liam snorted and shook his head, which Alix did her best to ignore. "Is this farmland?" she asked, running a finger along the map.

"Largely. A few bits of wood here and there, but the country is small and crowded, so most of the land is under cultivation."

"Good. Open territory will make travelling faster."

"It'll also make you easier to spot," Liam put in.

"I'm a trained scout, Liam. I don't need you to explain cover to me."

He sighed, raking a hand through his unruly hair. "I'm sorry. I'm not trying to be a prat. I just hate this."

"Of course you do, but that's not exactly new, is it? You hated it when Erik and I travelled to Harram too, just as I hated it when you were sent to Onnan. This is no different."

He scowled. "Is that supposed to make me feel better? Both of those missions ended in spectacular failure, on top of which, I seem to recall that we all nearly *died*."

"This is who we are, Liam. That's not going to change until this war is over." Turning back to Highmount, she said, "Go on."

Highmount's glance cut between them, but he wisely let that part of the conversation drop. "There is not much else to tell. Your brother will know better than I which routes are safest, and which best avoided. All I can offer you is this." Reaching into an inner pocket of his jerkin, Highmount withdrew a key and unlocked the top drawer of his desk. Inside was an iron box, unadorned, guarded by the most formidable padlock Alix had ever seen. Whatever was inside that box, Albern Highmount had taken great pains to ensure that it remained for his eyes only. He opened it and pushed it across the desk.

"Letters?"

"From an Aldenian royal guardsman, a man called Terrell. He was sent to live among the Andithyri, to join the cadre of guards assigned by our allies to keep watch over the boy. He posed as a farmer and sent these missives from time to time. As you can see, they are few, but perhaps you will find something useful in them to help guide your search."

"Thank you."

"And now, Your Highness, before you depart, there is something I would like you to consider. Another perspective, if you will, on the mission you are about to undertake."

Something in the chancellor's tone made Alix wary. "All right."

"Twenty-seven years ago, I gave a crucial bit of counsel to King Osrik. It went unheeded, to my lasting regret, a mistake that led directly to the delicate position in which we now find ourselves. Had His Majesty followed my advice, his heir would not now be bloodbound and locked away in his own palace. Indeed, there is a very good chance we would not be at war at all."

Alix regarded him coldly. "I presume you're referring to your suggestion to—how did you put it—*destroy the boy*?"

"Rodrik White posed a grave threat to the kingdom. He still does. More so, now that he is a man grown and Alden is at war. We know nothing about his character. It is not difficult to imagine that the enemy could persuade him to become a puppet king, or any number of other scenarios. I am sure I do not need to remind you how this country has suffered when a White brother, legitimate or otherwise, chooses to contest the crown. We have already known two such tragedies in our kingdom's brief history, the latest scarcely a year old. When you find Rodrik, you would do well to remember that, and consider carefully what comes next."

"What in the hells does that mean?" Liam snapped.

Highmount met his gaze unrepentantly. "It means, Your Highness, that a rescue mission may not be what is called for under the circumstances."

"He's joking. You're joking, surely? This is my brother we're talking about, Highmount. *My brother*. Do you understand that?"

The chancellor ignored him, turning his hawkish gaze back on Alix. *You know I'm right*, those eyes seemed to say. And a cold, logical voice inside Alix whispered, *I do*. But however much that voice might be in harmony with Highmount's, she could not heed it. Erik would never forgive her. And neither, judging from the look on his face, would her husband. "Erik told me once that he mourned his twin for his entire childhood. That's when he thought he had a stillborn sister. If he found out he had an identical twin, only to learn I'd taken that from him . . ." Alix shook her head. "It's Erik's choice to make, Highmount. Not mine, and not yours."

The chancellor seemed to expect that answer, for he merely nodded, as if to say, *On your head be it*. He rose, signalling that the conversation was over.

But Alix wasn't through quite yet. She kept her seat, gaze in her lap.

There was an uncomfortable stretch of silence. Highmount cleared his throat. "Is there something else, Your Highness?"

For a moment, she almost lost her nerve. But she couldn't hide from the truth forever; Highmount needed to know. "Before I go, there's something I have to tell you." She glanced at Liam. "Both of you."

Highmount resumed his seat.

"Varad's assassination," Alix said. "It was me."

Highmount's brows gathered. "What do you mean?"

"I killed him." Alix stared ruthlessly ahead. She could feel Liam's gaze on her, but she couldn't face it. Not yet.

As for Highmount, he betrayed no emotion beyond a slight narrowing of the eyes. "I'm afraid I still do not understand, Your Highness. How could you possibly have killed the King of Oridia, particularly since you were on your way back from Harram at the time of his death?"

"I had my spy do it. That is, I ordered my spy to see it done. He has networks in Varadast." She sat up straighter, forced herself to look Highmount in the eye. "It was a terrible error in judgement, and I take full responsibility."

"I see." Highmount's fingers formed a steeple, a gesture Alix had come to recognise as a sign of careful reflection.

Liam found his voice at last. "Allie, why would you—"

"I thought I was helping." It sounded childish, even to her own ears. "The Priest was already dead. I thought if the King were gone too, the Warlord would have no choice but to back down, at least for a while. As the sole remaining Trion, I thought Sadik would be too weak to continue. That I could end the war at a stroke." True, as far as it went, but not the *whole* truth. The real reason she'd done it was far, far simpler.

Vengeance.

She'd been exhausted. Afraid. Tired of feeling powerless. And then the news of the massacre at Raynesford, of the Warlord butchering children and women . . . So she'd done what she always did, acting without thinking, a true child of Ardin. It was just as Erik had warned her all those months ago: *One of these days, your recklessness is going to cost you dearly. Cost all of us, perhaps.* She'd played right into Sadik's hand. He was the sole remaining Trion, all right—and all the more powerful for it. If she'd bothered to consult Erik, she would have learned that Varad had been a restraining influence on Sadik. On top of which, the Oridian public, outraged by the assassination of their King, had rallied in support of the war effort. With Varad out of the way and his people behind him, the Warlord of Oridia was free to indulge his ambition to the fullest.

She cleared her throat. "When Erik is . . . when he's better, he'll have to deal with me."

"Deal with you, Your Highness?" Highmount lifted a bushy grey eyebrow. "What exactly do you believe His Majesty will do?"

"I don't know. It's hard to imagine what punishment could answer for what I've done. The Oridians were weary. They might have stood down. Only now, I've given them a martyr to rally behind. I've prolonged the war at the cost of who knows how many lives." Saying it aloud made her queasy all over again, and she found she couldn't quite meet the chancellor's eye after all.

Highmount sighed. "You give yourself rather too much credit, I think. We cannot know what might have been. Your actions were ill-considered, Your Highness, and I do regret them. It is true that the Oridian people are united as never before. But the Warlord is not known for his . . . *democratic* inclinations. The views of the public are not likely to weigh heavily on him. Can we truly say you have prolonged the war?" He made a dismissive gesture. "Speculation."

"But it's possible."

"Perhaps."

Alix waited for him to say more, but he only regarded her with that damnably closed expression, the one she could never read. "That's it?" she demanded. "That's all you have to say?"

He spread his hands. "What would you have of me, Your Highness? It is done. We cannot afford to dwell on it; we have more immediate concerns. Besides, I daresay there is little I could suggest that would be as severe as the condemnation you heap upon yourself."

That, at least, was Destan's own truth.

"If you will forgive an old man some unsolicited advice," the chancellor went on, "put this behind you—but do not forget. There will come a time when the memory of this regrettable incident is all that stands between you and another rash decision. Forgive yourself, Your Highness, but do not forget."

Liam reached over and squeezed her hand again, and when Alix met her husband's gaze at last, she found no judgement there. Her heart flooded with gratitude, her fingers tightening around his.

"And now, Your Highnesses, if there is nothing else, I suggest you continue your preparations. As for me, I have a great deal of correspondence to take care of. The council must be apprised immediately of His Majesty's terribly contagious fever."

Alix didn't envy him the task. It would take a deft hand to convince the council that the king was ill enough to require quarantine, yet not so ill that they needed to be concerned. If anyone could manage the balance, it was Albern Highmount. "Will I see you before I leave?" she asked him.

"I should not think so. Your departure must be as discreet as possible. My presence would not aid that cause."

"In that case, farewell."

Highmount rose, smoothed his doublet. Then he folded at the waist in a grave bow. It was the first time he'd ever bowed to her. "Take care, Your Highness. And good luck."

Alix thanked him, though she doubted there was enough good luck in the Nine Heavens to see her through.

TWO

"That man is incredible," Alix said, and even she wasn't sure if she meant it as a compliment. "I swear, you could tell Highmount the dragon was nigh and the world ending and he'd just look at you and say, *I see.*"

Liam threw the latch on their chamber door. "He's right, though. There's no point dwelling on it."

Alix forced herself to meet his gaze. "I'm sorry, Liam. I am so sorry."

"I know." He put his arms around her. "It's behind us, love."

That wasn't really true—it wouldn't be behind them until the war was over, and maybe not even then—but Alix loved him for saying it. She let out a long breath, tucked her face into the curve of his neck. The familiar scent of his skin was a tonic, soothing away the bitter trials of the day. Exhaustion crept into the spaces grief left behind. It wasn't even noon, and already she felt . . . spent.

Feeling her sag against him, Liam said, "Come on, let's lie down a moment. You need to rest."

"There isn't time . . ."

"Just for a moment." He led her through to their sleeping chamber, where they found Rudi sprawled across the foot of the bed. Liam shooed the wolfhound off before starting in on the buckles of Alix's armour. She began another weak protest, but it felt so good when he lifted her breastplate away that the words died unspoken. They curled up together, Alix's body tucked neatly into Liam's. *A perfect fit*, she thought, not for the first time.

"Do you ever wonder what it would have been like," he murmured, "if the war had never begun? For us, I mean. You and me." His fingers twined through hers, toying with the ring on her baby finger, the one that had once belonged to his mother.

She knew what he was doing, but she played along. The alternative was letting herself descend into dark thoughts. Whether she looked ahead or behind, there was only sorrow; better to steal a moment of peace in the small space between. "I'm not sure we would even have met," she said.

"Sure we would have. You'd have done your King's Service anyway, right?"

"Yes, but I doubt you and I would have crossed paths. You'd have been a knight, after all. Entirely too important to mix with a scout like me."

"How do you figure that?"

"Well, Arran Green only delayed your knighthood to keep you off the front lines. No war, no front lines, no banishment to the scouts."

He hummed thoughtfully. "Hadn't thought of that. Still"— his arms tightened around her—"we would have met."

In spite of everything, she felt a smile tugging at her lips. "What makes you so sure?"

"I'd have seen to it."

"We'd have been barracked on opposite sides of the compound. You'd never even have noticed me."

"Oh, I'd have noticed, believe me. Have you seen you?" He twisted a lock of copper hair around his finger. "You rather stand out, my lady."

"I see. My hair would have drawn your eye, is that it?"

"That, and your dulcet tones cursing out your opponent in the ring."

"Bugger off."

"Just so. Like a sweet songbird."

She rolled over to find his grey eyes dancing with mischief, mouth hitched in that crooked grin that had snared her so long ago. "All right," she said archly, "you'd have noticed me. What makes you think I'd have paid any attention to you?"

"Are you kidding? I'd have swept you off your feet even sooner. With no war getting in the way, how could you resist me? Especially since I'd be extra dashing, what with the knighthood and all."

"Extra dashing? One struggles to imagine."

"You can be sarcastic all you like, but you don't fool me. I dash like anything." Alix couldn't help it; she giggled. Liam rolled onto his back, hands tucked under his head. "Victory."

He'd said that to her before, in this very bed, though under different circumstances. The memory brought a flash of heat to her skin. She climbed on top of him, hair falling around them in a copper curtain.

He reached up and brushed a thumb along her mouth. "I thought your mind might go there."

"You hoped it would, you mean."

"I don't know what you're talking about."

"It worries me sometimes, how easily you play me."

The crooked smile again. "I am but a humble harper, my love." He drew her head down into a kiss.

Smug bastard. He played her body just as easily, and he was a relentless tease. Even now, as he kissed her, his fingers were ghosting up her sides, turning her skin to gooseflesh. His hands came to rest just under her breasts, but no farther—not yet. She knew from experience that if she shifted, tried to guide his hands where she wanted them, he would comply—but only for a moment. Just long enough to make it clear that he knew exactly what she needed, and would give it to her in his own good time.

She broke off from the kiss. "I mean it. Sometimes it's like you're reading my mind."

"I'm not reading your mind, Allie. I just pay attention." He raised her arms and pulled her shirt over her head. Then he rolled her onto her back and proceeded to prove his point. He knew just where to start, lips brushing behind her ear, thumb gliding over the bud of her breast. From there, he followed the cues, reading every hitched breath, every tensed muscle; a tracker on the hunt, answering with nips and kisses and firm fingers until Alix thought she would explode.

"Liam, by the gods, if you don't . . ." She gasped as his thumb moved in a slow, tormenting circle. "I'm going to kill you . . ."

She felt his laugh, hot breath on her skin. "Like a sweet songbird," he said, and slid inside her.

Alix woke to an empty bed. She got up, put on a dressing gown, and stirred the fire. Then she padded off in search of her husband. She found him standing at the hearth in the sitting room, staring into the flames. *So much for our moment of peace.* Aloud, she said, "How long did I sleep?"

"Not long. An hour, maybe."

"Thank you for that."

He glanced over, firelight playing off his features. "For letting you sleep?"

"For all of it."

He turned back to the fire. "I've been thinking," he said.

Alix knew what was coming. She lowered herself into a chair, tucking her bare feet under her. "I have to go, Liam."

"Hear me out . . ."

"I've heard you out, several times." She said it gently, trying to soften the words. "Nothing's changed, love. Someone has to get Rodrik out of enemy hands, and you've got to stay here and keep things in order while Erik is"—she faltered—"while he's not well."

"Highmount's managed on his own before. He and the council did a fine job when I was in Onnan and Erik in Harram. I don't see how this is any different."

"Yes, you do," Alix said patiently. "We could afford for you and Erik to be away at the same time because as bad as the situation was out there, at least things in Erroman were relatively stable. That's not the case anymore. The crisis is here now. There needs to be a White at the helm."

"The crisis is Erik's twin. So let me manage it. I'll go to Andithyri with the Wolves. We'll rescue Rodrik and kill the bloodbinder, and Erik will be free. I used to be a scout too; I know how to sneak about. I can do this."

Alix wrestled with mounting frustration. "I know you're worried, love, but—"

"Worried?" He turned away from the hearth, and it was as

if his eyes had absorbed some of the flames. "I'm not worried, Allie. I'm *petrified*. The more I think about this plan, the madder it seems. Four of you alone in enemy territory—"

"Three, actually. I've thought it over, and I've decided that Rona Brown should stay here with you and Highmount. She's a banner lady—you'll need her voice on the council."

"Even better! Come to think of it, are you sure you wouldn't just rather go alone?"

Alix scowled. "Now you're being silly. There are no good choices here, Liam. No easy tasks. I've got to do my part, just as you do."

"Your part doesn't have to be a suicide mission!"

"Let's not be dramatic—"

"I'm not. You *know* I'm not. It's insane and I can't let you do it." The flame in his eyes cooled, hardening into resolve. "I won't."

She paused. "I beg your pardon?"

"I should have a say in this. I'm your husband and your prince."

For a moment, she was stunned into silence. "You can't be serious."

But he was—perfectly serious. "I can't let you do it, Alix."

She rose slowly from her chair. Something stirred in her belly, cold and constricting like the coils of a snake. She knew this feeling. She'd had it in Harram, in the moments before she'd written that fateful letter to Saxon ordering the assassination of a Trion. A feeling of powerlessness. Of being merely a witness, a window through which great men were glimpsed in the midst of great events. "You can't let me do it," she echoed softly. "You think you can decide for me, is that it?"

"I can decide for the kingdom, can't I? Isn't that what being a prince is supposed to mean?" She heard the frustration in his voice, the desperation—just as he must surely hear the warning in hers. But neither of them seemed able to heed it, too caught up in the dangerous momentum building between them.

"So, what, now that you outrank me, I'm just your subject? Your wife? Property of Liam White?"

"Of course not. That isn't what I mean and you know it."

She barely registered the words. A roar like an avalanche filled her ears, drowning out everything but the rage hurtling toward her. It was as if something that had been looming over them for months had suddenly broken free, and now it crashed over her in a bitter torrent. "Aren't you forgetting something? Yours isn't the only claim on me. I'm also Erik's bodyguard. So I'm well and truly covered, aren't I? I belong completely to the White brothers!"

"Don't be ridiculous, you know that's not true . . ." Liam stepped toward her, hand outstretched, but she backed away.

"Isn't it?" Her voice spiralled ever higher, caught on the updraft of a mounting fury. "Ever since I came to this place, it's as if I disappeared, as if Alix Black were gone forever. And she is, isn't she? I'm Alix White now. If I'd married anyone, *anyone* else in the kingdom, I'd get to keep my name. But I marry into the one family that outranks mine, and suddenly I'm someone else entirely."

Liam stared, thoroughly taken aback. "I had no idea you felt this way."

"So much for *paying attention*."

He stiffened. "Very nice."

She regretted herself immediately, but as usual, that only put her more firmly on the offensive. "You used to be a squire. Surely you remember what it's like to live in someone else's shadow?"

"I don't even know what we're talking about, Alix. Is it being Erik's bodyguard you resent, or being my wife?"

"What? Neither, obviously—"

"Yeah, you know, for some reason I'm not finding it all that obvious just now."

The hurt in his eyes pierced through the red haze. Alix drew a deep breath, tried to gather herself. "That's not what I meant. But you can't just order me around, Liam. I'm a grown woman."

"Yes, you are, a grown woman who doesn't always make great choices."

"And what's *that* supposed to mean?"

"Come on, Allie. How many times have you done something rash and nearly gotten yourself killed in the process? Hells, nearly gotten *me* killed? Not two hours ago, you were begging forgiveness for having your spy assassinate Varad. A sodding *Trion*, and you had him snuffed without even consulting anyone! Can you blame me for being afraid of what you might do next?"

"You're going to throw that in my face?"

"I'm not throwing anything in your face. I'm stating a fact. I'm trying to make you understand that I'm *terrified*, Alix."

She drew another breath, deep and shuddering, trying to cling to some scrap of control. "I understand that. What I don't understand is why you're saying any of these things. I have to go to Andithyri. You have to stay here and protect Erik's crown. We owe him this, you and I. We owe him everything." And then, without thinking: "You, especially."

A crushing silence followed this addendum. Liam looked at her numbly. Too late, Alix realised what she'd done. She'd stabbed him in the place it hurt most, the secret wound he'd been trying so hard to overcome. He was a bastard, nameless, worthless in the eyes of the world until Erik acknowledged him. Still convinced somewhere deep down that he didn't deserve the new life he'd been given. And now Alix had made it sound as if she agreed, as if it were a debt he could never repay.

"Just so I'm clear," he said quietly, "is that because he gave me my name, or because he gave me my wife?"

"Gave you . . . ?" The rage bled away, leaving her insides scoured and empty. For a moment, she couldn't find her voice; when she did, it seemed to whistle through the cracks. "No one *gave* me to you, Liam."

"No? He never fought for you, not really. Tell me the truth: if Erik hadn't stepped aside, would you have . . . Would you and he . . ." Even now, he couldn't finish the sentence.

"How can you ask me that?" she whispered tremulously. "*Why* would you ask me that?"

They'd never spoken about it openly, not since the night Alix had made her choice, the night she'd come to Liam's bed and told him she loved him. Why would they? What possible good could come of it? Alix had proven her love again and again. At least, she'd thought so. But now here was Liam, standing before her in the apartments they shared as husband and wife, questioning whether she'd really made a choice at all. Whether when all was said and done, she wouldn't rather be with Erik.

"You almost married him," Liam said.

"But I didn't. I married you. That was *my* choice. No one else's."

The anger drained from him now too, but Alix could see that it left behind the same bitter residue. They both knew what they'd done. Some words, once spoken, can never be taken back.

Liam passed a hand over his eyes. "I don't even know why I said that. It's just . . ."

"You don't trust me," Alix said. "You don't trust *us*."

"That's not true."

But it was true, at least on some level, whether he admitted it to himself or not. Alix had thought the past was behind them, but she saw now that she'd been naïve. Liam had been carrying it with him all this time, an invisible weight around his neck. Or worse, a slow poison in his veins. *Maybe we can never be free of this. Maybe the only reason we've made it this far is that there are so many more important things going on around us.*

She looked at Liam and saw her thoughts mirrored in his eyes. And for the second time that day, Alix's heart broke.

It's behind us, love. So Liam had said little more than an hour ago. But nothing was behind them. Not now, and maybe not ever.

She turned away from him. There was too much to do and too little time. She withdrew, feeling as though she'd left more behind in that sitting room than her husband and his silence.

She felt it all over again the following morning when she rode out under cover of darkness with Ide and Dain Cooper, leaving a still-silent Liam on the steps of the keep.

THREE

† "I think it would be best," said Albern Highmount, "if you allowed me to do most of the talking, Your Highness."

Big surprise, that. Highmount barely trusted Liam to dress himself, let alone run a council meeting. He obviously thought his prince an irredeemable idiot—which verdict, to be fair, Liam probably wouldn't dispute just now. After all, he'd just let his wife ride off into mortal peril without him. Again. Only this time, he'd sent her forth not with a love letter, but with fatal doubts about their marriage. Bloody brilliant. Happy endings sure to follow.

"I sense I do not have your undivided attention, Your Highness," Highmount said.

"Yeah, well, you'll have to forgive me," Liam said tartly. "I've had a bit of a rough morning."

The chancellor was unmoved. "Her Highness is exceedingly capable. If anyone can accomplish this task, it is she."

"For what it's worth," Rona Brown put in, "I agree."

Liam sighed and shoved a hand through his hair, forcing himself to focus on the matter at hand. His gaze roamed over the oratorium, all stately pillars and polished stone and stained-glass windows. He could scarcely fathom a more intimidating room, yet Erik had always commanded it from the moment he walked through the door. Liam would have to find a way to do the same, even if he was only half the man his brother had been. *Half the man he is*, he corrected himself. Erik wasn't lost, not yet. Alix would fix this. Liam needed to believe that on so many levels.

The guardsman Pollard appeared at the door. "Ready, Your Highness?"

Liam looked at Highmount and Rona, the only two council members who knew the truth about Erik's condition. Could they hide it? Glancing from one steady gaze to the other, he thought, *Who are you kidding?* A chancellor and a banner lady, born and bred at court. He, on the other hand . . . *If anyone's going to cock it up, it's you.*

Green was the first to enter, as always, the rest of the lords and ladies following in the strict order protocol demanded. Liam found himself taking them in as if for the first time, measuring them up, deciding if they'd be friend or foe in the days and weeks to come.

Raibert Green. Cousin to Liam's fallen mentor, Arran Green. First among the banner lords. Green, at least, Liam knew he could trust. *Or can you?* Green was a good man, fiercely loyal to the king. *If he thinks you've betrayed Erik . . .* Next came Norvin Gold. Liam knew nothing about him save his rank as banner lord. Still less of Lady Stonegate, or Lord Swiftcurrent . . .

And then there was Sirin Grey.

She met Liam's gaze from across the room. Curiosity lit her blue eyes, but it was a cold curiosity, unpredictable and dangerous, like sunlight on a glacier. *Doing some measuring up of her own*, Liam thought. He had no idea where he stood with her. They didn't have much history together, but what they did have could hardly have filled Sirin with warm, cuddly feelings. Liam had been there the day her lover was executed—her lover, Tomald White, brother to Erik and traitor to the crown. It was Liam who'd caught her when she swooned, overcome by the sight of the Raven's blood running in rivulets between the flagstones. It was Liam who'd taken the Raven's place as Erik's heir. Meanwhile, her brother Roswald's role in the plot had cast Sirin's family into disgrace. Half their lands had been confiscated, their men-at-arms disbanded. By the time Erik and Highmount were done, their banner was all the Greys had left—and they were lucky to keep that.

Sirin Grey, Liam decided, had no reason to love him.

Which meant he had two, at most three, firm allies on a council of eight. Bad news.

"Thank you for coming, my lords," Highmount said when they had taken their seats. "Before we begin, are there any other items to be added to the agenda?"

Sirin Grey arched a delicate eyebrow. "You mean besides the absence of the king?"

"His Majesty sends his regrets," Highmount said. "Unfortunately, he has a touch of fever left over from his voyage to Harram." He might have been reporting the weather, so banal was his tone.

"A touch of fever?" Sirin's eyebrow climbed to perilous heights. "Is that why you have the corridor to the royal apartments sealed off?"

Cocked heads and bemused frowns rippled round the table. Lady Sirin was obviously better informed than most. Bad news, volume two.

Raibert Green glanced about as if noticing something for the first time. "And where is Lady Alix?"

"Sick," Liam said—maybe a touch too quickly.

"Hardly surprising," Highmount said, "given how much time she spends with His Majesty. Difficult to say which of them infected the other, but the illness is unmistakably contagious, which is why we have sealed off the royal apartments." He flashed a bland smile. "A precaution, at His Majesty's own insistence."

Norvin Gold harrumphed, as if personally inconvenienced. "Who has the Blacks' proxy?"

"I do," said Highmount, "as before. Now, if there are no more questions, perhaps we can begin—"

"I'm sorry, Chancellor, but I'm afraid I do still have questions, if you will indulge me."

Sirin Grey again. Liam forced himself not to react. Highmount, for his part, adopted a mildly annoyed expression, and

Rona Brown looked just plain bored. *Professionals, these two*, Liam thought.

"Sealing off the royal apartments seems a bit drastic for a *touch of fever*, don't you think? In fact, I'm surprised His Majesty would forgo the first council meeting since his return for such a trifle. King Erik is not known for being delicate with his health. If anything, he tends to push himself too hard."

Liam cursed inwardly. Sirin Grey had been engaged to Erik for years; she knew him better than just about anyone in the room. *She's dangerous, this one.* Fatal, even, were she to expose them. He and Highmount had locked the king in his chambers and usurped his crown. How would they ever explain that to the council? They couldn't possibly, not before Erik had their heads off. It wouldn't be the first time he'd executed a brother for treason.

The image came back to Liam, as vivid as if it were yesterday: the Raven's blood on the flagstones, Erik's bloodblade buried deep in the wood block that had cradled his brother's head . . .

A sheen of sweat broke out along Liam's scalp.

"He does tend to push himself too hard," Highmount said smoothly, "which is how he fell ill in the first place. To be frank, had Her Highness Lady Alix not also succumbed, I suspect we would not have been able to convince him to remain abed. In the event, however, I was able to appeal to his reason, by pointing out how very irresponsible it would be to risk infecting the entire council."

"That," said Rona Brown, "would certainly have been a disaster at a time like this."

"Indeed," said Lady Stonegate. "I have only just recovered from my own illness of last week. I thank you, Chancellor, for sparing me a repetition of that."

Sirin Grey started to say something, but Liam decided at that moment he'd had enough of being a spectator. "My lords," he said, cutting her off, "I've got rather a lot to do today, including looking after my wife, so if we could get under way?" He didn't mind playing the part of Petulant Prince. These people barely knew him; he could cast himself in any role he liked and no one would know the difference. A trick he'd picked up while playing the diplomat in Onnan, slithering around with the rest of the vipers. At least *some* good had come out of that gods-cursed trip.

"I do apologise, Your Highness," Highmount said, sounding almost sincere enough to give himself away. The chancellor had never apologised to Liam in his life. "I will endeavour to keep this meeting moving smoothly. And now, my lords, if we may begin . . ."

Liam watched Sirin Grey as Highmount unfurled the agenda and began reading it aloud. She sat perfectly poised in her chair, spine straight, silk gloves folded primly in her lap. Dark braids framed a face as coolly beautiful as a statue, a gaze as coolly calculating as a moneylender's.

As though sensing she was being watched, Sirin looked over. Her eyes met Liam's, and she did not look away. He held her glance just long enough to make it clear that he had nothing to fear. Then he looked back at Highmount, straining to hear the chancellor's words over the dull roar of his own blood.

"Really," Liam said disgustedly. "In the rose garden. You couldn't wait half a heartbeat until we were back in the courtyard." Rudi just looked up at him, nub of a tail wagging, apparently finding nothing amiss in leaving a nasty gift on the sparkling white gravel.

Liam was trying to decide what to do with the mess when the wolfhound's ears perked up and he took a halting step forward, growling. Liam tensed, hand going instinctively to his bloodblade. Ridiculously, his first thought was of Sirin Grey, but it was not her slender form that rounded the rosebushes; instead it was an unfamiliar figure in a dark hood. Rudi's teeth flashed into a snarl and the figure froze, one hand raised in a warding gesture.

"I should be grateful, Your Highness, if you could keep that beast at bay," said a rasping voice.

"Why should I do that?" In spite of his words, Liam rested a hand on Rudi's head. He'd seen what the wolfhound could do to a man, and he didn't fancy scraping guts off the gravel as well as shite. "Whoever you are, I'm fairly certain you're not supposed to be here."

"True enough, but I flatter myself to think your lady wife would be somewhat put out by my untimely demise."

Liam scowled. "Name?"

"Forgive me, but I would rather not say. Besides, I suspect you've already worked that out."

Liam thought so too, but just to be sure, he said, "Saxon?"

The man winced. "It is little better if you say it, Your Highness, the objective being that it isn't overheard."

"*My* objective is to know whom I'm talking to."

"And now that you do, perhaps you could see fit to quell your hound?"

Liam hadn't even noticed that Rudi was still snarling away. He had to give the spy credit; not every man would stand his ground in the face of those fangs. "Quiet, you." The wolfhound subsided, though he kept his yellow eyes riveted on the spy. Liam did the same, taking in the man's unremarkable form— middling height, medium build, commonplace clothing. Alix had always had trouble describing her spy, and Liam could see why. Aside from his grating voice, the man was utterly ordinary. "If there's someone nearby to overhear," Liam said, "we've got bigger problems than your name."

"True enough, I suppose."

"What do you want?"

"To remind you of my presence, Your Highness, and my devoted service." His tone wasn't sarcastic, exactly, but there was something vaguely mocking about it. Alix had mentioned something about that too, Liam recalled.

"Your service to my wife, you mean." Considering Saxon's role in the assassination of Varad, Liam didn't fancy himself part of their little arrangement.

"Were my notes on Onnan not helpful to you?"

"I guess," Liam said, a little ungraciously. "Didn't keep me from flaming out—literally. I'm sure you heard what happened to the Onnani fleet."

"Torched, down to the last galley." The spy nodded gravely. "I heard. Though I doubt there was much you could have done. From what I've been told, the dockies had been planning that action for months. The only reason they delayed as long as they did was to try to exact concessions from the Republicana.

That"—his mouth twisted wryly—"and they wished to put on a show."

"Yeah, well, they did. A big, fiery show. And for an encore, they got themselves thrown in the dungeons, leaving a bunch of inexperienced whelps working the docks. So if we're lucky, the fleet might be ready in, oh, eight months. By which time we'll all be speaking Oridian."

"So pessimistic?"

"Haven't had a lot of good luck lately."

"I am sorry to hear it, Your Highness, especially since it seems I must add to your woes."

Wonderful. "And how's that?"

"This morning's council meeting was the flipping of a timeglass. The sand is running, and it will not last long."

"What are you talking about?"

"His Majesty's condition."

Liam stiffened. Beside him, Rudi growled.

"A loyal beast," Saxon said dryly. "He is most attuned to you."

"Why should Erik's fever add to my woes?"

The spy's mouth took a sour turn. "Please, Your Highness, don't insult me." He dropped his voice until it was barely above a whisper, a rasp of flint on tinder. "We both know His Majesty is not suffering from fever."

"I don't know any such thing."

Saxon sighed impatiently. "Really, this is going to take far too long if we continue this pointless shadowfencing. I am a spy, Your Highness. Knowing secrets is my business. Lady Black rode out before dawn this morning, accompanied by two of your own White Wolves. I know your lady wife, and she would never leave the king's side were she not compelled by the utmost urgency. That, combined with earlier rumours about His Majesty's erratic behaviour . . ."

"There are rumours about Erik's behaviour?" *This just keeps getting better.*

"King Erik White is above all things a charmer, a gracious young man known for his charisma and political acumen. Yet he offends the King of Harram so badly that our allies turn him away without so much as a single legion to aid our cause. Not only that, His Majesty returns to us peevish and paranoid, suddenly the sort of king who upbraids his own chancellor in full view of the entire palace."

"Erik nearly died on that mission. The mountain tribes took him captive, and Alix too. He was barely able to talk his way out of being executed. Naturally he was rattled by the time he got to Ost, the more so when King Omaïd turned him away."

Saxon wasn't fooled. "Something happened to His Majesty in those mountains. Something dire. And now Lady Alix is trying to fix it." He paused, shrugging. "I am likely to put this together faster than most. But others will work it through eventually, and when they do, your neck will be on the block. Yours, and my lord chancellor's."

Liam's throat felt suddenly tight, as though his neck were already on the block. But he forced his voice to remain steady as he said, "I don't know what you think you've worked through, but you're wrong. Erik is ill. End of story. Alix rode out this morning, it's true, but there's nothing remarkable in that. She's going to see her brother, that's all."

"And yet you troubled to lie to the council about it."

Liam tensed again.

"Did Lady Black not tell you I had a tick on the council?" The spy laughed. "Really, do the two of you not speak?"

It was a little too close to the mark. "I'd go gently, if I were you," Liam growled. "It'd be a shame for the gardeners to have to scrub your blood off the king's nice white gravel." He was bluffing, of course. Probably.

"I am here to help, Your Highness. The sword is already balanced above your neck, whether you realise it or not. Certain facts are out in the open, which, though not terribly damning in isolation, are going to be woven together all too soon. And while the picture that emerges may not reveal the whole truth—I doubt even I have guessed that—it will be enough to land you in the Red Tower, or worse. Most of the council has not yet heard the rumours of His Majesty's erratic behaviour, but when they do—as they are certain to, for gossip is the very air the court breathes—they will begin to suspect. Should they discover Lady Black is gone, it will only deepen their suspicions. Your time is limited, Your Highness, so whatever you and your lady wife are about, I strongly suggest you *take care of it quickly*."

Liam turned his back on the spy, rubbing his jaw roughly. Saxon was right. He might not have guessed the whole truth, but he knew enough, and it had taken him less than a day to work it out. How long did they really think they could keep something like this from getting out? And when it did . . .

Blood on the flagstones.

When the spy spoke again, the mocking tone was gone. "Let me help, Your Highness. I daresay you need it."

Liam glanced over his shoulder. "How?"

"My tick on the council will feed me information. That will help us keep an eye on their mood."

Liam nodded resignedly. He felt dirty.

"Not all of them are your friends, Your Highness."

"You don't say. Most of them see me as a bastard or a fool or both. I don't care about that right now. What I am worried about"—he dropped his voice—"is Sirin Grey."

A pause. The spy considered him from the shadowed depths of his hood. "It is true, Your Highness, you do have something of a reputation for being glib. The assumption is that your political instincts are not strong."

"That's not an assumption, it's a fact."

"Hmm. I am inclined to doubt that."

"Because you know me so well."

"A man does not last long in my trade if he is not a good judge of character. You give yourself too little credit, I think. As do many others, and you can use that to your advantage. Let them underestimate you while you play the Hew-tongued fool. Meanwhile, I will feed you whatever I get from my tick on the council. That way, we will hopefully be forewarned when they begin to suspect."

When, not *if*.

"I should not linger here," Saxon said. "It would not help matters if you were seen with a spy. If you need me, leave a rose on your windowsill. I will find you."

"How romantic."

A smile drifted across the spy's face. "You are terribly well suited, I think, you and Lady Black."

The words were like a knife in Liam's belly. "That's really none of your business," he said coldly.

"As you like. Take care, Your Highness. You are being

watched, and I am not the only spy at court. Even a single ill-considered word could get you killed. From now on, treat everything you say, everything you do, as a matter of life and death."

So saying, the spy headed up the path and turned, cloak flapping, to disappear behind the roses.

FOUR

"That's it?" Ide said, looking up at the scarred timber façade of the Kingsword fort. "How in the name of Rahl did we hold off the Warlord with *this*?"

Good question, Alix thought, fighting her horse as it danced restlessly before the gate. The fort had probably never been impressive, but it looked positively crippled now, half-razed in the enemy onslaught three weeks before. Builders dotted its surfaces like insects, armed with hammers and saws and buckets of pitch, effecting hasty repairs in anticipation of another assault. It wouldn't be long, Alix knew.

Dain Cooper threw a friendly wave up at the ramparts; a pair of archers waved back. "That's General Black for you," Dain said. "Man's a genius."

Alix was momentarily surprised, but then she remembered: Before Dain had joined the White Wolves as Liam's second, he'd been a soldier here in the fort. He knew Rig—and respected him, obviously. She couldn't help smiling. "My brother is many things, but I'm not sure genius is among them. I think he'd be the first to admit that the secret to his success is less wit than luck."

"The secret to his success," Ide said, "is *balls*. Begging your pardon."

Alix laughed. In spite of her fatigue, in spite of the hurt brooding in the pit of her stomach, she found herself enjoying the company of her companions. Though it was impossible not to think of Liam while spending day after day with his men, Ide had been a friend since their days scouting together, and Dain was easy to like. Alix hadn't realised just how much she missed the scouts; having something like that fellowship again was a comfort, especially now.

A final scrape and judder heralded the opening of the gate, and Alix and the others rode into a cramped courtyard smelling of straw and smoke. The ring of a forge sounded somewhere nearby, and of swordplay too, soldiers practicing lunges and parries with spears and dulled blades. For all its crude lines and hasty construction, the scene reminded Alix a little of the bailey at Blackhold, as it had been in her youth.

More so when she heard a familiar voice call out from clear across the yard. "What in the Nine Hells are you doing here?"

Alix turned to find her brother making his way over in great strides, his expression a mix of concern and delight. After everything that had happened, the sight of him nearly brought her to tears; she was grateful when he enveloped her in a bear hug, shielding her face from prying eyes.

"Seriously, Allie," Rig's deep voice rumbled in her ear, "how worried do I need to be right now?" They hadn't dared send word ahead for fear of it falling into the wrong hands, but Rig was no fool. If she'd left Erik's side, it couldn't be good news.

"Not here," she whispered. "Someplace safe."

"Gods' balls." He drew back and gave her a long, appraising look. Brushing her cheek with a rough hand, he said, "Give us a smile, love, and a laugh if you can manage it. Can't have you standing there looking like you're about to cry. Bad for morale." His own features broke into a smile, dark eyes flicking meaningfully to the ramparts, where a handful of soldiers stood gawking at their commander general and his sister.

Alix did her best to laugh, though she doubted it was very convincing.

"Dain Cooper!" Rig clasped arms with the Onnani knight. "Didn't I throw you to the Wolves?"

Dain laughed. "You did, General. I'm still nominally Prince Liam's second-in-command, though by rights that duty belongs to Ide here."

Gracious of him, Alix thought. And true. Ide deserved better than to have been replaced for political reasons and Dain knew it. Though it was no fault of his, he must have felt terribly awkward about it.

Ide, though, was phlegmatic as always. "Rights got nothing to do with it, leastways not mine. Commander appoints who he will."

"He appointed you," Dain said. "They *made* him replace you, just to appease the Onnani."

Ide shrugged. "It's done. No use whinging about it." Saluting, she added, "Honour to see you again, General Black."

"I guess we'd better head inside," Rig said. "Not sure where we'll put you, but in the meantime, I can see that you get some food and hot water."

"Sounds brilliant," Ide said. "Got any wine?"

Alix rolled her eyes. Being knighted had obviously done nothing to change Ide's priorities in life.

Rig just laughed. "A woman after my own heart. It so happens I have a small private stash. I'll see to it you get some."

They followed him inside, to a room that looked remarkably like the common room of an inn. "Home," he said. "Now, about that food and water . . ."

Alix left Ide and Dain to wash up. What she had to say couldn't wait, so Rig took her up to his quarters, which looked to double as a war room judging from the table strewn with maps. She started to speak almost the moment he closed the door, but he held up a hand. "Washbasin. Wine. Then we talk."

Alix nodded wearily, allowing herself to be shown to a washstand in the corner. With the dust of the road gone and a cup of warmed wine in her hand, she certainly felt better. But that didn't make what she had to say any easier. "I don't even know where to begin."

Rig's eyes, as coal black as his hair, took her in carefully. "They usually say you should start at the beginning, but in this case, I think it might be best if you skipped to the end."

Alix took a sip of warmed wine. Swallowed. "Erik has been bloodbound."

A flicker of dark eyebrows, like lightning before the storm. "Explain."

"We were wrong. The Priest's cursed magicks didn't die with him. At least one bloodbinder in Oridia still knows how to pervert the bloodbond, and he's using it on Erik."

Rig paled. "Are you telling me Erik is a *thrall*?" Alix couldn't remember the last time she'd heard her brother whisper, but he was doing it now, throwing a nervous glance at the door.

"Not exactly, not yet. I think the bloodbinder must be too far away to control him completely. But he's . . . not Erik, either. He's erratic. Volatile, even. It's as if he's completely unable to keep his emotions in check. And then there's what happened in Harram . . ." She did her best to explain, pausing every few moments to take another sip of wine, as though its warmth could banish the chill inside her.

When she'd done, Rig launched himself away from the table, cursing a streak so foul that Alix winced. He looked like he wanted to snap someone in half. More than that, he looked like he actually *could*. "How is that even possible? Where did they get his blood?"

"Erik has a twin. Identical. It was kept secret, obviously— even Erik doesn't know. Rodrik—that's his name—was exiled to Andithyri as a baby so no one would ever know he existed."

Rig's mouth fell open. "You have *got* to be . . . First Liam and now this? How many secret children did King Osrik *have*?"

Alix couldn't help it; she burst out laughing—a hollow, bitter thing, perilously close to tears. "He did have his intrigues, didn't he?"

"So the enemy has this Rodrik and they're using his blood to control our king." Rig laughed too, both of them edging on hysteria. "It couldn't possibly be worse! Bloody Alerran himself couldn't have penned a finer tragedy!" He shook his head in awe. "Who else knows about this?

"Highmount, Liam, Rona Brown. Dain and Ide. A handful of my guardsmen." *Too many.* She saw the thought reflected in her brother's eyes.

"What are you going to do?"

The question tore something open inside her. Alix told him what they'd done, how they'd locked Erik away, barring his doors and guarding his windows . . . And now the tears finally broke free, sliding down her face, cold as betrayal.

More cursing. Rig sagged against the table. "Everything we've been through. The Onnani fleet burned, the Harrami refusing to help. Battle after battle, grinding us down by attrition. We barely survived that last fight, Allie. I've been tearing my hair out ever since, waiting for the Warlord to ram the rest of his army down our throats. And meanwhile, all this time, he's had a trump tucked up his sleeve, the play to end all plays." Rig looked at her grimly. "We are *completely* buggered, you know."

"Don't say that. We'll find a way. We have to. I swore on the blood of our family."

He sighed. "You're right, of course. It's just . . . this is a lot to take in." He paused, dark eyes pinning her. "But you didn't come all this way just to deliver a message. You're going after him, aren't you? Rodrik?"

Alix nodded, swallowing the terror that reared up in her throat.

Rig pursed his lips in displeasure. "Sadik's forces are close, Allie. Just a few miles across the river. And he has spies everywhere, even here in the fort."

"What?" She gazed up at him in dismay. "A spy in the Kingswords? Are you sure?"

"Positive. Meanwhile, Sadik's army will be on us any day, all twenty thousand of them. It could hardly be a worse time to go sneaking across the border."

"What choice is there? If we don't get Rodrik out of enemy hands, Erik is lost to us forever."

Alix watched her brother wrestle with denial, wracking his brain for some other solution—until, inevitably, he was defeated, swearing softly and shaking his head. "Liam must be thrilled."

She looked away. "Safe to say he's not."

"You argued?"

"You might say that." Alix squeezed her eyes shut. "I said some horrible things, Rig."

"He'll forgive you."

"I'm not sure about that. I don't know if we can get past this. Not the fight, but what it brought out into the open."

"Meaning?"

"What happened between Erik and me last year . . . I thought it was behind us, but I was wrong. It's not behind us at all. It's between us, and I don't know if we can get around it. I don't know how."

Rig was quiet a moment while he digested that. "Male pride is a fragile thing. It does heal, but it takes a long time. And I'd hazard a guess that this isn't all about you."

"I don't follow."

"I know you like to forget that Liam's a bastard, but I promise you he doesn't forget it, not for a moment."

"I know that."

"All right then, imagine what that's like for him. He's spent his whole life being told that he's less than Erik, unworthy of the White name. That's enough to give anyone a heap of insecurities. On top of which, show me a man who doesn't suffer by comparison to Erik White."

"Liam doesn't."

Rig gave her a sober look. "Better be sure he knows you feel that way, Allie."

Before she could reply, the door opened and a woman breezed into the room. She froze when she saw Alix, her glance cutting back and forth between brother and sister. "I beg your pardon. I didn't realise General Black had company." She was Onnani, attractive, with long black hair and fierce dark eyes. Her tone carried a touch of frost; that, along with the entitled manner of her entry, was very telling indeed. Alix shot her brother a wry look.

Rig met her gaze blandly, utterly immune to embarrassment. "Vel," he said, "may I present my sister, Lady Alix."

"Your sister? Oh, I . . ." Colouring a little, the woman dipped into an awkward sort of bow, as if she were meeting royalty. Alix arched an eyebrow. And wait . . . were those robes . . . ?

"You're a *priestess*?" Alix blurted.

A dusky blush flooded the other woman's features. "I am," she said, and the hint of frost was back—with reinforcements.

"Vel," said Rig, "will you excuse us? We're not quite finished here."

"Yes, of course. Apologies again, General." She looked only too happy to quit the room, closing the door with a decisive *snap*.

Alix and Rig stared at each other.

"A *priestess*."

"What of it?"

"You're bedding a *priestess*. An Onnani priestess, no less!"

"Who says I'm bedding her?"

"Rig."

He shrugged. "I don't see what business it is of yours."

"None. I just thought you were through with casual relationships. Responsibilities of a banner lord, so on and so forth."

Rig snorted softly. "Is this your subtle way of asking whether I'm serious about her?"

"Not at all, because I know you couldn't possibly be serious about her." Alix raised an eyebrow pointedly.

"Because she's a priestess?"

"A priestess. Onnani. Take your pick."

"This from the woman who married a bastard."

"This from the woman whose brother forbade her from marrying a bastard and would have forbidden it unto the end of the world had said bastard not become a *prince*."

"Well." He scratched his beard. "You have me there."

"On top of which," Alix added bitterly, "look how well *that* turned out."

Rig sighed. "Try not to be too dramatic, Allie. Give it time. You'll see things more clearly, and so will he."

"Unless I don't make it back from Andithyri. Or Liam is found out, and ends up in the Red Tower, or . . ." She clamped her eyes shut, shook her head.

She heard Rig stir, and a moment later, his arms went around her. Alix sank gratefully into her brother's embrace, knowing it was the last bit of comfort she would have for a very long time.

"You didn't tell me your sister was coming." Rig didn't miss the faint whiff of accusation in Vel's voice, nor the tense lines of her shoulders as she poured herself some wine.

He didn't miss it, but he didn't acknowledge it, either. "I didn't know," he said simply.

"Had a sudden urge for a visit, did she?"

"Not exactly."

Vel waited for more; when it didn't come, she took her irritation out on the wine jug, setting it down roughly enough to send liquid sloshing over the top. "My, you are wonderfully verbose this evening. And could you tell me what is so fascinating about that fire that you can barely be bothered to glance at me while we're speaking?"

Rig sighed and turned away from the hearth. "I've got a lot on my mind, Vel."

Her expression softened. "Bad news from your sister?"

"Something of an understatement, that."

Vel set her wine down and came over, slipping her arms around him. "Do you want to talk about it?"

"Some of it I can't discuss." He'd learned that it was best to be direct with her about such things. She could nearly always tell when he was holding back; lying about it only hurt her. Anyway, she seemed largely to have made her peace with it. He was, after all, commander general of the king's armies. Secrets came with the territory. "I can give you the basics, though."

"Tell me," she crooned in her priestess voice, that soothing cadence that thrummed along Rig's spine. "You'll feel better."

Rig doubted that, but he had reasons of his own for telling her. "Alix is planning to infiltrate Andithyri, she and the two knights she came with."

Vel drew back, eyes round with surprise. She knew better than anyone just how dangerous that could be, having done it herself only a month ago. "Why?"

"That's the part I can't tell you." He brushed a lock of dark hair behind her ear, an affectionate gesture to soften the blow. "But it's important, obviously."

"I thought your sister was the king's bodyguard?"

He needed to be careful here; Vel was too clever to overlook even small clues. "She is," he said, "but she's also the stealthiest scout we've got." He smiled, in spite of himself. "If it calls for sneaking, you can't do better than Alix Black. That's been so since she was small. A born thief, that one."

"I'd forgotten. You raised her, didn't you?"

"Since she was eleven. A royal pain in the ass, she was. Still is, I suppose. Headstrong as an old mule. A true child of Ardin."

"How could she be otherwise, raised by you?"

"You're hardly one to talk, my dear."

Vel feigned indignation, withdrawing to retrieve her wine. "Being passionate is one thing, being stubborn entirely another. Ardin has no domain over obstinacy; that belongs to Destan."

"Whichever Holy Virtue it belongs to, the Black family has never lacked for it," Rig said, accepting a cup of wine. "And neither do you."

She regarded him shrewdly from under long, dark lashes. "I may be stubborn, but I am also an ordained priestess of Eldora. When it counts, I am guided foremost by prudence, which is what allowed me to steal across enemy lines and contact the Resistance without being caught. But you already know all that." She sighed, her gaze dropping to her wine. "Which is why you're going to ask me to go with her."

Rig should have known she'd guess it. Too clever by half, this one. He took her wine and set it aside, covered her hands in his. Her fingers looked tiny and delicate in his grasp, like the pinions of a bird trapped in the paws of a beast. "Alix will never find what she's looking for on her own. She'll need help from the locals."

"By which you mean the Resistance. And you want me to act as go-between."

"I would never ask it of you if it weren't a matter of life and death. Not just my sister's, but . . ." He stopped himself, recalibrated. "There's a lot at stake, Vel. More than I can tell you."

"Yet you would ask me to lay down my life for it." He couldn't read her expression; it was too smooth, too penetrating.

"It's unfair of me, I know."

"But you know perfectly well that I'll do it." She pulled away. "And you know perfectly well why."

He did. Just as she knew that he couldn't return those feelings, at least not right now. Apparently, though, he wasn't above using her love as leverage. He hated himself for that, but . . . "This is war, Vel."

"Yes, it is." She drew herself up and met his gaze. Candlelight burnished her features, painting her in flaming defiance, a portrait of such fervid beauty that it took Rig's breath away. "And you needn't worry, General. I'll not be a bystander in this chapter any more than I was in the last."

Pride flared in Rig's blood. He took her face in his hands and kissed her, hard. Dimly, some part of him registered that it might have been wrong of him, but if Vel felt manipulated, she didn't seem to mind. She was fierce, his priestess, and matched his passion with her own, as if answering a challenge. And then of course she had to outbid his body into his, pressing her body into his, tugging suggestively at his armour. The thin thread of restraint snapped. Rig hoisted her onto the table, sending the wine jug teetering dangerously. She hiked her robes up around her thighs and wrapped her legs around him, ignoring the sound of fabric tearing as her hem caught the edge of his chain mail. That would have to come off, right now. Buckles, *so many blighted buckles*, stood between him and what he wanted, but Vel was practiced by now, fingers deft and sure; she stripped the armour from him piece by piece, letting it clatter to the floor. More fabric ripping, Rig wasn't sure where, but it didn't matter, she didn't care; his hands climbed the bare skin of her thighs, soft beneath his callused palms.

"We're going to spill the wine," she breathed.

She was teasing him. She knew nothing could stop him now, not the Warlord himself. He slipped his fingers inside her smallclothes, making sure the momentum wasn't his alone. She nipped his ear, near hard enough to draw blood, and he knew she was with him. Still, he took no shortcuts, kissing her throat while he stroked her, listening to her breath climb in pitch until she gasped, her whole body seizing. Then he scooped her off the table, just high enough to rid her of those last scraps of clothing in his way. Her fingers twined in his hair in anticipation. She threw her head back as he took her, neck curved invitingly, skin glowing bronze in the candlelight. Rig paused to savour the feel of her, the sweet ache of tension hurtling toward him in an ever-building wave.

She clutched at him, impatient.

Rig surrendered himself to instinct, riding the riptide to oblivion.

* * *

Sleep had almost claimed him when the guilt came rushing back.

"Vel."

She hummed in acknowledgement, rolling onto her side. Dark eyes peered at Rig through a mass of dishevelled black hair. Gods, she was beautiful.

"I hope I didn't . . . I wouldn't want you to think . . ."

She let him struggle for a moment before she took pity on him, full mouth curving into a smile. "I'm a grown woman, Riggard Black. I am capable of resisting your charms if I so choose."

"I wasn't trying to manipulate you, is all," Rig said gruffly.

"I would hardly think you capable of anything so subtle."

"I'm serious, Vel. I may be thoughtless sometimes, but I'm not a *complete* bastard."

She hitched a shoulder indifferently. "You're making an issue where there is none. Ardin was in your blood, and in mine. I see no need to complicate a most enjoyable couple of hours."

He sighed, gazing up at the ceiling. Somehow, he doubted she would see it that way a few days from now.

"It's not the lovemaking you feel guilty about," Vel said with cutting clarity.

"You're right, it isn't."

"It is unfair of you to ask me to go. I'll not spare you that. But I choose to believe I would have done it anyway, even if my feelings for you were"—she faltered briefly—"less than they are."

"I think so too." They both needed to believe that, though for very different reasons.

"The situation is obviously grave." Vel slid over and tucked herself into him, head propped on his chest. "Your sister's expression made that clear enough. She looked near to tears when I walked in."

"She was, though that had as much to do with personal problems as matters of war and peace."

"She would not wish you to tell me about it, I suppose."

"I shouldn't think so."

He fell silent, thoughts drifting back to his conversation with Alix. She'd always had a flair for drama, but this time, Rig had no doubt things were serious. That dull look in her eyes, how fragile she'd felt in his arms . . . He'd never seen her like that, and it hurt like hell. He'd spent his whole life protecting her, but he couldn't shield her from this. If his sister's marriage was in trouble, there wasn't a damned thing Rig could do about it.

Trust was everything in a relationship. If Alix and Liam had lost that . . . *Can you ever really get it back?*

"Get what back?"

Rig started; he hadn't realised he'd spoken aloud. "Sorry, I was just thinking."

"About?"

"Trust. How once it's lost . . . Do you think it can ever be rebuilt?"

He felt her tense. "Why do you ask?"

"Just something my sister said. Wondering if it's possible for a relationship to overcome the past."

A pause. "I certainly hope so."

"Me too," Rig said, and drifted into sleep.

FIVE

"Hard to say," Dain Cooper admitted, grimacing as he peered through the longlens. "Trees are too dense to see much of anything."

Dense and in the full exuberance of spring, a riot of fresh green in every possible shade. It should have been beautiful, but all Alix saw was menace, a thousand hiding places for enemy scouts. The Wolves felt it too, she could tell. Dain still had the longlens to his eye, tracking systematically back and forth, scanning the Andithyrian side of the river. Ide had her bloodbow strung, arrow in hand. Even the priestess, Vel, had her bottom lip drawn between her teeth, squinting across the wide expanse of the Gunnar as though she might see more with her naked eye than Dain with the longlens.

We should have waited a day, Alix thought. She could have studied Rig's maps a little longer, deliberated a little more carefully about whether she wanted a complete stranger for an escort. But there was little point in regretting her decision now. "If the enemy is out there," she said, "he'll show himself soon enough."

"We should go carefully," the priestess advised, "and not

only because of the Oridians. It was early in the season when I crossed. The river is higher now."

"How much higher?" Dain asked. "Can you tell?"

"About a foot, perhaps a little more. In which case it should be manageable. It came to just below my waist last time, and I'm the shortest among us." Looking Alix and Ide up and down, she added, "By quite some measure."

The remark nettled, as it had Alix's whole life—especially coming from someone as dainty as Vel. "What about those?" she said coolly, gesturing at the priestess's robes. "Not the most practical attire for wading across a river."

Vel gathered her robes, which Alix now saw were split down the sides, and swept aside the folds to reveal close-fitting leggings. Wrapping the loose flaps around her waist, Vel tied them off and out of the way. She shot Alix a highly expressive look before stepping confidently into the water.

"Better let me go first," Ide said, wading in beside the priestess. "I'm the one with the bow. Carry my pack, Dain?"

Alix brought up the rear, breath catching as the water climbed her thighs. Swollen with snowmelt, the Gunnar was scarcely above freezing; its touch stung like a whip. Alix had no doubt her legs would be numb by the time they reached the far bank.

They crossed slowly, choosing each footfall with great caution. The current was fast here, and their packs were heavy enough to make swimming all but impossible, especially with the frigid water shocking the breath from their lungs. Even a rolled ankle could lead to disaster. Ide did double duty in the point position, carefully selecting their path even as she kept her bow trained on the far bank. Alix's nerves prickled with every step, and not just from the cold. They were so vulnerable out here in the middle of the water, an easy target for any competent archer. And slow—gods, it was taking *forever*. The water dragged at Alix's wool leggings, and her boots felt heavy and clumsy. It was like one of those nightmares where her limbs wouldn't quite work, weighing her down even as she sensed some unseen threat looming. Her heart pounded, fear and the bitter chill of the water spurring her pulse to a gallop.

A rustle in the trees sent a bright arc of panic through her, but it was only a bird taking flight. It caught one of Ide's arrows square in the breast and plummeted like a stone. Ide cursed, annoyed at the waste of a shaft.

"You didn't have to kill it," the priestess said.

"Got the shot off before I knew what it was," Ide returned irritably. "And it's a bloodbow, isn't it? Not like I could miss."

Their voices carried dangerously across the water. *"Quiet,"* Alix growled.

At last, mercifully, they gained the far bank. Alix dragged herself out of the water, wincing as she dropped into a stiff crouch.

"Well, we made it," Dain said.

Alix couldn't manage to feel relieved. Gaining the far bank meant they'd crossed the border. They were in occupied Andithyri now. The Warlord's territory. And the deeper into it they forged, the greater the threat would become.

"The game trail picks up again just up there," Vel said, pointing.

"How long before we hit the farmlands?" Alix asked.

"I doubt we will reach the forest's edge before nightfall. Better to camp under cover."

As though I need a priestess telling me how to scout. Alix pushed the thought aside. She had more important things to worry about than her pride. However much it irked her, however strange it was to be walking into mortal danger with her brother's lover as her guide, she needed to make an effort to get along with this woman. There was too much at stake to be distracted by trifles. "And after that," she said, "how long until we find this Wraith?"

"He will find us, I should think, or rather his men will. He has scouts posted all along the river, keeping an eye on the Warlord's movements."

"Wraith," Ide muttered. "What kind of name is that?"

"Mysterious and unsettling," Dain said, "or at least, that's the idea. The Onnani rebellion used to do the same, back in the days of the empire. The most celebrated of the rebel commanders all had names like that—Viper, Deadeye, and suchlike. Seems kind of ironic that the white-hairs would take up the tradition."

"That they would adopt the practices of the very people who revolted against their rule?" Vel hummed thoughtfully.

"Yes, it does rather, now that you mention it." She smiled at Dain. "It is good to have one of my countrymen along on this journey, Commander."

"Just Dain, thanks. And I consider myself an Aldenian first and foremost, though I am proud of my heritage." He smiled back at her, adding, "It is nice, though, to not be the only Onnani in the party for once."

"Though you are the only bloke," Ide pointed out. "No getting ideas."

Dain rolled his eyes.

"If we could get back to the Andithyrian Resistance, please," Alix said dryly. "If they're likely to pick us up quickly, then we'd better be prepared. Anything we need to know, Vel?" There hadn't been time for a proper briefing before they left the fort; Alix had been too determined to strike out immediately. She could feel the hours slipping through her fingers, each one as precious as a grain of gold. Her king was bloodbound and locked away in his own palace. It was only a matter of time before he got out, or word of him did, and that would be the death of her husband. Her brother, meanwhile, was left holding the line against twenty thousand Oridians. Everything depended on what Alix did here, and how quickly she did it.

Which was why she'd let Rig talk her into bringing along a civilian—a priestess, no less. *She'd better pull her weight.*

As if sensing the thought, Vel's expression smoothed, all business now. "I'm not sure how much you already know about the Resistance."

"Only a little. They're a fairly new phenomenon, from what I can tell."

"Our knowledge of them is, at any rate," Vel said. "I have the impression that they are not quite as new as we suppose."

"A good bet," Dain said. "Seems likely they'd be around for a while before word reached our ears of it."

"White-hairs are a prideful lot," Ide put in, "being they used to rule the empire and all. Getting conquered can't sit well with them. Probably been working against the Trionate from the beginning."

"Though how organised they are," Vel said, "we cannot tell. Myself, I am not convinced that the Resistance operates as a single cohesive entity. General Black and I believe they may be more of a loose coalition of cells operating independently."

General Black. The priestess had yet to refer to Rig by his given name, or even as *your brother.* Deliberate, Alix judged, as was the reminder that she enjoyed Rig's confidence. *She knows how you feel about all this, and she's as uncomfortable with it as you are.* If anything, that only made things more awkward.

"How many are they?" Alix asked.

Vel shook her head. "I asked few questions of that nature. General Black did not send me for the purposes of reconnaissance, but rather to establish contact. I judged that asking too many pointed questions would strain our fragile trust."

She had good instincts for a civilian, Alix had to admit. "How fragile is that trust, exactly?"

"Stronger now, I think, after we worked together successfully in the last battle."

"Anything else I should know?"

"Not that I can think of, except perhaps to remember that these are hard, dangerous men. Wraith, especially. He is difficult to read. We should not anticipate a warm welcome. Nor, I think, should we anticipate charity."

"Meaning?"

Vel shrugged. "Only that his first priority is the freedom of his country."

"And my priority is Alden's freedom." *And the freedom of her king*, Alix added inwardly.

"May those two priorities never diverge," the priestess said, as solemn as a prayer.

They were making good time the following day when the priestess saw fit to stop—in the middle of a field, in broad daylight, where any Sam Stumble-Along could see.

"We need to keep moving," Alix said.

Vel scarcely seemed to hear. "I don't understand it. Wraith's men should have found us by now."

"*Someone* certainly will if we don't get out of the open."

"Maybe the Resistance has moved on," Dain said.

Alix shook her head. "That wouldn't make sense. This area

is teeming with Sadik's men. If the Resistance wants to keep an eye on them, this is where they'll be."

"They are nearby," Vel said. "I *know* it." To Alix's ears, it sounded more like wishful thinking than a statement of fact.

"Keep moving." Putting actions to words, Alix brushed past the priestess and continued across the field.

Highmount had been right about the terrain being open. And Liam, she was forced to admit, had been right about it posing a problem. Avoiding the roads might lessen the odds of bumping into Oridian soldiers, but it also made their party look suspicious, tracking through fields of winter wheat without hoe or harrow. *Maybe we should find a place to hole up for a few days*, she thought. *That might make us easier to find.* For the Resistance, but also, she realised, for the Warlord. Sadik would have spies out here as well as soldiers, and in the land of the white-hairs, Alix could hardly be more conspicuous. Even if she managed to keep her flaming red locks tucked under her hood, two of her party were Onnani, a rare enough sight in Andithyri to draw unwanted attention. *No getting around it*, she thought grimly. *Spotted is branded, and branded is most likely dead.*

Such were her thoughts when the soldiers appeared.

She knew them for Oridians the moment she saw them, even from clear across the field. They were on horseback, and in occupied country, only soldiers got to keep their horses.

"Dain," she hissed, but he didn't need to be told; he was peering down the longlens already.

"Five—no, six. They've definitely seen us. They're headed this way."

Alix reeled under a sickening wave of fear. Not for herself, but for the mission. She could not afford to fail.

Dain still had the longlens to his eye. "Can you take them, Ide?"

"Not at this range. Most I'd get is one or two before the rest found cover and started shooting back."

"Too risky," Alix said. "They won't assume we're a threat straightaway. Let them get close. It'll be easier to take them if we have to."

"Better let me bring up the rear, then," Ide said, "and keep a tight ring around me so they can't see my bow."

"Hide your packs in the wheat," Alix said. "We may yet talk our way out of this." The enemy soldiers didn't have a longlens, or if they did, they hadn't used it—their leisurely pace was proof enough of that. *Looking for some peasants to bully, no doubt. Well, let them try to bully us.* The thought brought a welcome fire to her belly.

They were drunk, Alix saw as the riders drew near; she could tell by the lazy way they sat their horses. A mixed blessing, that. Six to three was poor odds (the priestess didn't count), but drunkenness might just even things out. On the other hand, there were few things in the world more quarrelsome than a soldier in his cups. Alix slipped a hand under her cloak, felt the reassuring steel at her hip. She ran a thumb over the garnet buried in the hilt that marked her blade as blood-forged. Another advantage, assuming the Oridians didn't carry bloodblades of their own. *Not very likely*, she told herself. Too rare and valuable, especially now that the Kingswords had slain the Priest, greatest and most prolific of the enemy bloodbinders.

"Ho there!" the lead rider called in Erromanian. "What have we here?"

Alix ducked her head, the better to conceal her features. "Just humble farmers, my lord."

"My lord! I like that!" He swivelled in his saddle to look at his comrades. "You all can call me *my lord* from now on," he said, eliciting jeers and sloppy laughter. Turning back to Alix, he said, "Not afraid of us are you, all huddled up like that?" His accent was heavy, but he spoke the language well, even through his drink. An officer, Alix judged. "What's this now," he said, leaning forward with narrowed eyes. "Some fishmen, I see."

Damn. It had been too much to hope that the soldiers might overlook the dark skin of the Onnani in the party.

"Fishmen farmers? In Andithyri? That doesn't seem likely, now does it?" The officer's gaze sharpened; suddenly, he seemed very sober indeed.

"Not farmers," Vel said, throwing off her cloak to reveal her priestess's robes. "Missionaries, here to pray with our Andithyrian brothers in these dark times of war."

It was a good ploy, and it might have worked had Vel not shown a little too much skin in those robes. But there was no mistaking the leer that crossed the officer's face. He turned and said something to his comrades, and this time the laughter had a predatory edge to it. Alix's Oridian was poor, but she distinctly heard the word *treat*.

She tensed, fingers tightening around the hilt of her blade. "Ide."

An arrow hissed over her shoulder and caught the officer between the eyes; he was dead before he hit the ground. Dain's arm whipped out from under his cloak and a second rider fell with a dagger in his throat. The horses scattered amid shouts and the steel song of blades being drawn.

A rider charged at Alix. She got her sword out just in time to turn aside the blow, but the force of it knocked her off balance, sending her tumbling to the dirt. She barely managed to regain her feet before the rider was on her again. Alix threw herself back to the ground, swinging out at the horse's fetlocks as she fell, but she wasn't fast enough; the animal loped past and out of reach.

Rolling to her feet, Alix readied herself for another pass. So focused was she on one soldier that she nearly died on the blade of another; she spun just as a flash of steel came at her flank. Her sword was moving before her mind had fully registered the attack, meeting her opponent's blade with a clumsy *clang* that sent her stumbling back. The Oridian was on foot, his horse lying dead a few feet away, but that only made him more nimble; he threw himself at Alix in a flurry of blows. Caught off balance, she would have struggled to parry had she not wielded a bloodblade. As it was, even a sword enchanted to obey her every instinct was barely enough to keep her alive. Her foe was skilled, and if he was drunk like the others, it didn't seem to bother him. If anything, it lent him courage; his attacks were bold, furious, unpredictable. Alix gave ground quickly, without any idea what lay behind her. She couldn't even spare a glance for her comrades; a moment's distraction would be the end of her.

If her enemy hadn't stumbled on the uneven ground, she might have been overcome. But he did, and Alix didn't hesitate, driving her blade into his gut and twisting just enough to be sure of finishing the job.

She whirled in time to see a rider grab a fistful of Vel's long hair and drag her against his horse. A dagger flashed. Dain cried out in alarm.

"Enough!" The soldier holding Vel brandished his dagger menacingly. "No moving!"

Alix glanced around, breath harsh in her ears. Ide had thrown down her bow as soon as the battle began—it made her too vulnerable in a close fight—but her blade had seen action, judging from the smear of crimson on its edge. Dain and his foe faced each other warily, both of them bloodied, but neither seriously. That left one Oridian on horseback—the one with his dagger pressed against Vel's throat.

Alix's mind whirred. They could take the one on foot easily enough, but it would cost them Vel. That, in turn, might well cost them the Resistance. Swearing, she lowered her sword. "What now?"

"Weapons down," the rider growled. "All." His Erromanian wasn't as good as the dead officer's had been, but he made himself understood.

"Not much for maths, are you, mate?" Ide pointed with her sword. "There's three of us and two of you."

"You want this one dead?" He yanked Vel's hair, hard enough to draw a yelp of pain.

Just now, I might not mind so much. A fleeting thought, unfair. But there was no denying the anger that set Alix's cheeks aflame. The priestess had been careless, and now they might all pay the price. Aloud, she said, "How do we know you won't kill us the moment we lay down our weapons?"

He sneered down at the priestess in his grip. "You pray!"

Alix hesitated. A breeze sighed through the field, caressing it into rolling waves of green. In the heightened senses of the moment, Alix felt the soft brush of wheat against the back of her wrist, gentle as a lover. "All right," she said. "I'm going to lower my sword now." What choice did they have?

They laid their weapons in the long grasses with exaggerated care—none more so than Ide, who bent low enough that her short-cropped hair disappeared behind the stalks of wheat.

"Hurry up," the soldier snarled.

They were the last words he ever spoke. Ide shot up out of the grass like a snake, bow in hand, loosing a shaft before the soldier could react. He pitched backward off his saddle. The remaining Oridian tried to run, but Ide took him down before he got far.

Alix nearly doubled over in relief. "Thank the gods. I had no idea your bow was right at your feet!"

"Good bloody thing too, and that the wheat was high enough to hide it." She whirled on Vel, who sat in the grass looking dazed. "You almost got us killed, priestess! Why didn't you take cover? Instead you just stand there like a startled rabbit?"

Alix had never seen her so livid. Neither, apparently, had Dain. "Ide—" he began.

"No, don't defend her! It's common sense, isn't it?"

Alix knew she should intervene, but in truth she agreed.

"You think maybe there's a *reason* I chop off my hair," Ide went on, "or that Alix keeps hers in a braid? Nothing stupider in battle than giving the enemy something to grab on to."

"I'm not a soldier," Vel said.

That much is obvious. Alix retrieved her bloodblade, threw it into its sheath. "We need to move on."

Vel drew herself up on shaking legs. "I must pray for the dead."

Alix's mouth fell open. Ide launched into a string of curses. Even Dain looked taken aback.

"I am not a soldier," Vel repeated, ice crystals forming on the words. "I am a *priestess*. Leave me behind if you will, but I must do my duty."

Alix pressed her lips together, exchanging a dark look with the Wolves. Turning her back on Vel, she approached the nearest horse and gave it a whack on the rump, sending it loping off into the wheat. Though she would have loved to keep it for a pack animal, it would only draw more soldiers down upon them. "Make it quick," she shot over her shoulder. "We've lingered here too long."

SIX

The Resistance found them the following day. Or
rather, that was when Wraith's men chose to reveal
themselves. From the way they appeared—in numbers,
two groups in a flanking manoeuvre, materialising from
behind cover with bows drawn—Alix guessed they'd been following for a while.

"Drop your weapons."

Alix couldn't tell which of them had spoken; like her own
party, they all wore hoods pulled low over their faces. She
hesitated, every instinct screaming of threat. Then she felt the
cool kiss of steel under her jaw.

"Don't make me repeat myself," said the voice, right in her ear.

Alix went rigid. No one had ever managed to sneak up on
her like that.

"Getting a bit tired of being told to drop my steel," Ide growled.
"Be nice to go more than a day without stumbling across the
enemy."

"Don't be a fool," said Vel. "These aren't Oridians. Can't
you hear his accent?"

"Accents can be faked."

"Not by me," said the man with the sword, a trace of

amusement in his voice. "At least not while I'm sober." Alix felt a tug as her hood was yanked back. "Well now, there's a lovely head of hair. Goes with the jewel on your lovely sword, which I'll thank you to put down."

Alix had little choice but to comply, tossing her bloodblade a few feet in front of her.

"And the dagger," the man said, helping himself to the knife sheathed at her hip. Turning it over, he whistled admiringly. "Bloodforged as well. My, my, we are well kitted, aren't we? Now—the rest of you."

Reluctantly, Ide dropped her sword, as did Dain. Vel had no weapon to divest herself of.

The sword flicked away from Alix's jaw and a slight figure stepped in front of her. He pulled his own hood back to reveal a shock of white hair and the most unsettling green eyes Alix had ever seen. He was pretty even for an Andithyrian; with his fine features and high cheekbones, he looked almost fey.

"Asvin," said Vel, "it's good to see you again."

"And you, Daughter." The lack of surprise in his voice confirmed Alix's suspicion: they'd been following for a while, at least long enough to realise Vel was in the party. It was probably the only reason they'd shown themselves.

"I worried about your fate in the grain silo attack," Vel said.

The slight man cocked his head. "How did you know I led the grain silo attack?"

"A lightning strike designed to distract and confuse? Who better than the lightning-quick Asvin?"

"By Hew," said one of the Andithyrians, "she does pay attention."

"By Farika," Asvin said, "she does flatter."

Alix was in no mood for banter. "How long have you been following us?"

"Long enough," Asvin said. "Nice work with the roaches yesterday."

She scowled. "I suppose you mean the Oridians. Do I take it you stood by and watched that? Your friend the priestess here nearly died."

The green eyes regarded her coolly. "We had no notion of who you were. Still don't, aside from Daughter Vel here. General Black's men, I presume?"

"General Black's sister, in fact," Vel said conversationally.

Asvin arched a white eyebrow. "Is that so? The same sister who snuffed the Priest?"

Alix felt herself flush. "It wasn't I who killed him. It was my comrade, Gwylim. I just helped smuggle in the black powder."

"Now that," Asvin said, "was some *quality* sneaking. I should know."

"It does seem to be a talent we share," Alix said, not warmly.

"I'd fancy hearing that tale, but it'll have to wait." He sheathed his sword and gestured for his men to gather up the weapons. "You know the procedure, Daughter."

"Blindfolds." Vel nodded. "Please proceed."

It was more than a little presumptuous, but Alix let it go. It seemed her brother had been right, and Vel did know her way around these men. *Time to earn your keep, priestess.*

They were bound and hooded, loaded onto the back of an oxcart among sacks of turnips smelling of mould. Someone pulled a blanket over them, and they were off, jouncing along the narrow dirt track they'd been following when Wraith's men ambushed them.

"Bloody undignified, this," Ide muttered, but the rest of them endured it in silence.

After what seemed like forever, the oxcart came to a halt. Someone climbed up and set to cutting their bonds. As soon as her wrists were free, Alix pulled the sack off her head, squinting in the harsh sunlight. A shadow resolved itself into Asvin, looking amused. "Stiff?"

"Rather," she said, wincing as she worked her joints.

"I'm sorry for it. It's not that we don't trust you, but . . ." He shrugged.

"But you don't trust us enough."

His smile vanished. "Trust is death in occupied Andithyri, my lady. You'd best remember it." He leapt down from the oxcart and offered a hand.

Alix took in her surroundings. A remote farmstead, from the look of things, probably much like the place where Rodrik grew up. For that matter, it could have been just about anywhere in Alden, so anonymous were its features. Their base of operations, or simply a safe place to bring visitors? Alix supposed it didn't much matter. "Where is Wraith?"

"Not here. You'll have to settle for me for the time being."

Alix and the Wolves exchanged a look. It was Wraith they'd come all this way to see, but apparently that would have to wait.

They were shown into the farmhouse, a humble dwelling with little in the way of furniture. A door in the back hinted at a smaller room beyond, and a cot sat in the corner, but it didn't look to have been slept in recently. The only occupant was a falcon eyeing them keenly from its perch. Hunter or messenger? Knowing the white-hairs, the bird could even have been trained to attack. Alix kept her distance. Asvin, meanwhile, fetched a kettle and set to boiling water while the rest of his men waited outside.

"This can't be their headquarters," Dain said in an undertone while the Andithyrian busied himself with the tea. "Not enough room."

"This is where I was brought the last time," the priestess said. "Perhaps it serves as a vetting area."

"Vetting?" Dain echoed, frowning. "Vetting what?"

"Why, us of course."

Asvin poured tea, then dragged a chair up to the table to join them. Green eyes scrutinised them one by one, sharp and unreadable. "So," he said, "let's start at the beginning."

Alix growled in frustration and ran her hands over her face. "I already *told* you, I don't know. And even if I did, I wouldn't say. If my brother thought it wise to share such details about his forces, don't you think he would have done so by now?"

Asvin set his empty teacup aside, fixing Alix with that same inscrutable look he'd worn for the past two hours. "Essentially, what you're telling me is that General Black saw fit to send his sister, two White Wolves, and an Onnani priestess to beg a favour of the Resistance, in return for which he offers—" He spread his hands, empty.

"I'm sorry you feel that way," Alix said, "but I can't bargain with information that isn't mine to share." Rig would never forgive her, and anyway, these men had given her no reason to trust them.

"I've been hearing some variation of that refrain all afternoon," Asvin said impatiently. "You've deflected my every inquiry, no matter how insignificant."

"And yet you continue to ask."

"Does that surprise you? My comrades and I are scavengers, my lady. We spend our days scrounging for opportunities. A scrap of information here, a spot of luck there—anything we can use to strike at our enemies—and here I have the sister of the Aldenian commander general sitting across from me. A rare gift, one I cannot afford to pass up. So please—there must be *something*, some small detail you can part with, if only as a gesture of good faith."

Alix shook her head. This was going nowhere. There was too much at stake, and too little time, to sit here haggling like a couple of merchants. "I've told you what I can. If it's not enough—"

"Not enough?" Asvin's voice grew cold. "All you've told me is that you need our help to find a man called Rodrik who grew up in a village called Indrask. You won't tell me who he is, or why he's important. You won't tell me anything of what your brother plans, or what he thinks the Warlord plans. And in exchange for this *treasure trove* of information, you'd have us risk our lives."

"I sympathise," Vel put in dryly.

"Maybe it was a mistake to come here," Alix said, rising. "My brother thought you'd help us, but apparently the line between ally and mercenary is thin in Andithyri."

It was a mistake; she knew it as soon as she'd spoken. A glint of menace flashed in the green eyes, like a dagger unsheathed. "Careful, my lady. You will find no mercenaries here, nor will you find men who bear insults lightly."

"I have no wish to insult you, but I can spare no more time for this interrogation. I'd hoped you could help us. Apparently, you can't. So I'll ask you to blindfold us and pack us in your wagon, because we have a long and dangerous road ahead."

Vel and the Wolves took the cue, rising. Asvin, though, remained seated, boot propped casually on his thigh, gazing up at Alix with his unsettling eyes. "It's your call," he said.

Alix thought the remark meant for her, but then a door

opened at the back of the room, and a large, grizzled man with a close-trimmed white beard filled the doorframe. Hazel eyes met Alix's, held her gaze in an iron grip as their owner strode over, boots tolling heavily across the floorboards. From its corner, the falcon gave a keening cry, as though in greeting.

"Hello, Wraith," said Vel.

"Daughter." His eyes flicked only briefly to the priestess. They were too busy devouring Alix, stripping her to the bone. "This won't do at all," he said.

Alix swallowed, resisting the urge to back away. It wasn't so much his size—though he rivalled Rig in both height and bulk—but the sheer intensity of his gaze. Where Asvin reminded her a little of a fox, this one was a wolf—the kind that would set his pack on you without a thought.

"Sit," he said with a perfunctory gesture, and Alix complied.

Wraith. An incongruous name for a man such as this; Alix had a hard time imagining a more substantial figure. The room seemed suddenly smaller with him in it.

"This won't do," he said again, straddling a chair in front of Alix, meaty arms draped across the back. "It's very bad manners, my lady of Blackhold, to come into a man's home and start making demands."

"I'm not demanding anything. I'm asking for help."

He nodded. "Rodrik. Indrask. I heard. Only you won't say who he is or why we should care. So tell me, why would I risk the lives of my men to help you find him?"

"Does it really matter who he is?"

"Aye," Wraith said, leaning forward, "it does."

Alix glanced across the table at Dain; he gave an almost imperceptible shake of his head.

She couldn't tell Wraith the truth. Of course she couldn't. But if she didn't tell him *something*, he wouldn't lift a finger to help her. She could see that clearly, could even understand it. Yet without the Resistance, her chances of success were vanishingly small. The incident with the soldiers had convinced her of that.

Alix licked her lips. Made a decision.

"Rig wouldn't want me to say." An opening ploy. Destan himself wouldn't judge her for it under the circumstances—or so she told herself.

"I've not met your brother," Wraith said, "but he must be a good judge of character, else he wouldn't be able to play the Warlord the way he does. I've got to think he'd anticipate my position on the matter, yet he sent you my way nonetheless."

"I don't know . . ." Alix shot another look at her companions, openly this time. *Can't give in too easily, or he'll be suspicious . . .*

"There is little use belabouring the point," Vel said, unwittingly playing into Alix's hand. "Tell him or do not, but we have gone round this issue enough for one day."

Alix dropped her gaze to the floor as though weighing her options one final time. "Very well," she said. "Rodrik . . . he's a bloodbinder."

Asvin's eyebrows flew up at that, as did Vel's. Wraith just grunted.

"I thought Alden had only one," Asvin said.

"That's true, which is why Rodrik is so valuable. It seems he never declared himself. He went into hiding when the war broke out, to avoid military service." Plausible enough; it would hardly be the first time such a thing had happened. In peacetime, a bloodbinder's rare gifts ensured he would be comfortable and wealthy. But in times of war, he was little more than a tool, compelled to work day and night to equip his country's armies. Some bloodbinders remained in hiding all their lives to avoid such a fate. "This man could make an enormous difference to the war effort," Alix said. "We must get him to General Black as soon as possible."

"After he's crafted a few weapons for us, I would hope," said Asvin. "A nice bloodforged dagger like yours would come in handy. A knife that can't miss, quick and quiet . . ." He mimed a throw, smiling unsettlingly.

"I'm sure that can be arranged," Alix said.

Wraith eyed her for a long time, as though trying to wait the truth out of her. Alix did her best to meet that gaze unflinchingly, though her heart was hammering in her ears. "Something I don't understand," the big man said. "Why all the fuss a moment ago? Why not just tell us?"

"It's like Asvin said. Trust is death in occupied Andithyri." A weak answer, but it was the best she could come up with under the pressure of that stare.

Wraith rose and went to the falcon. He stroked its head meditatively, the bird closing its eyes in bliss. Then he said, "No."

The air went out of Alix. "Just like that?"

"Just like that."

"I don't understand," she said, hating how desperate she sounded.

"Then I'll make it simple. If I help you, the most I get out of it is a couple of enchanted weapons. Fine so far as it goes, but a bloodforged weapon can only be wielded by the man whose blood went into the making. Once he's dead, that weapon is useless. Most we could do with it would be to melt it down for the steel. I'll not risk the life of one man so another can have a better weapon for a few months, and that's the longest most of us can expect to live."

A crude, pecuniary calculus, yet Alix couldn't deny its logic.

"I told you not to expect charity," Vel said sourly.

"Gold, then," Alix said. "I brought some with me, and I can get more . . ."

Wraith was already shaking his head. "We're not sell-swords."

"Every army needs gold, even an underground one."

"True, but you won't have enough with you to make it worth my while, and as for what you can get . . ." He shrugged. "We're not moneylenders, either."

"But what else could we possibly offer?"

At that, the big man smiled. It was not a pleasant smile. "Now we're getting somewhere."

A prickle of dread crept down Alix's spine.

"Way I heard it told," he said, "you're the one managed to sneak those barrels of black powder into the Elders' Gate, right under the Priest's arse. Quite the explosion, they say. Probably still picking bits of him off the walls of the Nine Heavens."

Asvin laughed through his nose.

"Skills like that are rare," Wraith went on. "Skills like that I can use."

Alix and her companions exchanged uneasy glances. "What would you have of me?"

"Arkenn," said Wraith, throwing a meaningful look at Asvin. The smaller man's eyes widened, but he said nothing.

"Arkenn." Alix had heard the name, but for a moment, she couldn't place it.

"The governor?" Vel said.

"Governor of the Oridian Protectorate of Andithyri." In case anyone had missed the tone, Wraith spat on the floor. "A parasite, sucking the blood of Andithyri for his Oridian masters. He's holed up in the royal palace in Timra. Too much of a coward to set foot on the streets, so he has his thugs *keep the peace*." His lip curled into a snarl. "He mostly *keeps the peace* through hangings, though I hear he's taken an interest in the old imperial cages."

Alix shuddered. She'd seen drawings. Of all the torture devices employed by the Erromanians—and there had been many—the cages were surely among the worst. They hung in the squares, usually, or the village green, bars just far enough apart to admit the crows. By the time the prisoner died of dehydration, the birds would have long since plucked out his eyes.

Vel whispered something in Onnani and drew a sign against evil. Thousands of her ancestors, and Dain's, had met their ends in those cages.

"It sounds horrible," Alix said, "but I don't know what you want from me."

That was a lie. She knew what Wraith was going to say; already, the bile was rising at the back of her throat.

"You're going to help me kill him."

The room went very still then.

Alix could feel the eyes on her, all five pairs of them, scrutinising, judging. Even the falcon seemed to be watching, waiting for her answer. "I'm no assassin," she whispered, but the words tasted like a lie on her tongue, the biggest lie she'd told today.

Fate, it seemed, had a nasty sense of humour. *A sodding Trion, and you had him snuffed, without even consulting anyone.* Liam's voice a week ago, hurled like an accusation. The point of that spear was still lodged in her breast.

An assassin.

For a bodyguard, there was no fouler creature. Erik had nearly been killed by one; Alix had almost died protecting him from another. In ordering Varad's death, Alix had come perilously close to becoming the thing she hated most. Close, but not quite; *she* hadn't killed him, not with her own hands. A chain of spies stood between her and the deed. That distance mattered to her, was the only thing separating her from the monsters who'd tried to murder her king. And now . . .

"If you want my help," Wraith said, "that's exactly what you'll be."

"I can't do this," Alix said, tracing small circles on the table. She couldn't look up, couldn't meet the concerned gazes of her companions. "It's too much to ask."

Dain went to the window of the cabin. "Do you suppose they can hear us out there?" Their hosts had left them alone to discuss Wraith's proposal, but they hadn't gone far. "I see them. They're sitting on the back of the wagon."

"Let them listen," Alix said. "I don't care. I won't do this."

"Really?" Ide sounded puzzled. "Thought you'd jump at the chance to help snuff a man like that."

"Did you." Alix glanced up coldly. "And why would you think that?"

"Sounds like he deserves it and then some. Besides, he's the enemy, isn't he?"

"It's more complicated than that," Dain said. "It's one thing to face a man in battle, but to sneak into his home and kill him in cold blood?"

"Even if he tortures and murders people for a living?" Ide shook her head. "Don't see what's complicated about it. Besides, it's not as if they're asking Alix to go it alone. She's just supposed to help, right?"

Dain appealed to the priestess. "What do you think, Daughter?"

But Vel scarcely seemed to be listening. She gazed into nothingness, a troubled line creasing her brow.

"I'm not an assassin," Alix said again, as though repeating it would make it true.

"You ask me, that's just a word," Ide said. "Enemy is enemy, dead is dead. What difference does it make whether he's looking you in the eye when he dies?"

"Honour," Dain said.

"Honour is for duels. This is war."

"There's no honour in war?"

Ide rolled her eyes. "You telling me you never took a man from behind in battle? Or ambushed one with an arrow?"

"Of course, but—"

"How's this any different?" She made a dismissive gesture. "You got nothing to feel bad about, Alix, but if you don't want to do it, I can offer my services. I'm a trained scout too. Not as good as you, maybe, but good enough to help Wraith and his men sneak into the palace."

Alix was almost tempted. But no—she'd be using Ide just like she used Saxon, a tool to keep her own hands from getting bloody. *Either this is right or it's wrong, and if it's wrong, it's not fair to let your friend stain her honour in your stead.*

The trouble was, it didn't *feel* wrong. In fact, she agreed with Ide—Arkenn was obviously a monster. Moreover, as governor of occupied Andithyri, he was a legitimate military target. Or so she told herself, but was that wisdom, or rationalisation?

Would Erik do it?

She tried to imagine what he would say if he were here, if she could confide in him the way she used to. But the thought of Erik was too painful; she flinched away from it. She was on her own. "Dain, you served under my brother's command. You know the lay of things better than I do. If we took out Arkenn, it would help the Kingswords, wouldn't it?"

"It would stir things up in Timra, that's for sure. That might force Sadik to pull some of his men off the border, redeploy them to the capital to restore order. Anything the white-hairs do to keep the Warlord busy is good for us."

"But not quite as good for the people of Timra," Vel said, snapping out of her reverie. "If the Trionate's governor is murdered, we can be sure the Warlord will respond harshly. I have seen with my own eyes how brutal Sadik's reprisals can be. Is that something we can live with?"

"That's for Wraith to decide, isn't it?" Ide said. "His people. His idea. Our job is to look out for Alden. For the Kingswords."

"And for our own souls," Vel said. "Wraith might have more right than we to decide what is best for his country, but he cannot decide what is best for us. So I ask again, is this something we can live with?"

Alix sighed. "Let's hear from Wraith. I doubt we'll find any answers there, but I'd like to know he's at least weighed the consequences. Dain, if you wouldn't mind calling our friends?"

Vel's dark eyes followed Dain out of the cabin, growing unfocused once again. Alix would dearly have liked to know what was so damned important that the priestess couldn't concentrate on the discussion at hand, but she had bigger worries.

"So," the leader of the Resistance said as he walked through the door, "do we have a deal?"

Alix didn't bother to hide her resentment. "This is coercion."

"Way I see it, it's a simple trade. I do for you, you do for me." He shrugged. "Either way, I don't give a flea's teat how you feel about it. It's a military necessity. And I daresay General Black won't look ill on it, either. It helps your Kingswords, after all."

"So we've concluded," Alix said. "But it will certainly provoke a backlash against a lot of innocent Andithyrians."

"I saw what Sadik did at Raynesford," Vel put in. "I prayed over the corpses of children. Are you prepared to make such a sacrifice?"

For a fleeting moment, Alix glimpsed a different Wraith: grief-worn, weary to the bone. Then his lips pressed together, and the hard shell came back over his eyes. "My people have done nothing but sacrifice for the past two years, Daughter. I've buried family. Friends. If it's going to end, it's going to end with blood. I'd have thought an Onnani would understand that better than most."

It was a well-aimed shaft. The look that came over Vel was at once proud and serene. "My ancestors sacrificed a great deal, it's true. Many innocents had to die for their children and grandchildren to be free."

"Just so," Wraith said. "And it might have been my ancestors who had yours under the boot, but make no mistake— Andithyri and Onnan understand each other now. We've learned from you, and the greatest lesson is this: Strike where you can, when you can, even if it's a glancing blow, and eventually the enemy will bleed out." His gaze shifted back to Alix. "For what it's worth, I don't ask this lightly. If that bloody parasite had the balls to set foot outside the palace, it'd be simple enough. But he won't, which means we've got to go in there after him. That won't be easy. I've got a few men of skill, like Asvin here, but he can't do it alone. So I'm asking one last time: Are you in?"

Alix paused. Traced a final circle on the table. "We're in."

"Good," Wraith said. "We leave at dawn."

SEVEN

"I don't know," Liam said. "Piglet, maybe?"

"Piglet." The cook repeated the word as if he'd never heard it in his life. Then a delicate spasm of pain crossed his face. "Does His Highness perhaps refer to *suckling pig*?"

"That's it, exactly. We had it at the wedding. It was great."

"Very good, Your Highness." The cook made a note on his ledger. "Suckling pig it is."

"Hmm," said Albern Highmount, "I think not."

Liam's back teeth came together, hard. "You disagree, Chancellor. What a surprise."

It wasn't. It wasn't anything *like* a surprise, because Highmount had done nothing but disagree with every single sodding thing Liam said from the moment he'd been put in charge. "Can I ask why you have an issue with suckling pig?" *Childhood memories, perhaps? Not enough room at the teat?*

"I simply do not think it suitable for the occasion."

Even the cook looked perplexed. "It is a fine dish, my lord, worthy of the most distinguished of guests."

"I quite agree, Master Horna. One of my personal favourites, in fact. But I am afraid it would not be an appropriate dish to serve the Onnani ambassador, given its origins."

"Origins?" The cook's brow rumpled even further. "Why, it originates from right here in Erroman!"

"Precisely. It is, in fact, an Erromanian dish, dating from the days of the empire, and particularly associated with the imperial class."

Liam laughed incredulously. "You're worried the Onnani ambassador will be offended that we served baby pig because the white-hairs used to enjoy baby pig way back when?"

"Way back when the baby pig was being dished onto their plates by Onnani *slaves*. Yes, Your Highness, that is precisely what I am worried about."

Liam growled and rubbed his eyes. Bad enough he had to muddle his way through a diplomatic dinner, they couldn't even plan the sodding menu without worrying about the political implications. *How in the name of the Virtues does Erik do this all day?* Barely a week of trying to fill his brother's boots, and already he was going mad. "Whatever you think," he said, as though Highmount needed his permission.

The chancellor spent another few moments discussing the dinner before dismissing the cook. Liam didn't bother listening; he was getting the impression his presence was purely symbolic anyway. Was it like this for Erik, he wondered, or did Highmount actually give a damn what the *real* king thought? *Probably*, he decided. Erik had too much gravitas to be brushed aside. Liam, on the other hand . . .

"You must understand, Your Highness—" Highmount began, preparing to launch into yet another lecture.

A soft knock sounded, and Rona Brown poked her head into the study. "Am I interrupting?"

"Dear gods, no." Liam waved her in.

She took a seat across the desk from Liam, in the place Alix used to sit when conferring with Erik. She'd taken Alix's place as captain of the royal guardsmen too, more or less, working closely with Pollard. "All is well," she reported, "or rather, as well as it can be under the circumstances. The chamber guards changed over this morning—I've just come from debriefing them. His Majesty's spirits are . . . not improved. But he is eating again, at least."

Liam blew out a breath. "Thank the gods."

"Good news indeed," said Highmount. "I feared something drastic might be required."

Rona winced. "Yes, well, thankfully that won't be necessary. He took both supper and breakfast, and he's no longer wearing holes in the carpets with pacing. Apparently he just sits at the window now, staring out into the gardens."

A familiar jolt of fear arced through Liam. "We're absolutely *sure* no one can see him from out there?"

He'd asked the question half a dozen times, and Rona always gave him the same patient answer. "The gardens are sealed off. Even with a longlens, there's no way anyone but our guardsmen can get eyes on that window."

Liam nodded, comforted—for a few hours, anyway, until the next bolt of fear lit him up again. He'd be as grey-haired as Highmount by the time this was done. Assuming he survived.

"It would appear His Majesty has finally resigned himself to the situation," Highmount said. "That is for the best. I do not like to think of him suffering unduly."

Unduly. Such a sensitive man, Highmount.

Another knock at the door; this time, it was Pollard who looked inside. "I beg your pardon, Your Highness. Lady Sirin Grey requests a word."

The three of them exchanged a look.

"Bloody hells," Liam growled, "that's all we need." To Pollard, he said, "Show her in."

They received their guest in a cluster of plush chairs near the window, the better to convey how very unconcerned they were by her visit. She swept aside the shining folds of her dress as she sat, smoothing them down with jewel-studded fingers and arranging them *just so*. Her braids were bound up under a delicate net of freshwater pearls, and a pair of sapphires dangled from her ears, catching the sunlight. A bit much for midmorning, in Liam's estimation. Like an aging woman plastered in cosmetics, or a knight who insists on wearing armour that no longer fits, Lady Sirin was trying a little too hard to cling to the past—in this case, her family's lost prestige.

"To what do we owe the pleasure?" Liam asked, breaking out his most charming smile.

"I've come to pay my respects to His Majesty."

"Your respects?" Liam laughed awkwardly. "Did someone die?"

"How amusing," Sirin said, sounding about as amused as if Liam had spilled tea down the front of her frock. "It's so dreadful being ill, don't you agree? I should like to boost his spirits." She smiled sweetly.

"His Majesty will be gratified to hear it," Highmount said, "but alas, it is quite impossible. As we have already discussed, the risk of contagion is too great."

"My risk to take, surely?" The sweet smile never wavered, as fine-edged as a razor.

"Not really, no," Liam said. "If you fall ill, you may infect others, and the last thing we need is more council members unfit for duty."

A delicate furrow appeared between Sirin Grey's eyebrows. "I should think it unlikely that His Majesty would still be contagious after all this time. I must say, my lords, this seems like an overabundance of caution."

"When it comes to the health and well-being of His Majesty's closest advisors," Highmount said, "there is no such thing."

"I quite agree, Chancellor," Rona said. "If Lady Sirin or anyone else were to succumb after being permitted to break the quarantine, you would never hear the end of it."

"Well," Liam said, beaming until his face hurt, "that settles it. I'm sorry, my lady, but I'm sure Erik will be touched that you stopped by to wish him well."

"And who will inform him? One of the servants, presumably, since I'm sure you would not dare take the risk of exposing yourself to illness." Pale blue eyes met Liam's, locking him in an icy embrace. "Oh, but wait—the servants don't see His Majesty either, do they? Meals, laundry, everything passes through the royal guardsmen. Why, the servants' quarters must be positively abuzz!"

A month ago, Liam might not have recognised the threat. But he'd survived the crucible of Onnani politics, learned the rituals of courtly duels. He knew a challenge when he heard one, and Sirin Grey had just called them out. Not a gauntlet thrown, but a silk glove gliding silently to the floor.

I've got eyes and ears among the servants. The message

was clear: She knew the prince and the chancellor were up to something, and she was making it her business to find out what.

"I'll take my leave, my lords," Sirin said, rising. "Please be sure to keep my family apprised of His Majesty's condition. We do worry for him so." She was halfway out the door when she paused and turned back. "Oh, and do give my regards to Lady Alix, Your Highness." She smiled. "When next you see her." The door clicked shut.

Liam said something decidedly unrefined.

"*Really*, Your Highness," Highmount spluttered.

"I wouldn't have chosen quite the same language," Rona said, "but I certainly share the sentiment. We have a serious problem."

"Not an unexpected one," Highmount said, "nor am I surprised that it should be Lady Sirin who positions herself as our adversary. She obviously feels compelled to prove her loyalty to the king in the wake of her brother's treachery. On top of which, she has no love for me, given my role in Prince Tomald's execution. I feared she might be tempted to scrutinise our situation, though I had hoped we would not begin trading blows *quite* so soon."

Liam swallowed a sudden dryness in his throat. "What do we do now?"

"Nothing at all."

"Are you sure that's wise?" Rona asked. "She's made it clear she's getting information from the servants."

"The servants know very little that could worry us, at least for now. In fact"—Highmount made a steeple of his fingers—"I rather think this could be turned to our advantage. Servants delight in nothing so much as rumour and scandal. No doubt they have already devised a number of wild theories. We can encourage that by planting a few seeds of our own."

Liam had a feeling he was about to ask a stupid question, but . . . "Why would we do that?"

"Have you ever seen a garden overgrown with weeds, Your Highness? It is terribly difficult to spot the flowers."

Liam's brow smoothed. "That," he said, "is bloody *brilliant*."

"I am gratified you think so, though I daresay some of the most likely rumours will not please you."

"What do you . . . ?" And then he understood.

Alix.

She was behind those doors too, allegedly, with Erik. Alone, just the two of them, day and night . . .

Such talk would hardly be new. Rumours had followed them all the way from Greenhold. The gossip had waned after the wedding, but this would only stir it up again. In the kitchens, the stables, the laundry . . . everyone would be whispering. Every night, in someone's overheated imagination, Liam's wife and his brother would be . . .

"I need some air," he said, rising. "I think I'll take Rudi for a walk."

"Shall I come along?" Rona asked.

"No thanks. I'd rather be alone."

Erik spent the first three days of his captivity convinced she would come back.

She wouldn't leave him like this. Not Alix. She was too loyal, she loved him too much. As a brother only—it still hurt to admit that—but even so it was love, as fierce in its way as her love for Liam, or even Rig. She would realise what she had done and she would regret herself. This was Alix, after all. How many times had he been obliged to forgive her for doing something rash? He would forgive her again, and hold her as she wept, for it would be a bitter thing to watch her husband die for treason. But she would know that Erik had no choice, just as he'd had no choice with Tom, and she would understand. They would forgive each other.

So Erik had thought. So he had told himself for three long days, watching in silence as her guardsmen filed in and out, convinced each time that *this* changing of the guard would be the one to bring Alix back to him.

But she did not come. And gradually, he came to understand that she never would.

Erik spent the next three days of his captivity in a rage.

He paced the length of his apartments and back. His blood was a tempest, his thoughts a seething black swarm. He broke nearly everything he could get his hands on, taking petty delight in the way the guards flinched every time another priceless vase exploded in a fine mist of porcelain.

That had been unwise, though. Indulgent. For he soon realised that his only hope was to bargain his way out, but by then, he had alienated his captors. Squandered his only chance at escape.

That was when he stopped eating.

It was, he supposed, the weakness brought on by hunger that triggered it: whispers, at first, voices clawing at him from the inside, their meaning just beyond his reach. And then the visions . . .

"Not visions. Delusions. There's a difference."

Erik couldn't help smiling. Delusion or no, he was glad of the company. "You always were a pedant, Tom."

A faint smile flickered across his brother's face. Tom sat on the far end of the window seat, one leg propped on the bench, arm draped casually over his knee. He was clad in the crimson doublet he'd worn on the day of his execution. Tom normally preferred white, but he had not wanted the blood to stand out so shockingly. Practical to the end. "Being precise is never wrong," he said.

Erik snorted softly. "As though it makes any difference. Visions. Delusions. Either way, you're not here."

"No, I'm not. But you are, and you need me."

Just like that, their moment of camaraderie was over. It had ever been thus between them. "You've thought that your whole life," Erik growled, "and it hasn't been true yet. Speaking of delusions."

Tom just laughed. "Your tongue grows sharp in your despair, brother. But you should lower your voice, if there is any hope of convincing your guards that you are not, in fact, mad."

Erik glanced at his bedchamber door. The wood was thick enough that the guards ought not be able to hear, but Tom was right—it was best not to take chances.

"You brought this on yourself, you know," Tom said.

"So you keep telling me," Erik snapped. "If that's your idea of helping, you can leave now."

"It gives me no satisfaction to say it, brother. But you must own the truth, if things are going to be different from now on."

Tom's blue eyes were solemn, piercing. "And things *must* be different, Erik, because you can't leave this kingdom in the hands of our bastard half brother. You know that."

Erik closed his eyes. "I know."

"You always were sentimental," Tom sighed. "Just like Father. And I even admired you for it, though I don't suppose you'll believe that. But you must realise now that I was right."

Erik started to reply, but found he had nothing to say.

Tom rose from the window seat and crossed over to Erik's side of the room. He moved with the same feline grace he'd had in life; his eyes burned with the same intensity. Erik could almost have thought him flesh and blood—except he cast no shadow, even though his body blocked the light of the window. "I know you wanted us to be closer," he said.

"I wanted a true brother, that's all."

"I wanted that too, for what it's worth. I even think, if we had it to do over again . . ." He trailed off, shook his head. "But making Father's bastard your heir was never going to fill that hole. It was a terrible mistake."

Erik couldn't deny it. "Still, I don't blame him. How could he be otherwise, given what he went through? If I'd let Father take him in when he was young, he would have grown into a different man. He wouldn't have resented me so."

"What does it matter? That's not what happened. He grew up a bastard, dreaming of the chance to take your place. Now you've given it to him. He married the woman who should have been yours, an alliance that puts her brother, commander general of your armies, in his pocket. Right under your nose, he did it. And this"—Tom spread his arms—"is the result."

Erik glared at the apparition of his dead brother. "Do be sure to let me know when we get to the part where you're helping."

"I *can* help you," Tom said, "and I will, if you promise me you will do what's necessary."

"What do you mean?"

"We are at the end of it, brother. Our father's kingdom lies an inch from ruin, but it is not too late. Make peace. Consolidate your rule. Marry and make an heir. No more hiding from the difficult decisions. No more indulging your precious honour. Promise me you are prepared to do what you must to save this kingdom. Whatever it takes."

"I . . ." Erik shielded his eyes from the harsh glare of the window. His head buzzed like a swarm of flies. The harder he tried to ignore it, the louder it grew. He felt weak, dizzy . . . He hadn't eaten enough . . .

"Promise me."

Erik growled, digging the heels of his hands into his eyes. "*Enough.* You need not doubt me. I took your head, didn't I?"

The buzzing died away. Erik drew a relieved breath.

"You did," Tom said. "And now you must be prepared to take our brother's."

"I am, gods help me." The words settled around Erik like ash, as though he stood once more amid the smouldering rubble of the Elders' Gate, mourning his new brother. He'd thought Liam dead in the explosion, and the pain of it . . . He felt it again now as a fresh wound. He'd wanted so much for them to be a family . . . But that was gone, a dream left in ruin like the shattered remains of the ancient tower.

He opened his eyes, met the intensity of Tom's gaze. "I will take his head, and this time, I'll make sure all the city is there to see it. Let no one doubt what fate awaits those who would betray the crown." Sighing, he gestured at the door. "But there is still the small matter of my captivity. I'm afraid I can see no way out."

"There is always a way out." Tom smiled, held out a hand. "Come, brother, I will show you."

EIGHT

†It was strange, Alix thought, how one's state of mind coloured the world. She had expected Timra to be grand beyond description, as befitted the "City of Roses." The Andithyrians considered themselves the height of culture and civilisation, a narrative largely embraced by the rest of the continent (with the exception, perhaps, of the Harrami). Certainly Alix's parents, along with the rest of the Aldenian aristocracy, had spared no expense to furnish their estate with Andithyrian *everything*, from tapestries to wine to silverware. Even the harp Alix's music teacher had laboured fruitlessly to teach her was Andithyrian, as was the man himself. All her life, Alix had longed to set eyes upon the glittering city whence these glories came.

But Timra was a city under siege, capital of a nation under conquest, and Alix saw nothing grand about her—at least not from this vantage. Though the gates were as ornate as the tapestries depicted, and the towers did indeed stretch to the sky, Timra seemed to cower beneath the black belly of storm clouds gathering over her.

"That's gonna come down," Ide said. "Before dark, mostlike."

"Let's hope not," Asvin said, drawing the oxcart to a halt, "or we're going to freeze our bits off."

Ide made a face. "You sure we really gotta do this? Don't see why we can't just go in the front door with him." She hitched a thumb at Wraith.

"*You* could, sure," the big man said. "Maybe even Her Ladyship here, if you keep your mouths shut and don't let the accents give you away. But these two?" He gestured at Dain and Vel. "No way a pair of Onnani gets through the city gates without the roaches asking questions, and trust me—they're just waiting for a wrong answer. You want to ride with me, you're welcome. But your friends go through the storm drain."

"Dain's a Wolf," Ide said. "I go where he goes."

"We're all staying together," Alix said firmly.

"Fair enough. So quit your whinging and get out of my wagon."

Asvin hopped down off the driver's seat, and Alix and her party reluctantly followed suit, leaving only Wraith and two of his men. "Keep a low profile," Wraith said. "I don't want a bunch of corpses putting the roaches on high alert."

"One doesn't sneak into Timra without cutting a throat or two," Asvin said, "but we'll try to keep it to a minimum."

"You do that." Wraith twitched the reins and continued on, leaving Alix, Asvin, and the others standing in the road.

"This storm drain," Alix said. "Will it be guarded?"

"Not from the outside," Asvin said. "Inside the walls, maybe. The roaches know we've used the drains before, mostly to smuggle in weapons. It's a dance—we loosen the grate, they replace it, we loosen it again. Sometimes they post a man on the inside at night. If so, that's one of the throats we'll have to cut. Or rather, my comrades will. They'll be waiting for us inside the walls."

"Isn't there a curfew?" Dain asked.

Asvin nodded. "We'll have to stay out of sight. Anyone spots us in the streets after dark, we'll be shot."

Alix cast a worried glance at her companions. She and Ide knew how to get about without being seen, but she doubted the others were much practiced at stealth.

"Don't worry, my lady," Asvin said with an easy smile. "You and I are sneaky enough for all of us."

They approached the walls from the south, using the thick brush along the riverbank as cover. Their path wound lazily through the hills, so that dusk had already settled by the time they reached the walls, and the smell of wood smoke was in the air.

"Timra," Vel murmured, gazing up at the battlements. "How long I have waited to see it." There was a feverish, almost desperate gleam in her eye.

"For the relics, I suppose," Dain said. The Andithyrians had managed to whisk away many of the empire's treasures before fleeing Erroman, including the most sacred artefacts of the Nine Virtues. Onnani clergy often travelled to Timra to pray over them.

Vel blinked, as if woken from a dream. "I . . . yes, that's right. I had planned a pilgrimage."

"Probably didn't plan on having to crawl through the storm drains, though," Ide said, eyeing the iron grate ruefully.

Vel sighed. "That will smell awful, won't it?"

"Like rotting awful smeared with shite," Asvin said cheerfully. "You'll want to hike up those robes, Daughter."

They waited by the river until dark, the sky rumbling and flashing with the gathering storm. Dain cursed their luck as the first droplets began to fall, but Alix knew it was a boon. "The clouds blot out the moon," she explained, "and the rain will help cover the noise."

"You really are going to be perfect for this," Asvin said with a wink. "Now come on, it's time."

They slipped out from cover and rushed at the walls, following the shallow canal that connected the storm drain to the river. The drain itself was a low stone arch covered by an iron grate, just high enough to admit a man. Asvin knelt beside it and waited.

And waited.

"Well?" Alix whispered, glancing nervously up at the ramparts. If a guard should happen to peer down from the wall walk . . .

Asvin shook his head.

The rain began to fall harder, spattering noisily against Alix's hood. Still they waited. Her hands balled into fists, and not just from the cold. She could feel the time running like raindrops off her cloak. They'd wasted two days getting here, and it would be another three to reach Indrask, the village where Rodrik lived. And that was just the beginning of his trail—the gods only knew where he'd gone from there. How long would it take to find him? Would Wraith even keep his word? What if Liam had already been found out, or Erik had escaped, or . . .

Stop it. She couldn't afford to descend into panic. There was too much at stake.

A shrill whistle sounded, as of a bird calling. Asvin grabbed the grate and pulled, the iron coming free with a screech that made Alix wince. "Now you see why we waited," he said.

"The whistle—a signal?"

"Means the patrol on the wall walk has gone past. Now if you wouldn't mind . . ." He gestured at the drain. Grimacing, Alix got down on hands and knees and crawled inside.

The water was deeper than it looked. Freezing cold, and foul—*gods*, it was foul—the rain sweeping the filth from the capital's gutters, mixing it into a vile slurry that coursed through the sewers. The stone beneath Alix's hands was slick, and anonymous bits of debris brushed her bare skin as she moved. It was all she could do not to retch. The dark, at least, was a blessing, sparing her the sight of the sludge she crawled through. The water level was climbing rapidly with the rain, but the journey was blessedly brief. Already, Alix could feel a sharp breeze on her face from somewhere up ahead.

"Hold," Asvin called, his voice all but lost in the rush of the water.

Alix could see the grate now—all four inches of it. The rest was lost in a torrent of water. *We're going to have to put our heads under*, she realised in horror. Just for an instant, she heard her mother's voice, as clear as if she were still six years old: *A lady does not get mud on her dress, Alix Black!* She laughed ruefully, inaudible through the din.

A low scrape signalled the moving of the grate. Alix reached up, thinking to climb, and was startled when a pair of hands grabbed her wrists. The next thing she knew, she was being dragged through the filth and out into the street. She shook herself like a wet dog, casting about for something, *anything*, to wipe her face with. Then someone pressed a dry rag into her hands. She didn't even look to see who it was before towelling herself down.

"Not a pleasant journey," said an unfamiliar voice. "These days, we come prepared."

Alix didn't recognise the woman who'd handed her the rag, but her hair glowed white under the flashing sky. A second figure knelt by the drain, helping the next in line. Vel emerged, spluttering and gagging, and was handed a towel of her own.

The newcomers took turns helping Alix's companions out of the drain. Asvin was last, and he barely paused to wipe his face before crouching in the shadow of the wall to grab hold of something: the body of a guard. Alix hadn't even noticed it in the dark. Asvin and one of his comrades dragged it across the street and out of sight. "Let's get going," he said.

They moved through a warren of narrow, twisting alleys, keeping away from the main streets as best they could. The rain was coming down hard now, and several of the streetlamps had been snuffed out. Alix dared to hope they might make it all the way to the inn without being seen.

It was not to be.

"You there! Hold!" A voice of authority. *City guard*, Alix thought in dismay.

They broke into a run, making for the intersection ahead. The guard cursed in Oridian; moments later, an arrow whistled past, shattering against the wall ahead of them. Asvin banked left at the T. They pounded up the street, passing closed doors and shuttered windows. "This way," Asvin hissed, cutting into a branching alley.

Alix obeyed, not even daring to glance behind her until she reached the end of the alley, another unmarked T. "Asvin, which way—" She whirled, but he was gone.

"Hold, I say!" Lightning flashed, sketching the outline of a figure standing in the alley behind them, bow drawn. "Don't move!"

Rain streamed off Alix's face, sending icy tendrils down the back of her neck. "Ide?"

"Not before he gets you."

The guard started to make his way up the alley, bow still trained on Alix. "Why have you broken curfew? You must know the penalty is—"

He never finished. A slight figure rose up from the shadows and, in one liquid motion, stole up behind the guard and opened his throat. The Oridian hit the cobblestones in a clatter of armour.

Asvin knelt over the body, wiping his knife on the dead man's tabard. *One doesn't sneak into Timra without cutting a throat or two.* Alix hoped fervidly that two would be enough.

"This way," Asvin said. "We're nearly there."

The sign on the door read *closed*, but Asvin walked in anyway, knowing the inn had been cleared out by the Resistance for their own use. Wraith was waiting for them. "Glad to see you made it in one piece," he said.

"Barely," Alix muttered.

"Oh, don't be dramatic," Asvin said, sidling up to the hearth. "Two throats is a perfectly respectable tally."

"Human lives are not a tally," Vcl said coldly.

Asvin ducked his handsome head in a parody of deference. "Of course not, Daughter. Beg your pardon."

Wraith ignored them both. "I'll give you a moment to clean up," he told Alix, "then we'll talk. I got an idea how to get us inside the palace gates, but after that we're running blind. None of us has ever set foot in a place like that, but you—well, you're a king's bodyguard, aren't you? Reckon you'll have a much better idea what to expect."

So that's why I'm here, Alix realised grimly. "I thought you needed me for my sneaking skills."

"Those'll come in handy too, make no mistake. But good intelligence is worth half a dozen stealthy men."

Oh, he was cunning, this one, waiting until now to bring this up. She'd been emotional back at the farmhouse. Irresolute. Reminding her that she was a *king's bodyguard*, that it was precisely her experience protecting Erik that he intended to exploit, might have tipped the balance, provoking a knee-jerk refusal. Instead, he'd waited until it was too late for her to back out. He'd manipulated her as deftly as any courtier.

"Get cleaned up. Then I'll want your thoughts." So saying, he withdrew.

Alix glared at his back with a mixture of resentment and self-loathing. *Dear gods, what have I become?* She glanced over at Asvin, warming his hands by the fire as if he were merely passing a pleasant evening with friends. "Tell me something. Have you always been this cavalier about killing?"

The green eyes narrowed sharply.

"I'm not judging, truly. I just . . . I want to know if you started out like this, or . . ."

"Or if it just happens." He looked away, and was silent long enough that Alix wasn't sure he would answer. Then he said, "I honestly don't know. Would you believe I scarcely remember who I was before all this?"

"Yes," she said quietly, "I would."

He laughed, not unkindly. "You're not like me, if that's what you're worried about."

"How can you be so sure?"

"Well, for starters, I never would have asked the question." Another thoughtful pause. "But it does change you, this life. Has to, doesn't it?"

"Had you ever killed a man before the war?"

He shook his head. "Any thief worth his salt shouldn't need to get blood on his hands."

"You were a thief?"

"Where do you think I learned how to sneak about? When Wraith found me, I was one arrest away from the end of a rope. I was thinking I'd have to change trades, maybe start selling my body to the roaches." He looked over and winked, and for the life of her, Alix couldn't tell if he was joking.

"You and Wraith have served together a long time?"

"Not that long. It wasn't this Wraith who recruited me. It was the one before."

"I beg your pardon?"

"This one"—Asvin hitched a thumb over his shoulder—"has only been Wraith for about eight months. The man before him was a chap like me. Small, sneaky. Suited the name better, but he wasn't half the leader this one is. Probably why he ended up dead. This Wraith—he knows the business. Hard as rock too. Isn't afraid to make the tough calls."

"I don't understand. Wraith is a title?"

"In a manner of speaking. Whoever assumes the mantle of leader gets the name. Might be me next." He laughed suddenly, as if the idea had only just occurred to him.

"But why?"

"Well, he's immortal then, isn't he? The roaches can never kill him. Whatever they do, Wraith goes on. Inspires the hells out of the city folk, I can tell you."

"And frustrates the hells out of the enemy." It made sense. In fact, it was brilliant. In spite of everything, Alix couldn't help respecting these men. Ruthless, relentlessly single-minded, but committed to their cause. And effective. At least, Alix hoped so.

Tomorrow, she would find out.

NINE

†"What do you think?" Ide spread her arms, offering herself for inspection. "Do I look like a bloke?"
Ide always looked like a bloke, but it wouldn't do to say so. Alix cast about for something suitable, and came up with, "The livery is convincing."

"Gods bless the roaches for picking crimson as their colour," Asvin said, grinning. "Blood never really washes out."

"And gods bless my sewing skills." This from another member of the Resistance, a dark-haired man called Tag. "Wasn't easy, stitching up the mess you made." He patted himself down, scrutinising his handiwork. He too was dressed in the livery of an Oridian soldier, and like Ide, he'd been chosen for the job by virtue of his colouring, being one of the minority in this country who didn't have white hair.

"It's fine," Wraith said. "Now, any last questions?"

Vel started to say something. Stopped.

"Daughter?" Wraith arched a white eyebrow.

"The dungeons in the palace—will you be anywhere near them?"

"I certainly hope not. Why?"

She bit her lip. "Nothing. I just thought . . . There must be dozens of your brothers locked up in there, and many other innocents besides."

"No doubt, but we don't have the resources for a rescue mission. Anything else?"

Vel shook off her diffidence. "Not from me. Does anyone wish to pray before you go?"

Wraith grunted. "Aye, Daughter, now you mention it."

The other members of the Resistance murmured agreement, and the impromptu congregation gathered near the hearth. Even Dain joined in, leaving Alix alone with Ide. "Not interested?" Alix asked.

Ide shrugged. "I got nothing against prayer, but . . . a priestess, you know?"

"Strange," Alix agreed. "I don't think I've ever seen one before."

"Me neither, but you hear tales, don't you? She seems all right, but . . ."

"But still." Sighing, Alix shook her head. "I really don't know what my brother is doing. Or what she's doing with my brother, frankly."

"No mystery there. She's easy on the eyes, and General Black . . . well."

Alix lifted an eyebrow. "Well what?"

Ide shrugged again, awkwardly this time. "If you like those real red-blooded types, you know. Manly, like. Well built, and, er—"

"Okay," said Alix.

"Okay," said Ide.

The prayer session broke up; Vel had wisely kept it brief. Wraith and the others gathered near the door. A current of anxiety ran through them, connecting one man to another in a thrumming cluster of tension. "Everyone knows his part," Wraith said. "No mistakes." He pulled open the door, letting sunlight and the noise of the street tumble in. "Go."

They went their separate ways as soon as they quit the inn. Alix, Wraith, and Asvin turned west, taking a meandering path toward the palace. The towers were visible even from here, the pair of them jutting imperiously into the sky, each one branching near the top in a feat of engineering that was the envy of all Gedona. Designed to evoke the antlers of a stag, Alix recalled dimly, the onetime symbol of the imperial family. Her whole life, she'd dreamed of laying eyes on those towers, but the sight of them now made her physically ill. Somewhere in that palace was Arkenn, governor of the Trionate in occupied Andithyri. And they were going to kill him.

Oh, Alix, what are you doing?

She felt another wave of loathing for the man leading her through the streets. She'd come to him in desperate need, and this was the price he demanded. *Too high*, she thought. *Much too high*. Even so, some remote part of her acknowledged that in his place, she might have done the same.

"This way," said Wraith, turning into a narrow lane and pointing at a set of switchback stairs. "We can reach the rooftops from there. Keep low—there'll be archers on the palace walls."

Asvin went first, springing up to the roof with effortless grace before reaching down to help Alix. Wraith followed, and they belly-crawled across the tiles to the parapet. From there, they had a clear sight line to the palace gates on the far side of a small, meticulously landscaped courtyard. Set back from the road in an inverted U, the courtyard was a bubble of tranquillity amid the throng of the street, its patterned paving stones lined with trees and dotted with colourful spring flowers. At the bottom of the U stood the gates, an ornate row of spikes that offered a tantalising glimpse of the palace compound beyond. It was here that Wraith's part of the plan would unfold.

Asvin drew out a longlens and scanned the streets. "Got 'em," he said, pointing. "You see?"

It took Alix a moment, but then she picked out Vel and Dain loitering near a bakery up the street. Wraith's people were invisible in the crowd. Asvin tracked the longlens slowly. "And there's Tag and Ide."

The two of them were easy to spot, lounging nearby in their crimson tabards. Everyone was in place.

Asvin offered the longlens to Wraith. The big man put it to his eye and grunted. "Two guards outside the gate, six inside."

"Not so many as last time," Asvin said, "but it should still be enough of a crowd to get lost in."

"Better hope so." Wraith passed the longlens back.

They watched in silence for long moments. Then Asvin

twitched, hands coiling excitedly around the longlens. "Here we go."

Vel and Dain started along the street, strolling into the courtyard in front of the palace gates as if to admire the flowers. Alix could see Vel gesturing at the blossoms, Dain nodding, the two of them apparently immersed in casual conversation. The guards ignored them, just as Wraith had said they would. City folk often drifted into the courtyard to gawk at the palace; so long as they didn't approach the gates, the guards would let them be.

Meanwhile, the crowd on the street continued to flow past indifferently—until a man and a woman peeled off and started making their way toward Vel and Dain. Wraith's people: Alix recognised Gretia, the woman who'd handed her the towel the night before. Gretia's companion, a man called Fredek, shouted something. Alix couldn't hear it at this distance, but she knew it would be insulting, a racial epithet hurled at the Onnani. A common enough occurrence in Timra; though the days of empire were long gone, old prejudices lingered.

Gretia and Fredek crowded the Onnani couple, harassing them. An exchange of sharp words, Dain stepping protectively in front of Vel. People on the street were starting to notice; heads turned, and a few stopped to watch. One bystander tried to intercede, soon followed by another. Wraith's men all, slowly but surely accumulating in the courtyard.

At this point, things had escalated enough to trouble the palace guards. Alix could see one of them gesturing irritably, warning the group off. That was when Dain threw the first punch.

Even knowing what to expect, Alix was astonished how quickly things degenerated. Passers-by surged into the courtyard to break up the fight—or to join it. The two guards at the gate rushed in to control the situation, but were quickly overwhelmed in a flurry of flying fists. One of them went down hard. Enter Ide and Tag, hurrying to the rescue of their "fellow guards" and throwing punches at anyone and everyone. The sight of Oridian guards beating civilians drew even more angry bystanders into the fray. The original quarrel was all but forgotten now; it had turned into a full-scale brawl between the Andithyrians and their occupiers—and the numbers were not in the Oridians' favour.

"Come on, you cowards," Asvin growled, peering through the gates at the half-dozen Oridian guards posted inside. They could see what was happening in the courtyard, but had yet to make a move. "You just going to stand there picking your arses while your boys take a beating? *Come on.*"

At last, the palace gates opened, the guards rushing out to support their beleaguered comrades. In the meantime, the melee had swelled to at least twenty people. It must have been chaos down below, but from her vantage on the roof, Alix saw clearly the moment Ide and Tag slipped away from the crowd and ducked, unseen, through the abandoned palace gates.

"They're in," Asvin said, clenching a fist in triumph.

Alix blew out the breath she hadn't realised she'd been holding. "I had no idea you had so many men on this."

"Just the five you met," Wraith said.

"But there must have been two dozen people down there . . ."

Asvin grinned. "Timrans don't need much encouragement to beat on the roaches."

"Doesn't that land them in the dungeons, or worse?"

"Surely does. Gives you a sense of just how hated the roaches are, doesn't it?"

"Aye," said Wraith, "and that's how I know Timra is willing to pay the price for what we're about to do." He cocked his head over his shoulder. "Come along now, my lady. Time to earn your keep."

Alix hunkered in the shadows with Wraith and Asvin, her gaze fixed on the simple oak door of the servants' entrance. She'd been staring at it for so long that her eyeballs hurt, and her imagination had begun to conjure all manner of terrible fates for Tag and Ide. But at last a low scrape sounded, as of an iron bolt being moved, and Ide stuck her head out and waved. Alix and the others scurried like rats into the rear yard of the palace. "Hurry," Ide hissed. "Patrol will be back soon!"

"Bodies?" Wraith asked.

"In the gardener's shed. Reckon we don't got long before someone notices they're missing."

Alix glanced up at the empty guard post on the wall walk above. It was just dark enough that the patrol at ground level might not notice, at least not on the first pass or two. But Ide was right—they didn't have much time.

This is it. From here on, Wraith would be relying on Alix— her highborn education, familiarity with grand estates, and most of all, her experience as Erik's bodyguard—to lead them through the glittering maze before them. The thought made her dizzy, but she did her best to keep her breathing steady as she led them across the yard, flitting from shadow to shadow, gravel crunching damningly under their boots. To their left lay the citrus grove; the night was redolent with the scent of orange blossoms. Their sweet perfume, coupled with the soft chirping of insects, cast such an aura of tranquillity that Alix was momentarily disoriented, feeling as though she should be dining under the stars on the terrace instead of stealing into the palace to commit murder.

Tag was waiting for them at the door to the south wing. "No guards in there," he whispered, "leastways none I could see."

"That's the Imperial Gallery, isn't it?" Alix recognised the shape of the grand hall from many a painting.

"Gotta be guards, surely," Ide whispered. "All those valuables to protect?"

"I doubt it," Alix said. "At the palace in Erroman, we . . ." She stopped herself just in time. "Never mind. Suffice it to say that I'm not worried."

Wraith cocked his chin, indicating the far end of the hall. "Staterooms are just beyond, you said. Then the king's bedchamber. I'm asking you one last time: You sure? I don't want any surprises on the other side of that door."

Alix closed her eyes, thinking back to her studies. *The Imperial Gallery was built to impress visitors. They'd be obliged to walk the length of it in order to reach the state apartments, and then . . .* "No." Her eyes snapped open. "I forgot: There's a series of anterooms first, where they make the dignitaries wait."

"Bloody *hells*, woman."

"I'm doing my best," Alix said coldly. "I've never been here before. I barely remember reading about it. Perhaps if you'd read a book or two yourself, you wouldn't need me."

"Aye, if only I'd taken the time to educate myself, in between begging for coins and scrounging through street rubbish for something to eat." Wraith snorted and shook his head. "You two," he said, gesturing at Ide and Tag, "keep those exits clear."

They left Ide and Tag behind and slipped into the Imperial Gallery. Once again, Alix was in the lead, guiding them between the looming columns. It was surreal, jogging the length of that legendary chamber in the dark, blade in hand, footfalls muffled against the plush carpet. She couldn't help glancing up as she passed beneath the paintings, massive and shadowed, wondering how many she would recognise from books and replicas. The white-hairs had managed to spirit much of their cultural heritage away in the final days of the empire. Before the Oridian invasion, Aldenians had come to Timra in droves to admire pieces like these. *But they're so huge—how in the world did the white-hairs transport them?* A thought so absurdly out of place she almost laughed aloud.

They paused at the far end of the gallery. "This is it," Wraith whispered. "You know where you're going?"

"I'll work it out. The main corridor will be guarded, but if we manage to stick to the anterooms, we should make it most of the way without being spotted."

Wraith nodded. "I'll keep an eye on this door. You and Asvin do your thing."

"This isn't *my thing*," Alix said between clenched teeth, but it was a waste of venom and she knew it.

They slipped into the first anteroom, a small chamber littered with shadows in the vague shapes of furniture. Opposite them stood a plain-looking door; Asvin started toward it, but Alix grabbed his arm and shook her head. He paused, only now realising there were two more doors to choose from. "Which one?" he whispered helplessly. Unfamiliar with the elaborate protocols of court, he had no idea how to interpret the scene before him.

To Alix, though, it was as simple as reading a sign that said, *Dignitaries this way, servants that way.* The grandest of the doors would lead to the first stateroom, while the humblest would give onto the corridor—and the guards. She chose neither of these, instead taking the door on the left. As expected, it led to another, slightly more distinguished anteroom. And another after that, on and on through a series of anterooms, each one adjoining a stateroom of increasing prestige. The grandest of them all, the final room in the chain, would be the king's own chambers—now the bedchamber of Arkenn, Governor of Occupied Andithyri.

They had gone a little more than halfway when Alix reached for a door and found it locked. The door to the stateroom was barred too. She swore under her breath.

Asvin put his lips to her ear. "Guess we make our way on open ground from here." With that, he winked and reached for the last door, spilling them out into the corridor.

They'd gone only a few steps before Alix grabbed Asvin's elbow and dragged him down behind a sideboard, mouthing, *Guards.*

A pair of them stood at the far end of the corridor, flanking what must have been the governor's door. In the low light, Alix could make out the glint of plate and mail, the jutting shapes of swords at their hips.

Asvin narrowed his eyes, assessing. Putting his lips to her ear once more, he said, "How are you at throwing that knife?"

She showed it to him, tilting it so the muted glow of the lamplight glinted off the bloodred jewel in the hilt. Asvin grinned; he'd forgotten it was bloodforged.

She hadn't owned it long—less than two weeks—but after the ambush in Harram, Alix swore she'd never be caught unprepared again. She'd set Nevyn the task of crafting the weapon barely twenty-four hours after her return to Erroman, and he'd been only too happy to oblige, having recommended it many times before. A bloodforged dagger couldn't miss.

But there were two guards between them and the governor's bedchamber, and Alix had only one knife. She cocked her chin at Asvin, eyebrows raised. *What about you?*

He rolled his eyes. *Please.*

Alix peered around the sideboard. About one hundred paces, she judged. Too far to throw, and not enough cover to sneak up on them, even in the relative gloom of the low lamplight.

Lamplight.

One lamp on the sideboard beside her, another on what looked to be a matching piece of furniture at the far end of the corridor. Alix reached up, grasped the lantern, and twisted—*slowly, slowly*—letting the flame flicker as though the oil were about to run out. After a pause, she shut it altogether, plunging their side of the corridor into darkness.

A muttered oath from the far end. One of the guards quit his post, stomping down the hall to relight the offending lamp. Alix glanced at Asvin. She could barely make him out in the sudden dark, but the tip of his dagger flashed as he rested it meaningfully against his chest. *I'll do it.* Alix nodded her understanding. They coiled, ready.

The guard reached the lamp, barely a handspan away from Alix's hiding place. There was a squeal of hinges as he fumbled in the dark. Asvin sprang from his crouch and rammed his dagger under the guard's jaw, clamping his other hand over the Oridian's mouth. But the guard's weight proved too much for him, and the dead man slumped to the floor in a rustle of armour. In the silence of the sleeping hallway, it might as well have been a shout.

The other guard called out softly; when he was met with silence, he started down the corridor to investigate.

Alix moved.

She'd never been so swift, so silent, hurtling through the shadows like death on wings. She got close enough to see the whites of the man's eyes as they widened, his lips parting as he prepared to shout. She whipped the dagger, blade flashing in the light of the remaining lamp. It took him in the throat before he could call out. But there was no one there to break his fall; his knees buckled, and he toppled straight into the wall.

For a heartbeat, everything was still. Then a door opened, a figure emerging drowsily from one of the staterooms. Too young to be their target, but an enemy nonetheless: Asvin was on him before Alix even had time to react, driving the Oridian bodily back into his room and opening his throat before he could give the alarm. Alix ducked in behind them, ready to meet another foe, but the shadows were still. The dead man had been the room's only occupant.

She started to turn, only to feel a blade against her own throat.

"Back up," a voice growled. Alix took a step, but an arm snaked around her chest, pinning her. "Not you. The white-hair."

Asvin had gone very still. He stood there, blade half raised, tunic soaked with another man's blood, a look of such cold hatred in his eyes that Alix would have shuddered had she dared. "What a coincidence," Asvin said. "Just the man we're here to see."

"Here to kill, you mean," said the voice in her ear.

Arkenn. It was the governor himself who held her, who pressed the tip of his knife against her neck at precisely the point where her pulse thrummed.

"Slowly, if I had my way," Asvin said, "but it doesn't look like we've got that kind of time."

"Perhaps you might have considered making a little less noise," Arkenn sneered.

"Sorry," Asvin said. "We're new at this."

How can he be so cavalier? Maybe because it wasn't his throat the governor's knife was pressed against.

"Drop your weapon," Arkenn commanded.

"Why should I?"

The governor brandished his dagger. "Because I'll kill her, that's why!"

Asvin raised his eyebrows. Hitched his shoulders indifferently.

Alix's blood turned to ice.

She should have seen it coming. She knew where this man's priorities lay. Where Wraith's priorities lay.

"You're bluffing." The blade, warm and sticky, dug into Alix's flesh.

"Afraid not. Her job was to lead me through this maze, and she's done it. Now it's time for me to do mine."

The arm around Alix tightened. "Stay back . . ." Arkenn's voice climbed, shrill with fear. *"You stay back!"*

Asvin smiled.

TEN

✝ "**S**top!" the governor warned a final time. Alix could feel her pulse against the unyielding edge of the blade. Asvin advanced, bloodied knife raised.

Arkenn's hand made a slashing motion—and the dagger sprang from his grasp and clattered to the floor.

Calmly, Asvin moved Alix aside and drove his knife into Arkenn's belly—*again* and *again* and *again*, a brutal, wet sound Alix would remember for the rest of her days. By the time she turned and saw the governor's face, he was already half dead: eyes bulged, mouth gaping, hand clutching at his killer's shoulder as he slipped to the floor. Alix didn't know what she'd expected a monster to look like, but it wasn't this—a terrified old man dying in his nightshirt with a bubble of blood on his lips.

Asvin knelt and wiped his blade on the governor's shirt, a violent smear of crimson against white. He whispered something Alix couldn't hear, for which she was profoundly grateful. Then he picked up the dagger, the one Arkenn had held at her throat. "Your knife, my lady."

Alix took the dagger with numb fingers. Her dagger. Her *bloodforged* dagger. Arkenn must have pulled it out of the dead guard outside his door. He'd grabbed the nearest weapon to hand—of course he wouldn't have noticed the garnet that marked it as enchanted. Not in the dark, in the frenzy of the moment. He wouldn't have realised that the dagger would never obey him, forged of someone else's blood.

"You . . ." Alix whispered tremulously. "You knew?"

Asvin's eyebrows went up. "You didn't? Poor thing, you must have had a fright." He grinned and planted a kiss on her forehead. "You were brilliant. Couldn't have done it without you. Now let's get the fuck out of here."

They darted out of the stateroom and back up the corridor, leaping over the body of the first guard they'd killed. Back through the maze of anterooms to the foot of the Imperial Gallery where Wraith was waiting, eyes burning with anticipation. Asvin nodded, and Wraith permitted himself a brief, toxic smile.

They had just met up with Tag when the screaming started.

From the staterooms, Alix judged, a woman wailing out the window. The layout of the palace was not in their favour; the labyrinth of anterooms twisted about such that they emerged only a few hundred feet from the screaming. By the time they found Ide in the orange grove, the shadows were swarming with guards.

"Way out's been blocked," Ide snapped. "Have to fight our way through." She had an arrow nocked and ready. Alix and the others drew their swords.

Bells clamoured; beacon fires blossomed all over the grounds. A dozen or more guards scurried along the wall walk toward the servants' entrance, swords flashing in the orange glow. Already, half a dozen heavily armoured guards blocked the narrow doorway.

Ide's bow twanged. A guard cried out and went down. And then the night was full of arrows, from the door, from the wall walk, from somewhere behind them. Alix found a new speed, crashing into the thicket of bodies in the doorway and taking out a guard who hadn't dropped his bow in time. After that it was chaos, shoulders and limbs and the clash of steel, too frenzied to follow. For Alix, it was more of a shoving match than a battle, and somehow she managed to squeeze through the doorway. But that left her alone and exposed on the far side of the wall, and she paid the price: An arrow slammed into her shoulder, dropping her to her knees.

Ide barrelled through the door, spun, and loosed a shaft at the wall walk; a guard pitched forward and hit the pavement with a sickening *crack*. "Come on," she said, helping Alix to her feet.

Wraith and the others managed to fight their way out while Ide peppered the wall walk with arrows. They started up the street—only to find the intersection ahead blocked with guards. Then a voice called, "This way!" and a familiar figure waved frantically from a branching alley.

"What in the hells is *she* doing here?" Ide growled, half dragging, half carrying Alix.

"The way is clear," Vel said. "Hurry!"

Dain was waiting for them in the alley, and he slipped his shoulder under Alix's other arm. They made it back to the main street, where more of Wraith's men stood ready to cover their escape. What happened after that Alix never knew; a triumphant battle cry propelled Wraith's men forward, and then she was clear, fleeing into the night, stumbling along with the taste of metal on her tongue and blood pounding in her ears.

Alix sucked in a breath as the needle pierced her shoulder.

"Almost done," Vel said, tugging at the thread. "Are you sure you wouldn't like some spirits?"

"I'm sure." In the common room downstairs, the ale was flowing freely, but Alix didn't feel like celebrating, or even taking a drink to dull the pain. She deserved that pain and worse.

"There is a poultice I use," Vel said. "It will help the wound heal more quickly."

Alix glanced over her shoulder. "Does it smell horrid, by any chance?"

"It sounds as if you know it."

In spite of everything, a smile found its way onto Alix's face. "I think so. A friend of mine used to make it. He was almost a priest."

"Almost?"

Alix flinched again as Vel pulled another stitch through. "He quit just before being ordained."

"Which order?"

"Eldora, like you."

"That explains it." Vel snipped the thread. "The secret of that poultice is jealously guarded by our order."

"The way Gwylim told it, everything in the priesthood is jealously guarded. It was part of the reason he quit—all that politicking among the orders, jockeying for position."

Vel laughed. "That sounds familiar. My brother nearly . . ." She trailed off.

"Your brother?"

"It doesn't matter. Give me a moment, I'll fetch the poultice." She slipped out of the room.

Alix perched on the edge of the bed, listening to the muted sounds of singing from below. She recognised the song—they sang it in Alden as well, a shared piece of history from the glorious days of the empire. Dain would know it too. Alix wondered how he felt about the white-hairs singing an imperial song. He didn't seem as sensitive as some—as Vel, say—but he had taken a second name, Cooper, still a relatively unusual step in Alden. That said a lot about his politics.

"Here we are," Vel said, returning with the poultice.

"Sounds as if they're having a grand time down there."

"Doesn't it. As though death is anything to celebrate." Something cool touched Alix's back, and the familiar stench of Gwylim's miracle poultice filled her nose. It was every bit as vile as she remembered, yet it still brought a sad smile to her face, reminding her vividly of the friend she'd lost.

"Do you think I was wrong to be part of it?" she found herself asking, as though it were Gwylim tending to her instead of a woman she barely knew.

Vel was silent for a moment as she dabbed at the wound. "It's a difficult question, even for a priestess. Many would call what you did justice. I might even be among them. But I would not have guessed justice would feel so . . ."

"Wrong?" Alix sensed the other woman's nod.

"Though perhaps it should. Perhaps that is the toll we are meant to pay." Vel sighed. "I just wish we knew what will happen to the people here. How the Oridians will react."

"If they're smart, they won't react at all. Having their governor assassinated where he sleeps makes them look weak. In

Sadik's place, I'd keep it quiet, replace Arkenn without any fanfare."

"You would not seek vengeance?"

"Eventually. In the meantime, I would find ways of clamping down without admitting weakness."

Vel hummed thoughtfully. "That has more of Eldora than Ardin, I think. I'm not sure Sadik will see it that way. Nor am I sure it would be better if he did. Your method sounds more patient, but no less chilling." With a final dab of poultice, she added, "Done. It's just the bandage now."

"Thank you. And for earlier too, helping us get away." Alix glanced over her shoulder. "What were you and Dain doing there, anyway?"

"I had . . . thought to reconnoitre the dungeons."

Alix twisted abruptly, prompting a sharp tug at her stitches. "You followed us?"

"It wasn't Dain's fault," Vel said coolly, sensing rebuke. "I told him I was going and he felt obliged to help me."

"I'm sure he did! What did you think you were going to accomplish, anyway?"

"I don't know," Vel said, ramming the stopper back in the jar. "Free some innocent people, perhaps? Regardless, I don't have to account to you for my actions."

"Maybe not, but I would dearly like to know why you would let my husband's second put his life at risk for the sake of something so patently unrealistic."

"There is no point in trying to explain. You made up your mind about me a long time ago, and I have neither the will nor the energy to try to change it."

"Not even for Rig's sake?" A cheap shot, and she knew it; Alix kicked herself inwardly.

An icy calm descended over Vel. She sat up a little straighter, held her head a little higher. "Not even for his sake. It would be foolish indeed to exert myself over something so *patently unrealistic*."

Alix sighed. "I'm sorry, that was unfair."

"Do not concern yourself, *Your Highness*." Vel rose and began clearing up her things. "You have more important things to worry about than an Onnani priestess."

"Vel." Alix put a hand on her arm, then withdrew it awkwardly. It seemed too possessive a gesture, too entitled. "I really am sorry. It was a reflex, nothing more."

"I am quite accustomed to the reflexes of persons such as yourself."

"Steady on. No need to get nasty." But it had already gotten nasty, and it was her own fault. Alix drew a breath, tried again. "The fact is, I'm being a hypocrite anyway—"

"About acting rashly, or about taking a lover beneath your station?"

Alix was too stunned to reply; she just stared, open-mouthed, as Vel finished packing up her things and swept out of the room.

A moment later, Asvin entered. "Now that," he said, "is one pissed-off priestess. What did you say to her?"

"Nothing she deserved," Alix muttered, angry with herself. "But she's not in a mood to hear an apology."

"Is this about your brother?" He smiled wickedly, dropping down onto the bed. "She's his lover, isn't she? I *knew* it!"

"I am not gossiping with you, Asvin. Is there something you need?"

"He could do worse. She's got fire, that one. Bet she's a tempest between the sheets."

"Asvin."

His smile turned wry. "Just having a little fun with you, my lady. In case you haven't noticed, we're in something of a celebratory mood down there."

"In case *you* haven't noticed, I'm not."

"Not feeling bad about it, are you? That roach got better than he deserved, I promise you."

"I'm not, actually, and that's part of the problem. But what really worries me is what comes next. I need to get out of here, Asvin. I need to find Rodrik. Right away, before . . ." She stopped herself in time.

"Ah, yes." The slight man leaned back against the headboard, hands folded behind his head. "The bloodbinder."

Alix pretended not to hear the note of scepticism in his voice. "Wraith promised me that if I helped with Arkenn, the Resistance would help with Rodrik. But if we're to have any chance of finding him, we have to leave immediately. At dawn."

He considered her with a shrewd eye. "Why don't you tell

me what's really going on? I've seen your expression when you think no one is watching. You're on the brink of panic half the time and a towering rage the rest of it. Nobody gets that worked up over a stray bloodbinder."

Alix looked away, avoiding the scrutiny of that unsettling gaze. "There's a lot at stake."

"We're not fools, my lady. Leastways, I'm not. King Erik could have sent anyone after this bloodbinder. White Wolves, or any of a dozen handpicked knights. Do you expect me to believe he sent his personal bodyguard, his *sister-in-law*, behind enemy lines for a sodding bloodbinder?"

"I don't give a fraction of a damn what you believe. We made a deal. I expect you to honour it."

Asvin rose and gave a mocking bow. "Wraith respectfully requests Your Ladyship's presence downstairs. I believe he'd like to go over the plans for tomorrow. Those parts of it you care to trust us with, at any rate."

Alix plucked moodily at the bedsheet. "Trust is death, you told me."

"I forgot to tell you the rest of it. Which is that mistrust is death too." So saying, he left her.

She found Wraith sitting in a relatively quiet corner of the common room, as far removed from the drunken carousing as it was possible to get. Asvin was with him, all traces of amusement gone from his pretty features. Over near the bar, Ide looked to be having a grand evening, and even Dain seemed to be enjoying himself. Vel was nowhere to be seen.

"You want to leave at dawn, Asvin tells me," Wraith said as Alix took a seat across from him.

"I'd leave now if I thought it was practical. Time is slipping through our fingers, and I can't emphasise enough how precious it is."

"So I hear. But if you want to get out of the city tomorrow, we'll have to leave well before dawn. The guards will be out in force after what happened at the palace tonight."

"Will we have trouble getting out?"

"Shouldn't, not if we make use of the same road we took in."

She sighed. "Wonderful."

"It's not a glamorous business we're in." Wraith stitched his meaty fingers before him on the table. "Now, why don't you tell me what we're in for?"

"I'm not sure I follow."

"I think you do. I think there's more than a little you're holding back." Alix started to protest, but he held up a hand. "You did your bit back there. Now it's my turn. If you don't want to tell us the whole truth, there's not much I can do about it." He leaned in, and once again Alix had to fight the urge to recoil. "But I will insist, my lady, that you tell me what we're walking into, and whether it's like to get me and my men killed."

"I . . ." She wet her lips. "I'm not sure. I think Indrask should be fine, being such a small place, but everything depends on where Rodrik went after that." She hesitated. Made a decision. "Where he was taken."

She owed them that much, and besides, they wouldn't be much good to her if they weren't expecting trouble.

"Taken." Wraith's eyes bored into her.

"We believe the enemy has him. You know how valuable bloodbinders are."

"Aye. If the enemy has him, they won't part with him lightly." He scratched his beard. "So it's to be a fight, then."

It was going to be a gods-sight more than that, but Alix had already told them more than she'd planned. So she just said, "Most likely."

"Well, all right then." He rose, stretched. "I'm off for a bit of a kip. You should do the same, if you can. We leave in three hours."

He pours her another glass, ignoring her protests. "If you're going to be my bodyguard, Alix, you're going to have to learn to hold your wine. Courtly occasions and so on." He's smiling—he knows he's talking rubbish. She would never drink on duty.

"We're going to regret this in the morning," she says, but that doesn't stop her from taking a sip.

"Actually," Erik says, "I seem to be curiously immune."

She snorts, a little indelicately. She's several drinks past delicacy. "Why doesn't that surprise me?" She eyes him closely, grinning. "Not immune to the drink, though, Your Majesty."

His smile is radiant, blue eyes dancing. "No, I daresay I'm not. And I'm sure the hangover part will catch up with me one day too. But until then." He hoists his glass, winks.

The room is spinning a little. She can't tear her eyes away from him. She's never seen him like this, so relaxed and unrestrained. The effortless charm flowing from him—this is who he truly is, she thinks, beneath the royal mask. Or at least who he once was, before the war. Small wonder he's broken every heart at court. Such a pity this part of him is so rarely glimpsed.

She's been staring. He raises his eyebrows, laughing. "What?"

"Nothing. I was just thinking about what you said earlier, about how things were different before the war. How you were different. I'll bet you were like this all the time."

"Drunk?"

She laughs. "No. Just . . . free, I guess."

"Free . . ." His smile fades. "I wouldn't go that far. I don't think I've been truly free since I was a child. Perhaps I haven't always been the stern creature I am these days, but that's not quite the same as being free, is it?"

"No," she says, "I suppose it isn't."

His gaze takes on a faraway look, glassy with liquor. "Do you ever wonder what it would be like if you weren't you? If instead, you were . . . ?" He gestures vaguely.

"Whom?"

"Nobody." He laughs, shaking his head. "Absolutely no one at all. I think it might be quite wonderful."

"Hmm. You could be on to something there. No arranged marriages, no stuffy courtly events . . ."

"None of those horrid little fish the Onnani ambassador insists on serving . . ."

She's laughing now too, hard enough to bring tears to her eyes.

He sighs, still smiling, swirling the wine in his glass. "Still, being king isn't so terrible. Not when I have you to protect me." He holds out a hand. "I can't tell you what a comfort it is to have you here. Promise me it will never change."

She takes his hand, squeezes it. "I'll always be there to protect you. I swear it."

"I'm grateful. But I didn't only mean that, Alix. I meant . . .

us. Supporting each other. Confiding in each other. After everything that's happened, having someone I know I can rely on . . . You can't know what it means to me. Promise me we'll stay true to each other, whatever comes."

She opens her mouth to say the words, but no sound emerges. Her throat is too dry to talk. She takes a sip of wine and tries again, but still the words won't come. He's looking at her expectantly. She goes to take another sip, but she's clumsy and clutching; the glass shatters in her hand, scattering crimson droplets everywhere. It's all over his face, his doublet, flowing down her hand, and she can't tell how much of it is wine and how much blood . . .

A knock roused her from sleep. Ide's voice sounded on the far side of the door; it was time to leave. Alix rolled out of bed and pulled on her boots, pausing only to wipe the tears from her face.

ELEVEN

†   "We understand your dilemma, my lord," Albern Highmount said patiently, "but I fear there is nothing to be done."

"Nothing to be—" Osmond Swiftcurrent pounded the table, startling the beast sleeping beneath. Rudi growled, then flashed a bit of teeth for good measure. It was a more effective rebuke than Highmount could ever hope to deliver; Swiftcurrent shot an uneasy look at the wolfhound and lowered his voice. "How can that be, Chancellor? I'm offering twice what that flour is worth."

"It is not a question of gold," Highmount said. "The summer harvest is still two months away and the city is critically low on grain. We have none to sell, not at any price."

"I'd give it to you for free if we had it," Liam put in. "But the chancellor is right, we just don't. We still haven't recovered from the shortages last year. We lost most of the spring planting season in the Brownlands, and—"

"I know what the problem is," Swiftcurrent snapped. "What I don't know is how I'm meant to deal with it. My people are starving, my lords."

Liam cursed inwardly. Wasn't this exactly the sort of thing

the crown was supposed to fix? But Liam couldn't see how. He couldn't see how to fix *any* of the problems that had been put before the council that day. He felt so helpless. Even more so than he'd felt in Onnan, and that was saying a lot. Not so long ago the only thing he'd been accountable for was staying alive, maybe jabbing his sword into an enemy soldier every now and then if he could manage it. He'd been good at that. Effective. But now . . . it seemed like the more authority he had, the more powerless he felt. *Probably a profound bit of wisdom hiding in that observation*, he thought wryly. Aloud, he said, "What about the rest of you? Anyone have grain to spare? Even just a little?"

The lords and ladies around the table stirred uncomfortably.

Oh, for the love of . . . "What about you, Lord Gold?" Liam raised his eyebrows pointedly. "Your lands haven't been touched by the fighting."

Norvin Gold picked at an invisible speck on his clothing. "My lands are not nearly as fertile as some. That being said"— he smoothed his jerkin—"I can perhaps spare a few bushels."

"Excellent," Highmount said. "That is resolved, then."

"I would hardly call a bandage over a mortal wound *resolved*," Swiftcurrent growled. Grudgingly, he added, "Still, I am grateful for the assistance."

"Moving on," Highmount said. "I trust you have all reviewed the missive from Newmarket." The grim looks around the table confirmed that they had.

"Horrific," said Lady Stonegate. "Truly horrific."

Raibert Green shook his head. "It wounds me to the core that Aldenians would prey upon each other this way. Opportunistic banditry is bad enough, but to take over a whole town, butchering anyone who stands in your way . . ."

"War brings out the worst in people," Sirin Grey said.

"Perhaps," said Green, "but I would not have thought our worst was so base as this."

"We can all agree that the reports are harrowing," Highmount said. "The question is, how shall we respond?" He spread his hands. "Proposals, my lords?"

"Seems pretty simple to me," Liam said. "Those people need help."

"Agreed," said Rona Brown. "We should dispatch a battalion as soon as possible."

"Dispatch them from where?" Green asked. "It's not as though we have a reserve loitering about."

"Such a grave misfortune that His Majesty was unable to persuade the Harrami to aid our cause," said Lady Stonegate, setting Liam's teeth on edge. Her Ladyship seemed to think it her duty to remind them daily of the White brothers' failure to secure help from abroad: Erik from the Harrami legions, Liam from the Onnani fleet. As though anyone could forget.

"That trip was just full of *grave misfortunes*, wasn't it?" Liam said coldly. "My brother and my wife being held prisoner by the mountain tribes, for example. I'm guessing His Majesty found that a bit *distracting*."

Lady Stonegate was unmoved. "Nevertheless, without reinforcements, our hands are all but tied."

"We cannot divert resources from the capital, that is certain," Highmount said. "Even if we could spare the men, it would take them nearly a week to reach Newmarket. We dare not place them so far out of range, where they cannot return immediately in case of need."

"From Pir, then," Liam said. "It's only a few days' march from Newmarket."

"Surely not, Your Highness!" exclaimed Norvin Gold, aghast.

"The citadel is our greatest defence at the border," said Sirin Grey.

"Well, sure, but—"

"That seems altogether too risky," Lord Swiftcurrent said. "We dare not weaken the citadel's defences, not with an attack on our borders imminent."

"I concur," Highmount said gravely. "Lord Black would not thank us, I am certain."

"Respectfully," said Rona Brown, "I'm not sure I agree . . ."

She might as well not have spoken. The mutterings around the table grew in volume, circling around two inescapable conclusions: One, they couldn't possibly deplete the citadel's forces, and two, Prince Liam was an irredeemable twit for even suggesting it. (They didn't say that last part aloud, obviously; it was more of an *atmosphere*.)

"Is there nowhere else we could draw from?" Sirin Grey asked.

Liam started to answer, but Osmond Swiftcurrent spoke over him.

"None of the nearby garrisons is large enough to do any good, not if the reports from Newmarket are accurate. Though for the life of me, I can't imagine how there could be fifty such unspeakable villains in the entire kingdom, let alone gathered in a single band of brigands."

Green's brow furrowed. "So we do nothing? This cannot be allowed to stand, my lords. Not only would we be turning our backs on innocents, it would only embolden other criminals."

"Exactly," Liam said, "and—"

"From Canterwick, then," said Highmount. "It is four days away, and guarding an iron mine of middling importance."

"There are only a handful of men at Canterwick," Green said. "What good would they do?"

"You said it yourself, my lord," said Lady Stonegate. "We must do *something*. Alas, it would seem this is all that is within our power to do."

"So we are decided, then?" Highmount arched a bushy eyebrow.

Liam opened his mouth. Closed it with a snap. No one gave a damn what he thought.

"Good," said Highmount. "Next on our agenda . . ."

Rona Brown found him in the rose garden, throwing sticks for Rudi. (Well . . . throwing sticks, anyway. Rudi just sat on his haunches and watched, casting the occasional dubious glance up at his master.)

"I thought you might be here," Rona said.

"It isn't as if I've anything better to do. Highmount's got things well under control, obviously." Liam threw another stick, sending it spinning into the duck pond. Any day now, the ducks would be back, and taking Rudi for a walk would become a lot more interesting. Liam had eaten rather a lot of duck last summer.

Rona sighed. "You let them bully you."

"Nonsense. I let them ignore me. Hardly the same thing. Say, do you think I could slip away without Highmount noticing? Head down to the front and do something *useful* for a change?"

"Commander . . ."

"We'd have to find a replacement to take my seat on the council, of course. I'd suggest Rudi, but he's a bit too opinionated. A potted plant, perhaps. Yes, I think that would do admirably."

Rona ducked her head, trying to hide her smile. "You mustn't say things like that."

"Surely you've realised by now that I'll say anything for a laugh." His smirk turned sour. "Especially when it's not far from the truth."

"But that's not so and you know it. Tell me, what were you going to suggest earlier, about Newmarket?"

"You heard what I suggested. Redeploy a battalion from Pir. Apparently that was blithering idiocy. Not my first blither of the day, either, if Highmount is anything to go by. Seems I blither a lot."

"I meant after that. You didn't need Sirin Grey to tell you the citadel is our most important defence at the border. You'd already taken that into account."

"Of course."

"And?"

"And I thought . . . oh, what difference does it make?" He tossed another stick.

Rona folded her arms stubbornly. "Shall I tell you what you thought, Commander? You thought that the citadel was not only our most important defence, it was our strongest, and therefore the last place the Warlord would strike when there are so many other weaker, more tempting points along the border. You thought that even if the enemy did attack, a single battalion wouldn't make much difference if the citadel were besieged by a force of twenty thousand. Is that more or less it?"

"Er . . . more or less." More or less *exactly*. It was a little unsettling, actually.

"And you were right."

He scowled. "If you thought so, then why didn't you say anything?"

"Do you honestly think they would have listened to me if they weren't listening to you?"

"Fine, so we agree. They wouldn't have listened to me."

"They would have, if you made them. You're the prince. That's *your* council in there."

"But it's not, is it? It's *Erik's* council in there."

Rona sighed. "And that, right there, is your problem."

"Sorry?"

Her glance dropped to her boots. "I know it's impertinent, Commander, and I apologise, but I feel it's my duty to tell you the truth. On top of which, I hate to see you treat yourself this way."

"What way?"

"As *less than*. Less than Highmount, or any other member of the council. Less than King Erik. I thought, in Onnan . . ." She shook her head, still not meeting Liam's gaze. "It seemed to be going better. You seemed . . ." She trailed off. Silence stretched between them.

"I seemed what?"

"I'm sorry. It isn't my place. Please forget I said anything."

"A bit late for that."

"I spoke rashly. It was inappropriate."

He gave her a wry look. "Have I ever told you how much you remind me of my wife?"

"You have, actually," she murmured, a furious blush flashing over her skin. She was like Allie in that way too.

"It's good to know I'll never want for someone to tell me when I'm acting like a prat."

She knew he was teasing, but she rose to the bait anyway. "I never said that. I just think it will be difficult to convince a man like Albern Highmount to believe in you if you don't believe in yourself."

Liam sighed. Alix was constantly saying things like that too. But they were wrong, both of them. "I do believe in myself. Or at least I used to, before all this . . ." He gestured at the palace grounds.

"I know you feel out of your element, but—"

"You don't understand. It's more than that. It was bad enough standing in Erik's shadow. Now I'm trying to fill his boots. When those lords and ladies look at me, they don't see Liam White. They see not-Erik White. And it's not just them.

Sometimes, I think even my . . ." He trailed off. That wasn't a thought he cared to finish, especially not in front of Rona.

Apparently, though, he didn't need to—he could tell by the flicker of hurt in her eyes that she understood him well enough. She started to say something, but changed her mind, biting her lip and glancing away. She looked so troubled, as if the wound were her own. Liam was touched by her empathy.

Touched, but also annoyed with himself. It was unprofessional of him to be whinging to someone under his command. (He winced inwardly to think what Arran Green would say.) Yet he couldn't deny that it felt good to have someone to confide in, and Rona was just so . . . understanding. *She gets me*, he thought. Alix was gone, and the way things stood between them . . . Could anyone really blame him for needing to talk?

Still, he'd let himself get carried away. *That's quite enough out of you, Commander Crybaby.* "We should head back," he said, gesturing at the path. Rona nodded and fell in step beside him, Rudi trotting along ahead.

When they reached Erik's study, they found a messenger waiting for them. One look at the man was enough to send Liam's heart to the floor and back, for it was clear from the state of him—weary, crusted with dirt and sweat—that he'd ridden hard to get here. Urgent news was bad news, in Liam's experience. "Message from General Black, Your Highness," the man said with a swift bow.

Liam dismissed the messenger before the man collapsed on Erik's pretty rug. Then he sliced open the seal, dread pooling in his stomach. He skimmed the handwriting, seeking out only one word, and when he found it his pulse skipped a few beats. He scoured the paragraph with his wife's name in it, looking for words like *dead, hurt, missing* . . . But by the time he reached the last line, it was clear that there was no fresh news of Alix and the Wolves since she'd crossed the border a week ago. Not exactly a comfort, but better than he'd feared. Liam paused long enough to take a steadying breath. Then he started reading from the beginning.

"Well?" Rona asked when he'd done. "What does it say?"

Liam shook his head grimly. "Nothing good. Rig still

hasn't rooted out the spy in his ranks, and he's feeling more vulnerable than ever now that the Warlord knows the location of the fort. He says the enemy is still massing at the border, someplace called Ennersvale." Liam read the next bit aloud. "'I can't tell you exactly when Sadik will strike, but I'd make it a week or two at most. And this time, the fort will fall. The enemy knows where to find us, and he's had a good long look at our defences. You should prepare yourself for the worst, Your Highness, and start preparing the city too. The Warlord is coming, and once he breaches my lines, there will be nothing standing in his way. You will have very little warning, so my advice is to activate our contingency plans as soon as you read this letter.'"

"Gods preserve us." Rona had gone quite pale. "This is really happening, isn't it?"

"Looks like."

She swallowed, eyes round and fearful. "Erroman can't survive another siege."

Liam would have liked to reassure her, but he couldn't. Even if he were willing to lie, there would be no point. Rona was a soldier. She saw the military reality as clearly as he. And it was bloody *terrifying*.

"A week . . ." Her gaze fell to her lap. "You always think you'll have more time, don't you? To say and do all the things you meant to."

"Yeah, I guess you do." He thought of the way he'd left things with Alix, how he'd let her ride off in silent misery, wondering if their love could survive. The last words they'd spoken had been in anger. "You tell yourself you'll get another chance, at least one more . . ."

Rona looked up, meeting his gaze. "And then the next thing you know, a week is all you have left . . ."

They stared at each other for a long moment. Something uncomfortable stirred at the edge of Liam's awareness. "Rona . . ."

And then something entirely different occurred to him, obliterating every other thought in his mind. "We have less time than that."

"What do you mean?"

"I'll have to share this news with the council."

"Of course." Her brows came together. She wasn't following—yet.

"News like this . . . It's a matter of the gravest importance. A matter for the *king*. They're going to insist on it." Liam's hand clenched spasmodically, crumpling the letter. "The moment this gets out, the council is going to demand that Erik resume his duties, and no excuse in the world is going to placate them, least of all some yarn about his delicate health."

The colour drained from Rona's face. "You're right. Oh gods . . ."

"If we let them see Erik, it's over. If we don't, they'll know something is wrong, and it's over." He stared at the treacherous piece of parchment in his hand. "This letter is my death warrant, Rona," he said numbly.

"No." She was on her feet. "We'll just keep the news to ourselves, that's all. No one will know this letter ever existed. Give it to me." She held out a trembling hand, shot a look over her shoulder at the hearth. "Give it here."

He shook his head. "You heard what it says. We need to start preparing the city. Evacuations. Mobilisations. Even if we keep the letter secret, the council will never authorise actions like that without Erik's say-so. They'll want to hear it from *him*."

"Well, that's too bad," Rona snapped. "They'll be hearing it from the prince."

"What will that buy us? A few days, maybe a week? And even if by some miracle Sirin Grey is willing to accept that line, what happens when Sadik actually does attack?"

"By then it will be too late. We'll have bigger concerns than treason."

Liam wanted very badly to believe that, but he knew better. "Erik executed the Raven a matter of days before the Siege of Erroman."

"So what do you suggest, Liam?"

She spoke so sharply that it brought Rudi to his feet, barking. Liam waved the wolfhound down, eyeing Rona in mild astonishment. He wasn't sure what surprised him more—that she'd called him by his given name, or that she'd come so thoroughly undone. He'd never seen her like this, not even during that horrible business with the fleet. He gestured for her to sit. "You needn't glare at me as though I'm enjoying myself," he said. "It's my neck, you know."

She scowled at her lap. "What are you going to do?"

"What can I do? Try to stay alive." He smoothed out the letter on Erik's desk. "Now . . . we'd better call for Highmount."

TWELVE

† "Not much to look at, is it?" Ide said, leaning out the back of the wagon. According to the map, the cluster of wattle and daub up ahead was Indrask, the village where Rodrik had been taken as a baby. Ide was right, though—it didn't look like much. A dozen buildings or so, the kind of village where the only stone structure would be the temple. So small, indeed, that it would have taken much longer to find it without Wraith's help, map or no. They'd turned off anything resembling a proper road ages ago, and asking for directions would have been tricky, Andithyrians being understandably suspicious of foreigners these days. *At least Arkenn wasn't for nothing*, she reasoned. The thought was some comfort, at least.

The letters Highmount had given her, the ones from the royal guardsman called Terrell, indicated that Rodrik had remained here until at least age twenty. That was when the letters had dried up, as Highmount had known they would one day, when their author passed away. What happened to Rodrik after that was anyone's guess, an uncertainty that wound itself into a hard knot in the pit of Alix's stomach. She could only hope that in a village this small, people kept track of one another, and that if Rodrik had moved away, someone would at least know where. "How many live here?" she asked.

Asvin shrugged, swaying with the rhythm of the oxcart. "No idea. None of us had ever heard of this place before you turned up. Had a time finding a map that even mentions it. The town will be more than what you see here, though. Most people probably live scattered across these farmsteads, come into the village when they need something."

"An ideal arrangement for someone who wishes to remain anonymous," Vel said, echoing Alix's thoughts.

The road stood empty as the cart pulled into the village, and no one emerged to greet them. At first Alix took the place for deserted, but no—smoke curled from a nearby chimney. Someone was home.

"They're afraid," Dain said.

"Hiding from the roaches." Wraith swung down from the driver's seat. "These days, folk hear hoofbeats, it's time to disappear."

Asvin pulled off his hood, revealing his shock of white hair. "Come out, come out! No roaches here!"

They waited, but no one appeared. All was silent but for the clucking of chickens, the bleating of a single goat. Wraith squinted at the buildings. Pitching his voice to carry, he said, "Look at that, lads. The place is deserted. Villagers must have fled."

"Guess they won't be needing this goat, then," Asvin said. "Or those chickens."

Wraith spread his arms wide, feigning triumph. "We feast tonight, lads!"

An obvious ploy, but an effective one. Grudgingly, a voice called, "What do you want?"

It took Alix a moment to locate the source: an older man with a pitchfork and a fresh scar down the left side of his face, standing half concealed behind the corner of a house.

"Just want to talk, elder," said Wraith.

"We're friends," Asvin added.

"You're no friends of mine." The man's eyes had a dull, hard cast to them, like battered iron.

"We're the Resistance," Asvin said.

"I know who you are."

"In that case, a little gratitude would be in order."

"Gratitude." The man leaned out and spat, slowly, deliberately, on the ground. "There's your gratitude. Take what you came for and be gone."

"Haven't come to take anything," Wraith said. "I told you, we just want to talk."

The villager didn't look convinced, and Alix couldn't blame him. Wraith was hardly a reassuring figure, with his bulky frame and grizzled features. She, on the other hand . . . Stepping forward, she said, "We mean you no harm."

The iron gaze shifted to her. "Doesn't much matter what you *mean*. Every time your kind come through here, we pay the price." He gestured with the pitchfork, and for the first time Alix noticed the burnt-out husk set back from the main road. The temple, she guessed, judging by what was left of the foundations.

She threw an uncomfortable glance at Wraith. "Who did this? Not the Resistance?"

"They weren't the ones lit the fire," the old man said, "but they might as well have."

"The roaches," Asvin said. "Villages that are branded as sympathetic to the Resistance are punished."

"Sympathisers, aye," the old man echoed with a sneer. "That's what they called us. Feeding the rebels, they said. As though we had any bleeding choice. Not bad enough you carry off our livestock, you bring the soldiers down on us too."

"We've brought nothing down on you, old man," Wraith said. "Whoever took your livestock had nothing to do with us."

The villager just shrugged resentfully.

Alix could see others now, watching from the shadows, peering around doorways and through windows. None of the gazes were friendly. She had assumed Wraith and his men would be welcomed with open arms in every village and town in Andithyri, but she saw now that was naïve. To these people, the Resistance weren't heroes; they were dangerous men who brought nothing but trouble.

She took another step forward, removing her hood. Perhaps if the villagers saw she wasn't one of them . . . "I'm very sorry for your troubles, and I swear we'll do our best not to add to them. We're not here on Resistance business. These men"—she gestured at Wraith and Asvin—"are helping me to look for someone, a farmer who grew up here. His name is Rodrik—do you know him?"

The man's eyes narrowed sharply, and the knuckles on the haft of the pitchfork went white. *I'd say that's a yes.* Aloud, Alix said, "He was taken, wasn't he? By the enemy?"

"Who are you?"

"My name is Alix. I'm . . . well, I'm from Alden." There was no point in lying about it. If her hair didn't give her away, her accent would.

A look of genuine confusion crossed the man's face. "Alden? What's Rodrik to do with you?"

"I can help him," she said, evading the question. "Tell me what happened, and I promise I'll do everything I can to find Rodrik and see that he's freed." She risked another step toward him, palms spread. "We're on the same side, elder. Let me help him."

"Not good enough," said a new voice, and a woman stepped out of one of the houses. She didn't look much younger than the man with the pitchfork, though it was always hard to tell with Andithyrians and their white hair. Young or old, she had a fierce way about her, a glint her in eye like that of a mother bear protecting her cubs. "Rodrik never set foot outside Indrask," the woman said. "Not from a babe, leastways not until the soldiers came for him. How does an Aldenian even know of him?"

Alix could feel Wraith's gaze on her, and Asvin's too. Even Vel was looking at her strangely, a small crease between her eyebrows. This was new information, and it didn't fit with what Alix had told them. There would be questions, she knew. She'd anticipated that, and she would have to deal with it—in due course. One problem at a time. "It's a very long story," she said, "and there isn't time. I'm not asking you to trust me— that would be too much, I know. All I'm asking is that you tell me what you can about Rodrik's arrest."

The woman scowled. "Why should we? You say you want to help Rodrik, but you could be lying. We got no way of knowing, do we?"

"I suppose not. But here's what you *do* know: He's in enemy hands right now. The Oridians came and they took him, against his will. I'm betting he put up a fight. Maybe some of his loved ones got hurt trying to protect him." She paused, and the pained look that came into the other woman's eyes told her she'd guessed right. "Wherever he is, he's in danger. So what is there to lose? If there's even a chance I'm telling the truth, and I really can help him, isn't it worth taking?"

The woman's hands twitched, the muscles in her jaw working. *Come on*, Alix willed her silently. *See reason.* A tall order given what these people had been through, but without their help it would be all but impossible to find Rodrik. Alix needed some scrap of information, however small, to guide her, or she'd be fumbling in the dark.

Surprisingly, it was the man with the pitchfork who came to Alix's rescue. "Lady's got a point, Marelda. Can't get much worse for Rodrik, now can it?"

A shimmer of tears came into the woman's eyes. "And what about the little one?" She was looking at Alix, but her words were for the old man. "She's the only one who saw what happened. You really want to put her through it all again? Make her remember?"

"Not as if she's like to forget," the man said gently.

The woman hesitated a moment longer. Then she blinked back her tears and straightened, the fierce she-bear again. "Come on, then." She levelled a finger at Alix. "But take my warning, stranger: If you harm a hair on that girl's head, any of you, I'll kill you myself."

Alix nodded gravely. "Fair enough."

The girl's name was Ana, and when Alix saw her face, she wanted to hurt someone very, very badly.

It wasn't just the yellowish-green shadows along her temple and cheekbone, lingering vestiges of an impact so brutal that it left its mark even now. It was the other ways she was marked: the hunted look, the flinching manner, and worst of all, the way she started shaking the moment the two strangers entered her home. Even though Alix and Vel had come with the woman Marelda, whom the child clearly knew, Ana stood with the table between her and the newcomers, eyes darting to the corners as if looking for an escape route.

"Dear child," the priestess murmured, "what have they done to you?" She might as well have been speaking a foreign tongue for all the comprehension that touched the girl's features. She looked to be about twelve, though perhaps her vulnerability made her seem younger. Certainly, she was too old to be Rodrik's daughter. His sister, perhaps—though obviously not by blood.

"Ana, dear." Slowly, Marelda made her way around the table, taking the girl's hands gently. "These women aren't here to hurt you. They're friends." She shot a severe look at Alix and Vel, as if to say, *You'd better be, or you'll be sorry.* "They want to help find Rodrik. Isn't that wonderful?"

Ana nodded dutifully, but her gaze remained flat, untouched by hope or even surprise. *By the Virtues, when I find the whoreson that did this . . .* Alix left the threat unfinished, even in her head. The odds of her singling out the one responsible were vanishingly small.

"They just want to ask you a few questions," Marelda said.

The girl threw a fearful glance at the strangers. "I don't want to," she whispered.

"Just a few." Marelda squeezed her hands. "Please, sweet one. For your brother. For Rodrik."

Ana seemed to process that; she nodded slowly. "And Mama."

Marelda bit her lip. "Yes, sweet one. Your mother too."

"They took the child's mother as well?" Vel asked, but Marelda shook her head.

Alix started to ask a question, but thought better of it. She was already intruding on Ana's tragedy. There was no point prodding where it was not absolutely necessary.

Marelda drew the girl out from behind the table and stood her before Alix and Vel. "Ana," Alix said, "can you tell us what happened?"

The girl stared at her in silence.

Vel lowered herself down to the girl's eye level. "Ana," she said, "my name is Vel. I am a priestess. You probably haven't heard that word before, but it just means that I am a priest who is also a woman. You know what a priest is, don't you?"

Ana nodded mutely.

"Good girl. And this"—she gestured behind her—"is my friend Alix."

The girl's gaze drifted over Alix's armour, settling on the sword at her hip. Alix kicked herself; she should have left the weapon outside. "She's not a priest," Ana said.

"No, child. She is a guardian. She protects people." The priestess's voice was low and soothing, almost musical, as if she were intoning a prayer. The fear receded a little from the girl's eyes. "We want to protect your brother, child, but first we need to find him. Do you understand?" When the girl nodded, Vel glanced over her shoulder. *Your turn.*

Following the priestess's lead, Alix knelt. "When the men came for Rodrik, did you recognise any of them? Had you seen them before?" A long shot, but she had to start somewhere.

Incredibly, the girl nodded. "They were the same ones who came before, to take the sheep. The big one and . . ." Her voice broke, fear sweeping back into her eyes.

"Tell us, child," Vel cooed. "It's all right. He's not here now."

Ana swallowed. "The one with the yellow hair."

Is that who gave you those bruises? Alix's instincts said yes. Maybe she would get a chance to repay the cur after all. "You said they came before, to take the sheep. When did this happen?"

Marelda answered that one. "About two months back. A group of them went through the village like locusts. Took what little the Resistance left behind, except a goat and a few chickens. The soldiers she's talking about—I know the two she means. They're with a unit camped down at Gertswold, about a day's ride from here. They come through now and again. The big one—he's the one set fire to the temple. Last winter, that was. Not surprised he was involved."

"So the big one and the yellow-haired one—they took Rodrik?" The hope in Alix's breast felt almost like an alien presence, it had been so long.

"Not by themselves," Ana said, "but they were there."

"It's not the first time soldiers have made off with someone from the area," Marelda said. "Girls, mostly. This was different."

"Because they took a man?" Vel asked.

"That, and they came and went without stopping by the village proper. None of us even knew they'd been, until Ana here . . ." Marelda trailed off, throwing a grief-stricken look in the girl's direction. "Almost as if they came here just for

Rodrik. But that can't be, can it? What would they want with him, withered right arm and all?"

Alix tried to avoid the question, but Marelda was looking at her expectantly. "He's . . . special," she said lamely.

Ana nodded, as if there were nothing unusual in that statement; just for a moment, she reminded Alix of herself, the way she'd worshipped Rig growing up. Marelda, though, wasn't satisfied with that answer. "Rodrik was . . . *is* . . . a good man. But I wouldn't call him *special*."

"He grew up in Indrask, then?" Vel asked.

"He did."

Alix cursed inwardly. This line of questioning was unwelcome. "I think—"

But Vel was faster, firing off her next question before Alix could interrupt. "Was he born here?"

Marelda considered that. "I suppose not, now you mention it. But he grew up here from a baby. Pastora and Rab couldn't have young ones of their own, or so they thought, so they adopted the babe from an orphanage in Timra. It was another fifteen years until they had Ana." She reached out and stroked the girl's hair. "Her little miracle, Passy called her."

"How old is Rodrik now?" Vel asked. "What does he look like?"

Alix tried again to intervene. "I know what he looks like—"

"He's the handsomest man in the country," Ana declared.

Marelda smiled. "There's a sister's pride. She's not wrong, though—he's a fine-looking fellow. Beautiful blue eyes, and that hair of his . . . Nothing like that around here. Gold with a hint of red—"

"I know what he looks like," Alix said again, firmly. "I'm sorry to cut this short, but we have to get moving. We've no time to lose. Marelda, if we head to Gertswold, are we likely to find the men who took him?" She pretended not to notice the way Vel was looking at her.

"I suppose so," Marelda said. "Unless they're out terrorising someone."

The words were too bitter, too sharply spoken, for poor Ana's nerves; the girl burst into tears.

Stricken, Marelda gathered the girl in her arms. "Oh, sweet one. Oh, honey, I'm sorry . . ."

"We'll leave you," Alix said. "Thank you, Ana. I know this was difficult. But I swear to you, I'm going to do everything I can to find Rodrik." The girl's watery eyes fixed on her, but whether the words registered, Alix couldn't tell.

Vel placed a hand on the crown of the girl's head and whispered a few words in Onnani—a blessing, most likely. Then they left the pair to their grief.

Alix had just closed the door behind them when Vel gripped her arm. "You and I are going to talk," the priestess said in an undertone, "and by the Virtues, you are going to tell me what's really going on here."

"Is that so?" Alix wrenched her arm away, shot an uneasy glance at the wagon where their companions waited.

"That is so," Vel said, "at least if you want me to voice my concerns privately. If you'd rather I aired them in front of Wraith, then by all means, let us discuss it all together, as one happy family."

Alix glared at the priestess. "Did it ever occur to you that I might have a very good reason—that *Rig* might have a very good reason—for not telling you everything?"

Vel was ready for that, and parried easily. "I'm tired of risking my life for people who don't trust me. Either I am a part of this, or I'm not. Your choice."

She left Alix standing in the yard.

THIRTEEN

✝ "So," Wraith said conversationally, "a bloodbinder, is he?"

Alix kept her expression neutral, gaze focused on the task of unfurling her bedroll. She'd been prepared for this, even before they reached Indrask. Their enquiries in the village had been a vital starting point, but there was always the risk that they would turn up inconsistencies with her story. She'd known there might be questions, and she had her answers ready. "If you've something to say, Wraith, get it over with. I'm tired."

"All right, then. You told us we were tracking down an Aldenian bloodbinder who fled across the border to hide in Andithyri. Now we find out he grew up in that little piss-pot of a village. Never even set foot outside it, they said. You want to explain that?" In the amber glow of the firelight, his grizzled features looked more menacing than ever.

Alix paused in her work, eyeing him levelly. "Actually, that's not what I said. I told you Rodrik was a bloodbinder, but I never said he was Aldenian. That part you assumed for yourself. All I said was that Alden only had one bloodbinder, and we needed another. I never said where he came from, only that he'd never declared himself."

"Hang on, then," Asvin said. "Are you saying this bloke is *Andithyrian*? We're helping you track down an *Andithyrian* bloodbinder?"

The others were gathering around now too, including Vel and the Wolves. "That's right," Alix said. She resumed fussing with her bedroll; it gave her an excuse to avoid their gazes. "You can understand why I left that part out, perhaps."

"Because he's not your resource to exploit," Wraith growled. His anger was a good sign—it meant he was swallowing this new lie.

"Maybe not," Alix said, "but we need him, and it's not as though the Resistance can make good use of him. You're too few to make any real military difference, at least on your own. On top of which, with the risks you take, he'll just end up getting captured again, back to bloodforging weapons for the enemy. He's safer in Alden, equipping our armies. You'll get him back when the war is over and Andithyri free."

What does it say about me that lying comes so easily? A stray thought, irrelevant. Alix swept it aside.

"How do we know that's true?" Tag demanded. "How do we know we're not helping you smuggle our last bloodbinder out of the country, never to return?"

Alix gave him an exasperated look. "I guess you don't, but if Alden fails and Andithyri stays under the Warlord's boot, having Rodrik around won't do you much good, will it?"

"It's a straightforward question of strategy," Dain said, coming to Alix's aid. "You back the army that's got a chance of winning. Unless you think you can overthrow the Oridians with assassinations and supply raids, we're your best chance."

Wraith scowled. "I don't like being lied to."

"And I don't like being forced to assassinate people," Alix snapped, "but here we are."

A good deal of grumbling ensued, but no one challenged this new version—at least not openly—and after a while they dispersed, each one claiming his own bit of space. All except Vel, who lowered herself presumptuously onto the foot of Alix's bedroll. "That was a pretty piece of fiction," the priestess said without preamble. "And now I'd like the truth."

"What makes you think that wasn't the truth?"

Even in the dark, she could sense the other woman's smirk. "Aside from what I heard earlier, there is the matter of how Alden became aware of a secret Andithyrian bloodbinder. You had better consider how you will deal with that question, because it will come, once our friends have had a chance to digest what you just told them. If I were to put gold on it, I would say Asvin will be the one to ask."

You and me both, Alix thought sullenly.

"Apparently," Vel went on, "you even know what Rodrik looks like. How is that, I wonder?"

Dread and anger mingled in Alix's stomach, a potent brew. What had started out as an inconvenience was fast becoming something much more serious. "I have letters," she said through gritted teeth. "From a man called Terrell, who used to live in Rodrik's village. He was Aldenian, a friend of Chancellor Highmount's. He's the one who reported Rodrik to us."

Vel nodded slowly. "A workable explanation. Wraith should be satisfied with that, presuming you have the letters to back up your claim."

"I do." A number of them were vague enough that they could be shown without fear of giving anything away.

"You're very good at this, Lady Alix." Vel's tone was unreadable, her features masked in shadow. "You would make a cunning spy."

"You're an expert on espionage, are you?"

"What I am is observant. Shall I tell you what I observed this afternoon? I saw a young girl of about twelve, whose brother, according to Marelda, was fifteen years old when she was born, making him around twenty-seven today. A handsome fellow, we're told, with blue eyes. Nothing remarkable so far. But then there's the hair. Gold with a hint of red, I believe she said. An unusual shade for an Andithyrian. An unusual shade *anywhere*. Foreign blood, perhaps?" Vel's smirk had acquired an edge, her tone unmistakably challenging.

Alix tried to speak, but found her mouth had gone dry.

"Even more unusual," the priestess continued, "he has a withered right arm. No doubt that explains why he was put up for adoption. A fascinating tapestry these threads weave, don't you agree? But it was you who gave me the final thread, Lady

Alix, just now. An Aldenian man—a friend of Chancellor Highmount's, no less—happens to live in the same tiny, out-of-the-way hamlet as this twenty-seven-year-old man with blue eyes and reddish-gold hair. *Quite* a coincidence. Almost as much of a coincidence as the undeniable resemblance this description bears to a certain eminent personage whose personal bodyguard you just happen to be."

In the silence that followed, in the clinging dark of a starless night, Alix felt her hand stray to the dagger at her belt. The priestess was the only one who'd heard the physical description. Without it, no one could possibly guess the truth. Without Vel, Erik's secret was safe . . .

It's your duty, a hard voice inside her whispered. *You must protect the king.* Alix's pulse raced. Her fingers curled around the hilt of her dagger. In the dark, Vel's face was featureless, anonymous. A shadow. A threat.

The blade hissed out of its sheath. Alix lunged.

She drove her dagger into the dirt an inch away from the priestess's thigh, burying it to the hilt. She held it there for long moments, looming over Vel, eyes boring into the other woman. Briefly, she flicked a glance over Vel's shoulder, but no one had stirred. No one had seen. Leaning in even closer, Alix whispered, "Do we understand each other?" She didn't wait for an answer; Vel was shaking so badly that Alix had no doubt she'd made her point.

She sat back. Sheathed the blade. Vel sat there, trembling.

"Here." Alix passed her a flask, the last remnants of her brother's wine. Vel downed it without a word. Alix waited a few moments for the shaking to pass. Then she said, "You understand what's at stake now. And you know where my duty lies. Don't make me choose, Vel. For both our sakes, don't make me choose."

A long pause. Tremulously, Vel said, "You have already chosen, at least for now. I am fortunate to be alive, it seems." She twisted to her feet and crossed the campsite, leaving Alix alone in shadow. It was then that she too began to shake.

"I'd have done it," Ide said, throwing a dark glance across the campsite at the priestess. The others were packing up their gear, giving Alix and the Wolves a rare moment of privacy. Alix had filled them in as quickly as she could, pretending not to notice Vel pretending not to notice them.

"Would you really?" Dain gave Ide a troubled look. "You'd have killed her? Just like that?"

"Don't know what you mean, *just like that*. It's not like it's a whim or something. For starters, she's Onnani . . ." Dain scowled and started to object, but Ide waved him off. "Don't get your smalls in a scrunch—I don't mean the colour of her skin. I mean she's a *foreigner*. And a priestess on top of it, and now she knows the most dangerous secret in the kingdom. What's to stop her telling Wraith or anybody else? Puts the king's life at risk, doesn't it? Hells, puts the whole country at risk."

So Alix had thought in the heat of the moment. But now . . . "You really think I should have done it?"

Ide hitched a shoulder. "Not saying that, necessarily. Your brother trusts her, and that's gotta count for something. I'm just telling you what I would have done."

"What about you, Dain?"

"I'd have thought about it, maybe. But actually go through with it?" He shook his head. "I couldn't do something like that."

"I could have," Alix said. "Gods help me, I almost did."

Dain gave her a sympathetic look. "What stopped you?"

"A decision like that . . . you can never take it back, can you? I wanted to make sure I'd had a chance to think it through."

Ide lifted a straw-coloured eyebrow. "Since when?"

"Incoming," Dain murmured, and a moment later Vel arrived.

She stood before them in silence, spine straight as a poker, an unlikely mixture of pride and apprehension. "I came to apologise," she said.

Alix stared. "You're . . . apologising for having your life threatened?"

"Certainly not. For my ill-considered words. I must have sounded terribly smug to you. Threatening, even. But I assure you that was not my intention. I was exceedingly pleased with myself for having worked it all out, and I let that childish excitement get the better of me. I did not consider how it would come across, or the position it would put you in. For that, I apologise." She paused, her gaze falling to the ground. "Though I don't expect any of you to believe it, I *am* on your side."

Alix sighed. "I want to believe it, Vel. I really do." Not just for Rig's sake, but because she needed all the help she could get. Even so . . . "This is going to be hard to get past, though, isn't it? For both of us."

The priestess raised her eyes; they bore a hard, practical look. "Yes, it is. But this is bigger than us, so we had better try." With that, she spun on her heel and headed for the wagon.

Ide grunted. "I'll say this for her: She's got balls."

"That she does," Alix said. "I just wish I knew whether that was a good thing." She would have said more, but she was interrupted by a harsh voice on the far side of the camp.

"My lady of Blackhold!" Wraith gave a mock bow, gesturing impatiently at the wagon. "If you're through gossiping with your retainers, can we get on the road? I'd like to make Gertswold before dark."

"Ready?" In the shadows of the alley, the hard angles of Wraith's face were sketched in charcoal, his beard a dusting of ash.

Alix eyed the golden light of the tavern windows. She wasn't ready, not remotely. But it was too late to back out now. She gave a curt nod in answer.

"Remember," Wraith said, "low profile. No questioning the locals, no getting fancy. Just find yourselves a table, have a few drinks, and keep an eye out for our yellow-haired friend. That's all there is to it."

"That," said Asvin, "and avoid getting killed."

"We won't be far," Wraith said.

"Be through that door before you know it, something goes wrong," Ide added, patting her bow for emphasis.

Words. If something went wrong, Alix had little doubt that she and Asvin would be dead before their friends could come to their aid. For all intents and purposes, the two of them were on their own, in a strange town, walking into a tavern full of drunken enemy soldiers. *Gods, I must have been mad to agree to this.*

"What if he doesn't show up?" Vel asked. "Alix and Asvin are putting their lives at risk on a hunch."

"It's more than a hunch," Wraith said. "This ain't my first horse race, Daughter. We've been doing this kind of thing for months, and trust me—there's nothing occupying soldiers like better than drinking and whoring. He'll show. You'd better hope so, anyway, because after this our best shot of finding our roach is in his nest, and I don't fancy taking on a whole barracks full of soldiers."

"Now *that* would be risky," Asvin said.

Alix growled under her breath. "Let's just get this over with."

Asvin stepped into the street and gestured with mock gallantry at the tavern. Throwing a final, uneasy glance at her companions, Alix headed for the door.

She kept her gaze on the floorboards as they entered, hoping it would pass for shyness. She didn't trust her expression not to give her away. The tension screaming inside her must surely be visible to anyone, even overconfident soldiers well into their cups. She resisted the urge to tug at the hood of her cloak for the tenth time. The cowl was generous, her hair pulled back in a severe braid. No one would see. *Casual,* she reminded herself. *Unremarkable.*

She crossed the common room in carefully measured steps, like a doe picking her way past a pack of wolves, hoping they were too sated to stir. It felt as if every pair of eyes in the tavern were pinned to her, each one a cold needle piercing her flesh. She imagined bodies rising from chairs, hands straying to swords. Pure fancy, she knew. Gertswold was a decent-sized town; strangers were commonplace. No one would take any notice of her if she didn't give them a reason to. So her mind told her, but somehow, her nerves weren't convinced. Only a supreme act of willpower prevented her from glancing about to see who might be watching.

Somehow, she made it to a table in the back without attracting the attention of the predators. "We should have a good view from here," Asvin said, pulling out a chair.

The barmaid came by with mugs of ale; she didn't even ask before thumping them down on the table, and she was gone before either of them could say a word. Alix feigned a wave at the girl's retreating back, giving herself an excuse to scan the room for the first time. No one seemed to have taken any notice of them. The place was crowded, and judging from the flushed faces, most of the patrons had been here awhile. Soldiers were scattered throughout, with a cluster of six near the bar who appeared to account for the majority of the noise. Alix scrutinised them one by one, but didn't see their quarry.

"Something to eat?" The barmaid was back. She had a nervous way about her—furtive movements, downcast eyes. Alix didn't blame her. Being a serving girl in a tavern full of foreign soldiers had to be stressful work.

"No thanks," Asvin said, "but I'll think of another excuse to bring you back to us by and by." He winked, setting the girl's cheeks on fire. She hurried away.

Alix scowled at him. "This is your idea of keeping a low profile?"

"In a tavern full of happy people drinking? Why, yes it is. You, on the other hand, sitting there with your hood pulled low and your drink untouched, that sour look on your face . . . Which of us is doing the better job of blending in, I wonder?"

He was right, of course, but Alix couldn't help it. "What do you want from me? This place is full of *soldiers*."

"That's the idea."

"I know, but—" A burst of rough laughter startled her; she nearly upended the table in fright. *So much for making a cunning spy.* Saxon certainly wouldn't be impressed.

Asvin growled under his breath, dabbing at the ale she'd made him spill. "Relax, would you? I've done this a hundred times. No one has any reason to suspect us. We're just ordinary townsfolk having a drink."

"Not many ordinary townsfolk in here. The Oridians have practically taken the place over."

"Which is exactly why we're here," Asvin said impatiently. "Look, this isn't my idea of a pleasant evening either, but it's our best chance of finding the men who took Rodrik. Everyone we asked gave us the same story: *This* is where the roaches come to drink. Sooner or later, our yellow-haired lad will show up, and when he does . . ."

"And when he does, we'll follow him, and very likely find that he's the *wrong* yellow-haired lad."

Asvin rolled his eyes. "My lady of optimism. You got a better idea?"

She didn't. Wraith was right—there were too many of them to fight. Thirty in the garrison, if the townsfolk they'd spoken to had it right. Getting into Gertswold had been easy enough;

the soldiers weren't holding the town so much as using it as a base, and people came and went freely from the surrounding farmsteads. But attacking would be folly. *We'll do this quiet*, Wraith had said. Alix had agreed readily—until she'd learned what he had in mind.

"Regretting volunteering?" Asvin said into her thoughts.

She shook her head. "This is my mission. It's only right."

"Well, then." He hoisted his flagon. "Try to loosen up a little, will you?"

She did as she was told, taking a long draw of her ale. Maybe it would help calm her nerves. *This is no different than when you used to go down to the Crooked Mast to listen to gossip*, she told herself. Except, of course, that the Crooked Mast hadn't been packed to the crow's nest with enemy soldiers.

Time passed. Alix drank her ale. It tasted like fermented nuts, but it did seem to slow her racing pulse just a little. She glanced at the bar every now and then but generally kept her head down.

Until Asvin kicked her under the table, and slowly, as casually as she could, Alix looked.

Three more soldiers had just walked in. One of them, a thickset fellow who stood well over six feet, thumped his chest and roared something in Oridian that earned a round of cheers and raised flagons from his comrades.

"There's a big bloke," Asvin murmured. "And what do you know? Take a look at his mate."

She was already looking. She could see nothing else. "Yellow hair."

"Yellow hair, in the company of a big bloke." Asvin grinned. "You were saying, my lady of optimism?"

Alix's blood spiked, a sensation unsettlingly similar to desire. This was the man who'd hurt Ana. Alix barely knew the girl, but she was young and vulnerable and she was Rodrik's sister. Erik's niece, after a fashion. Alix owed the girl her shield. Her sword, if necessary.

In that moment, her nervousness melted away. She was the predator now. She settled in and waited.

It was a long wait. Dawn had broken over Gertswold by the time the yellow-haired soldier stumbled out of the tavern, still in the company of the two comrades he'd arrived with. By that time, Alix and Asvin had slipped outside, having had the benefit of a good long look in a well-lit room. Sure of their target, they could afford to retreat to the shadows with the others.

When the yellow-haired man appeared, Wraith signalled to Alix and Asvin, and the three of them followed, leaving the rest to find their way back to camp. It wouldn't do to have all eight of them tailing the soldiers at once—they'd be spotted for certain, no matter how drunk their quarry might be. Still, Alix didn't relish the idea of attacking three on three; she hoped the yellow-haired man could be separated from his companions before they struck.

Their chance came when the Oridians veered toward a brothel. Two of them went directly inside, but the yellow-haired man lagged behind, ambling up to the side of the building to relieve himself. Wraith slipped behind the Oridian and hooked a meaty arm around his neck, taking full advantage of his considerable bulk to wrestle his prey into an alley. He ground the Oridian's face into the wall and pinned his arm behind his back.

"Look at that," Wraith growled. "I always knew you roaches had tiny pricks."

The Oridian's face twisted into a snarl, but he didn't struggle. He knew his attacker could break his arm with no effort at all. Still, he dared a threat. "I am a soldier of the Trionate, white-hair. You are a dead man."

"You'd be surprised how often I hear that." Wraith glanced over his shoulder. "Asvin, keep watch on the brothel." Then, to Alix: "Ask your questions, but make it quick."

She closed in, bringing her lips close to the man's ear as Wraith had done. He smelled of beer and stale sweat. "Indrask," she said.

"What?"

In reply, Wraith took a fistful of yellow hair and slammed the Oridian's face into the wall.

"Indrask," Alix repeated. "The man you took from there."

The Oridian spat blood. "I have no idea—"

Impassively, Wraith slammed the man's face into the wall again. His nose broke open, loosing blood over his mouth and chin.

"Andithyrian," Alix said, "but not white-haired. Withered right arm. You took him from Indrask. I'm not asking."

The Oridian squirmed pointlessly. "What about him?"

"Where did you take him?"

"I do not— *Wait!*" He was theirs now; Alix could tell by the panic creeping into his voice. "I swear, I do not know. He was sent to the *Tartir.*"

Alix glanced at Wraith, but he shook his head; he didn't know the word, either. "*Tartir.* What is that?"

"The *Tartir.* Sadik."

Wraith scowled. "You expect us to believe Sadik himself is interested in this man?"

"That is what they told me!" The Oridian's voice was too high, too strangled, to doubt him. "The commander said he had orders to take the cripple straight to the *Tartir!*"

"Which is where?" Alix demanded.

The man shook his head.

"Tell us," Alix said, "and we'll spare your life."

"I do not know where they took him. The *Tartir* comes and goes as he pleases. To meet with spies, they say, or his witch."

Alix's breath caught; she seized the man's collar. "The witch—what do you know of him? A bloodbinder like Madan?"

"Like Madan, yes. The *Tartir* would go to see his experiments."

"*Would* go. He doesn't anymore?"

"They are together now. At Ennersvale, with the bulk of our forces." His voice dropped to a fearful whisper. "The men do not like it. The witch is evil, they say."

Alix's heart raced. This was it. It *had* to be. "Ennersvale . . ."

"At the border," Wraith said. "About where we started. Roaches have been there a while."

It made sense. It also meant another three days lost as they retraced their steps back to the border. Alix cursed inwardly, feeling another handful of sand slip through the timeglass.

"Let me go," the Oridian said. "I told you what you wanted."

Alix hesitated. It was true—he'd told her what she wanted. But this was also the roach who'd hurt Ana. Who'd struck a twelve-year-old-girl so hard that the bruises still showed more than six weeks later. *But he's powerless now, and you told him you'd spare his life . . .*

Wraith drew his dagger and opened the Oridian's throat. The man sagged, gurgling and thrashing, blood soaking his crimson tabard.

"Why did you do that?" Alix snapped. "It was my decision to make!"

Wraith whirled on her so suddenly that she recoiled. In that moment, she hardly recognised him; he scarcely seemed human at all. He loomed over her, thrumming with menace, his hulking form seeming to take up every inch of space between them. *Not Wraith*, she thought dimly. *Wrath.*

"That's a roach," he snarled, gesturing with his bloodied dagger. "An enemy. His people occupy my country. They murder and they rape and they do whatever they please. Killing him is not only my right, it's my fucking *obligation*. This is war. Do you understand that? *War*. It makes no difference if this sack of shite is pinned against a wall or coming at me with a spear in melee combat. He's fair game either way. So spare me your self-righteousness, *my lady*."

When he backed away, Alix's lungs seemed to fill with just a little more air.

He stalked off, melting into shadow. All Alix could do was follow.

FOURTEEN

† "There will be panic," Osmond Swiftcurrent said. There was a faint note of denial in his voice, as though he didn't quite believe what he was hearing. He wasn't alone in that; the faces round the table all wore the same horrified look, as if Liam had just announced that he planned to give the contents of the royal treasury to charity.

"We will avoid panic if we manage the announcement properly," Highmount said with his usual cool assurance. "And provided that we here, as members of the King's Council and representatives of the crown, do not ourselves give in to it." His hawklike gaze did a slow tour of the table, subjecting each council member to a long, piercing look. "I will not have you retreating to your family estates, my lords. Our place is here."

"Our place is with His Majesty," said Sirin Grey. "And yet His Majesty is not here."

Liam resisted the urge to glance at Rona. This was the moment they'd dreaded. They'd spent two full days planning this meeting, since how they navigated it could well determine whether Liam and Highmount lived to see another sunrise. *Steady, Your Highness. You knew this was coming, and you know what to say.*

Sirin Grey continued. "This council has been remarkably indulgent, my lord chancellor, in accepting excuse after excuse for His Majesty's absence. But a matter of this gravity? You cannot seriously expect us to authorise an evacuation of the capital on your say-so alone."

Raibert Green cleared his throat uncomfortably. "I'm afraid I must concur, Chancellor. I quite understand the caution you have exercised in the matter of His Majesty's health. But surely that concern pales in comparison to what is before us now? This could be the end of the Kingdom of Alden. She needs her king."

"She has her king."

All eyes swivelled to Liam.

He took a moment to return those gazes, one by one, as Highmount had done. He lingered on Rona's, drawing strength from it, her voice still fresh in his ear. *I know growing into this role hasn't been easy for you, but you're out of time. It's now or never.*

The great lords and ladies of the realm gazed at him expectantly, and just for a moment, his nerve deserted him. It was like one of those nightmares where he found himself standing naked in the sparring ring before a crowd of jeering onlookers. Except this crowd would do worse than jeer if he didn't take control of the situation. *Now or never*, he reminded himself.

"With respect, Your Highness—" Sirin Grey began.

"She has her king," Liam repeated firmly. "And she has her prince. My brother has always trusted in the wisdom of this council, and I have done the same. I ask that you continue serving as you have, with prudence and conviction. I welcome your questions and your criticisms. But make no mistake, my lords, it is I who will take the final decision here, as prince of the realm, acting with my brother's proxy." He paused to let that sink in, praying to all the gods that it sounded more convincing than it felt.

A gentle flutter round the table, a frisson of disapproval. The horrified looks were back too, with that same hint of denial. Those expressions would turn his bone marrow to liquid if he let them. Arranging his features into his best Battle Face, he deliberately squared off against the scariest among them, meeting Sirin Grey's eye levelly. It was the look he used on his enemies, the one that let them know he was a foe to be feared. *Come at me if you dare*, that face said. *I'm ready.*

Norvin Gold harrumphed into the silence. "You intend to proceed with Chancellor Highmount's suggestion, then? Evacuate the capital?"

"I do, and precisely in order to *avoid* panic. You don't wait until you're attacked to reposition your forces. That ends up in chaos. People tend not to follow orders very well with the enemy waving weapons in their faces. But if we act now, while we have the luxury of time, we can move in a measured, organised way."

"That sounds very well, Your Highness," Sirin Grey said coolly, "but words are easier than deeds. In ordering the city evacuated, we are sending a clear message that we expect it to fall."

"Not necessarily," Highmount said. "It is a matter of how we communicate. If we simply order evacuations and leave the public to develop their own narrative, then yes—they will likely conclude the worst. But if we do not surrender that space, if we instead fill it with a carefully crafted message, we stand a reasonable chance of casting this as a tactical manoeuvre that will help us defeat the enemy."

Lady Stonegate hummed sceptically. "You give the people too little credit, Chancellor. They are not fools."

Highmount's expression suggested a differing opinion, but luckily Rona Brown spoke up first. "Not fools," she said, "just human beings who desperately want to believe everything will be all right. They will cling to any scrap of hope you give them, and gladly."

"Very true," said Raibert Green. "I've seen it a dozen times on the battlefield. Men will gladly suspend their disbelief if their commander gives them half a reason to."

"How fortunate," Sirin Grey said, "since half a reason is all we have."

Liam swallowed an irritable reply. "Chancellor Highmount and I will begin preparing an address to the public, which I will deliver personally once we've worked out the details. As to those—Lord Green, I'd like you and Lady Brown to oversee manoeuvres on the walls. The men have been idle for too long—let them hone their edges. Lords Gold and

Swiftcurrent, I want to see a proposal for the reinforcement of the gates. Make sure to consult the clergy—they have some interesting tricks up their sleeves. Lady Stonegate, the chancellor tells me your estate here in the city has an impressive vault."

Her Ladyship nodded gravely. "That is so, Your Highness."

"Good. We've no chance of getting the contents of the treasury out of the city altogether, but if we're discreet, we should be able to hide it on your estate for a time, if the worst comes." Liam glanced round the table again. "Have I forgotten anything?"

"You have not assigned me a task, Your Highness," Sirin Grey said.

"Oh, I'm sure I'll think of something." *Ideally involving flint and tinder and Your Ladyship's noble arse.* "If there's nothing else, my lords, we're adjourned." He stood, effectively rendering his last remark rhetorical. The lords and ladies filed out of the oratorium.

"Now that," Rona grinned, "is more like it."

Even Highmount gave him a look of grudging respect. "Well handled indeed."

"It helps to have a good battle plan," Liam said. "Thank you for your help these past two days, both of you."

"Plans are of little use if not executed properly, and you carried them off smoothly. It seems you have begun to hit your stride at last, Your Highness."

Praise from Albern Highmount? Liam might have fainted clean away had Sirin Grey not reappeared at the door.

"A word, Your Highness?"

Liam's pulse faltered. He should have known it had been too easy. "Please," he said, gesturing at a chair.

"We are rather pressed for time," Highmount said. "What can we do for you?"

She smiled. "Where is the king?"

Her bluntness was calculated to shock, and it worked. The question struck Liam like a body blow, stealing the air from his lungs.

Highmount, though, weathered it masterfully enough for both of them; he merely lifted an eyebrow. "I am afraid I do not understand the question. You know where His Majesty is."

"Quarantined in the royal apartments, yes." She smoothed a fold in her dress. "Except I don't believe that, I'm afraid."

Liam scowled, letting his anger mask his fear. "What exactly is so hard to believe about it? Has Erik never fallen ill before?"

She turned her glacial gaze on him. "Of course he has, Your Highness. He has had consumption, a broken leg, and even a bout of Red Fever. And never, in any of those instances, did he allow himself to remain bedridden for days on end, let alone weeks. Our good king finds it impossible to sit still for more than a few hours at a time, whatever his condition. And yet now, with his kingdom facing the gravest crisis in its history, His Majesty falls so gravely ill that no one has seen or heard from him in over two weeks. Meanwhile, the chancellor continues to claim that the sickness is not serious. So which is it? Is the king at death's door, or is he merely suffering from a sniffle?"

"We don't have time for this," Liam growled. "We've got the Warlord at our doorstep, and—"

"Let us not play games, Your Highness," Sirin said coldly. "I know the truth."

Liam's heart froze in his breast.

A long, thin thread of silence quivered between them. Sirin Grey glared at Liam. Highmount made a steeple of his fingers. Rona gripped the arms of her chair until her knuckles went white.

"You have played your hand well until now, Your Highness, but your luck has run out. Even the most artful rumours circulating among the servants have exhausted themselves. The council grows suspicious. Your story loses credibility with each passing day, and the vultures have begun to circle. If you would bring the situation in hand before it is too late, you will tell me the truth."

"That sounded like a threat," Rona said, folding her arms in a manner that just happened to jostle her armour.

Sirin paled, but her expression didn't change. She was tough, Liam had to admit.

"Tell me," Highmount said, "what exactly is this truth you claim to know?"

"Come now, Chancellor. It is obvious what's happened. Frankly, I am astonished you would be part of it."

Liam felt like throwing up. Maybe that wouldn't even be such a bad thing. At least it would bring a swift end to the conversation. If he was going to be accused of high treason, he'd rather get it over with.

"I would have thought you'd have better judgement . . ."

Here it comes . . .

". . . than to let His Majesty leave the city."

Liam stared. He had no words. He didn't even have breath.

"Don't look so surprised, Your Highness. You forget, perhaps, that I was engaged to Erik White for years. I know perfectly well his elaborate code of honour, not to mention his penchant for boyish adventure. He couldn't stand to remain here, tucked away safely in the palace, while Riggard Black took the weight of the kingdom on his shoulders. He's gone to the front, and your lady wife has gone with him."

Liam realised his mouth was hanging open slightly; he closed it with a snap. He cast about for something to say, but thankfully, Highmount spared him the effort.

"I assure you it is more complicated than that, Lady Sirin. His Majesty is not merely indulging some misguided sense of principles, let alone an appetite for adventure. You can be certain I would indeed have no part of that. I am afraid that a very serious matter has arisen at the front, one that requires his personal attention."

Liam scratched his chin just to make sure his mouth wasn't hanging open again. He had never seen anyone lie so seamlessly. Without even missing a beat, Highmount had fabricated an entirely new story to fit Sirin Grey's assumptions.

"I fail to see what could possibly be more important than presiding over the evacuation of the city," Sirin said.

"We did not anticipate the need arising quite so soon," Highmount said, "but His Majesty's letters from the front indicate that the Warlord could make his move at any time."

Her eyes narrowed. "But I still don't see—"

"I am certain I do not need to tell you, Lady Sirin, how terribly important it is that you keep this information to yourself." Highmount regarded her gravely. "Your family has ever had a reputation for doing its duty, recent aberrations notwithstanding."

Gods, the man was an *artist*. Sirin Grey wanted nothing more than to restore her family's reputation, so thoroughly ruined by her brother. With a few choice words, Highmount was subtly offering her a way to do just that, while simultaneously suggesting that if she didn't, she was little better than her traitorous sibling.

Sirin drew herself up stiffly. "My loyalty to the crown is what brought me here, Chancellor. I could easily have voiced my suspicions to the council."

"And the crown salutes your devotion," Highmount said. "I am certain that when His Majesty returns, he will wish to thank you personally."

He left that little carrot dangling, tantalisingly vague. It was all Liam could do not to shake his head in awe.

Sirin narrowed her eyes. "I will keep your secret, my lords, for now. But I warn you: if His Majesty does not return forthwith, or if I believe the kingdom to be at risk, I will not stay my tongue."

"Fair enough," Liam said with a taut smile. "Now, if you don't mind . . ." He gestured at the map lying on the table before him. "War planning and whatnot."

With a swish of silk and the soft ring of footsteps, Sirin Grey quit the oratorium.

"Well," said Rona, "that was terrifying."

"I can't believe we're still sitting here," Liam said. "With our heads and everything."

"For now," Highmount said, his gaze lingering on the door. "She will not be satisfied with that for long. A few days at most, I should think."

Liam put on a brave face. "Given that our goal is to live long enough to be killed by the Warlord, I'm inclined to take it one day at a time, Chancellor." Just the sort of glib nonsense that was expected of him. Inside, though, he was saying a silent prayer—not to the Virtues, but to his wife.

Hurry, Allie. For the love of all the gods, please hurry.

"I dreamed of her last night."

"I know," said Tom, a note of boredom in his voice.

"Of course you do." Tom existed only in Erik's mind;

naturally he would know all that transpired there. "Forgive me. Sometimes I forget you're not real."

"I don't recommend that, brother. Then you truly will be mad."

"Isolation and boredom will do that to a man."

"Indeed." Tom toyed with the sumptuous velvet of the curtains. As usual, he sat propped in a corner of the window seat, gazing listlessly out into the garden. "If it helps you to speak of it, feel free."

"Of the dream? Very well." Erik got up to fetch himself a cup of wine, resisting the impulse to offer one to his imaginary brother. "It was the day we met Rig on the battlefield in the Brownlands. We had a sort of banquet that evening in my pavilion, to celebrate."

"I remember."

Erik started to say, *You weren't there*, but of course that made no sense. The real Tom hadn't been there, but he wasn't here now, either. He was the product of an overtired, overstressed mind. He was also a tremendous comfort, an escape from the dark whispers that clawed at Erik night and day. They had always been there, those whispers, in some form or another. His father's voice, sometimes, and later, Tom's. Highmount's occasionally, or Arran Green's. Even Alix's. Anyone who had ever counselled Erik this way or that, tried to make of him what they would. True, the voices were different now—stronger, more insistent, almost an audible presence. They tied his insides in knots in ways they hadn't before. But that was only to be expected, given his situation. In his captivity, in his doubt and self-recrimination, those whispers were his only company.

Those, and his dead brother.

Erik sank down into his favourite stuffed leather chair, letting his mind wander back to the dream. "I might as well have been invisible, for all the notice Alix took of me that evening. All her attention belonged to Rig. After so long apart, worrying that he might be dead . . . And now here he was, safe and sound, eating as if he hadn't seen a crumb in months. The way Alix looked at him . . . She *glowed*, Tom."

"You always thought so."

"This was different. I'm not talking about beauty. I'm

talking about love. She was so happy to see her brother alive and well. And it was in his eyes too, when he looked back at her, that same glow. This incredible bond between them. I remember thinking, isn't that what it's supposed to be like between siblings? Might it have been that way with my twin, had she lived?"

Tom rolled his eyes. "Not this again . . ."

"Liam was there too, though of course that isn't how it really happened. But in my dream, he was there, and he was just as fascinated as I, both of us examining these strange specimens. It was as if we were trying to figure out the trick to it. As though, if we paid close enough attention, we might work out how to be brothers."

"Why do you do this to yourself, Erik? This fantasy of yours, of having an ordinary family, an ordinary life . . . why torture yourself with it? It was never going to be. You are king."

"As though I need you to tell me," Erik said coolly. "I thought you were going to listen to my dream?"

"This dream I've heard. Many times."

Erik ignored that. "When supper was over, Alix stayed behind in my tent. She had something important to tell me, she said. She had to leave my service. To join up with Rig, to lend him her sword."

"That never happened."

"Not in real life, but in my dream it did."

"And in the dream, you were stunned."

"Of course! But your sword is mine, I said. You swore me an oath. She said her first duty was to her brother. That it always had been. Part of me rejoiced to hear it, but another part was furious. How can your first duty not be to the king, I asked her?"

"A reasonable question."

"Do you know what she said? She told that me that her brother would be king soon enough."

"Riggard Black. King." Tom snorted softly. He and Rig had never got on.

"Dreams are strange," Erik said. "Rig was standing in for Liam, I think. In reality, Alix abandoned me for my brother; in the dream, she abandoned me for hers. Either way, this fraternal love I'd been longing for my whole life . . . it had betrayed me. Alix had betrayed me." His gaze dropped to the cup of wine in his hand; his reflection, distorted and bloody, gazed back up at him. "I was devastated. After everything we had been through together . . ."

"Sentimental tripe," Tom scoffed.

"We argued—"

"Enough, brother, this isn't—"

"—and I killed her."

Tom fell silent. Erik could feel his brother's eyes boring into him.

"I called her a traitor. I pulled her own sword from its scabbard and plunged it into her breast." Erik gazed a moment longer at the dark, twisted reflection in his cup. Feeling a sudden chill, he took a swallow, letting the wine trail fire down his throat. Tom watched in smouldering silence. Softly, Erik said, "What do you think it means, brother, this dream of mine?"

"It means you're ready."

A knock at the bedroom door.

"Impeccable timing," Tom murmured.

The guardsman Meinrad entered. He had the ledger with him, Erik saw. That was a good sign. "Your Majesty. This belongs to you." He set the ledger on a side table.

"You read it, then?"

"I did, sire." As usual, he would not meet Erik's eye.

"And did you confirm what I told you? That it is written in the chancellor's own hand?"

The guardsman nodded.

"Well, then." Erik rose, regarding the other man with a grave expression. "You know the truth now. And what do you make of it?"

A strained look knitted the guardsman's face. "This isn't . . . I shouldn't have read it, sire. It's not my place . . ."

Erik sighed, letting his gaze soften with sympathy. "I am sorry, Meinrad. I have put you in a difficult position, I know. It cannot have been easy, reading that. But it is important that you know the truth. The whole kingdom must know it. The Priest may be gone, but his dark magic lives on, and it could be used against any of us. The people must know how it works, that they might protect themselves. Not just from the Oridians, but from those who would take advantage of the situation and prey upon people's fears, as my brother has done. Think of it,

Meinrad—as it stands now, anyone can accuse his enemy of being bloodbound and no one can disprove it, because they do not know how the magic works. This ignorance is a terrible danger."

"I understand that, I do." The guardsman's expression grew still more strained. "But, sire, why then did you keep it secret? Why ask the chancellor to put it down in a ledger and hide it away in a trunk in your chambers? Why not trumpet it far and wide?"

"It was wrong of me. I thought . . ." Erik shook his head regretfully. "We believed the threat had passed. That when the Priest died, his magic died with him. I did not want it rediscovered. I feared that by releasing this information, I might unwittingly help others to replicate his work. It seemed wiser to keep it quiet. Put it down in a journal, that what we learned might not be lost, but keep it safe, that it might not be abused . . ." He closed his eyes, allowing a fleeting look of pain to cross his features. "But I see now it was a mistake. Keeping that secret has been my undoing. It has allowed my brother to condemn me with lies that no one can contradict. I was naïve in that, as I was in my brother, thinking a bastard could be made a prince and all would be well."

That last bit had been Tom's suggestion. *Remind him of Ysur the Bastard and the White War. Remind him that a half-breed was nearly the doom of this kingdom.*

The guardsman pressed his lips together, gave a tiny, almost imperceptible shake of his head. *Careful, Erik.* It had taken him nearly a week to get this far; if he pushed too hard now, he would break the spell. It took patience, this, like trying to coax a wild animal to eat from his hand. One false step would scare his quarry off. But if there was one thing Erik had always been able to count on, it was his way with people. *You've been relying on your charm all your life, brother,* Tom had said as he handed Erik the ledger. *Why stop now?*

"You have read the journal," Erik said. "You understand how the magic works, and you know that I cannot possibly be under the enemy's control. They would need my blood, a great deal of it." He spread his arms. "And as you can see, I am quite whole." He smiled, a sad, wounded thing. "If still you doubt me, ask the bloodbinder Nevyn. He will confirm what the ledger says."

The guardsman's hands twitched into fists by his side. "But, sire, what would you have me do? I can't free you. If it were up to me . . . But I *can't*." He cast a furtive look over his shoulder, afraid one of his comrades might overhear.

"I would never ask that of you, Meinrad. It would be unfair. But there is another way you can help me. A small task, one that leaves the difficult decisions to others, that you need not carry the burden on your shoulders."

The guardsman drew a series of short, heaving breaths. He was on the verge of panic, but Erik knew that for a sign of victory. He could feel Tom's gaze, fierce and triumphant, from across the room.

"You can take this letter to Lady Sirin Grey . . ."

FIFTEEN

† "How many?" The look on Wraith's face was more wolfish than ever, lips drawn back in a grimace, eyes following the soldiers hungrily. Alix wouldn't have been surprised if he'd licked his chops.

"Too many," Asvin said, lowering the longlens. "That's a whole army, that is."

Wraith spat on the ground and snatched the longlens for himself, resting his elbows atop the pasture wall to steady his view. He grunted, but otherwise kept the fruits of his reconnaissance to himself.

Alix shielded her eyes and squinted into the distance. Without the longlens, all she could make out was a clutter of shadow and metal, but she'd been a scout long enough to know that Asvin was right. "Fifteen thousand at least, and probably more nearby. So what now?"

"We need eyes on Sadik," Wraith growled.

"We need eyes on *Rodrik*. He's the one we came for."

Wraith didn't answer. The longlens was still glued to his eye.

"We should go back to the others," Asvin said. "There'll be enemy scouts nearby, and if they spot us, we're dead."

They scurried back down the rise to where the rest of their party waited, protected from view by the swell of the land.

"Well?" Vel asked.

Asvin shrugged. "Not much to say. It's the whole sodding Oridian army, isn't it?"

"So," said Tag, "we're buggered."

"Not buggered." Wraith's gaze was unfocused, but no less intense for it. "We just need a plan."

Asvin made a wry face. "If by chance the plan involves myself and Her Ladyship sneaking into the camp, you can forget it. Fifteen thousand pairs of eyes is a few too many, even for me."

"After dark, like," Tag said, as though it were an innovative suggestion.

"We don't even know for certain Rodrik is with them," Alix pointed out. "Our first priority is to find out."

"We should be able to manage that much," Asvin said. "We just need to get close enough to get a better look with the longlens."

"I want eyes on Sadik," Wraith said again.

Alix swallowed a sharp reply. They were too close to their goal for her to risk antagonising Wraith now. "We'll do what we can."

"I'll come with," Ide said. "Things go sour, you'll need someone can shoot." Alix nodded her thanks.

"No more than three," Asvin warned. "As it is, I'm worried about those damned dogs."

Alix winced; she'd managed to put them out of her mind until now. She hadn't seen one since Boswyck, but she remembered only too well what they could do to a man. The Kingswords used dogs too, but mainly as sentries. Oridian warhounds, on the other hand, were bred for battle, fiercely disciplined and ludicrously vicious. If they caught so much as a hint of unfamiliar scent, they'd go wild. They were the bane of Kingsword scouts and the terror of Kingsword infantrymen. And this camp would have dozens of them. "We'll have to stay downwind," Alix said, "and make sure we have nothing on us that will catch us out." The jingle of a buckle, even the mere creak of leather might be enough to give them away. And if the wind should suddenly change direction . . .

Not worth thinking about, Alix told herself. *Focus on the things you can control.*

They fell back to the nearest cover, there to wait for nightfall. Alix used the time to check her equipment, tightening straps and discarding unnecessary metal, including her bloodblade. Unwieldy and shiny, it was too risky to bring along; her bloodforged dagger would have to do. *Just like old times.* A bittersweet thought, bringing Liam to mind. What she wouldn't give to have him here at her side—and at her back.

Night fell. Alix tossed a few blades of grass in the air, then struck out with Ide and Asvin in the direction of the wind. They gave the camp a wide berth, cutting low across the fields for nearly a mile before swinging back toward the orange glow of campfires. Above, a glittering track of stars seemed to light a path toward their goal; Alix chose to view that as a sign the gods were with them.

They dropped to the ground well out of longlens range, crawling the rest of the way on their bellies. Across the open plain, a low murmur of voices could be heard, and the smell of roast meat drifted down the wind. In the distance, a coyote yipped.

"What do you think?"

Alix started badly, though Asvin's voice was barely a breath. "A few more feet," she whispered.

This close to the camp, the glow of the fires was no longer soft and diffuse; instead, a dozen searing points of light burned holes through Alix's night vision. The voices too had become distinct; Alix caught a familiar word here and there.

The coyote yipped again, and this time it was answered: a bone-chilling howl went up from the far side of the camp. *The dogs.* Alix shuddered.

"Least they're way over there," Ide said in an undertone.

"Longlens," Asvin whispered, but Alix raised it to her own eye. This was *her* bloody mission, after all. The instrument smelled of the river mud she'd smeared on it to keep it from catching the light. Blinking away bits of dirt, she looked.

It was the most orderly camp she'd ever seen. Instead of the random constellation of tents she was accustomed to, the Oridians had theirs staked out in neat ranks, about twenty tents to a square. Between the squares ran well-tended dirt tracks, wide enough to permit the passage of a wagon. A single pavilion, slightly larger than the others, stood at the northwestern corner of every square—the officer of the unit, presumably—and each boasted its own cluster of tables and cooking fire, complete with roasting spit. Wraith had said the bulk of the Oridian army had been camped here for a while; it certainly showed.

This is good, Alix thought. *The more organised they are, the easier it will be to find Rodrik.* Unless of course Sadik expected them to come looking, in which case Rodrik could be hidden in any one of those fifteen thousand tents. Her pulse fluttered unpleasantly at the thought. It was possible. After all, Erik had been locked away in his chambers; the bloodbinder must realise by now that his influence had been discovered. Might Sadik not anticipate this response?

Alix could feel herself sinking into panic. She couldn't afford that. *Be rational about this. Think it through.* Rodrik couldn't be in just any of these tents, at least not all the time. The bloodbinder needed space to work. On top of which, a bloodbinder was too valuable a resource to yoke to a single man, even one as important as Rodrik. The Priest, who'd single-handedly bloodbound thousands of thralls, had still found time to bloodforge weapons for his army. Sadik would no doubt have his pet bloodbinder doing the same.

Alix's pulse settled back into a steady rhythm. "We're looking for a smithy."

Asvin grunted. "Makes sense."

Alix swept the longlens over the camp again. She recalled only too vividly the pavilion the Priest had used in the field last summer. There had been an open wooden structure beside it, with a stone forge beneath . . . "There."

"You see it?" Asvin's eyes glinted excitedly.

"No, but I do see smoke, too thick for a cooking fire." Handing the longlens to Ide, she said, "Past the crimson pavilion, on the left. See how it blots out the firelight? And just past it . . ."

Ide swore expressively.

Asvin scowled; he didn't like being left out. "What is it?"

"The forge is on the far side of the camp," Alix said.

"The *dog* side of the camp," Ide added.

"Figures." He held out a hand for the longlens. "Am I permitted to look now?"

Alix watched him scan the camp. "No, not there. To the left. Can't you see it?"

"Just getting the lay of things," he murmured, continuing his slow arc from right to left. He paused, tensing, but whatever he saw, he didn't give voice to it; he passed the longlens back in silence.

"Did you see it?" Alix asked.

"I saw enough."

"We need to be sure," Alix said.

Ide sighed. "Meaning you want to get closer."

"We'll head toward the river. That'll keep us downwind of the dogs."

Asvin glanced up at the sky. "We're going to run into dawn if we're not careful."

"Then we'd better be careful."

Olan was riding high among the stars by the time they cut their way back toward the far side of the camp, his gleaming silver shield bathing the countryside in the holy light of courage. Maybe the brightness of the moon explained the excitement of the coyotes, still yipping away upstream. Whatever the reason, Alix thanked Olan and all the Virtues, for the Oridian warhounds were driven to distraction by the shrill mockery of the coyotes in the distance. Low barks and deep-throated howls marked out the kennels as surely as smoke marked out the forge, and fortunately, the two were not as close together as Alix had feared. She and her companions were able to settle in barely two hundred feet from the fringes of the camp, beyond the greedy glow of cooking fires and the still-smouldering pit of the forge.

"That's got to be it," Alix breathed into Ide's ear. "See that pavilion beside it? Looks a lot like Madan's, doesn't it?"

Ide's straw-coloured mop bobbed in the dark.

"That's definitely the bloodbinder's forge. I'll bet he even sleeps in there." *I'll bet they're in there right now, he and Rodrik . . .* Alix's whole body tensed. The urge to try her luck right here and now was almost overwhelming, but she knew it for folly.

Asvin pointed at the moon. *Time to go.* Nodding, Alix wriggled backward into the night.

She could feel Wraith's gaze tracking them through the darkness as they approached their modest campsite by the creek. No fire for them so close to the enemy camp; only a single tallow candle wedged into a rotting log provided light. With her night vision well tuned, it was enough for Alix to make out the anxious features of her companions.

"Success," Asvin said, flopping soundlessly to the ground. "I could use a drink."

"You found him?" Wraith's wolfish gaze was pinned to Asvin. The smaller man looked up, and an expressive glance passed between them. "Think so," Asvin said.

"Did you actually see him?" Dain asked.

Alix shook her head. "But we found a pavilion with a forge outside. It looked much like the tent Madan used for his rituals, minus the religious trappings. I'm fairly certain that's where the bloodbinder plies his trade."

Fredek, who rarely said much of anything, asked the obvious question: "So what do we do about it?"

"I see only one alternative," Alix said. "We need a distraction."

"Aye," said Wraith. "Problem is, we don't have much to work with here. The rest of my men are back at the farm, and that's a half day's ride from here. Even then, it wouldn't be enough. I'd need time to muster the irregulars."

"The irregulars?" Alix and the Wolves exchanged blank looks.

"Civilians. Part-timers, you might call them. Same folk we used to put together that decoy your brother asked for a few weeks back. They're willing enough, but they're scattered. Would take a few days to gather them up."

Alix was shaking her head even before he'd finished. "We don't have that kind of time. For all we know, it's already . . ." She looked away, swallowing a sudden lump in her throat.

"In case you haven't noticed, we're outnumbered about fifteen thousand to one. Unless you've got a better idea . . ."

"I do," said Vel.

All eyes swung to the priestess.

"Will nine thousand Kingswords do? General Black is a day's ride across the river, after all."

Wraith snorted. "You know a lot of useful things, Daughter, but fighting obviously isn't one of them. General Black would be a fool to risk his already outnumbered army for a single man, even a bloodbinder."

"You obviously don't know General Black," Vel returned smoothly, "nor any number of other relevant factors, because I am quite confident he *would* risk it. Particularly if his sister is the one doing the asking."

"She's right," Alix said. "Rig will help us, I'm sure of it."

Wraith grunted, scratched his beard. "Someone would have to ride to the fort. We can probably muster up a horse around here someplace, but not a falcon."

"I'll go," Vel said, a little too eagerly.

"No, Daughter," Dain said, "I'll go. I'm a fast rider, and besides, Rodrik will most likely need your healing skills."

"Oh? Do you think the enemy will have mistreated him?"

Alix and Dain exchanged a look. Vel knew more than the Resistance, but she still didn't know all. "Probably," Alix said. "To force him to do their bidding."

Vel looked like she wanted to argue, but she just bit her lip and nodded. "Very well."

"That's settled, then," Dain said. "I'll start out as soon as I can. Now, where do we get this horse?"

"Alix."

She glanced up to find Vel's slender silhouette framed by the thin rays of dawn. Patting her bedroll, Alix said, "Please."

The priestess lowered herself down and smoothed her robes around her. "I'm sorry to intrude."

"No intrusion. I wanted to talk to you anyway. I have for a while, actually, ever since . . ." Alix could feel her skin warming; fortunately, it was too dark to see. "Well," she finished awkwardly, "you know."

"That is behind us."

"That's kind of you to say, but it's not really true. It couldn't be, not after what I did. I think . . ." She plucked at the grass beside her bedroll. "I *know* I could have handled that better."

"We both could have." Vel drew her knees up under her chin. "We are in an awkward position, you and I, and I daresay neither of us is terribly accustomed to holding her tongue."

Alix regarded her brother's lover in silence. She was, Alix had to admit, rather remarkable. "You're being awfully gracious about this. I'm not sure I could be, in your shoes."

Vel hitched a shoulder. "I know what it's like to feel fiercely protective of someone. To be prepared to do anything, *anything*, to keep them safe, even things that stain your soul . . ." She trailed off. Alix started to ask a question, but Vel continued, "Which is why I think we should be wary."

Instinctively, Alix shot a glance across the camp to where Wraith and his men were gathering up their bedrolls. "Wary of what?"

"If what the soldier in Gertswold told you is correct, Sadik is in that camp."

"Most likely."

Vel lowered her voice. "Remember what I said about Wraith and the Resistance. You've surely seen evidence of it yourself by now. Like you and me, they are prepared to do whatever it takes to protect their people."

"Meaning?"

"If I were Wraith, I would find the prospect of eliminating the Warlord more than a little tempting. That has never been a goal within his reach, but now . . ."

Alix thought back to the way Wraith had acted earlier—that feverish hunger, his insistence that they needed eyes on Sadik. "You're probably right, but there's not much I can do about it."

"Except to be watchful, and not assume that Wraith or his men will be there for you when you need them."

Alix shook her head bitterly. "Because this mission wasn't mad enough."

"I will pray for you." In the low light of dawn, Vel's eyes glinted like coal.

"Thank you, Daughter," Alix said, and was half surprised to find that she meant it.

SIXTEEN

T he constant hammering was driving Rig *insane*.
It began before dawn and did not cease until dusk.
Hour after hour, day after day of relentless banging, until
it felt as though the blows fell inside his skull, beating
against his very eardrums. Even after the hammers went silent
for the night, Rig could still hear them, pounding, pounding,
like a terrified heartbeat. Like a countdown to doom. Like a
thunder of enemy hoofbeats bearing down on the fort.

You're a proper sodding poet this morning, aren't you?

Growling, Rig rubbed his eyes and sat up. It was no good
lolling around in bed feeling sorry for himself, letting his
thoughts swirl in the same old dark dance. Even though it was
not yet dawn, he could already feel the worries of the day
weighing down on him; he might as well face it like a man. He
washed in cold water and scrubbed his teeth. Confronting his
reflection in the looking glass, he debated trimming his beard,
as he did every morning. Decided against it, as he did every
morning. Then he snatched up his greatsword and headed for
the ring. He desperately needed to bludgeon something.

The infernal hammering accompanied him out of the barracks and into the yard, each blow answered with a ricochet

of sound off the opposite wall. The repairs were nearly complete, and for that Rig was grateful. He would reward the men with ale and cheese and the last of the salted pork. And then he would make a bonfire of every fucking hammer within a tenmile radius.

When he reached the ring, he was surprised to find it already occupied: Commander Wright had claimed the leaded wooden longsword and was alternating between half-handed thrusts and two-handed chops on a straw dummy. "Ho there," Rig called. "Fancy hitting something that hits back?"

Wright turned and saluted. "Good morning, General. An early start for you as well, I see." Early enough, indeed, that mist still clung to the ground, rolling off the perpetual pool of rainwater the men had dubbed Lake Black. Rig had been after the engineers to find a drainage solution for weeks, but the repairs on the wall had effectively crossed that off the priority list. That, and the fact that the fort would likely be razed by the enemy in a matter of days.

"Hard to sleep with that racket," Rig said, ducking between the rails and into the ring.

"Indeed. But their diligence has paid off, it seems. I'm told the repairs are nearly done."

"Let's hope so. The Warlord has already given us more time than I expected."

Wright nodded solemnly. "It is a blessing."

The words brought Vel to mind. Hardly surprising; Wright was her closest disciple and spoke with the same slight Onnani accent. Though if Rig were honest with himself, plenty of things brought Vel to mind lately. He'd expected that—up to a point. But it ran deeper than he would have guessed, an uncomfortable realisation that he wasn't quite ready to deal with.

Just one more reason he needed to get on with bashing something. "Up for a little sparring, then?"

Wright smiled ruefully. "I've barely recovered from the last round, General. I fear my shoulder will never be the same."

Rig winced. "Sorry about that. I did try to break the momentum at the end there, but . . ."

"You needn't concern yourself. Every wound is a lesson, isn't it?"

"And what lesson was that?"

"Parry."

Rig laughed, exchanging his bloodblade for the wooden version. "Always good advice." Taking the practice weapon two-handed, he swung it about his shoulders a few times to loosen up, enjoying the low hum as it cut through the air. He missed fighting with a greatsword, but alas—single combat was a rare occurrence for a commander general. These days, he was more likely to find himself on horseback, or on the walls. If it weren't for his daily routine in the ring, he'd be soft as a stableboy by now.

Planting his feet, he squared off. "Ready?"

They traded leisurely blows for a while, easing themselves into it, the cracking of wood joining the cacophony of percussion in the yard. Gradually, though, the momentum overcame them, each move a little more aggressive than the last, escalating steadily until they were properly pummelling each other. Wright was surprisingly nimble for a man of middle age, and he'd been well trained; Rig could tell by the way his glance kept dropping to the ground, reading his opponent's footwork. He obviously didn't have much experience with greatswords—he let himself get tied up once or twice in the parrying hooks, each time costing him a blow to the flank—but he held his own.

Rig took a couple of good cuts himself, but he didn't mind. A few bruises were a small price to pay for one of life's simple pleasures. Attack and riposte, lunge and retreat—it was a dance he never grew tired of. The immediacy of it, the straightforward sequence of action and reaction, everything tangible and predictable. Few things in Rig's world were as clear-cut. Not love, and certainly not warfare. Not when you had a spy in your ranks. When one of your *own men* had sold out his country to the enemy. What could prompt a man to such betrayal was simply beyond Rig's fathoming. As for unmasking him . . . One out of nine thousand. Like searching for a flea in a farmyard. He would never—

A hard blow rang off Rig's armour. Swearing, he pivoted and brought his weapon scything across his body, sending Wright stumbling back. Before the older man could regain his balance, Rig charged, getting off a rapid succession of unanswered jabs.

The momentum was his now, and he took full advantage, alternating side to side, high and low, forcing Wright to give ground.

His rhythm restored, Rig's thoughts drifted back to the spy. He should have talked to Allie about it while she was here. She had a good head for intrigue, though how she'd come by it, he couldn't imagine. The Blacks weren't exactly known for their political acumen. But Allie saw the angles somehow. She read the landscape of court the way Rig read the battlefield—capabilities, interests, opportunities. Vel had a similar talent, come to think of it. They probably made a good team. If anyone could recover Erik's twin, it was those two. Even so, Rig couldn't stand to think of them out there, surrounded by the enemy. It made him sick to his stomach, a familiar surge of dread washing over him . . .

Which was how he ended up on his ass.

A low chop to his calves spilled him like a sack of apples; he landed awkwardly, driving his shoulder into the hard ground and blasting the air from his lungs.

Wright leaned over him, hands propped on his thighs, breathing hard. "I sense your mind is elsewhere, General."

"Looks like." Rig had let his thoughts get drawn into that same old dark dance after all. He lay on his back a moment, contemplating the sky and his own stupidity, before hauling himself gracelessly to his feet.

"The spy?"

"That obvious, huh?"

"It's what I would be thinking about in your place. That, and worrying for my sister and my . . . er . . ."

"I'm worried for all our people," Rig said, sparing them both having to endure some ridiculous euphemism for *lover*. He and Wright had largely managed to avoid talking about Vel until now, and Rig hoped to keep it that way. It was hard to say which of them would find the subject more awkward.

"I'm sure they will be fine," Wright said. "Daughter Vel is exceedingly clever, and Lady Alix has a reputation for being a capable warrior. On top of which, they have a pair of White Wolves as an escort." He paused again, and Rig could tell he was debating whether to ask *why* this clever, capable duo had been sent under White Wolf escort into enemy territory, but he managed to restrain himself. Wright was a military man; he understood the need for secrets. Especially when there was a spy among them.

"I just wish I could think of some ploy to flush him out," Rig said. "The spy, I mean."

"And I wish I could suggest something, but the truth is, without at least some small clue to go on, we're utterly blind."

Rig replaced the practice sword on the rack and grabbed a towel. "It's got to be someone with access to logistics of some kind, or he wouldn't be able to communicate with the Warlord. That narrows it down some. Ordinarily, I'd do as you suggested the other day—plant a seed of misinformation and watch to see who reacts. But with these close quarters, and the rumour mill whirling away like it is, we could never control where that seed ended up. It'd be like blowing a dandelion into the wind and trying to keep track of where it sprouts."

Wright grunted. "An excellent analogy."

"I seem to be feeling lyrical today," Rig said sourly, glancing up at the ramparts where the guard was changing over. The men coming off looked frayed at the edges, and those coming on didn't look much better. The anxiety of waiting for their doom to come knocking was wearing them all down. "Frankly," Rig said, "it matters less each day, with the Warlord on our doorstep."

"I suppose that's true. Now that Sadik knows where we are, we have few secrets left to tell. The damage is largely done."

Rig paused. "Which is what, exactly?"

"Sorry?"

"The damage." He scratched his beard, musing. "When you think about it, there hasn't been much. If anything, we've been able to use the situation to our advantage, feeding the enemy rumours and lies. It might not have unmasked the traitor, but it did allow us to manipulate Sadik."

"A testament to your cunning, General. You turned a liability into an opportunity."

Rig snorted. "If the options are between my being brilliant and the other guy being a fool, I'm inclined to think it's the latter."

"You lack grace with a compliment, General," Wright said, smiling.

"I lack grace in every way, Commander." Cocking his head in the direction of the wall walk, he added, "Join me for the rounds?"

They toured the wall walk, surveying the state of their defences. Not an activity likely to improve Rig's mood, given how paltry those defences were in comparison with what would be thrown against them. Sadik had at least twenty thousand men at his disposal, more if he gathered up the forces occupying Timra and elsewhere. With or without siege engines, he would ride roughshod over them, a destrier thundering across a patch of daisies. It was simply a question of numbers. If Erik had managed to convince the Harrami legions to come to their rescue, or if the Onnani fleet were ready to set sail . . . but those things hadn't happened. Alden was on her own, and Rig couldn't defend her, not anymore; it was like trying to stanch a fatal wound with his bare hands. The best he could hope for was to keep her alive a little longer so that someone more skilled could save her.

Someone like Erik. But first, someone would have to save *him*.

Which brought Rig's thoughts right back to his sister, and Vel, and the whole dark dance began all over again.

By evening, a second round in the ring was beginning to look tempting—that, or a round of serious drinking. Rig was trying to decide which when a shout went up from the gates.

"Kingsword rider coming through!"

Rig froze midstride. The horses—what was left of them— were stabled within the walls. There shouldn't be any Kingsword riders outside the gates. A message from the capital, perhaps? But no, that would have come by pigeon. Rig braced himself for bad news.

At least, he thought he was braced. But when Dain Cooper rode through the gates alone, Rig's knees nearly gave out.

"General!" The Onnani knight saluted and swung down from his horse. "I bring news from Lady Alix."

Rig blew out a relieved breath. "She's all right, then?"

"Everyone was well when I left them, General."

"But the fact that you left them at all doesn't augur well."

Lowering his voice, Dain said, "Is there somewhere private we can talk?"

Back in his quarters, Rig listened in glowering silence as Dain Cooper recounted the events south of the border. Rig had spent all day listening to bad news, but that had been children's rhymes compared to what he was hearing now. One close call after another, Alix at the sharp end of all of them. And when he heard about Governor Arkenn, what Wraith had forced his sister to do . . . Rig set his wine cup aside lest it shatter in his hand. "I'll kill him. I swear by Ardin, I'll choke the life out of him."

"I wouldn't stop you, General, at least not once we have Rodrik in hand. But for now, we need him. And we need you."

"How?"

"We followed the trail to Ennersvale. That's where the Warlord's main camp is."

"I'm aware." It was a smart choice. Well positioned for water and roads, and perched on a swell in the land, offering a decent view in all directions, barring a few dips here and there. "It's as strategic a location as you can find on an open plain."

"It's also where he's holding Rodrik."

"Strange." Rig frowned. "I'd have thought he'd want to keep his prize somewhere safe."

"Who knows—maybe he did. Maybe he's gathering his pieces for the final play. We're closing in on the end, after all."

"That we are," Rig said. "One way or another."

"Obviously, we can't just storm the camp, and we can't sneak in either, not without a distraction."

"Which is where I come in."

"We hope so, General."

Rig raked at his beard. "Shit."

"Yeah." Dain eyed him uncomfortably; he understood the position this put Rig in. "Wraith figured you'd be a fool to risk the men."

"He figured right." Rig sighed ruefully. "But it would hardly be the first time, would it?"

"So you'll do it?"

"I don't see that I have much choice. Without Rodrik, our king is lost. On top of which, my sister will go into that camp with or without my help, and that's two sacrifices too many." *Three*, he amended silently, *since Vel will never let her go alone.* "But I'm not prepared to risk more than a battalion or two, even for Alix. If we fail, there has to be enough left at the border to slow the enemy down while Liam evacuates the capital."

"All we need is to keep Sadik busy for a half hour or so."

"In that case, a small hit-and-run strike should be enough." The gods knew he'd had more than enough practice at that. "How much time do I have to plan?"

"They go in tomorrow night. Some of us argued for at least one more day, but Lady Alix wouldn't hear of it. She's pawing at the turf as it is."

"I'm sure. Erik's situation is bad enough, but she's got to be terrified for Liam. His neck is exposed. Any day now, those preening peacocks on the council are going to realise something is up, and when they do . . ."

Dain nodded grimly.

Rig threw back the last of his wine. "So. We have one day to plan something reckless that might lose us the war. In other words, just another night at the Kingsword fort." He sighed, gazing into the empty cup in his hand. "How many times do you think a man can tempt fate, Dain?"

The other man shrugged. "As many times as it takes, General."

SEVENTEEN

† Alix clawed restlessly at the dirt, feeling the stutter of her heartbeat against the cold earth. The taste of metal sat at the back of her tongue, and a tendril of sweat crawled along the curve of her spine, even though she shivered against the chill. The Oridian camp was a quilt of darkness, each square studded with its own flaming orange jewel. A scene of tranquil, deadly beauty.

At least it would have been, if the dogs would leave off their barking.

All night they'd been at it, driven to distraction by the relentless taunting of the coyotes. Or so Alix supposed—she couldn't actually hear much of anything through the racket the dogs were making. Though she knew it was a blessing to have them so preoccupied, the clamour frayed at her nerves, reminding her every moment how near were those teeth, those claws, those ten stone of muscle. The Oridians were no happier about it; more than once, Alix heard the crack of a whip and a torrent of swearing, but the hounds would not be silenced. *All to the good*, she told herself. *Just make sure you're nowhere near those kennels when the time comes.*

She didn't doubt for a moment that the time *would* come.

Commander general or no, Rig was her brother and loved her fiercely. He would be here. It was distantly possible that he might come alone, or with only a few volunteers, rather than risk his men. If so, Alix would understand. But Rig was a master of military deception, well practiced in the art of goading and harassing much larger forces. And Alden needed her king. With Erik restored to them, they had a sliver of a chance. Without him, they had none at all.

A sudden movement in the darkness, quick as a viper: Ide's hand clamping down over Alix's. Ide glared, her message clear: *Stop fidgeting.* Alix looked down at the soil beneath her fingers; she'd torn it up as though she intended to plant something. Chastened, she nodded an apology. On the other side of Ide, Vel watched the exchange with dark, unreadable eyes. The priestess must have been terrified, but she didn't show it; if anything, she seemed more serene than usual. More . . . just *more.* There was a presence about her, a gravitas, as if she'd donned her prayer mask and was no longer merely a person, but a *priestess.* Not so very unlike Erik's royal mask, Alix decided. An enviable gift, one she would dearly have liked to possess just now.

Her fingers started to twitch again. The waiting was killing her. It didn't help that she couldn't see Wraith and his men. They were supposed to be positioned about three hundred feet to the southwest. Alix had no reason to believe they weren't . . . except a worm of doubt that had been eating away at her ever since her conversation with Vel.

And then a shout went up, and the time for doubt was over.

At first Alix couldn't see what set it off, but once the alarm was given, the whole camp was alive with it, swarming like a nest of hornets. Bells rang out in the darkness. Men scattered in every direction. The dogs went properly crazy now, their vicious baying turning Alix's guts to water. Then she saw it: a wing of shadow sweeping past like a deadly breeze. All along the fringes of the camp, men were dropping under an invisible hail of arrows. Horse archers. Rig's scarcest and most precious resource, used to lethal perfection. How had they fallen upon the camp without the dogs giving warning?

"Look!" Ide pointed.

A pack of Kingsword wolfhounds tore into the camp. A dozen of them at most, too few to do much good, unless . . . Alix looked at Ide and found her own grin matched on her friend's face. Even Vel understood, and she fairly glowed with pride.

Rig, you bloody genius!

The Oridian dogs *had* noticed the approach of the horses, and the wolfhounds too. They'd done their job, giving the alarm, but by then no one had paid any heed. Rig must have had his wolfhounds barking on the far side of the river all night, whipping the Oridian dogs into a frenzy so that when the time came, the enemy camp was deaf to the warning cries of its best sentries.

Alix felt the thunder of hoofbeats beneath her chest. Springing to her feet, she saw a second wave of horse archers scouring the near side of the camp. For a moment she stood mesmerised, watching in awe as the horses swooped in like a flock of birds to loose a volley of arrows before curving away gracefully into the night, shapes more felt than seen, sketched in gleaming shadow. Vel ran a few steps toward them, robes caught up in the draught of their passing, hair streaming out behind her, gazing after the riders as though she might spy Rig among them.

It all happened in a heartbeat, and a heartbeat was all Alix could spare. It was time to move.

They made straight for the bloodbinder's pavilion. Wraith would be matching the manoeuvre from the other side of the tent, ensuring that whichever way the bloodbinder tried to run, he would be intercepted. Alix kept her eyes riveted to her target, all but blind to the mayhem swirling around her as the Oridians tried to assemble themselves into something resembling a fighting force. Nor were the soldiers any less blind to her; in the chaos, she was just one more figure darting through the shadows.

As they neared the pavilion, Alix reached for her dagger, expecting the bloodbinder to flee at any moment. Yet the tent remained quiet, an island of stillness in a sea of motion. Alix experienced a momentary pang of dread. What if they had guessed wrong? What if this wasn't the bloodbinder's pavilion after all? But no—a pair of knights flanked the entrance. Whatever was inside that tent, it was worth guarding.

Ide's bow twanged; one of the guards staggered backward with an arrow in his throat. The second guard cried out before he charged, drawing the attention of a passing soldier. Alix's dagger found the eye of the unlucky passerby, while Ide brought down the charging guard with another arrow.

For the moment, they were clear. Alix retrieved her dagger, gaze raking the shadows for any sign of Wraith. She found none, but there was no more time to waste; with a final glance at Ide and Vel, she plunged through the tent flap.

Black.

It smelled of blood. Alix crouched, raising the tip of her sword blindly. She heard a rustle beside her as Ide moved away from the door. Alix did the same, looking to put the tent wall at her back. She debated trying to throw her dagger, but she doubted the enchantment would work. The bond was between weapon and user; if the user was blind, it stood to reason that the weapon would be too. The same would be true of her sword. That left her vulnerable. The space around her felt close, oppressive. Her breath sounded absurdly loud in her ears.

Something stirred. Alix's grip on her bloodblade tightened, but she could see nothing through the impenetrable darkness.

"Water." Though it was barely a whisper, the voice startled Alix so badly that she nearly lost her balance. "Please, I'm so thirsty . . ."

A breath of silence. Then a scramble at the back of the tent, like a wild animal starting from the brush. A slice of moonlight appeared, blocked by a shadow as it slipped out into the night. Wraith and his men should be there to intercept, but . . .

"Ide!"

The other woman was already moving, crashing and swearing her way past unseen obstacles to bolt out the back door in pursuit. The momentary flash of light gave Alix an idea; she slashed at the canvas walls until slivers of moonlight shot through the shadows, picking out a table here, a chair there. Her gaze fell upon a narrow cot near the back of the tent. She rushed at it, nearly stumbling over it in her haste, bracing herself inches from a face nearly as familiar as her own.

"Erik!"

It burst from her in a sob before she could stop herself. Because of course this *wasn't* Erik. This man was a stranger to her, and she to him. Her mind understood that, but her heart did not; all it saw was Erik, red-gold hair and ashen skin, ice blue eyes beneath fluttering lids. Her heart saw Erik, and it broke into a thousand pieces. "Oh gods," she breathed, kissing his forehead. "Oh, what have they done to you . . ."

"We must hurry."

Vel's voice, steady but urgent, wrenching Alix back to the here and now. She drew her dagger and began sawing at the ropes that bound him. His wrists . . . dear gods, they were raw meat . . .

Vel found a jug of water and poured the contents of a small pouch into it. Helping Rodrik to sit, the priestess said, "Drink."

His gaze was unfocused, but he obeyed without hesitation, as though he were accustomed to following orders in such a state. Which, Alix realised grimly, he almost certainly was.

A rage was building inside her unlike any she had ever known. This man might be a stranger, but he was her prince, brother to the men she loved. "I'm going to get you out of here," she whispered fiercely.

He seemed not to hear. "The water," he murmured, "tastes strange . . ." Erik's voice, but with an Andithyrian accent.

"Don't worry," said Vel, "it's only a mixture of salt and sugar. It will help restore you. Take a little more, if you can."

Outside, chaos continued to reign, but Alix knew it wouldn't last. Rig would only dare a handful of passes, a few swipes at the enemy's flank while the camp boiled and seethed with confusion. He needed to be gone by the time the Oridians organised themselves or he'd never make it back across the river alive. "We have to go," Alix said. "Rodrik, can you stand?"

"Who are you?" His gaze was rapidly coming into focus, wariness creeping in.

"A friend. I'll explain, I promise, but we need to get you out of here."

"Dargin. Where is he?"

Alix shook her head. "I don't . . . Please, Rodrik, we have to hurry."

Shouting sounded outside the tent, a flurry of footsteps

rushing past. Rodrik seemed to process that. His gaze sharpened still further, a steely look coming into it that Alix recognised only too well. He hopped down off the cot . . . and
promptly buckled. Alix and Vel caught him—too easily, his
wasted frame weighing far less than it should. "I'm all right,"
he said. "I can do it."

"We don't have time, Rodrik. Please, let us help you."

He hesitated, and for a moment Alix thought he would
refuse. They were strangers, after all; he had no reason to trust
them. But they were trying to take him away from here, and
what could be worse than this place? Alix could almost read
the thoughts in those unsettlingly familiar blue eyes. He nodded resignedly.

They helped him toward the back of the tent. Wraith and
his men should be waiting for them outside, covering the exit
to keep it clear.

Except he wasn't.

Alix's step faltered, the realisation washing over her in a
sickening wave. It was just as she'd feared. Wraith had abandoned them. To go after Sadik, presumably, not that it mattered. What mattered was that they were alone: Alix, a
priestess, and a man who could barely stand, smack in the
middle of the entire Oridian army.

We'll never make it out of here alive.

A poisonous thought; she shoved it aside and started for the
sea of darkness at the edge of the camp, half dragging, half
carrying Rodrik, praying to all the gods that no one would
notice them. But of course that was too much to ask. Though
it was still dark, they were conspicuous now, hobbling along
with an injured man propped between them. A soldier rushed
over to help, only to find himself face to face with two women.
Vel might have passed herself off as a camp follower, but Alix
was clad in leather armour and had a pair of blades strapped
to her belt. Armed women had no business in an Oridian war
camp. The soldier went for his sword.

Alix's instincts took over. Shoving Rodrik and Vel behind
her, she drew her blade. A spike of dread went through her, a
momentary weakness in the knees. She tried to take comfort
in the familiar weight in her hand, in the reassuring knowledge

that she wielded a bloodblade against an opponent armed with ordinary steel. It was a well-worn refrain, one that had never failed to gird her against the inevitable fear of battle. Yet this time was different. It was not only herself she had to protect. Rodrik was weak as a lamb, Vel almost equally defenceless. The fear she felt for them was heavier somehow, more toxic. So much so that when the soldier came at her with a weak cut, she scuttled backward rather than parry. *The dagger. You should have thrown the dagger.* But it was too late now. By the time she exchanged it for her sword, she'd be dead.

The soldier lunged; Alix batted him aside, but narrowly. Her nervousness was getting the better of her, dulling her reflexes. *Bite down, Alix, damn you.* She'd scarcely processed the thought before he was on her again, a swipe at her midsection that forced her to leap back. But Alix didn't miss the way he overextended, leaving himself exposed. *Sloppy,* her mind registered. He took her for easy prey, and why not? She'd given him every reason to. It gave her an idea.

She pivoted sharply, forcing her attacker to do the same. She made a halfhearted chop to sell it, then braced for the counterattack. He obliged, and she let herself be driven back, drawing the Oridian away from Rodrik and Vel. The priestess saw her opportunity; she and Rodrik slipped around the side of the pavilion. Alix waited until they were out of sight before sidestepping suddenly, catching her foe off guard. She knocked his sword wide, almost hard enough to jar it from his grasp. He was so surprised that he stumbled, and that was enough: Alix lunged and drove a clean thrust through a joint in his leather armour.

She caught up with Vel and Rodrik on the far side of the pavilion. "This way." Rodrik took her arm, but he didn't put much weight on it; he stood a little taller, eyes lit with grim determination.

Seeing that, Alix felt her own resolve harden, so that when another Oridian blocked their path she brushed aside her fear and stepped out confidently to face him. So focused was she on her target that she didn't notice the danger until it was too late.

A blur of motion in the corner of her eye, something

hurtling toward her. Alix started to turn, but someone shoved her out of the way, hard enough to send her sprawling. Even as she fell, the sounds told the story: vicious baying, a woman shrieking, Erik's voice crying out in pain. Alix scrambled to her feet to find Rodrik pinned beneath the massive bulk of an Oridian warhound, its jaws clamped over his arm as he tried to fend it off. The soldier who'd blocked their path was moving in for the kill. Alix rushed at him, her ears filled with the screams of Erik's twin and the cracking of bone beneath powerful jaws. She rained blow after blow down on her foe, scarcely aware of anything but the sounds, the snarling and the screaming, the thump of a bow and a high-pitched yelp, and then another, and the snarling stopped, though the screaming went on.

When her vision cleared, Alix stood over a dying Oridian soldier, Ide stood over a dead warhound studded with arrows, and Vel knelt over a man curled into a bloody ball of agony.

"Farika's grace," Ide breathed, grimacing.

Alix flew to Rodrik's side. Vel clutched at his mangled arm, a look of pure panic in her eyes. Blood . . . gods, there was so much blood . . .

"I need a belt!" Vel cried. *"Now!"*

Ide yanked hers free. Vel worked quickly, but not quickly enough; Rodrik's cries of torment were drawing looks from across the camp.

"We have to go," Alix said.

"Fucking Wraith," Ide spat. "I'll skin him for this."

"The bloodbinder?" Alix feared she knew the answer.

Ide shook her head. "Lost him."

Alix's gaze raked the camp. The swarm had moved on, mustering on the north side where the bulk of the attack had been concentrated. Across the deserted rows of tents, she spied a slight figure moving like liquid shadow. He paused and their glances met; for the briefest instant, Alix thought she saw regret in Asvin's eyes. And then he was gone, vanishing between the tents, a hunter stalking his prey.

Alix knelt beside Rodrik. He was losing consciousness; he'd never be able to move on his own. "Ide, can you carry him?"

"Take my bow." Crouching, Ide did as Alix had done on that fateful day at the Battle of Boswyck, when she'd slung her wounded king over her shoulder and staggered off the battle-field. It was like watching herself in a dream, and for a moment, Alix stood motionless, overcome with heartache and memories. But she couldn't afford that. Rodrik couldn't afford that.

"This way," she said, and led them off into the night.

EIGHTEEN

"We have to stop," Vel said. "Ide, you have to put him down."

Ide gave a curt shake of her head, teeth bared under the strain. "Too close to the camp," she said, pausing only to hitch Rodrik higher on her shoulder. He groaned softly, barely conscious. "Bad enough we had to go back for our stuff." Their packs were too bulky to bring on the rescue; they'd been forced to stash them nearby. Going back for them had cost precious time.

"Can't you see his bandage is soaked? His arm has been crushed. Tourniquet or no, if we don't cauterise the wound, he will bleed to death." Appealing to Alix, Vel continued, "A healthy man couldn't survive this, let alone one who is already dangerously weak. You must let me tend him."

Alix glanced at the sky. Dawn was breaking over the horizon, but it was dark enough yet for a campfire to glow like a beacon. "We don't dare light a fire, not for an hour at least. Isn't there something you can do for him in the meantime?"

"We need to keep moving," Ide cut in. "If the enemy decides to follow, they'll be on us in a heartbeat. There's no place to hide out here."

"The trees," Vel said. "Our campsite from last night—"

"—is in the wrong direction. We need to make the river."

"Are you mad? The river is crawling with soldiers!"

Ide continued to lurch along stubbornly. "Which is why we need to keep moving. Need to get well east of the ford before we try to cross."

"And if Rodrik dies in the meantime?"

"Then he dies."

That was too much for Alix; she froze midstride. "Stop."

"Alix . . ."

"*Stop.* Put him down." The steadiness of her voice belied the sickening swirl in her gut. She wasn't sure what appalled her more—the idea of Rodrik dying or Ide's cool acceptance of it. "Do what you can, Vel, but hurry."

The priestess didn't need to be told; she was bending over Rodrik even as Ide lowered him to the ground. "In my pack, some fresh bandages. And a glass vial, about so big. It will help with the pain . . ."

Alix obeyed, taking refuge in the simplicity of the task, like shutting a door in her mind. On the other side of that door a flood raged, fear and guilt and the white-hot anger of betrayal. So long as she kept the door closed, she could function. That meant focusing on the charge she'd been given, narrowing her world to Vel's pack and its contents. Above all, it meant not looking at Rodrik—his ashen skin, those familiar features contorted with pain . . .

"Alix." Ide cocked her head in the direction of the river. "A word?"

Alix hesitated, but there was nothing more she could do for Rodrik, and the priestess was completely absorbed in treating her patient. Reluctantly, she followed. "What is it?"

"That wound is a mess. Even if we cauterise it, it'll likely go septic."

Alix scowled. "So you're a healer now?"

"I'm a soldier," Ide returned impassively. "Seen it a dozen times, and so have you."

"What do you suggest? We can't just leave him here. He's Erik's *twin.*"

"That's what makes him dangerous, isn't it? Enemy finds us, he falls back in their hands . . ." Ide shook her head. "Maybe it's better if he dies."

"Don't say that. Don't you *dare*." Alix's voice dropped to an angry hiss. "It's *treason*."

"I'm trying to protect our king. How is that treason?"

"Rodrik is our prince."

"It's not like I want him to die," Ide said impatiently. "You gotta be practical, Alix. Our mission was to get him out of enemy hands. We did that. He gets recaptured, we failed our mission, right?"

"Of course, but—"

"If the Oridians find us out here—which they will, we keep dithering like this—that's what's gonna happen. On top of which, he's not our only problem."

Alix's anger cooled into a lump of dread. "Meaning?"

"The bloodbinder. I chased him for a ways, but I had to let him go. He got himself tucked in all nice and snug behind a wall of soldiers, too many for me to handle. He fled the camp under guard, like he had an escape plan all laid out, just in case."

"So?" As much as Alix would have liked to dispatch the worm, her priority was Rodrik. She couldn't see how the bloodbinder was an immediate concern. Unless . . .

"So he had this jug in his arms. About so big, like the ones the Erromanians used to store wine in. Looked heavy, way he was carrying it."

"And you think . . ." Alix brought a hand to her mouth. "Oh no . . ."

"Gotta be. Big, bulky jug like that slowing you down? Must be something in there worth risking your life over, something like Rodrik's blood. Which means the bloodbinder can still work his spells."

"We have to find him," Alix said numbly, as though Ide needed to be told.

"He was running that way, last I saw." Ide pointed north. "Made certain I had a line on him before I came back to find you. That's what took me so long. Only . . ." She frowned, shook her head. "I can't figure why he'd be headed for the river. Why wouldn't he just wait until we'd gone, then circle back to camp?"

That, Alix realised, was an excellent question. "Do you suppose he thinks another raid might be on the horizon? Or that battle is imminent?"

"Could be. Wouldn't be wrong about the second part, anyway. Battle's coming soon enough. Maybe he figures he's safer on his own."

"Maybe he is." Alix paused. An idea was tapping at her, insistent as a woodpecker, but she couldn't quite make out the shape of it. "If you think about it, he *was* safer on his own, back when Sadik had him stashed away in Gertswold. It would have been all but impossible for us to find him there, with so many places to hide. Why risk bringing Rodrik to the front lines?"

Ide grunted. "Pretty stupid, actually."

"Unless . . ." Alix's brow cleared as the realisation broke through. "The Priest. He put himself at risk too, remember? At the Elders' Gate, and before that, in the Brownlands. He needed to be close to his thralls in order to control them. That's what we figured, anyway." It was the only explanation for the Priest's otherwise reckless behaviour. He exposed himself because it was necessary in order for his dark magic to work.

"Then how come this bloodbinder can control our king from all the way out here?"

"That's just it—he can't. Not fully. Erik's not a thrall, at least not yet. His mind is under the influence of the magic, but there's still some part of the real Erik in there. That must be because the bloodbinder isn't close enough to control him completely."

"So you reckon he wants to get closer?"

"It explains why he travelled to the front, and why he's headed for the river." It also explained why Erik had grown so much worse on the journey back from Harram. As they'd drawn nearer to Erroman, they'd drawn nearer to Andithyri too. Nearer to the bloodbinder. His power over Erik had grown with every step they took. *If only I'd known* . . . They could have turned around. Taken him out of reach . . .

"Either way," Ide said, "that's where he's headed, and we gotta stop him. That means picking up the pace."

They returned to Vel and Rodrik. "I've done what I can," the priestess said. "The bleeding has been brought under control for now, but we need to seal the wound as soon as possible."

The sight of him was almost more than Alix could bear. He lay on his side, pale and wasted, mangled arm trussed up against his body. He looked for all the world like a corpse, and it was impossible not to imagine Erik lying there, dead, as if she were living out her worst nightmare. "The wound." She spoke softly, as though she might wake him. "Will it turn septic?"

"Given the severity of it, and how he got it . . . That is very possible."

"Maybe we should cut his arm off," Ide said. "Not much good to him when it was healthy, shrivelled like it is."

"We may have to," Vel said, "though I doubt it would save him. We would have to take it above the elbow, and that would just leave us with another dangerous wound. We need to get him somewhere safe where we can tend him properly."

"We're a long way from safe," Alix said. Alone, they could make the border in a day or so. But with Rodrik in this condition . . . "At the rate we're moving, it will take three days at least, and that's just to the river. Another day to the fort."

"Except we're not headed for the fort," Ide said. "If that bloodbinder's got any sense at all, he'll give the Kingswords a wide berth, try to cross someplace out of sight."

"Bloodbinder?" Vel glanced between them. "I thought that was just a ruse to get help from the Resistance?"

There wasn't much point in trying to keep it from her now; they were in too deep. "There was a bloodbinder," Alix said, "it just wasn't Rodrik. We were supposed to kill him, but he fled out the back of the tent."

"I don't understand. What would a bloodbinder want with Rodrik?"

Alix and Ide exchanged a glance. "Rodrik is King Erik's identical twin."

"Obviously, but . . ." Then her hand flew to her mouth, and Alix knew she'd understood.

"The bloodbinder got away," Alix went on, "and we think he still has some of Rodrik's blood. We need to destroy it, and him."

Vel closed her eyes and whispered something in her own language. Alix didn't speak Onnani, but she was fairly certain she shared the sentiment. "How will we find him?" the priestess asked.

"We got a general idea where he's headed," Ide said, "and Alix and me are trained trackers. One man would be tough, but he's got an armed escort. Muddy riverbank, unfamiliar territory and all—we'll find 'em. But it'll take time."

"Rodrik doesn't have time," Vel said.

Neither does Liam, Alix thought. Nor Erik, nor the kingdom itself for that matter. Time was the scarcest, most precious thing in all the world, and it was bleeding out as surely as Rodrik's wound. "Let's keep moving," she said. "We'll build a fire after sunrise."

If she closed her eyes, she could almost imagine Liam was with her. The crackle of the fire, the soft sigh of wind through the leaves, a coyote calling in the distance. How many times had she listened to those sounds in a Kingsword camp, under an Aldenian sky, with her fellow scouts gathered around her? Even Ide's snoring was a familiar strain, for like Liam, she'd been with Alix from the beginning.

She could call his voice to mind so easily. Laughing at his own jokes, or trading banter with Gwylim. They were a delight to listen to, those two, Liam's playful spark against Gwylim's dry tinder. And then later, after the others had gone to bed, a different tone in Liam's voice, one reserved only for her. Even before they became lovers, she'd noticed that difference, and it made her feel special. It made the relationship feel special, as if two closer friends had never been. And when he'd finally worked up the nerve to kiss her . . . She could still hear the words as clearly as if he spoke in her ear. *Do you have any notion of how beautiful you are?* It sent the same bright shiver running through her even now.

And then, inevitably, the golden glow of memory faded, and she was alone in the dark, standing watch in enemy lands.

A hollow space opened in her chest, a great cavern of nothing between her ribs. She could almost feel the cold air passing through. *Oh, Liam, how did we let this happen?*

Movement nearby pulled her out of her reverie. Rodrik was stirring. She brought him water, helped him to sit. He took a few tentative sips before tipping the water skin back and gulping it down. "Careful," Alix murmured. "Not too much at once."

He passed the skin back breathlessly, wiping a hand across his beard. Even in the low light, Alix could see a vigour in his eyes that hadn't been there before. She knew better than to suppose that meant he was out of danger, but at least he was lucid. "How do you feel?" she asked.

His glance dropped to his arm, assessing. It must have been excruciating—crushed bone, severed tendon, burnt flesh—but he regarded it impassively, as if merely trying to recall how he'd come by it. He'd barely been conscious when they cauterised the wound; Alix wondered if he had any memory of the ordeal. She hoped not, for his sake.

"Should I wake the priestess? She can give you something for the pain . . ." Alix started to move, but Rodrik raised his good hand in a staying gesture.

"No more potions. I've been under their spell too long. At least with the pain, I know for certain I'm awake and not back in that never-ending nightmare."

Alix winced. They'd probably kept him drugged the entire time, rousing him only for food or water. And when he did wake, what he must have seen through the haze of pain and potions . . . a never-ending nightmare indeed.

"That beast," he said. "A warhound?"

She nodded grimly. "Trained to kill. If you hadn't pushed me out of the way . . . You saved my life. Thank you, Rodrik."

The blue eyes focused on her, clear and alert. "Who are you?"

She hesitated. "I'm not sure this is the time . . ."

"You promised me you would explain. What's happening to me?"

Alix sighed and lowered herself down beside him. "I'm not sure where to begin. The Oridians . . . do you know what they were doing to you?"

"Witchcraft." He shuddered, curling over himself protectively. "They were using my blood for witchcraft."

"That's right. The man who took your blood—"

"Dargin." A glimmer of hatred came into Rodrik's eyes. "His name is Dargin."

"He's a bloodbinder." Alix paused to let Rodrik process that. "Only he wasn't making weapons. He was performing a perversion of the spell, one that was discovered by the Priest of Oridia. Instead of controlling weapons, it controls men, and—"

"The king," Rodrik said. "They were using me to control the King of Alden."

A long silence, punctuated only by the crackle of the fire. "You knew?"

"I heard them talking. I was awake a lot of the time, even when they didn't realise it. But I couldn't move." He shuddered again, and Alix had to fight the urge to put her arms around him. It was unsettling, having to constantly remind herself that *this was not Erik*.

Even so, she was beginning to notice tiny differences, ones that went beyond the beard or his illness. He had a scar near the tip of his nose, and his eyebrows were slightly different. A little more feathered, perhaps, with higher arches. Alix had no doubt these subtleties would be lost on just about anyone, but to her, they were as plain as the beard on his face.

"They spoke of it often," he said. "I tried to understand, but I was so groggy . . ." He shook his head. "Even now, I can't fathom it. Why me? Why my blood?"

Alix bit her lip. For a fraction of a moment, she debated not telling him—but that wouldn't be fair. "This isn't going to be easy for you to hear, but you deserve the truth."

He regarded her warily.

"You've probably spent your whole life believing you were born in Andithyri, but that's not so. You were born in Alden. To Osrik and Hestia White." She paused, but the names washed over him without meaning. "You have a twin," she continued, and that *did* register; he jerked forward, eyes widening. "Your name is Rodrik White, and you are twin brother to King Erik White of Alden."

If she lived to be a hundred, Alix would never be able to describe the look that passed through Rodrik's eyes in that moment. The near-instantaneous progression from shock to disbelief to acceptance, as if this missing piece fit snugly into a mysterious gap in his life. The confused jumble of emotions—fear and wonder and anger. Most of all the profound *disorientation*, as though his entire world had just mutated into something unrecognisable. Which, Alix supposed, it had. In that blink of Rodrik's eyes, she watched a man's very identity come undone.

"You must have a thousand questions," Alix said, "and I

wish I could answer them, but the truth is we only learned of your existence about three weeks ago." *Dear gods, has it only been three weeks?* It seemed an age since she'd left Erroman.

Rodrik's gaze dropped to the ground, and there it stayed for a very long time. When finally he spoke, his voice was surprisingly devoid of emotion. "I do have a thousand questions, yet you still have not answered my first." He raised his eyes to her. "Who are you?"

"My name is Alix Black. Well . . . Alix White, now."

His glance flitted over her face, as though truly taking her in for the first time. "You are my sister?"

"Sister-in-law. My husband is Liam White, your half brother. And Erik . . . King Erik is my . . . that is, I'm his . . ." She stumbled ridiculously, as though there were anything complicated about it. And yet somehow, there was. "I'm his bodyguard," she managed at last.

He nodded as if he understood, but Alix could tell he didn't, not truly. He was too numb and too weak; already, his eyelids were drooping again, his shoulders wilting. Then he surprised her by saying, "I always wanted a brother. And now it seems I have two."

A simple sentiment, and yet it undid her. Tears sprang to her eyes. It was too close to the bone. To Erik's lifelong search for closeness, first with one brother, then another; to Liam's secret fantasies of adventuring with his brothers. Even Tom and his doomed quest to overcome whatever chasm separated him from Erik, and from their father. Four brothers, kept apart by so much, yet all nurturing virtually the same heart's desire: for family.

"I should very much like to meet them," Rodrik murmured through a haze of pain.

Alix helped him to lie down. "You will," she whispered, pulling the blanket over his shoulders. "I promise."

NINETEEN

The blade bit deep into the wood, sending chips flying. Liam didn't let it linger; he jerked it free and spun
his wrist, bringing the sword down on his left side to meet
the next target. The horse tilted obligingly—a little *too*
obligingly, throwing Liam's timing off. He nearly skewered
himself on the dummy's spear, but he managed to arrest his
momentum, holding his body upright in the saddle just a fraction longer before leaning out to cleave the wooden head from
its shoulders. Pressing his left leg into the stallion's flank, he
canted right to meet the final target, rising a little in his stir-
rups for a better angle. He judged it perfectly, driving a clean,
hard thrust deep into the wood; had it been flesh, he'd have
buried it to the hilt. As it was, he was forced to release the
blade as he rode by, turning the courser in a loping arc to
survey his handiwork.

Two headless, one limbless, and a couple of nice torso hits,
plus his sword quivering satisfyingly in the throat of the final
dummy. *Not bad for a single pass*, he thought smugly.

Then he heard Arran Green's voice in his head. *A boastful
stunt, leaving yourself weaponless like that. On the battlefield, it would be the end of you.*

Liam sighed. Even in death, Arran Green wouldn't let him have any fun.

"Nice," said a voice, and Liam turned to find Kerta Middlemarch leaning against the wall of the armoury. "Though that last bit didn't seem very practical."

Liam swung down from his horse, grinning. "It *looked* brilliant, though, didn't it?"

"You always look brilliant," she said obligingly. "Though I prefer watching you on foot."

"You and me both. I still haven't quite got the hang of this thing." He hooked a thumb over his shoulder at the stallion. A gift from Erik, he was an exquisite animal, but a little too soft in the flanks for Liam's liking. He'd grown up riding brutes, not sensitive, high-strung coursers like this. "Not sure fighting on horseback is my cup of tea, to be honest. At least when it's just me, the only clumsiness I have to worry about is my own."

"Clumsiness indeed. You're a dancer with that sword and you know it."

"Hmm. Can we agree on a manlier metaphor?"

"A poet, then."

"Funny."

Kerta smiled up at him, all freckles and blond curls and daintiness. She looked out of place in the yard, surrounded by dirt and horseshite. But Liam knew better. That sword on her hip wasn't for decoration. "In the scouting leathers, I see," he said.

Her smile grew strained. "Off to the front in about an hour. That's why I'm here—I came to say good-bye."

"Oh." Liam felt his own smile falling away. He hadn't seen much of Kerta these past couple of weeks, but it still felt like a loss. The gods knew he had few enough friends in the capital right now.

"I hear you're making a speech today," she said. "I'll be sorry to miss it."

"Not as sorry as the poor sods who'll have to listen to it."

"You'll be wonderful," she said, putting a reassuring hand on his arm. "I know it."

"I'll be lucky to make it all the way through without throwing up."

Kerta laughed. "Oh, Liam, I will miss you." A shimmer came into her eyes. "Take care of yourself, will you?" Squeezing his arm one final time, she left.

Liam was on his way back to the keep, head swimming with half-memorised bits of speech, when a servant collided with him.

"Profound apologies, Your Highness," said a rasping voice. Hands fluttered over Liam's clothing, as though to smooth it. And then the man was on his way, moving fluidly through the ever-present bustle of the bailey.

Liam blinked after him in mild astonishment. Then he turned back toward the keep—and raked his hand across something sharp. Sucking in a breath, he looked down and found a rose tucked into his pocket. It was the thorns that had attacked him, leaving a string of bloody beads from thumb to wrist. Nor was the flower the only thing waiting to ambush him: Reaching into his pocket, Liam found a folded note.

Your Highness,

This rose is a subtle way of asking you to join me in the rose garden at your earliest convenience.

A friend

Liam scowled at the patronising bit of paper. Then he made a hard right and headed for the royal gardens.

He found the spy waiting for him on the bench by the duck pond. "You know, I'm fairly certain I could have worked it out without the note."

"It pays to be certain, Your Highness. You are new at this, after all." The ever-present hood tracked from left to right as the spy scanned the ranks of rosebushes.

"There's nobody here," Liam said. "The gardens are closed, remember?"

"And yet here I sit."

Liam grunted. "Fair point."

Saxon continued to survey the garden, fingers twitching anxiously at his sides. He was a far cry from the cool, wry figure Liam had spoken with last time—which had to be a bad sign.

Liam sighed as he lowered himself to the bench. The fear that settled over him was as familiar as an old suit of armour by now: still heavy, but no longer capable of setting his heart racing. It was just too commonplace. "I'm guessing whatever's got you so worked up is the reason you called me here."

"You are in danger, Your Highness."

"Yeah. Not news."

"*Imminent* danger," the spy said impatiently. "Something is amiss in the council."

"Could you be more specific?"

"No, and that's what worries me. A pall of silence has fallen over them, individually and collectively. They have convened in secret, twice now, to unknown purpose. Meanwhile, my tick refuses even to meet with me. That is unprecedented, and a very ill omen indeed."

Secret council meetings. Without the prince or the chancellor. Rona must not have been invited—she'd certainly have said something. Which meant they didn't trust her, either. Liam cursed inwardly. *Ill omen* didn't begin to cover it. "And you have no idea what they're discussing?"

"All I can tell you is that the meetings were convened by Lady Sirin Grey."

"Shocking," Liam said dryly. Still, maybe that wasn't entirely bad news. "We told her that Erik had gone to the front. Alix too. As far as I know, she believes it. Maybe that's what she's telling the council."

Saxon considered that. "It's possible. In which case, though it might not earn you the affection of the council, your neck would at least be safe."

"That must be it," Liam said with a confidence he didn't feel. "Otherwise they'd have confronted me by now, right?"

The spy said nothing.

"Either way," Liam said, "there's not much I can do about it."

"You could find someplace else to be, Your Highness."

"Run?" Liam shook his head. "That'd mean leaving the kingdom headless. The council means well, but when it comes to military matters, they're hopeless. Raibert Green is the only one who knows a sword from a gardening trowel, and he's too mild-mannered to impose his will on the likes of Sirin Grey." He sighed. "No, I'm here to the end, one way or another."

A stretch of silence. Then Saxon said, "If things do not develop as we hope, Your Highness . . . that is, if they go badly . . ."

"You'll need to find someplace else to be."

The spy looked at him; for the first time, Liam could see the colour of his eyes, black as pitch. "I hope you understand."

"If it weren't for this whole running-the-country thing, I'd probably be right behind you."

"Somehow, I doubt that."

Liam rose. "I'd better go. I've got a speech to make." He started up the gravel path toward the keep.

"Good luck, Your Highness," the spy called after him.

Liam started to ask what he meant—good luck with the speech, or good luck staying alive—but decided he really didn't want to know.

A chill wind darted up the Street of Stars, collecting in whirls of dust at the corners of the temple square. The crowd shifted and huddled deeper into their cloaks. They looked miserable, fearful expressions gazing out from under hoods, from above white knuckles clutching at collars. Try as he might, Liam could not meet those gazes, even though he knew instinctively that was what Erik would do. He would connect with one pair of eyes after another, lingering just long enough to snuff that cold flame of fear before moving on. Liam had seen his brother do just that on the morning of the Battle of Boswyck, though he must have known the Kingswords couldn't possibly prevail. You did that when you were king—gave people confidence even when you didn't feel it. But as Liam stood on that dais, banner lords arrayed on one side of him, clergy on the other, confidence felt as far beyond his grasp as the Holy Virtues themselves.

Rudi stirred at his feet, nearly as uneasy as his master. Liam would have preferred to leave the wolfhound at home, but Highmount had insisted. Apparently, the chancellor didn't think Liam looked royal enough on his own; they needed a symbol of old King Rendell at his side to remind everyone that Liam was, in fact, prince of the realm.

He resisted the urge to glance one final time at the speech Highmount had prepared. He looked over at Rona Brown instead, but even that didn't help; the sight of her in brown silk, instead of her customary White Wolf armour, only served to remind him how grave an occasion this was. As did the presence of Alithia Grey. For the past several weeks, the holder of the Grey banner had been content to delegate matters of state to her daughter, but not today. Sirin, meanwhile, was nowhere to be seen, which had to be a bad sign.

But Liam couldn't worry about that right now. The crowd was getting restless. He cleared his throat again.

"Good people of Erroman. These past two years have been the darkest in our history. The flames of war have scoured our lands. Robbed us of our sons and daughters, husbands and wives. Left our children hungry. We have been forced to flee our homes, to abandon our hard-won livelihoods. And yet, through all these trials, we have been strong. We have endured."

He paused, awaiting the applause Highmount had told him to expect. Instead, he was slapped with a grim wall of silence. The crowd might have been spectres, so pale and motionless were they. Swallowing, Liam continued.

"We have endured because our defences are strong. Our Kingswords are the mightiest army in all of Gedona, trained professionals equipped for war. Our walls are the thickest and sturdiest, having been crafted by our imperial forefathers centuries ago. Even today, entire quarters of our great city remain unchanged by the whims of time, every stone placed just as it was at the height of the empire's glory. These great walls shielded us when the enemy came to our doorstep last summer. Though the Priest threw fifty thousand men against us, his armies broke like a wave over the rocks."

More or less, give or take a few thousand deaths, some shattered gates, and enough rubble to repave the Imperial Road. Liam kept that bit to himself.

"The walls of Erroman are our greatest protection," he went on. "Greater even than the citadel at Pir. And that is why, in our hour of need, we shall call upon them again. We will lure our enemies here, to our great walls, and here we will break them!"

Again Liam paused, and again he was met with terrible silence. He forged on.

"We will evacuate the city. Not because we are weak, or because we are afraid, but because we wish the Warlord to think so. Let him leave the safety of his positions at the border, thinking us easy prey. It will be a deception. We will be waiting for him, ready to meet him where we are strongest and he is most vulnerable. And by the time he realises his mistake, it will be too late."

A smattering of applause followed these words, but it was a far cry from the roar of triumph Liam had been hoping for. A sick feeling reared up in his gut. He glanced at the banner lords but found no help there; Raibert Green looked troubled, and Norvin Gold wouldn't even meet his gaze. Highmount stared straight ahead, hands folded behind his back. Rona Brown, for her part, had an almost desperate look in her eyes.

Liam surveyed the crowd. They stared at him, as if to say, *Is that it? Is that meant to inspire us?* He felt naked before them, just like in his nightmares. He felt like a *fraud*.

Silence coiled around him like a serpent. The rest of the speech fled from his mind, evaporating like mist under the searing glare of the crowd. His pulse skittered, on the verge of panic. Then he felt a nudge at his hand: Rudi had risen to his feet, either from boredom or tension, and gazed up at him, nub wagging, as if it were just the two of them on a leisurely stroll in the rose garden. Liam scratched the wolfhound's ears. Drew a long, deep breath. The next line of the speech came back to him; in his mind's eye, Liam held the scroll before him, Highmount's meticulous script flowing across the page.

In his mind's eye, Liam crumpled the scroll and threw it away.

"I won't lie to you," he said, raising his voice as if he were addressing the Wolves. "Everything I've just said was carefully thought through. Designed to make you feel better about what's to come."

He felt Highmount stir beside him, but Liam refused to look. For good or for ill, every word he spoke from now on would be his own.

"The truth is, none of us knows what the future holds. Least of all me. I'm standing before you as your prince, but right now, I don't feel like a prince. I feel like what I am: an Erromanian born and raised, scared out of my wits but ready to face the fight that's coming. I don't know if we'll win. I don't know if, someday soon, the Kingdom of Alden will be a relic of history. What I do know is that this city is my home, and its people deserve every last ounce of my strength, my courage, and my loyalty. And I swear to you now, upon my blood, you shall have it!"

He started to say more, but a murmur of encouragement from the crowd gave him pause. Thus fortified, he continued, "That's all any of us can promise, isn't it? To give everything we have so that our loved ones can be free. We can't control the future, but we can control our actions, and our hearts. That's what makes us who we are, and it's something the Warlord can never take from us. So I ask you, people of Erroman, to summon your courage and do your part to give us a fighting chance. Return to your homes and pack up your belongings. Take your time—leave nothing of value behind. Vacate the city and find whatever shelter you can, so that we who remain can defend our homes without fear for our loved ones. In return, I pledge you my sword." He drew his bloodblade, held it high. "I pledge you my life."

Hearing a whisper of steel at his side, Liam turned to find Raibert Green and Rona Brown holding their own swords aloft. Then Pollard drew his blade, followed by all the royal guardsmen. And suddenly there were blades everywhere, even in the crowd, glinting defiantly in the sun as the long-awaited cries of triumph went up, a wave of sound that rolled off the temple walls and tumbled along the Street of Stars. Liam wanted to laugh. And cry. And throw up. He did none of these things, holding himself still as a glorious statue while the crowd cheered and his dog barked and Albern Highmount looked at him with something perilously close to *approval*.

Liam nodded respectfully to the clergy and stepped down from the dais, Pollard and the royal guardsmen closing in around him. They were no match for Rona Brown, though; she shoved her way through the ring and threw her arms around him. "You were brilliant," she laughed. "You were so brilliant!"

"Pardon me while I write that down. I don't hear it often."

"It was finely done indeed," said a voice—cool, regal, and nearly as familiar as his own.

Liam's heart froze in his chest.

Erik stepped between the royal guardsmen, splendid in full armour and a white satin cape. Behind him stood Sirin Grey, looking grim but determined. "I thank you, brother, for handling a delicate task so admirably."

"Your Majesty," Rona breathed, as pale as if she'd seen a ghost. Which was not far off, Liam realised once he saw past the gleaming armour. Erik had the wan colour and gaunt cheeks of a man recovering from long illness.

"Sire," said Highmount, "I do not think you should be . . ."

Erik glanced over, and the look in his eye was enough to silence even Albern Highmount. Turning back to Liam, he said, "Perhaps you would not have made such a disastrous king after all, brother."

"Erik, before you say anything else . . ." Liam took a step toward him, but the guardsman Meinrad blocked his path. Rudi didn't like that; he sprang at the guardsman with a snarl. It was all Liam could do to hold the wolfhound back.

"Dispose of that beast," Erik said, and the guardsman drew his sword.

"Wait, Erik, *don't*!"

But Erik just motioned at the guards. Hands gripped Liam from all sides. Meinrad took a step toward the wolfhound. Rudi hauled against his lead, baying viciously, oblivious to the danger.

Meinrad hesitated, the point of his sword levelled at Rudi's throat.

"Gods' blood," Erik said impatiently, "it's only a dog. I'll do it." He drew his bloodblade.

"Sire, please, I'll take him!" A peasant pushed through the ring of startled guardsmen. He bowed his hooded head respectfully. "I've always wanted a wolfhound, Majesty," said a rasping voice. "Such a fine specimen, I'd be honoured to take him. He need never bother you again."

Erik scowled down at Rudi. Then, with a disgusted motion, he said, "Fine, take him. But mind yourself, or you're liable to lose a hand."

"Thank you, sire. What a handsome beast he is! You are most generous." The hooded figure grabbed the wolfhound's lead and dragged him away.

The king's icy gaze met Liam's, and it was like looking into the eyes of a stranger. "Your hound is fortunate to have escaped death, brother," Erik said. "Alas, the same cannot be said of you."

TWENTY

† "They definitely crossed here," Alix said, rising from her crouch and scanning the riverbank. "I make it half a dozen or more."

"Those are poor odds," Vel said. Glancing at Rodrik, she added, "I'm not sure he can make it across in any case. The current is strong here, and—"

"I can make it," Rodrik said. "And I will thank you not to speak of me as if I were unconscious."

Not unconscious, perhaps, but certainly not strong. He was pale as death and shining with sweat, stooped over his mangled arm with a permanent grimace of pain. Vel had offered to give him something stronger to help cope with his injuries, but Rodrik wouldn't have it; he preferred to remain as lucid as possible. Given what he'd gone through these past weeks, Alix couldn't blame him, but his suffering was terrible to witness.

"I'm trying to protect you, Rodrik," Vel said. "Many battles have been fought on this river, and there are corpses all along its banks, especially upstream of here. Your wound could become septic."

"It's already septic," he said wearily. "As you well know."

Vel bit her lip and glanced away. Ide threw Alix a grim look that said, *I told you so.*

"We need to get across," Alix said. She refused to let the tumult inside reach her voice, or her eyes. "Are you sure you can manage, Rodrik?"

He gave her a resigned smile. "Do we have a choice, sister?"

"No," she said, starting toward the water's edge. "No, we don't."

So they dragged themselves across the Gunnar, Rodrik braced between Alix and Ide, each step a delicate negotiation of fast-flowing water and loose rock. By the time they reached the far bank, even Alix was too exhausted to continue; she called a halt on the rocky shore, giving them half an hour of rest. She knew she should feel relieved—they were back on Aldenian soil at last—but there were still so many hurdles before them. Only when the bloodbinder was dead and Erik's twin safe in the palace would she have fulfilled her vow to her king. Right now, however, both of those charges seemed very uncertain indeed.

Seeing Rodrik close his eyes for a spell, Alix took the priestess aside. "The arm," she said in an undertone. "Should we . . . ?"

Vel shook her head. "I doubt he would survive it, weak as he is. If we could get him to the fort, I might be able to help him, provided the poison has not already spread to his blood. But out here . . ."

Alix squeezed her eyes shut, pushed her hands slowly through her hair. She could feel herself coming apart stitch by stitch. In a way, she was surprised she'd lasted this long; perhaps the only thing holding her together was fear. "I don't know what to do," she whispered, and the confession hurt more than a blade.

"None of this is your fault. The bloodbinder kept Rodrik on the brink of death for nearly two months. It's a miracle he's doing as well as he is. He must have been very strong before all this began."

"Like Erik. He was strong in every way . . ."

"He still is, I'm sure," Vel said, gently but firmly. "Don't give up. We are not beaten yet, Alix."

A muffled cry from Rodrik cut them short; he curled over

himself, teeth gritted in agony. "I'll prepare another dose of powder," Vel said. "But it will only dull the pain. The sepsis . . ."

"I know," Alix murmured. And the worst part was, so did he.

"Is it time to leave already?" he asked as she sank down beside him.

"Not quite. Vel is preparing you some tonic. Just try to rest."

He glanced at her out of the corner of his eye. "Please don't look at me like that."

"Like what?"

"I don't know how to describe it. Pity, I'm accustomed to. I've faced it my whole life." He held up his withered arm by way of explanation. "But that look on your face . . . it's more like remorse. As if you're apologising to me with your eyes every time you look at me."

She sighed. "Perhaps I am."

"But why? You have nothing to atone for, sister. You saved me."

Not yet, I haven't. Aloud, she said, "I'm doing my best, but we have a long road ahead. The bloodbinder—"

"Dargin." That glint of hatred again, like the last time he'd said the name.

"He has your blood, and that means he can still work his magic. On you, or . . ."

"Or on my brother." Rodrik nodded slowly. "I think I understand now. It's not me you're apologising to, is it? It's him. My twin."

"I'm sorry. It must be so strange for you. But when I look at you . . ."

"You see him."

"And you," she was quick to add. "I also see you, Rodrik. I feel as if you're both here, somehow."

He was quiet for a time. Then: "Will you tell me about him? What is he like?"

"He . . ." Alix swallowed against a knot in her throat. "Erik White is the best man I've ever known."

Rodrik raised his red-gold eyebrows. "High praise. How so?"

For a moment, Alix grappled with how to answer. But then

she realised it was really very simple. "He is endowed with every single one of the Holy Virtues. Courage and wisdom and honour. And strength . . . by the gods, he's strong. He carries the weight of the world on his shoulders, and with such grace . . ."

"You love him very much."

Alix could only nod.

"So what is it you're apologising for?"

"Pardon?"

"That look in your eye," he said. "The remorse. What is it for?"

She opened her mouth, but no sound came. How could she possibly explain what she'd done, how she'd betrayed his twin and her oath? Even if she could find the strength to confess her sins, it wasn't fair to burden Rodrik with the details of the evil that had been wrought with his blood.

"Never mind," he said. "It's unfair of me to ask. It's only that I would like to get a sense of him, in case . . ." He paused, his gaze falling to his bandaged arm. "In case we are not destined to meet in this world."

"Don't say that." Alix gripped his good hand fiercely. "You will."

He nodded, but Alix had the sense that was only because he was too tired to argue. "And my other brother—Liam, you said it was?"

The name brought an ache to her heart and a smile to her face. "You'll like him. Everyone does. He's . . ." She shook her head, still smiling. "He's Liam."

Rodrik laughed, and though his smile was Erik's, the sound was all his own. "That's exactly how I would describe my wife."

"You're married?" For some reason, the thought had never occurred to her.

"I was," he said, his smile turning sad. An old pain, clearly. "She died three years ago, along with our daughter."

"I'm sorry."

"At least she didn't have to see this war. It would have crushed her. She would never have wanted our daughter to be born into this world."

"What was her name?" It felt important to ask.

"Haillie. And our daughter was Sella."

"That's a beautiful name," Alix said.

"My little sister chose it," Rodrik said, and here was a fresh pain; his face crumpled in grief.

He doesn't know what became of her. Oh, Alix, you self-centred fool . . . "I'm so sorry," she said, taking his hand again. "I should have told you straightaway. I just wasn't thinking. Ana—she's all right."

His eyes widened. "You saw her? You saw my sister?"

"That's how we found you. She's fine. Shaken, but well. Marelda is taking care of her."

"Oh, thank the Virtues . . ."

Alix put an arm around his trembling shoulders. Vel came over with the tonic and he drank, but his gaze was a million miles away, lost in memories and grief. Or so Alix thought, until her hand brushed his skin. *Fever*, she realised grimly.

"Time to go," she said, rising. "We need to find that blood-binder."

And they needed to find help, or Rodrik White was going to die.

"We're losing them," Ide said, gesturing disgustedly at the pile of cold ashes at her feet. "If they got this far by last night, it means they're at least three hours ahead of us now. We got to pick up the pace, Alix."

"What would you have me do?" Alix snapped. "Conjure a horse out of thin air, perhaps?"

"If they make it to the Imperial Road, we'll never pick up the trail. All they gotta do is ditch their crimson tabards and no one will ever be the wiser—"

"Do you think you're telling me anything I don't know?"

"Enough." The priestess's voice, quiet but commanding. She gestured behind her to where Rodrik stood propped against a tree, head bowed, shoulders drooping. "This isn't helping."

"Nothing is helping," Ide said. "He's getting slower and slower. We should—"

"Don't say another word."

"What in the hells is the matter with you?" Ide glared at Alix the way she'd glared at Vel when the priestess had nearly got herself killed. "I know you, Alix. You got more sense than this. Deep down, you know I'm right."

Alix did her best to keep her voice low, but it trembled with raw emotion. "Erik would never forgive me. *Never.*" She shook her head angrily. How could she make Ide understand what this man meant to Erik? What Erik's forgiveness meant to her?

You can't. There were only two people in this world who could possibly understand, and neither of them was here. So she drew a deep, shuddering breath and said, "I won't have that kind of talk again, Ide, do you hear me?"

Ide thumped out a bitter salute and stomped off through the undergrowth.

Alix fetched her waterskin and offered to it to Rodrik, but he shook his head. "I can't," he said. "It aches."

"You must bear it," Vel said. "You need to drink or the fever will worsen."

"Maybe we should camp here," Alix said.

"We've fallen too far behind already." Rodrik lifted his head slowly, as though it cost him a great effort. "She's right, you know," he said, cocking his chin after Ide. "We're losing precious time because of me. You should leave me behind."

"We're not leaving anyone behind, least of all you. We came all this way to get you, Rodrik. I'm not quitting now."

"I'm not going to make it to Erroman, sister. We all know it. What matters now is catching Dargin. If you promise me you will make him pay for what he's done, I am content to let it go."

"Well, I'm not," Alix said, furious at the tremor in her voice. "I'm not *content*, so we keep moving for another hour, and then we make camp." Before he could argue, she snatched her waterskin back and headed after Ide.

Somehow, they managed to keep going until sunset. Rodrik nearly collapsed onto his bedroll, but at least Vel managed to coax some broth into him before he fell asleep. Alix took the first watch, prowling restlessly through the woods in a wide circle, letting the night sounds fill her ears and trying not to think about anything at all. Each time she passed the cluster of slumbering forms, she paused to listen, half expecting to hear Rodrik stirring, but it seemed exhaustion had triumphed over pain, for his bedroll lay still.

Ide took over when the moon was high. Alix was sure she wouldn't sleep; there were too many shadows chasing each other across the grim canvas of her mind. But exhaustion triumphed over her too; she had scarcely pulled her blanket up over her shoulders before she slipped into darkness.

If she dreamed, she had no memory of it. But she woke to a nightmare.

Someone was shouting at her, as if from a great distance. Alix tried to understand, but everything was dark and muffled, as if she'd been swaddled in layer upon layer of spider's silk. And then something seized her shoulder, tearing her from the cocoon of sleep; in an instant, she was on her feet, dagger flashing.

Vel stood before her, wild-eyed and dishevelled. "He's gone!"

"What?" Alix shook her head, throwing off the last silken threads of sleep. Dimly, she registered that it was just before dawn.

"Rodrik! I went to give him his tonic and he's gone!"

"What do you mean, gone?"

"His bedroll is empty! Look!"

Ide stirred, groaning. "What in the Nine Hells?"

Gone. Rodrik is gone. For a moment, Alix struggled to comprehend it. Then the realisation dashed over her like a bucket of icy river water. "The bloodbinder. Oh gods . . ."

"What do you mean?" Vel said. "What's happening?"

Alix was very nearly sick then, doubling over and clutching at her middle. *How did I not see this coming?* She'd been so focused on Erik, so sure that the bloodbinder would be doing the same, she hadn't even seen the danger. "He's using the bloodbond on Rodrik. He's calling him back!"

Ide scrambled to her feet with a string of blistering oaths. "We gotta find him! Get your things, priestess. Hurry!"

"But why would he do that?" Vel snatched up her blanket even as she struggled to process what was happening. "Surely every drop of Rodrik's blood is precious now. Why would he waste it on this?"

"It's worth it if he can get Rodrik back," Alix said. "Harvest his blood one more time before . . ."

"Before he *dies*," Ide finished cruelly. "This is exactly what I was afraid of. I told you we should have finished it. Now he's a thrall, on his way back to enemy hands. Already there, maybe!"

Alix didn't bother arguing; they hadn't the time, and she hadn't the heart. She just grabbed her things and started running.

Trees whipped by, branches snatching at her clothing and flaying her bare skin. Her mind barely registered the world around her; it was too busy playing out her failure from the night before. *He must have stolen away while you were doing your rounds. Your watch . . .*

Rodrik had trusted her, just as his twin had. She'd promised to protect him, just as she'd promised to protect Erik.

And she had failed them both.

TWENTY-ONE

"The execution will be tomorrow," Erik said.

The faces around the table were ashen. No one would meet the king's eye. That was to be expected, Erik supposed. Liam had been well liked before his treachery came to light; it was only natural that the council members would need time to accept the harsh truth. On top of which, personal feelings aside, the execution of a prince on the eve of battle was an ordeal a kingdom should never have to confront, let alone twice within a year.

Raibert Green cleared his throat. "Forgive me, sire, this must be terribly painful for you. But I have to ask—is this wise? A public spectacle, I mean. Prince Liam—"

"The traitor," Erik corrected.

Green shifted. "His private agenda notwithstanding, he did well in the temple square yesterday. We were right to delay his arrest until after the speech. The people are evacuating smoothly. If we make public the situation with"—he faltered briefly—"with the traitor, all our careful measures to avoid panic will have been for naught."

"Respectfully, sire," Sirin Grey put in, "I agree with Lord

Green. The traitor must certainly face justice, but if we make his execution public, we may rue the consequences."

A soft snort drew Erik's glance. Tom leaned casually against a pillar, arms folded, mouth twisted sardonically. "*We.* She is presumptuous, isn't she, my beloved? As though she or anyone else has a say in the matter."

With an effort, Erik ignored the apparition of his dead brother. "I understand your concerns, my lords, but I have committed this error once already. Tom was executed privately, without spectacle. Most of the city did not hear of it until after the siege. And now, scarcely a year later, here we are again, in precisely the same situation." He spread his hands, inviting them to draw the appropriate conclusions. "We may indeed rue the consequences of a public execution, but not nearly as much as we would rue the consequences of a private one."

"Oh, I don't know," Tom said languidly. "The danger is probably past. You've quite gone through your stock of brothers, I think."

Erik fired him a withering look, but did not otherwise rise to the bait. "I will not take that risk again," he told the council. "Instead, I will send an unambiguous message about what happens to those who would betray the crown." His gaze did a long, slow tour of the table. *Including any of you.*

Norvin Gold stroked his moustaches fretfully. "It will be a beheading, then?"

"I think it wise to make a stronger statement this time."

The council stirred uncomfortably. Lady Stonegate seemed to be voicing the general sentiment when she enquired, "What could be stronger than cleaving a man's head from his shoulders?"

"The emperors of old had a way with such things."

The shocked silence that greeted this statement was more than a little satisfying. It promised an even greater reaction tomorrow when he carried out the brutal act itself. No one would dare challenge him after that.

"My dear brother," Tom murmured, "how you have grown."

A log slipped in the hearth; Sirin Grey flinched as if startled from a nightmare. "Your Majesty . . ."

Erik waited for her to continue, but she just sat there, staring at him in dismay. *She regrets herself now*, Erik thought, not unkindly. *This must be difficult for her, remembering Tom.*

"Difficult and painful," Tom said, reading Erik's thoughts. "Yet she does her duty anyway. You could learn much from her, brother."

I have learned that lesson already, brother, Erik retorted in his mind, and Tom conceded the point with a grave nod.

Raibert Green was the next to brave the silence. "What about Lady Brown, sire? I know you believe her to be one of the co-conspirators, but—"

"Chancellor Highmount and Lady Brown have committed high treason and will be punished accordingly. Eventually, Alix Black will have to be dealt with as well. However, it is my brother who is at the centre of this plot, and who corrupted the others. He alone will face imperial justice."

Green winced. "But, Your Majesty—"

"The matter is decided," Erik said, rising. "And now, my lords, it remains only for me to thank you for your loyalty and dedication in this difficult time. You will all be rewarded in due course. For now, I suggest you spend what little time remains with your families. This council is hereby disbanded, with gratitude for its service." So saying, he headed for his study.

"You handled that well," Tom said, falling into step beside him.

"Rare praise," Erik said dryly, keeping his voice low so as not to alarm his new bodyguard. Thankfully, Meinrad kept a much more respectful distance than Alix had ever done.

"I judge things as I see them," Tom said with a shrug. "My feelings have never had much to do with it."

Erik started to reply, but a voice called after him down the corridor; turning, he found Sirin Grey sweeping toward him with all the haste dignity would allow. "A word, Your Majesty?"

Checking a sigh, Erik gestured for her to follow him into his study.

"I don't wish to intrude," she said. "But I am . . . concerned. You don't look at all well, if you will forgive me for saying so."

"I went several days without eating or sleeping, even longer without sunlight or exercise, and it certainly shows. That is why

I allowed the traitor to address the people in my place. The sight of me in this condition would hardly inspire confidence."

"You are thin, it's true. But it's not only that. You seem very . . . inflamed. That's only natural, of course, given everything that has happened, but I wonder if perhaps you aren't allowing your anger to influence your decisions."

"You believe my judgement is clouded?" Erik asked mildly.

Her gaze fell to her lap. "Forgive my impertinence. I only want what is best for the kingdom, and for you."

"I know." Reaching across the desk, he took her hand, gave it a reassuring squeeze. "But I need you to trust me now. You know me better than anyone on the council. I ask you—have I ever struck you as a vindictive man?"

"Not at all. If anything, you have allowed your good nature to be taken advantage of."

Erik's mouth quirked. "I hear Tom in those words. Nevertheless, you're not wrong. My rule has known too much of Farika and not enough of Rahl. I simply cannot allow that to continue."

"I understand, of course. But imperial justice . . ." She shuddered.

"It's terribly brutal, I know. But don't you see? That's just the point. An act like this is a powerful deterrent. Done once, it need never be done again." He squeezed her hand a second time, choosing his words as carefully as he had with Meinrad. "What happened with Tom . . . It is a wound I will carry with me for the rest of my days."

A shimmer of tears came into her eyes. "I know."

"You know because I let you see it. I let everyone see just how much it hurt me to execute my brother. I let them doubt my strength, my resolve. And now I pay the price. Had I dealt with Tom as I should have, Liam would never have dared to conspire against me. I will not make that mistake again, Sirin. This must be done, for the good of the kingdom."

She swallowed. Nodded. "For the good of the kingdom," she whispered, and she left him.

"Aina," said Rona Brown.

The word pierced a silence that had lingered for . . . how

long? Liam had lost all sense of time in here. A small window had been cut from the stone—more like an arrowslit, really—but the walls of the Red Tower were thick enough that it was impossible to tell the angle of the sun. All Liam knew for certain was that it was afternoon, and most likely his last in this world.

Rona sat next to him in a pose identical to his: back to the wall, arms propped against her knees. They'd left the straw pallet to Highmount; he lay with his hands steepled on his chest, staring at the ceiling. Liam would have paid good coin to hear his thoughts, but the chancellor kept his own counsel. "Sorry," Liam said, glancing at Rona, "what did you say?"

"Aina. She's barely seventeen. That's too young, don't you think?"

Liam wasn't following. "To be married?"

"She's already married, a few months back. No, I meant that she's too young to inherit the banner."

"Don't think like that," he said—a little more harshly than he'd intended.

It didn't matter; she was barely listening anyway. "I hope Raibert Green will take her under his wing."

"You're not going to die, Rona." It sounded childish even to him, like a petulant toddler refusing to be put down for a nap. Still, he persisted. "It's me Erik wants. If I go willingly, he should be satisfied with that."

"Don't be ridiculous, this has nothing to do with King Erik." Her tone was utterly flat, which only drew attention to the uncharacteristically sharp words. "It's what the blood-binder wants that matters, and he'll take the opportunity to destroy as many prominent figures as he can."

Liam wanted to deny it, but of course she was right. She would die too, and it was his fault. She was only here because of him, because of her loyalty to her commander. "I'm so sorry, Rona," he said, dropping his head into his hands.

"Don't." She grabbed his hands and pulled them away, forcing him to look up. "I know what you're thinking, but don't. It was my choice to make." Her dark gaze roamed over his features as if she would memorise them. And then, for some reason he couldn't fathom, she smiled. "Well," she said wistfully, "maybe not quite a choice."

Liam didn't understand. Then she reached for him, fingertips brushing the side of his face, and all of a sudden, he did. And a moment he thought couldn't possibly get worse became *so much worse*.

He could feel the realisation blooming in his eyes; saw it answered in hers, with resignation and a deep, long-concealed pain. "Rona . . ." he began, and there was simply no way he could finish that sentence.

She smiled again, sadly, and slumped back against the wall. "I know. It's all right."

He'd never heard anything so ridiculous in his life, because it wasn't all right—it was *so very far* from all right—but he couldn't bring himself to argue with her. Instead he closed his eyes, fighting off a flood of memories from the past year, every moment when he should have known but didn't, because he was a bloody *idiot*.

The thing was, it made no sense. That was why he hadn't been able to see it. How could someone like Rona—highborn, capable, one of the most powerful figures in the kingdom—be interested in a clod like him? He was having a tough enough time accepting that he'd won Alix. He'd written it off as a stroke of blind luck, spent the last year living in fear that his wife would wake up one day and realise she'd made a terrible mistake. But now here was another amazing woman with feelings for him. Feelings she knew he couldn't possibly return, and so she'd done her best to keep them hidden, at least until now.

Females, Liam decided, were utterly unfathomable. And wonderful. And he'd just doomed two of their most remarkable specimens to a traitor's death.

"Maybe it's not so bad," Rona said.

Liam laughed, on the verge of hysteria. "How is that, pray?"

"The Warlord is coming. He's almost certainly going to destroy us. If I have to die, I'd rather it be by King Erik's hand."

But it's not Erik, Liam wanted to scream. *You just said so yourself!* He held his tongue. If Rona had found some scrap of comfort to cling to, he certainly wasn't going to take it from her.

"It will be tomorrow morning, I suppose," she said.

"At dawn, I should think," Highmount put in, choosing that moment to rejoin them. "It is traditional."

Beheading. That was traditional too. At least it would be quick.

Rona straightened suddenly. "Did you hear that?"

"Footsteps," Highmount said, sitting up on the pallet.

Liam could hear them now, echoing off the stone stairs outside. A hasty step, as of guards. His insides slumped into ash. *Too soon*, he thought dully. *It's too soon . . .*

Highmount rose, smoothing his doublet gravely. Rona stayed where she was. Liam closed his eyes, hoping to conjure Alix's face one last time.

The door squealed on ancient hinges. "Now is not the time for a nap, Your Highness," said a rasping voice.

Liam's eyes snapped open. Saxon stood in the doorway, dressed in a servant's livery and looking decidedly put out. For a moment, all Liam could do was stare.

"We are in something of a hurry," the spy said.

Liam scrambled to his feet. "What in the hells are you doing here?"

"I've grown tired of feeding your dog," the spy said sarcastically. "What do you *think* I'm doing? Your lady wife pays me a great deal. I cannot simply stand by while they dash your head off. That would be terribly poor client relations. So if you please . . ." He gestured elaborately at the door.

Liam didn't need to be told a third time. Grabbing Rona's hand, he lunged out the door, Saxon and Highmount close behind. He hesitated at the top of the steps, blinking past a wave of vertigo. Below, the tower spiralled down and down and still down, disappearing into shadow. There would be guards at the bottom of the stairs, he supposed. "What about the—"

"Asleep," Saxon said. "I drugged their food."

"Good thinking. But just in case, do you have a—"

"Here." The spy pressed a dagger into Liam's hand.

Liam paused. "You're frighteningly good at this."

"Yes."

They started down the stairs.

The scene at the bottom was pretty much what Liam had expected: four guards slumped over their midday meal, snoring loudly. "What about outside?" he asked.

"Clear but for the usual activity. There is a horse cart across the square. Slops from the stables. You can conceal yourselves beneath the blanket."

"Across the square is a long way to go without being seen."

"I should have liked to wait for cover of darkness, but the guard will be doubled from dusk until dawn, and by dawn . . ."

"By dawn they'll come for us. You're right, it's now or never." Reaching for the door, Liam uttered a silent prayer. Then he dropped his shoulder and barged through.

The square was empty but for a pair of stableboys carrying pails of water, but if they wondered at the group scurrying like rats across the square, they didn't let it interrupt their duties. The cart stood tantalisingly close; Liam could smell the shite already. *By the Virtues*, he thought, *we might actually make it . . .*

He should have known better than to tempt fate.

Half a dozen royal guardsmen materialised from under a stone arch, blades drawn. Liam recognised their leader as the man who'd nearly skewered Rudi yesterday. He'd been a favourite of Alix's once. Meinrad, his name was.

The guardsman's gaze raked over Liam and the others contemptuously. "His Majesty was right. The spy did come."

You fool, Liam. Of course the king would know about Saxon. Allie and Erik told each other everything.

There was no point in resisting. Even if by some miracle he and Rona managed to take them, he wasn't willing to be responsible for the deaths of six of Alix's guardsmen. They were only doing their duty. "I don't suppose I could convince you to stand down?" he asked wearily. "Because trust me, you're on the wrong side of this."

Righteous anger flashed in Meinrad's eyes. "I am on the side of the Kingdom of Alden," he said, and the hilt of a sword swung at Liam's temple.

TWENTY-TWO

The last hour before dawn found them in the Green-lands. About half a day northeast of the fort, Alix judged, though it was hard to be sure. She'd clung to a thin strand of hope that they might find help out here, maybe even come across some Kingswords, but that had been naïve. The land was all but deserted this close to the front, most of its people having fled north. As for Kingswords, they had no reason to be here; there was nothing strategic nearby for them to protect. Alix and the others hadn't seen a single flicker of fire or lamplight all last night. They were on their own.

At least the Oridians were staying well clear of the Imperial Road. They would have been impossible to track once they joined the highway, but it seemed the bloodbinder feared discovery by the Kingswords more than he feared his pursuers. *That's his mistake*, Alix told herself as her ragged trio made its way along the edge of the woods. *And he will pay for it dearly.*

"Rodrik's gotta be somewhere close by," Ide said. "He only got a few hours' head start, and he can't be moving fast, shape he's in."

"He's a thrall now," Alix reminded her grimly. "No fear. No pain. He'll be stronger than you think."

"Until he isn't," Vel said. "He's been on the move for a full day and night. His body will give out eventually."

Like a horse running itself to death, Alix thought with a shudder. The worst part was, the Oridians wouldn't even care. "He only has to make it as far as their camp, live long enough for Dargin to harvest his blood."

"Dargin," Ide echoed. "That the bloodbinder?" When Alix nodded, she pulled an arrow from her quiver and brandished it. "What a coincidence. I got a shaft called Dargin right here."

A weak smile touched Alix's lips. "It's nearly daybreak. Let's pick up the pace. Maybe we can catch them before they strike camp."

"Think Rodrik's already met up with them?" Ide asked.

"No way of knowing. Whether he's there or not, Dargin is our priority." *And this time he's going to die, if it's the last thing I do in this world.*

A bloodred splinter appeared on the horizon, the first hint of dawn. Alix paused to reorient herself—which was how she happened to glimpse a flash in the mid-distance. "Did you see that?"

Vel squinted at the horizon. "What?"

"I'm not sure. I thought . . . a candle, maybe? Through the trees, right there."

"You saw a candle from here?" Ide lifted an eyebrow sceptically.

"Does it matter? I saw *something*." Alix was already moving.

They covered the distance in silence, and the closer they drew, the more certain Alix was that someone was in those trees. Several *someones*, by the sounds of it; she drew her dagger.

Surprise was in their favour; attacking now would certainly be to their advantage. But Alix had no way of knowing who was in those trees, whether friend or foe. A year ago, a month even, she wouldn't have given it a second thought— she'd have struck first and asked questions later. But things were different now. She'd had one too many bitter lessons.

This time, she was bloody well going to be sure whom they were dealing with, and how many, before she made her move.

She motioned for a halt at the edge of the trees. The shadows were deeper here, but they'd definitely found a campsite. In a short while, it would be light enough to make out whose. Crouching, Alix settled in to wait.

Dawn hadn't yet cleared the walls, but a crowd had already gathered in the courtyard of the Red Tower. Liam would have supposed the city all but deserted by now, but there were almost as many people in the crowd as there had been for his speech two days ago. Apparently, the execution of a prince was a spectacle not to be missed.

He felt strangely calm as they marched him across the square. Maybe that was because some part of him had always known this was how things would end up. The timeglass had started running the moment they'd hammered that bar over Erik's door; the chances of rescuing Rodrik before the sand ran out had always been remote. They'd known that, all of them, and they'd tried anyway. He was proud of them.

Or so he tried to tell himself as they wrenched him to a halt in front of the dignitaries. He kept his chin up and his shoulders back, and if his heart was working just a little harder than usual, that was only because it was weighed down with the thought of never seeing Allie again.

The banner lords—minus the Blacks and the Browns, naturally—stood assembled in a grim line with Erik at their centre. The king looked solemn. Sad, even. And when Liam caught his eye, he thought he glimpsed a little of his brother in there, behind the stranger who was about to execute him.

Erik stepped forward, his gaze roaming slowly over the crowd. Even now, Liam couldn't help marvelling at it: how regal he was, how effortlessly he held them all in his sway. *How could you ever have thought to replace this man?* It was laughable, really.

"My people," Erik said gravely. "These are dark times. Once again, we find ourselves betrayed by those we trusted most. By those whose oath, whose very blood, should bind them to us forever. A kingdom should never have to endure such treachery, let alone endure it twice. And yet, here we are." His gaze fell to Liam and there it rested, as though they were the only two people in that square. "I called this man my brother once. I acknowledged him before all of you, brought him into my home and my confidence. In return, he staged a coup. He and the others before you committed high treason, and for this, they are condemned to die."

Erik hesitated, a spasm of pain flickering through his eyes, and for the briefest moment the ice seemed to crack, revealing the roiling waters beneath. It was over in an instant; the surface froze once more, a cold glass surface in which Liam saw nothing but his own reflection.

"Rona Brown. Albern Highmount. You are hereby sentenced to death by beheading."

Liam looked over at his companions. Rona was pale but composed. Highmount looked the way he always did, cool and hawklike, his gaze locked on Erik as though he might chisel through the ice by force of will alone.

"The same sentence has been pronounced upon Alix Black in absentia, as well as upon her servant." Erik made a dismissive gesture at Saxon, whose name he didn't even know. "Her sentence will be carried out at the earliest opportunity."

Liam closed his eyes and swallowed hard. *Words*, he told himself. *Allie will never come back to this place. She'll hear what happened and she'll ride to the fort. Rig will keep her safe.* Liam would have given anything to see her one last time, to take back all the terrible things he'd said, but that wasn't to be. *At least it'll be quick*, he thought.

But Erik wasn't through. "As for the traitor Liam, whose lust for power lies at the centre of this tragic conspiracy, it is our decision that he will face imperial justice."

Liam stiffened. He had no idea what that meant, but he dreaded it instinctively—the more so when he looked to Highmount and saw the old man's composure shattered at last, his eyes wide with horror.

"Your Majesty—" Highmount began.

"The condemned will not speak!" The words cracked over them like a whip; even the banner lords flinched. Erik paused, as if to compose himself. Then he continued, "I should have liked to honour the traditions of old by constructing the Ram of Destan."

A wave of shock rolled over Liam, sickening in its intensity. For a moment he thought his knees might actually give out. Mercifully, he managed to remain upright, but the world seemed to tilt around him. There was noise in the crowd, and Rona crying out, and Raibert Green looking like he was going to be sick on the dais. Liam registered it all through a haze, his mind's eye fixated on the image of the Ram of Destan, that most infamous of Erromanian torture devices, a beast-shaped furnace that was said to bellow and snort smoke as the man boarded up inside roasted to death.

"We had not time to build one," the king went on, "but we will evoke it in spirit. The traitor shall be burned at the stake."

Liam blinked slowly. He felt as if he'd been swallowed in a bubble. Outside, sound was muted, colours diluted; inside, his breath was as loud as if he'd slipped underwater. There was a commotion on the dais, but he couldn't make it out. Already they were pulling at him, dragging him across the flagstones toward the pyre that he'd somehow failed to notice before now.

"The sentence," Erik said, "will be carried out immediately."

Ide stirred restlessly, scowling at Alix in a look that clearly said, *Now.*

But Alix shook her head. She needed to be sure. Dawn was blooming in the sky, but it had not yet penetrated the cover of the trees; Alix could see little of the figures moving in the gloom. She couldn't tell if they were armed, and their murmured voices were too low to make out. They could be refugees. They could be Kingsword scouts. They could be anyone. So she waited.

Eventually, light began to filter through the trees. The men—seven of them, by Alix's count—had almost finished packing up their camp. Definitely armed, she could see now. One of them, a burly fellow who looked to be in charge, was pointing and giving orders. Alix strained to hear the words, but he was deliberately keeping his voice low. *It's got to be the Oridians,* she thought. But what if she was wrong?

And then one of them moved to the edge of the camp to relieve himself, and the decision was made for her. Alix wasn't sure what caught his attention, but he frowned and took another step, calling a warning back to his companions. In Oridian.

He was dead before he'd finished his sentence. One of Ide's arrows caught him between the eyes, dropping him noisily into the brush.

The men scattered. Vel took cover. Alix had little choice but to spring out of hiding, hurtling headlong into the enemy's nest.

She barely looked before throwing her dagger, but as always the bloodbond did its work, guiding her blade to the precise spot marked by her glance. An Oridian went down with its jewelled hilt protruding from his skull. Alix pivoted, looking for a new foe, but the rest had already dissolved into the brush. They wouldn't go far, she knew. She'd taken them by surprise, but they outnumbered her; it wouldn't be long before they regrouped and seized the initiative. In an instant, she'd gone from hunter to prey. All she could do now was crouch and wait.

She didn't wait long. A rustle of branches brought her swinging around to meet her enemy in a clang of metal. She sensed movement at her back, a second swordsman rushing in for the attack, but Ide took him down before he got too close. Alix focused on the foe before her, trusting Ide to cover her as best she could.

He wielded a bloodblade. The realisation was a cold fist on her heart, but she tried to shake it off, squaring her feet and coiling, sword at the ready. They circled each other warily. Alix rarely struck first, let alone when she faced a knight with a bloodblade, but she could feel the time flowing through her fingers like sand. She hadn't seen the bloodbinder, and that meant he could be getting away even now. So she swallowed her fear and lunged. The Oridian batted her away and got off a quick riposte, driving her back. She tried to pivot around him, but he sidestepped, cutting her off. She was vulnerable here and he knew it. The trees were too close behind her, the shadows too deep. She could hear crackling in the brush.

She dove in again, trading blows with her attacker, trying to ignore the cold claws of threat raking at her back. The undergrowth rustled and snapped as the enemy moved into position. She could feel their eyes on her, waiting for their opening . . .

They came at her from both sides, erupting from the bush like a pair of charging boars. Ide's bow sounded a steady pulse, like a heartbeat. One man dropped where he stood. The other blundered into Alix, driving her bodily to the ground. She tried to roll the dead man over, but his armour weighed too much. And then a boot crashed down on her wrist. Alix screamed, her sword falling from numb fingers.

The bow thumped again, followed by the meaty *thunk* of an arrow meeting wood. The knight must have ducked behind a tree. Alix wriggled out from under the dead man and picked up her sword, but she knew the moment she lifted its weight that it would be all but useless to her now. Pain radiated up her forearm to her elbow; it was all she could do to keep the tip of her blade up. And then an arc of metal was flashing toward her, and though she managed to meet the blow, the jolt of agony up her arm was enough to send her reeling backward with a cry. She waited for the sound of Ide's bow, but it didn't come. A moment later, she understood why: A stutter of swordplay sounded from Ide's position. The enemy had charged her. She'd been so busy covering Alix she hadn't noticed them closing in, and now they were on her, leaving Alix alone and injured, facing a knight with a bloodblade.

Alix backed away, holding her sword two-handed, her heart hammering in her ears. *One man*, she told herself. *It's only one man . . .*

Then a shadow fell over her. Sunlight kissed red-gold hair, glinted against a blade clutched firmly in a white-knuckled hand. Dead blue eyes stared out from a beloved face. There was no hint of recognition in Rodrik's gaze. No hint of humanity at all.

He started toward her. Behind him, the sun rose steadily, shafts of light piercing the shadows like a hail of arrows. Alix had the fleeting, terrible notion that it might be the last dawn she ever saw.

"Your Majesty, I beg you to reconsider."

It was Sirin Grey, of all people, who pleaded with the king as they dragged Liam onto the pyre. The rest of the dignitaries were still clustered around the dais. Liam could see Highmount arguing with Green, Rona's shoulders shaking with sobs, but they were too far away to hear.

The king barely seemed to register Sirin's presence. "I will do this myself," he informed Meinrad. "It is only right. Fetch me the torch." The guardsman looked a little queasy, but he obeyed.

"Your Majesty. *Erik*." Sirin grabbed his elbow. "You'll regret this, I know you will. Please, this isn't you."

Liam couldn't help it; he burst out laughing. Not a *real* laugh, obviously—the completely manic sort, the laugh of a man about to be burned at the stake. "Yeah, well spotted. Do you think that might have had something to do with us locking him away for a time?"

"Silence," said the king.

"Or what? You'll burn me at the stake?" Liam could feel himself losing his grip, but really, what did it matter now?

"You have only yourself to blame for this," the king said.

"Do you think so? I tend to think the bloodbinder holding you in thrall has rather a lot to do with it."

Sirin Grey sucked in a breath. "What did you say?"

"The same nonsense he's been saying for weeks," the king growled. "Pay it no mind."

It was incredible. The face was Erik's, and the voice, but at that moment the man before Liam bore no meaningful resemblance to his brother. Even through the fear—the roaring, nauseating fear—Liam felt a terrible sense of loss. The sheer injustice of it, that a great man should be brought to this . . . It was more than he could bear. "The worst part is, I know you're in there somewhere, Erik. I saw it." Only for an instant, but still, it had been there, a glimpse of humanity peeking through a tiny crack in the ice.

"Enough," said the king.

"Allie is going to find that bloodbinder and she's going to kill him. And when she does and you're free of the magic, you're going to remember all this and . . ." Liam broke off, tears brimming in his eyes. Not for himself, but for his brother. Because he *would* remember all this, every detail. And he would never forgive himself. Liam squeezed his eyes shut and shook his head. "I'm so sorry, Erik. I tried."

"Oh gods," said Sirin Grey.

The ropes bit into Liam's arms. In spite of himself, he started squirming, though he knew it was pointless. Panic was climbing his chest, closing around his throat, a sensation so much like drowning that he actually tipped his head back. He fought it down as best he could. Erik needed him to be strong now. "It isn't your fault," he said between gritted teeth. "Remember that when you wake up from this nightmare. Remember that I died knowing it wasn't your fault!"

"Oh gods . . ." Sirin Grey whirled toward the dais. *"Green, come quickly!"*

"It isn't your fault, Erik," Liam said again, trying to sear the words into his brother's memory.

The king paused. A flicker of doubt lit his eyes. "Liam . . ."

Meinrad appeared with the torch. Erik took it as though he didn't quite know what to do with it. The flames guttered and snapped, black smoke curling maliciously into the morning sky.

"Erik," Liam said pleadingly. *"Brother, please."*

Erik grimaced, clutching at his head as though it pained him. He looked from the torch to his brother, and in that instant the ice shattered. Horror flooded his gaze, and for a moment, Liam dared to hope.

Then Erik gasped. His head snapped back, and he went rigid as a corpse.

"Sire!" Meinrad put a steadying hand on his arm. "Are you well?"

Slowly, the king lowered his head. His gaze met Liam's once again. The eyes were completely lifeless.

Liam sagged against the ropes.

The king advanced toward the pyre, moving as mechanically as every other thrall Liam had ever known.

A thrall. Your brother is a thrall. You're going to die.

Liam tried very hard to pass out then, but the gods refused to grant him even that. Sirin Grey was weeping, Raibert Green was rushing toward them, but it was all too late. The king raised the torch for all to see. Then he turned back to the pyre.

And collapsed like a puppet shorn of its strings.

The torch clattered to the flagstones in a shower of sparks, missing the pitch-soaked pyre by inches.

"Erik!" Liam struggled fruitlessly against his bonds. *"Erik!"*

THE BLOODSWORN · 215

"Don't just stand there, you great fools!" thundered Albern Highmount from across the courtyard. "Someone help His Majesty!"

Alix fought on two fronts—or rather, she defended herself on two fronts. It was all but impossible for her to attack, even with two hands braced on the hilt of her sword. She had all she could do just to parry, each blow sending a bright arc of agony through her injured wrist. She couldn't keep this up for long. With every deflection, her reflexes were a little slower, her limbs a little heavier. She was like a wounded stag holding off a pack of coyotes; any moment now, she'd be too exhausted to continue, and then they'd have her.

She pivoted, trying to keep Rodrik between her and the Oridian. He was weak and not a trained swordsman; using him as an obstruction was the only thing keeping her alive. But even as she did so, Alix was painfully aware that she was not the only one being worn down by attrition. Every moment of exertion brought Rodrik one step closer to death.

The Oridian lunged, forcing Alix back. Then, quicker than she would have thought possible, he spun around and came at her again, landing a hard blow that sent her stumbling back into Rodrik. It might have ended right there, but Rodrik was slow to react, and they tumbled together to the hard ground. Alix's bloodblade jolted from her grasp; she scrambled for it, but the Oridian kicked it aside. He loomed over her, in no hurry now. His eyes blazed with triumph—before widening in shock as his body jerked violently. He staggered forward with a cry. Behind him, Vel stood as if paralysed, arm half raised, frozen in the moment when she'd plunged her dagger into the Oridian's back.

It was all the distraction Alix needed. She rolled, grabbed her sword, and thrust it into the Oridian's side; he collapsed in a heap on top of the still-prone Rodrik. Alix dropped to one knee and hauled the dead man off her prince. He was unconscious, his skin deathly pale, but he was alive. As for the priestess, she remained stock-still, her expression suspended somewhere between horror and grim determination.

"The bloodbinder," Alix said. "I have to find him . . ."

Vel blinked as if waking from a dream. She pointed at the brush nearby.

Cautiously, gripping her sword with both hands, Alix picked her way over.

A man sat cross-legged in the undergrowth, concealed in the foliage like a newborn fawn. His head was bowed, hands folded in his lap, and though his eyes were open, they stared sightlessly at the ground. Alix had seen this near-catatonic state once before, on the face of the most frightening human being she'd ever encountered. The Priest had been unable to stand on his own when Alix had burst into his tent, too drained by his dark magic even to raise his head without difficulty. Even so, she had failed to kill him.

Not this time.

Alix drove the point of her sword between the bloodbinder's shoulders, hard enough that it erupted through his chest and bit deep into the dirt below. She barely noticed the pain in her wrist; it was incinerated in the blaze of her wrath.

For Erik, you twisted son of a bitch.

And then, in an instant, her rage was spent, and with it her strength. Alix's knees buckled; the sword tumbled from her grasp. She had to grab a tree to steady herself.

Moments later, Ide crashed through the brush, bloodied but apparently unharmed. Warily, she took in the scene. "That him? The bloodbinder?"

"It's him," Alix said. "It's done."

TWENTY-THREE

†"**Y**ou sure?" Ide kept her sword levelled at the corpse as though it might spring to life at any moment. Alix didn't answer straightaway, watching anxiously as Vel knelt over Rodrik. "How is he?"

The priestess shook her head. "Alive, but beyond that it's difficult to say. His pulse is weak, and the fever is worse than ever."

Alix closed her eyes briefly. *Farika have mercy on him. He has suffered so . . .* "Does he have a chance?"

"There is always a chance, but it would take a miracle."

Ide still hovered over the dead bloodbinder. "We need to be sure this is our man."

"It's him," Alix said. "He was in some kind of trance. I don't think he even noticed me—he was too busy concentrating on his magic."

"Lucky you found him," Ide said.

"I didn't. Vel pointed him out, right after she saved my life."

Ide didn't bother to conceal her surprise. "How's that?"

Alix nudged the dead Oridian with her boot. "Vel got her dagger into this one."

"I stabbed him in the back." The priestess's tone was

strangely distant. She gazed down at her hands as if they were someone else's. "I must pray for him," she said. "For them all."

For once, Ide didn't object, or even make a face. She just gripped Vel's shoulder and said, "Bloody well done, anyway."

Vel didn't seem to know what to say to that. She knelt by the body of the Oridian knight.

"Wouldn't've thought she had it in her," Ide said in an undertone.

"I think she's just as surprised as you are," Alix said, feeling sorry for the priestess.

"So what now?"

"We get Rodrik home."

Ide sighed. "He's not going to make it to Erroman, Alix."

"We have to try. We owe it to him, and to Erik."

Erik.

Alix gasped. She'd been so busy worrying about Rodrik that she hadn't fully processed the implications of what had just happened. "He's free!"

"What's this?"

"Erik! He's free of the bloodbond!" And a thought that should have brought a flood of joy brought only dread. Because Alix had no way of knowing what was happening in Erroman. "Oh, Ide, what if we didn't get to him in time? What if—"

"We did. Commander's fine, you'll see." She said it with such staunch conviction that Alix couldn't help hugging her, even though she knew Ide would stiffen like a board. Which she did.

"Okay," Ide said, patting Alix's back awkwardly.

Once Vel had finished her prayers, Alix helped her to make Rodrik comfortable. He needed rest, and for the moment at least the time pressure had eased. Whatever had happened in Erroman, there was no changing it now. As for the Warlord, Alix and the others were as safe from him here as anywhere. Which was to say, not safe at all.

"Your arm," Vel said when they'd finished tending to Rodrik. "Let me see it."

Alix glanced down at her wrist. A streak of purplish red ran from her forearm to her palm, and the swelling had turned her hand into a ham with five fat sausages. She didn't need the priestess to tell her it was broken.

"How in the name of blessed Olan did you hold a sword with that?"

"Not courage," Alix said. "Fear. And I don't think I can do it again."

"Let us hope you won't need to. I have a poultice that will reduce the swelling and help with the pain, but there is not much else I can do beyond immobilising it." Turning to Ide, she said, "I will need wood for a splint . . ."

It was a measure of their exhaustion that no one, not even the priestess, objected to spending a few hours resting at a campfire surrounded by enemy corpses. They said little, each lost in her own thoughts, their glances straying every now and then to the pale form lying in a swaddle of blankets near the fire. But when noon came and went and still Rodrik showed no sign of stirring, Alix knew it was time to move on.

"We'll need to make a litter," she said. "I'll see if I can find some rope around here, but I'm in no shape to chop wood."

Ide glanced down at her sword ruefully. "It'll ruin the edge."

"Use his," Alix said with a weary gesture at one of the dead men.

Satisfied with this solution, Ide wandered off in search of a good bit of timber. Vel, meanwhile, stood over Rodrik looking worried.

"Building the litter is the easy part," she said. "But we're in no position to carry it, and dragging it through this brush will be difficult."

Worse than difficult, Alix knew. They had a lot of forest to get through before they reached the Imperial Road, a journey that would have taken days even without an injured man to carry. But what choice did they have? It was the quickest way to find help, and she was determined to get Rodrik to Erroman, no matter the cost. Though his chances of a full recovery grew dimmer by the hour, she refused to allow Erik's twin to die before the brothers even had a chance to meet.

So they did the best they could. Alix and Vel pulled the litter like a pair of oxen, ropes tied round their waists. Even with Ide hacking a path through the undergrowth with her borrowed blade, the sled slipped and jarred and snagged in the brush, forcing them to stop frequently to reposition Rodrik. Alix's hips were soon raw and bleeding from the chafing ropes. Vel must have suffered even more with only her thin robes to shield her, but she didn't complain.

You'll never make it, the coldly rational part of Alix's mind argued. *You're only prolonging his suffering.* She shoved the thought aside, bent her head like a beast of burden, and slogged on.

Gradually, the terrain began to swell on either side of them, herding them into a long, narrow valley with an ancient river-bed at its bottom. The going was a little easier here, the trees a little more sparse. As they continued north, the valley wid-ened and the bluffs grew steeper until they found themselves at the base of a broad bowl dotted with wildflowers. A mem-ory lurked at the edge of Alix's thoughts, but she couldn't quite grasp it. The pines and steep bluffs reminded her of her homeland, the riverbed and wildflowers of the tribal lands of Harram. But no, the memory stalking her now was something darker, more visceral . . .

She stumbled over a hard edge sticking out of the dirt. Stooping, Alix found the broken remnants of a half helm. And then the dark thing at the edge of her memory gripped her in its cold talons, and she knew where she was.

"Farika's grace," she breathed.

Ide turned, a question on her lips. Then she saw the broken helm in Alix's hand, and her gaze did a slow tour of their sur-roundings. She took in the steep bluffs, the wide clearing. Recognition dawned, and she swore softly. Like Alix, she'd been so focused on the gruelling task at hand that she hadn't even noticed.

"What is it?" Vel asked. "Where are we?"

Wind sighed through the pines, and it seemed to Alix like the whispers of the dead. Glints of metal peeked through the swaying grasses; here and there, the hard white of bone. The earth felt suddenly cold beneath her feet. "Boswyck Valley," she said, and she shuddered.

Vel's gaze flitted over the battlefield. "I read about what happened here."

What happened here. Alix wondered how they'd described it, those who saw fit to record the horror. *Massacre. Treachery.* The day the tide of the war turned and a king lost his innocence.

"A great act of heroism took place in this valley," Vel said. "It will live forever in scroll and song."

"Heroism," Alix murmured. "That's not how I remember it."

"Heroes rarely do, I suspect."

It was only then Alix registered what the priestess was talking about, and she felt herself colouring. "What happened with Erik . . . That wasn't . . . I wasn't—"

"A hero," Ide said, turning back to look at her. "Saved the king's life. Carried him off the battlefield. Stuff of bloody legend and no mistake."

Alix stared, searching her friend's face for some sign of mockery. "*That's* what you remember about this place?"

"Not the only thing." Ide's gaze took on a faraway look. "I remember the Raven sitting up on that bluff watching our brothers die. Nik and Gwylim throwing themselves down the hill, screaming like bloody fiends. I followed them without even thinking. Stood on a rock somewhere over there and just . . ." She mimed firing her bow. "And then after . . . I remember Liam thinking he'd lost you, that it was all his fault. Remember them carrying the king away to the healers, and Arran Green using a tree to put his arm back in its socket. I remember running and thinking half the world lay dead behind me."

A ribbon of wind raced through the valley. The grass sighed, as though in sympathy. Gradually, Ide's gaze came back into focus. "What you did was the only good thing happened here, so yeah—that's what I choose to remember." She turned away, cutting through the grass with her head bowed, lips moving silently in memory or prayer.

Alix looked out over the valley. *So many dead.* Thousands upon thousands, each and every one a story cut short. How could hers count any more than any other?

When she found her voice again, it cracked with emotion. "What happened here . . . it wasn't the stuff of bard song. It was a tragedy, Vel. A *massacre*."

"Those who fought here must carry those memories forever," the priestess said gravely. "It is part of their sacrifice. They bear the burden of the darkness, that the rest of us need remember only the light."

"The lie has value, is that what you're telling me?"

"Not a lie." Vel laid a hand on Alix's arm. "Just one memory among many. Those who perished here will be honoured and remembered. But when this is over we must rebuild, and no one ever built anything out of ash." Vel squeezed her arm. "I will pray for the dead," she said, "and for you, my friend."

A touch on her shoulder startled Alix out of sleep. Though it was too dark to see, she knew instinctively that it was Vel. And she knew why the priestess was waking her in the middle of the night. "Rodrik."

"It won't be long now. I'm sorry, Alix. I did everything I could."

A cold ache filled Alix's breast. She'd known this was coming, but she'd forced herself to deny it. As though she could change Rodrik's fate through sheer stubbornness.

"He's awake," Vel said. "He asked for you."

Alix rolled to her feet, pausing to let the bracing night air fill her lungs. She needed to be fully awake if she was going to be able to face this. She took a step toward the bundle of blankets on the far side of the fire, then paused to look back at Vel. But the priestess shook her head. "This is for the two of you alone," she said.

Steeling herself, Alix crossed the camp to kneel at the side of her dying prince.

He trembled with fever, and though Vel had left his side only moments ago, he'd already fallen into a fitful slumber. He started awake at Alix's approach, a look of wild terror in his eyes. "Rodrik," she whispered. "It's Alix. You're safe."

Liar, a voice inside her whispered.

He struggled to sit. "Save your strength—" Alix began, but he brushed her off.

"It doesn't matter now," he said, his voice grating from disuse.

She gave him some water. He held it to his mouth, but did not drink. The ache in Alix's chest gripped her so tightly it was hard to breathe. "We're on our way home," she said, for want of something better.

"Home." He spoke the word as if it were foreign on his

tongue. "They say home is where your family is." He raised his eyes to her; they looked thin and watery in the low light.

"If that's true, then you have many homes. And many people who love you."

He didn't seem to hear. His gaze flitted over the campsite as though seeing it for the first time, and a hint of fear came into his eyes. The fever was toying with his mind, as subtle and pernicious as the bloodbond.

Instinctively, Alix reached for him, stroking his hair back from his forehead as if he were a restless child. Rodrik closed his eyes. He might have drifted back into sleep, for he didn't speak again for a long while. But when he opened his eyes again, they were sharp and lucid. "You're still here," he said. "Good."

Alix forced herself to smile. "I'm not going anywhere."

"I was afraid I would . . . that it would be over before I could say thank you."

The words were like a knife in her belly. Alix's body seized in a silent sob; she had to look away so he wouldn't see her wrestling with tears. "I don't know what you'd be thanking me for," she whispered tremulously.

His hand slipped over hers, gripping it with surprising strength. "I know this is hard for you," he said, and at that moment, he looked so very much like Erik that it took her breath away. "You think you've failed, but you haven't. I would have died on that table sooner or later. In the meantime, the gods only know what evil my blood would have wrought. You saved us both, my brother and me."

The tears were flowing freely now; Alix could do nothing to hide them. Rodrik's eyes, his grip on her hand, demanded that she meet his gaze, however painful it might be.

"Will you give him a message for me?"

Alix sucked in a shuddering breath, nodding. She could hardly see him through the blur of her tears.

"Tell him I'm sorry. I tried to hold on . . . I so wanted to meet him . . ."

"He wanted to meet you." She could give him that, at least. "They told him you were stillborn, but he mourned you anyway. He always wondered what it would have been like if you'd grown up together."

Rodrik smiled. Erik's smile. "Tell him I'll see him in good time. He's my twin—we will go to the same Domain. He can meet my wife and my child . . ." He was fading now, the words slurring as exhaustion claimed him again. "My sister will come one day too, and we can be a family . . ."

Alix's hands tightened over his, her head bowed in silent agony as she watched him slip into blackness.

They buried Rodrik White at the foot of a mammoth pine tree overlooking Boswyck Valley. It seemed somehow appropriate that he should lie here, in this place that held so much significance for all three of his brothers. It felt right that the tens of thousands of Kingswords resting in the valley below should have their prince watching over them.

None of that gave Alix any comfort. Erik's twin was dead. The brother he had longed for his entire life had slipped forever beyond his grasp, and she had been powerless to stop it. It was a grief as sharp and heavy as any she had ever borne, just one more burden to carry with her forever from the shadowed slopes of Boswyck Valley.

TWENTY-FOUR

Rig held the longlens to his eye, cursing a streak so vivid that even the hardened soldiers at his back shifted uncomfortably. The view before him was of fields and more fields and yet more fields—empty. It was just as the scouts had reported, but he still couldn't quite believe it. "It doesn't make sense," he growled. "Where *is* he?"

"Nowhere nearby, that's for certain," Dain Cooper said. "Territory doesn't get much more open than this."

"Perhaps they have fallen back," offered Commander Wright.

It certainly *looked* as though the enemy had fallen back. Ennersvale was completely deserted. Rig would have sworn they were in the wrong place were it not for the evidence of an army camp all around him: the crisscrossing lines of muddied turf, the squares of flattened grass and the charred remains of cooking fires. Most of all, the lingering smell of shit from shallow latrines. This was it, all right—the place where fifteen thousand Oridian soldiers had been camped only a few days before. The very spot where Rig and Dain and a battalion of horse archers had swooped in under cover of darkness to scour the unsuspecting ranks of the enemy while Alix mounted her rescue.

This was the place, but the only sign of life was a coyote and a few crows picking about in search of scraps. Sadik was long gone.

"They've been here for weeks, and now suddenly they pack up and leave?" Rig shook his head. "The Warlord doesn't withdraw, especially not when he's got us by the balls. This is a ploy."

Wright sighed. "Regrettably, I concur."

"Well," Dain said, "I don't suppose glaring at this field all day is going to help us figure it out. We need intelligence."

That was an understatement. Rig had never felt so utterly blind in his life. He had no idea whether Alix had been successful in her rescue attempt, or whether she was even alive. He knew nothing of events in Erroman. Nor was he any closer to rooting out the spy in his ranks. And now, on top of everything, he'd somehow managed to lose fifteen thousand men in an open field. "We need more than intelligence. We need an all-seeing eye. And me without my priestess of Eldora." Rig winced inwardly at his own choice of words. He'd meant it as a throwaway, the sort of glib remark he was known for. But the truth was, Vel's absence gnawed at him nearly as much as his sister's. At first that had irked him, suggesting as it did an inconvenient truth that he wasn't quite ready to face. But now, weeks on and with no news of her fate, Rig was through worrying about inconvenient truths. He wanted Vel safe in his arms and that was that.

"The last people to see my sister and Vel alive were also the last people to have eyes on that army," Rig said.

"The Resistance." Dain nodded. "As good a place to start as any, assuming they're still alive. But how do we get in touch with them?"

"We go that way," Rig said, pointing.

Wright's eyebrows flew up. "Are you sure that's wise?" Lowering his voice, he continued, "What if the spy is among us? We could lead him straight to the Resistance."

Gesturing at his escort, Rig said, "The odds of the spy being among these twenty-four men are virtually nil. Besides, from what Dain tells me, we'll be blindfolded before we get anywhere near the place. But there's no point in both of us putting ourselves at risk, Commander—take your men and head back to the fort. I'll see you tomorrow."

Wright eyed him sceptically, but he held his peace, turning away to round up his men.

"Let me go, General," Dain said. "I'll take a few men and—"

"I've got business with Wraith." The dark tone of Rig's voice gave away more than he would have liked.

Dain started to say something, then thought better of it.

Rig gave him a wry look. "Permission to speak freely, soldier."

"I don't think you need me to say it, General." The remark reminded Rig so much of his former second that he found himself giving the Onnani knight a newly appraising look, which Dain misread as irritation. "Sorry, General, but I always figured you for a man who'd rather hear truth than treacle."

"You figured right. But I'm still going to have a chat with our friend Wraith." So saying, Rig put the spurs to his horse.

He almost hoped they'd stumble across the enemy along the way. At least then the mystery of the missing army would be solved and they could hightail it back to the ford. But the fields between Ennersvale and the place Alix and the others had been "found" by the Resistance remained stubbornly, eerily empty. Rig and his small party kept to the trees near the river—he wasn't *completely* reckless—but if there were enemy scouts using the woods as cover, they were well hidden.

It's as if they just vanished into thin air. Which meant they could be anywhere, poised to strike. It was like being sent into melee combat blindfolded. Rig's nerves couldn't have been more frayed if they'd been coated in honey and chewed on by rats.

It was a little past midday when Dain said, "Here."

Rig glanced around. "Where?"

"Just here."

"What, in the middle of the trees?"

Dain nodded. "They'd been following us for a while, set an ambush of sorts for us in the trees. After that, we were blindfolded. But I reckon we can make a good guess of it."

"I hope so, or we've come a long way for nothing." Rig glanced behind him; his escort was about ready to fall out of their saddles. They'd been on the road since well before dawn, and nobody was sleeping much these days. It was hard to catch a proper kip when you were sure each night was going to be your last.

"We started off on this dirt track," Dain said, pointing. "It was late morning. By the time we got there, though, the sun was at our backs. I remember being uncomfortably hot."

Rig glanced up at the sky. "East, then."

"Southeast, more like. For about three hours."

"In an oxcart on open ground. I'd say that's more than enough to go on. Good work, Commander."

Dain gave a brisk nod, almost managing to conceal his pleasure at the praise. He knew Rig didn't serve it up lightly.

They followed the narrow dirt track for about an hour until one of the scouts pointed out a set of wagon ruts in the wheat, heading east. Dain reckoned that was about right, so they veered off the track and followed the wagon across open farmland.

Rig fully expected the Resistance to have sentries, so he was only a little startled a couple of hours later when a trio of archers sprang up out of the grass, bows trained at his heart. He jerked Alger to a halt and raised a hand, warning his men not to do anything rash. "Riggard Black to see Wraith," he said dryly.

The sentries exchanged a glance. "*General* Riggard Black?"

"The same."

"How do we know it's really you?"

Rig rolled his eyes. "If the livery and banners aren't enough for you, maybe you recall seeing this knight before? I imagine you don't get many Onnani round here."

Dain considered the sentries. "I've never seen these two before, but the woman was with us in Timra. Name of Gretia, if I recall."

"I remember you, fishman," she said.

"But you don't seem to remember your manners," Rig said. "This man is a Kingsword knight. You will show him the proper respect."

Gretia glared up at him sullenly. "I can't take you to Wraith. Not without a blindfold."

"Get on with it, then." Rig swung down from his horse.

They made the rest of the journey on foot, blundering their way through the wheat with nothing but an occasional hand on their elbows to guide them. It did little to improve Rig's opinion of the Resistance, or its leader.

When the blindfolds were removed, they found themselves standing outside a small farmhouse. "This is it," said Dain. "Same place as before."

"Better tell him we're here," Rig said to the sentry. "Wouldn't want things getting dramatic."

Gretia gave him a smug look. "We sent word hours ago. Been watching you since the river."

"Good," Rig said, stepping around the startled sentry and barging through the door.

Inside, he found a slight man lounging at a table. "Welcome," the white-hair said casually, gesturing for his visitor to sit.

Rig declined with a snort.

Dain appeared at Rig's shoulder. "Hello, Asvin."

Green eyes widened. The man called Asvin remained seated, but his hand twitched subtly near his midsection. Going for a dagger, most likely.

"You look surprised to see me," Dain said. "Your sentries told us they'd sent word."

"Of approaching men-at-arms. They weren't specific." His manner was cool but wary, hand still resting against his midsection.

"Your sentries need to brush up on their livery," Rig said. "The Kingsword banner is pretty unmistakable. As is my own." He gestured at the swatch of black silk hanging from his left shoulder.

The white-hair paled. "You."

"Me. Now get up. I want to see your boss."

"He's not . . . I don't . . ." Asvin was having some trouble finishing a sentence. It might have had something to do with the look in Rig's eye, which probably communicated his mood well enough.

"The back door," Dain said quietly.

Rig glanced at the back of the room. Raising his voice, he said, "Maybe this peek-and-hide bollocks impresses your usual houseguests, but I'm not a patient man."

"So I've heard, General," said a voice, and an imposing shadow darkened the doorway behind Dain. *How in the Nine Hells did he get past my knights?* Rig did his best not to look nonplussed as the figure strode through the door. He had a falcon on his arm, the same type he'd sent north with Vel a couple of months ago.

"Wraith, I presume?"

The big man deposited his falcon on a perch in the corner. "An honour, General Black."

Rig's mouth twisted, but he managed to keep himself in check, saying only, "We have business to discuss."

Wraith exchanged a guarded look with his lieutenant. "What sort of business?"

"Various sorts." Rig dragged out a chair, dropping himself into it and propping a boot on his thigh. Dain sat across from Asvin, his hand resting casually on the hilt of his sword. A nice, relaxed meeting, this. "Let's start close to home," Rig said. "My sister. What do you know of her fate?" He put every bit of menace he could muster into his voice, the better to conceal the terrified lump in his throat. There was a fair to good chance he was about to hear that Allie was dead, and he honestly didn't know what that would do to him. Or what he would do to the man sitting across from him.

"Last we knew," Wraith said, "she was alive and well, her and the priestess and the other one."

Rig's lungs filled in relief, but he kept his tone hard and his questions clipped. "Last you knew. Which was when?"

Another glance passed between the white-hairs. "Night of the attack," the big man said, "when you so kindly provided a diversion."

"And the rescue?"

This time, it was the smaller man, Asvin, who answered. "They found Rodrik, I can tell you that much. I saw the four of them trying to make their escape. I tried to get to them"—his gaze dropped—"but there were too many soldiers between us. After that . . ." He shrugged.

"You don't know if they made it out."

Asvin shook his pretty head. "Sorry."

Wraith, for his part, said nothing.

Rig narrowed his eyes. There was something they weren't telling him. Dain thought so too, judging from the thoughtful frown he wore. But Wraith's craggy features promised only stonewalling, so Rig moved on. "What about the Warlord? What happened after the Kingswords retreated?"

"We looked for Sadik," Wraith said. "Combed that sodding camp from end to end. Couldn't find him anywhere."

Rig lifted an eyebrow. "And if you had?"

"I'd have cut his throat and fed his entrails to his dogs."

It was all Rig could do not to laugh. Did this self-important thug really think he could have bested Sadik? The Warlord of Oridia, a vicious killer who had earned his place by systematically exterminating all rivals? "I doubt you'd have found him easy prey."

"Maybe not, but I'd have died trying."

Rig grunted. "I can respect that," he said, and he meant it. "So you fled the camp, presumably."

"Wouldn't call it *fleeing*, General," Wraith said between his teeth. "We left when it was clear we weren't going to find Sadik."

"What can you tell me about numbers?" Rig asked.

"Your sister estimated fifteen thousand."

Rig scowled. It made no *sense*.

"I know what you're thinking," Wraith said. "Sadik had twenty thousand there a month ago. What happened to the other five?"

"What happened to any of them? I'm sure you're aware that as of two days ago, that army picked up and left Ennersvale."

"We're aware."

"Any idea where they've gone?"

"We were hoping you could tell us," Asvin said.

Rig swore and scratched his beard.

"Sorry, General," Wraith said. "Looks like you came a long way for nothing. We don't know what happened to your sister, and we don't know where Sadik took his army."

Rig met the other man's gaze, held it like a too-firm clasping of arms. "I'm disappointed, I won't deny it. But I'm not quite through. There's one more thing I'd like to know."

"And what's that?"

Rig leaned forward. "I'd like to know if you can give me one good reason why I shouldn't snap your fucking neck."

For a single, quivering moment, all was still. Then Asvin went for his dagger, but Dain beat him to the draw, springing to his feet with blade in hand. They faced each other across the table, coiled like a pair of serpents ready to strike. Rig and Wraith stayed where they were, eyes locked in a deadly embrace. "Expecting that, were you?" Rig asked mildly.

"Putting myself in your place? Aye. But don't mistake that for tucking tail, General."

"I don't give a pig's ass where your tail is at. You betrayed my sister."

"I don't see it like that."

"She came to you in need and you took advantage of her. Forced her to kill for you."

Wraith's mouth twisted wryly. "Never figured you for a sentimental sort. Your sister is a soldier. Killing is part of the business. Besides, it was a fair trade. Her help for mine."

"Help? From what I just heard, it sounds as if you were too busy hunting for the Warlord to be much help." His gaze swivelled to Asvin. "The night of the rescue. How is it that you found yourself on the far side of the camp when my sister was trying to escape with Rodrik?"

Asvin's eyes dropped to his boots.

"That's what I thought. She could have been killed. For all I know, she *was* killed, along with Vel and Rodrik and everyone else who tried to help her."

"I fulfilled my part of the bargain," Wraith said. "Without me, it would have taken her twice as long to find Rodrik, if she found him at all. As for the rest, I did what I had to do. I won't apologise for it."

Rig paused. Then he launched himself across the table, hands grasping the white-hair's throat as they both tumbled backward over Wraith's chair. Rig landed with his knee in the other man's gut, driving the air out of him. He slammed the back of Wraith's head against the floorboards, once, twice, before his left hand snapped out to seize the fist swinging for his temple. He gripped the fist and twisted sharply, feeling a satisfying *crack* that was drowned out by Wraith's howl of pain.

"Stop." Asvin's voice, cutting coolly through the distressed shrieking of the falcon. "I'll open his throat." Rig didn't have to turn around to understand the lay of things.

He hovered over Wraith, their faces barely an inch apart, teeth bared at each other like a pair of wolves. "You're a disgrace," he snarled.

Wraith swivelled his head and spat on the floor. When he turned back, his teeth were pink with blood. "I'm a commander general, same as you. Tough decisions come with the job. Ask me to choose between my people and yours and it's no choice at all. You'd do the same."

"You have no idea what I'd do. The choice is nothing. The tough part is living with the consequences. And this right here? It's a consequence." He slammed his fist into Wraith's nose, opening it like a spigot.

Rig lurched to his feet. "We're done here." He fired a look over his shoulder at Asvin, who still had his blade against Dain's throat. "If you think this wasn't owed, you can go ahead and bloody your hands, but I think you know better. Either way, you spill so much as a drop, it'll be the last thing you ever do."

Asvin lowered his knife. "When you put it that way."

"Just be thankful my sister wasn't the one settling the accounts. I promise you she wouldn't have stopped at a couple of broken bones."

"Oh, I believe you," Asvin said, and strangely enough, he smiled. "Give her my regards, General."

Rig strode through a tense knot of soldiers and Resistance fighters waiting in the yard. He offered no explanation for the noises they must have heard. He just said, "Kingswords," and let his men fall in behind him. One of the Andithyrians started to say something about blindfolds, but a look from Rig silenced her.

He mounted up, pausing to shake out his right hand. Already, his knuckles were turning red; he'd be feeling that for days. Not that he minded one damned bit. He'd have done worse if he didn't need the son of a bitch to keep making trouble behind enemy lines. With the Onnani fleet delayed and the Harrami legions off the table, he needed all the help he could get. So much so, indeed, that he wondered fleetingly if he'd made a mistake. If so, it was the most satisfying mistake he'd ever made.

"Where to, General?" Dain asked.

"North. We'll make camp near the river, then head back to the fort in the morning."

"And after that?"

"After that, we wait. We might not know where the Warlord is, but we damned sure know where he's going."

"Home," Dain said grimly, kicking his horse into a gallop.

TWENTY-FIVE

O nce, when she'd been about fourteen, Alix had ridden through a fever village. She'd been on her way to Karringdon to spend the summer with her aunt, one of Rig's early and swiftly abandoned schemes to have his sister instructed in the art of being a lady. About half a day north of the river, they'd passed through a deserted husk of a town overgrown with weeds. Abandoned, her governess had explained, in the Year of the Great Fever, the fourteen-month nightmare that had claimed the lives of nearly half the population of the Blacklands. Alix recalled it vividly: the crumbling hovels dotting the field like tombstones, the naked bones of the temple with its gaping mouth of a doorway and dark, empty sockets for windows. Even more than the images, she remembered the *feeling* of the place. Eerie. Bitter. Mournful.

Erroman had that same feeling on the morning Alix, Ide, and Vel rode through her gates.

From the road, the city looked the same as always; if anything, it was a little busier than usual. The walls buzzed with more activity, and the guard at the portcullis had been doubled since Alix's departure a month before. But passing through the gates was like entering another world. Lower Town stood empty, gutted of its inhabitants and left to rot like the discarded bones of a fish. Every window, every door was boarded up. The only movement was the occasional rustle of pigeons. So complete was the silence that the clatter of their horses' hooves actually made Alix wince.

Even the palace grounds felt subdued, though the customary bustle of servants moved about the yard. No one took any notice of the three riders. They dismounted on their own, and Ide had to go off in search of a groom to take their horses. But Alix had more pressing concerns, so with a hurried farewell, she left her companions and rushed up the steps of the keep.

She made straight for Erik's study, footfalls ringing down the corridor. A muted bark sounded from the other side of the door; opening it, she was nearly bowled over by ten stone of wolfhound. Rudi yelped excitedly, wagging his nub and dancing about in a circle.

But the wolfhound's greeting would have to wait; a hand on his collar dragged him aside, and then Alix was in her husband's arms. "Thank gods," Liam breathed, clutching her close. "Oh thank you, Virtues." He buried his face in her hair, whispering his thanks over and over.

"Welcome home, Your Highness," said Albern Highmount from somewhere over Liam's shoulder. "I will let you have your privacy." With some difficulty, the chancellor squeezed past the tangled couple and out the door, closing it behind him.

Liam took her face in his hands, grey eyes flitting over her as though he couldn't quite believe she was really there. "When we knew Erik was free, I told myself that it had to mean you were all right. That you'd killed the bloodbinder and were on your way home. But I couldn't be sure. I was so afraid for you . . ." He clasped her to him again.

"And I for you," she said, her voice breaking. "I had so much no news until a few days ago, and then only from an innkeep who sold us some horses. Liam . . ." She pulled back. "He said you almost . . . That Erik almost . . ."

"But he didn't." Liam managed something just short of a smile. "He didn't, thanks to you. You saved us both. Again."

Tears pricked her eyes. She had so much to tell him, but she hardly knew where to begin.

But no, that wasn't true. She knew exactly where to begin. "I love you, Liam. I love you so much . . ."

His eyes were filling now too. He gathered her up again, and there they stayed for the gods knew how long, clinging to each other, whispering all the words of love and regret they'd held in their hearts for the past month.

Liam led her to the upholstered chairs near the window and they curled up together, doing their best to keep Rudi's excited affection at bay. Alix rested her head on her husband's chest, listening to the gradually slowing rhythm of his heart. She let herself bask in his nearness—the warmth of his arms, his voice, his scent—for as long as she dared before forcing herself back to reality. "Erik. I've got to see him."

Liam's voice hummed against her ear. "He'll want to see you too."

"I thought I'd find him here with you and Highmount."

"He doesn't spend much time here these days." Liam paused, as though choosing his next words carefully. "He doesn't spend much time out of his chambers at all. He's . . . different, Allie. You'll see."

She sat up in alarm. "What do you mean, different?"

"No, not like that. He's himself, just . . . well, you'll see. He's still struggling with what happened."

"That's to be expected."

"Maybe, but that doesn't make it any easier to watch. He's torturing himself with guilt, and nothing I say seems to help. Maybe you can get through to him. He listens to you more than anyone."

That had been true once, but now? Alix wasn't so sure. "All I can do is try." She rose and held out her hand, but Liam stayed where he was.

"Maybe it's better if you go alone. I think he'd appreciate having you to himself for a little while." Squeezing her hand, he added, "He needs you more than ever, Allie."

"He's got me. He's got us both."

Liam stood and planted a soft kiss on her forehead. "I'll see you tonight."

"What will you do until then?"

"Oh, you know." He gestured vaguely. "Govern."

Alix smiled. Squeezing his hand one more time, she headed off to find Erik.

At first, her steps were self-assured, purposeful. But as she drew nearer to the ancient oak doors, her gait faltered. She hadn't been here since *that day*, when Pollard and the others had nailed a wooden beam across those doors and sealed the king inside. Her heart tightened painfully at the memory. The look in Erik's eyes, the sound of his voice on the far side of the door. *I would rather have died than see this day . . .*

Erik might need her, but would he truly welcome her after what she'd done? He would *understand*—of that, Alix had no doubt. His head would tell him that she had done what was necessary. But in his heart, he would always carry the knowledge that she was capable of betraying him. How could things ever be the same between them after that?

A pair of royal guardsmen flanked the king's door. They were more than a little surprised to see their captain, but they stood aside wordlessly, recognising her obvious intent. They did not go far, however, and Alix was keenly aware of their eyes on her. They understood only too well the import of the reunion that was about to take place.

She paused, a slight tremor in her hand as it hovered over the door. *You'd think there was a horde of thralls behind that oak panelling.* Steeling herself, she knocked.

"Who is it?"

"It's . . ." Her throat closed over itself. Swallowing, she said, "It's Alix."

Silence.

She wondered if he'd heard. She was about to repeat herself when the door swung open and there he was, standing before her with wide eyes. "By the gods," Erik breathed, "is it really you?"

She might have asked the same. For a moment she couldn't find her voice, as overcome as when she'd first laid eyes on Rodrik. She'd been taken aback by how very much he looked like Erik. Now it was the reverse that shocked her into silence.

He had lost nearly a stone, enough so that it showed in his cheekbones and the set of his eyes. His skin was pale, as though he hadn't set foot out of doors in an age. But it was the week's growth of beard that sealed it, a thick dusting of reddish gold over the too-sharp angles of his jaw—that, and the haunted cast of his gaze, the look of a man who has known true suffering.

What have they done to you? The same words she'd spoken over Rodrik, only this time, she counted herself among those responsible.

Slowly, without really thinking, Alix sank to her knees before her king. Bowing her head, she whispered, "Forgive me."

He made a small, choking sound and grabbed her hand, pulling her to her feet. "Don't you dare," he said, his voice catching. "Don't you dare, Alix."

He threw his arms around her, clutching her as close as Liam had done, and Alix finally broke. All the pain and guilt she'd struggled with for so many weeks—for Erik, for Liam, for Rodrik—came pouring out of her in a rush of bitter grief, and in that moment, she forgot that Erik needed her. *She* was the one who needed *him*, his love and his grace and most of all his forgiveness.

Sinking into his embrace, Alix could feel all those things, and knew they were hers.

"We buried him at Boswyck Valley." Alix's voice still trembled a little, but she forced herself to meet Erik's eye as she spoke.

"How fitting," he murmured. He was quiet for long moments, staring into the hearth. Then he said, "I'm sorry you had to go through that. It must have been terrible for you."

"It was terrible for everyone. Rodrik most of all."

"Still, I'm glad you got to know him a little. I have that, at least."

As though a secondhand memory were any kind of consolation. Alix shook her head bitterly. "I can't tell you how sorry I am."

"Alix." He reached over and took her hand. "Listen to me. What you did for me . . . I cannot even put it into words. Your strength, your loyalty . . ." His fingers tightened around hers. "Nothing I can ever say or do will show you the measure of my gratitude. Know that I will carry it in my heart for the rest of my days."

The words were a balm to her aching soul. Still . . . "I told Rodrik I would get him to Erroman. I *promised* him, Erik. But I couldn't . . ." She trailed off, tears threatening to overtake her again.

Erik smiled sadly. "You are the most formidable person I've ever known, but you cannot control everything."

She blew out a shaking breath, somewhere between a laugh and a sob. "I'm not sure what to make of that coming from you. I've never met anyone who takes more on his shoulders than you do."

"I am king," he said softly, and he shuddered.

Alix paused, taken aback by the strange note of revulsion in his voice. "You *are* king. And a great man."

"A great man." He passed a hand over his eyes. "I wonder, what does that mean?"

"I can tell you what it doesn't mean. A great man isn't infallible, or incapable of being hurt."

"No, but at the very least, he should be able to trust himself."

"You can trust yourself."

Blue eyes met hers, sharp and clear and brimming with pain. "How can you say that after what I've done?"

"You're not responsible for what happened to you. You know that, don't you?"

"On some level, yes. But the fact remains that I nearly burned my own brother at the stake."

Alix went rigid.

"Ah." Erik looked away. "You haven't had the details yet, I see."

"I . . ." She faltered briefly, unable to conceal her shock. "I heard that Liam and the others were nearly executed. I assumed . . ."

"You assumed I would deal with him as I dealt with Tom. But that wasn't good enough for me, you see. I wanted to make a statement with Liam's death, so I decided to burn him at the stake." Erik squeezed his eyes shut, a spasm of pain wracking his features. His hands gripped the arms of his chairs until his knuckles went white. "Did they tell you, Alix? Did they tell you just how close I came to murdering my brother?"

"Not you. It was never you, Erik."

"It doesn't matter . . ."

"Of course it matters!" Alix dropped to her haunches before him. "Now it's your turn to listen to me. The enemy tried to kill Liam. *The enemy*, not you. They used your body as a weapon. You were no more a part of it than if you'd been tied to a chair and forced to watch."

"I know that. I do. And yet somehow . . ." He shook his head.

"Give yourself time."

He sighed. "Time is the one thing we don't have, Alix."

There, she could not argue.

Silence stretched between them. Gradually, a wry smile crept over Erik's face. "Aren't we a pair? What do you say, Captain—shall we agree to absolve one another?"

If only it were that easy. Aloud, she said, "That sounds like a good idea."

He stood and stretched. "I should turn in. As should you. You've had a long journey. Thank you again, Alix." He smiled.

Alix knew the royal mask when she saw it, and this time she wasn't playing along. She put her arms around him, rested her head on his shoulder. "Rodrik asked me to give you a message," she murmured. "He said he'd wait for you in your Domain. He wants you to meet his family."

She felt the air go out of him, felt his shoulders convulse in a silent sob. Alix held him tighter. "You still have family," she said. "Liam loves you. And I love you. Very much, Erik."

Alix held her king until he stopped shaking. It was a long time.

"How is he?"

Alix sighed. "I thought you were asleep."

"I was," Liam said, rolling over. "I heard you pouring your bath."

"Sorry."

"Most wonderful sound I've heard in weeks." He pulled aside the blanket, resting his hand on the empty space beside him. Empty no more. Alix slid into bed, curling her body into his and sighing as if she'd been holding her breath for a month. *I'm home*, she thought, sinking into him in relief. *My bed, my husband. My perfect fit.*

Except it wasn't, not quite. Their customary position pinned her injured arm under her. "Can we roll over?"

He obliged, and Alix tucked up behind him. Yet it still didn't feel right. *You're just not used to it*, she told herself.

But it was more than that. Something lay between them now, a whispering chasm filled with the echoes of bitter words. *Give it time*, Rig had said, but even a month apart hadn't been enough. The distance between them wasn't going to close up on its own; it would have to be bridged somehow.

Alix started to say something, but the words eluded her. She stared at the back of Liam's shoulders, a broad wall of smooth muscle. Silence pooled around them. Then Alix recalled something else her brother had said that day: *Show me a man who doesn't suffer by comparison to Erik White.*

Liam doesn't, Alix had said.

Better make sure he knows you feel that way, Allie.

She bit her lip. Then she said, "Lord Swiftcurrent told me about the speech you made. He said it was incredibly inspiring."

"He's being generous. It wasn't a disaster, but I wouldn't say it was the stuff of legends, either."

"Even so, I'm proud of you." Her arms tightened around him. "I'm so proud of you, Liam."

He rolled over, visibly surprised. It was not the reaction Alix had expected, and it cut her deeply. *Have I really never told him before?* "Thanks," he said. "It means a lot."

She started to squeeze him again, but the motion sent a shock up her arm; she hissed in pain, cradling her injured wrist.

"What's this? Are you hurt?"

"You didn't notice the bandage?"

"Sure, but I didn't realise it was that bad."

"Broken wrist. A roach tramped on it while I was fighting him."

Liam arched an eyebrow. "That must have been some roach. Taking revenge for all his squashed brethren, was he?"

She smiled. "It's what the Andithyrians call their conquerors. Guess I picked up the habit somewhere along the way."

He took her injured hand and kissed her fingers. "How long ago?"

"About a week."

"It'll be a while before you can hold a sword properly."

She growled under her breath. "Wonderful timing, isn't it? Some help I'll be to Erik like this."

"What a pity you have no other useful qualities."

"Sometimes I wonder."

For a moment the conversation seemed destined to spiral into darkness, but Liam wasn't having it. "Are you fishing? Very well, my lady, I'll indulge you." He lay back, folding his hands behind his head and adopting a thoughtful expression. "For one, you're quite clever, or so I'm told. Being something of a dullard myself, I have to rely on the testimony of cleverer types. Also—and this one I've witnessed for myself—you're decisive."

Alix knew she was walking into it, but she asked anyway. "And when exactly did you witness this?"

"Oh, plenty of times. But I think the one that stands out in my mind is the time you grabbed my manhood in the woods."

"*That's* your example?" she laughed, her indignation only half feigned.

"We'd barely exchanged our first kiss," he said with mock wistfullness. "Still in the delicate, tender phases of young romance, and the next thing you know . . ." He gestured below his waist, making a fist.

Alix reached down and grabbed him just as she'd done that night in the woods, delighting in the way his whole body stiffened. "It *is* one of your more useful qualities," she murmured. She watched the desire kindle in his eyes, gripping him firmly until it felt as though she clasped the hilt of a sword.

"See there," he said, "no need to worry. You're ambidextrous."

And just like that, the distance between them seemed insignificant, a divide she could easily conquer with nothing more than her body. Slipping her nightgown over her head, Alix pressed herself against him. She let her hands roam, lingering in the places where their bodies touched, hard against soft. Her lips ghosted along the planes and ridges of his chest. "You're beautiful," she whispered. "You know that, don't you?" He started to answer, but she shifted and let him sink into her, stealing his breath. He closed his eyes, hands gripping her hips until he was buried to the hilt. Alix paused. For a moment she was content just to look at him—the muscled chest, the strong cheekbones, that perfect nose. *Beautiful.* And . . . she laid her hand against his heart, felt its answer against her fingertips. *Beautiful.*

His eyes opened, locked with hers. All thought fled from her. Alix moved against him, slowly at first, then faster, her breath growing ragged in her ears. Her hair cascaded around her, head bent, hand braced against his chest, unable to tear her gaze from the sight of him climbing toward ecstasy. His hands moved to her breasts, but it was his eyes that drove Alix over the edge: the glaze of desire, the flutter of long lashes as he bucked beneath her. Alix moved one last time, gasped, and collapsed against him, feeling his heartbeat hammering against her chest.

"Allie," he whispered. She waited for more, but he seemed to have run out of words.

As for her, she had too many words. So much she needed to say, and no idea where to begin. Silence filled the spaces between gradually slowing breaths. And then he rolled onto his side, and her chance was gone.

Alix fell asleep with her head tucked up against the broad wall of her husband's shoulders.

Twenty-Six

† "**G**eneral."

Rig looked up, expecting bad news, but the expression on Dain Cooper's face was merely apprehensive. "Message from the capital," he said, holding out a pair of scroll cases. "Two, actually."

Rig reached for them with all the enthusiasm of a man taking the lead of a vicious dog. *Dear gods, please don't let it be bad news.* But when he unfurled the first scroll and saw the familiar, tidy script, he nearly collapsed in relief. "It's from Erik." Scanning the page, he added, "He's recovered."

"Thank the Virtues," Dain said. "And the commander?"

"He's fine," Rig said. "Highmount and Rona Brown too. Though"—his brows gathered—"there's not much detail here."

Dain whispered a prayer of thanks in Onnani, glancing briefly to the ceiling. "What exactly does it say, if you don't mind me asking?"

"Damnably little. Basically, it's just the king telling me he's well and thanking me for my foresight in suggesting the evacuation of Erroman." Rig put Erik's note aside and took up the second scroll case. "Looks like this one's from Highmount." *Probably wants to confirm the authenticity of Erik's note, just in case.* A sensible precaution. Though the previous letter unmistakably came from Erik, Rig would have no way of knowing whether the king was genuinely free of the blood-bond, absent independent confirmation from Liam or the chancellor. "Bloody hells," he murmured as he read. Dain remained dutifully silent until Rig elaborated. "Alix and the others must have found Rodrik, but only in the nick of time. Says here that Liam was a matter of moments away from being . . . *Bloody hells!*"

"General?"

Reading aloud, Rig said, "'His Highness was very nearly taken from us, but fortunately, the kingdom was spared that sorrow.'" He snorted and balled up the letter. "Albern sodding Highmount. 'The kingdom was spared that sorrow.' I imagine Alix and Erik would have taken it badly as well, not to mention Liam himself."

"I've never met the chancellor, but from what I hear, he's not known for being sentimental."

"I've come across hailstones with more warmth." Rig started to add more, but a knock interrupted him. "Come."

He didn't recognise the soldier at his door. "Beg your pardon, General, but a messenger just arrived from the west. Says it's urgent."

Rig and Dain exchanged a grim look. "Who's the ranking scout?" Rig asked.

"Lady Kerta Middlemarch. She's waiting for you in the yard."

The name hadn't meant much to him, but Rig recognised the woman as soon as he saw her, standing in a corner of the yard with Commander Wright and the messenger. She was one of Alix's former unit, and one of only three survivors of the failed mission to Harram. He hadn't realised she was a Middlemarch, though he should have guessed from her prim carriage that she was highborn. "Lady Middlemarch," he said, acknowledging her with a nod. "A friend of my sister's, aren't you?"

She coloured a little, pleased to be recognised. "Yes, General. An honour to meet you at last."

"I gather we've news from the west?"

"From the scouting post, yes." Nodding at the messenger, she said, "Tell the commander general what you've just told me."

"It's the enemy," the messenger said, wide-eyed and breathless. A mere boy, he was—sixteen at most. *Are we plucking such green fruit now?* Rig thought wearily. "They've crossed the border, General. A host of five thousand."

The boy paused as though bracing for an emotional outburst, but Rig just sighed and raked at his beard. He'd been expecting this news for weeks. If anything, he was surprised it had taken this long.

"There's our missing five thousand," Wright said.

"Where did they cross?"

"The Blacklands," said Lady Middlemarch. "The same place as before, from the mountains. They must have used the western ford."

"Meaning the Harrami tribes gave them free passage again." Rig shook his head in disgust. All this time he'd been worrying that the Harrami weren't helping, but he'd been wrong. They were helping, all right—just the wrong side."

"I have to admit, General, I'm surprised," Middlemarch said. "I was with His Majesty and Lady Alix in the Broken Mountains, and the tribe that took us captive considered it their sworn duty to defend their territory from foreigners. King Erik barely managed to negotiate our release, and only then by persuading the village council that the Oridians were a threat. It seems strange that the tribes would let Sadik's men through a second time."

"Strange or not, it's the only explanation." Not that it mattered anyway. Whichever route they'd come by, the Oridians were here. "What about the garrison I posted at the ford?"

"Completely overrun," the messenger said, dropping his gaze. "That's why you didn't get a pigeon, General. There was no one left to send it."

"May they find peace in their Domains," Wright said gravely.

"I take it the news comes from a returning scouting party?" Rig asked.

Lady Middlemarch nodded. "They spotted the enemy in the woods south of Greenhold. When they rode back to the garrison to report it, they found nothing but a smouldering ruin."

"When was this?"

"Two days ago. The attack must have been two days before that, given the enemy's location when they were spotted."

"Disposition?"

She shook her head. "The forest was too dense, but the scouts estimate at least half cavalry."

I'll bet it's more than that. If Rig were leading a small host across the border, he'd want as many horses as possible.

"Host of five thousand, half on foot . . ." Dain looked skyward, calculating. "Reckon that puts them somewhere north of Boswyck Valley now, assuming they're headed for Erroman."

"A safe bet," Rig said.

"But it makes no sense, General," said Commander Wright. "Why send such a small host? They can't hold any significant territory with that. Why not invade in force?"

"Because," Rig said, "it's not an invasion, not yet. It's a trap."

"Definitely a trap," Dain agreed. "But do we have any choice?"

"None at all. That's what makes it a good trap. There's nothing standing between that host and the capital. Even assuming Erroman has the manpower to repel them, we don't dare let the enemy chip away at the walls. Too many weak spots as it is. On top of which, if I know the Warlord, they'll have orders to loot and burn along the way. That leaves me no choice but to intercept."

"Leaving the border underdefended," Wright finished grimly. "I see."

"That's why Sadik broke camp," Rig said, thinking aloud. "He wants to keep us guessing. With his forces unaccounted for, we've no way of knowing whether he'll hit the fort or the citadel." *Or both,* he amended darkly. The Warlord had the manpower to make it happen.

"What are you orders, General?" Dain asked, sounding remarkably calm for a man whose homeland was about to be conquered.

"Three battalions."

The messenger paled. Lady Middlemarch's eyes widened. Wright said, "You don't intend to defeat them, then."

"Can't hope to, not unless I pull major resources off the border, and that's just what Sadik wants. Best I can do is slow them down for a while, give the capital time to prepare." It reminded him all too much of last spring when he'd ridden out of Blackhold with a paltry force of Blackswords, just enough to keep the enemy busy while his household got to safety. "We'll

THE BLOODSWORN · 249

tie up that host as long as possible, then wait for Sadik to make the next move. That's the only way I'll know where and when to redeploy."

"Wish we knew how many horses with them," Dain said.

"You and me both, but there's nothing to be done." Turning to Middlemarch, Rig said, "Pick your best. You're with me. Wright, I'll need you here, along with Rollin. If Sadik comes at you—"

"We will give him the fight of his life," Wright said solemnly.

"Bollocks. I'll not have you or any man throw his life away on a fool's errand. We're too few as it is. If you think you can hold out, fine. Otherwise, retreat. We'll regroup north of here."

"As you wish, General."

"As for you, Commander," he said, turning to Dain, "fancy a promotion? I'm in the market for a new second. I'm sure Liam won't mind."

Dain flushed, his gaze dropping briefly to his boots. He would be the first man of Onnani blood ever to hold a post of such rank, and he knew it. But when he looked up, he just smiled. "Thought you'd never ask."

They rode hard all afternoon and much of the night, stopping only when the moon was high. It helped that Rig knew the terrain nearly as well as he knew his own lands, and had taken the trouble to clear a makeshift road along the Gunnar, the better to reposition his forces in haste. The enemy would be hampered by the dense woods and steep slopes of Boswyck Valley, obliged to swing north in order to reach open terrain. Rig, meanwhile, led his forces almost due east, hitting the Imperial Road shortly after dawn and bearing north at speed. If they moved fast enough, they could intercept on a terrain of Rig's choosing. That came at a cost, however, for it meant there was no time to send scouts ahead. Rig would be going in blind. It was a gamble he had no choice but to make.

They came upon the enemy host deep in the Greenlands, stretched out in a wide, well-defended column.

"They're expecting us," Kerta Middlemarch announced, quite unnecessarily.

"Trap," Rig reminded her. Swivelling in his saddle, he

raised his arm, calling his men to a halt. When he turned back, he caught Middlemarch surveying the Kingsword column with a troubled expression. Doubtless she was having difficulty imagining what Rig could possibly accomplish with fifteen hundred men. *Plenty*, he answered inwardly. *Not enough.*

"You've timed it well, General," Dain said, lowering his longlens. "If we send the horse archers ahead, they can position along the bluff over there."

"That's the idea," Rig said, and with a whistle and a wave, he sent them on. "I want some longbows up there too."

"Aye, General." Dain cantered down the line to pass on the order.

"How long do you think we can hold them?" Middlemarch asked.

"Depends. If they've got enough cavalry, this could be the shortest battle in history. Best-case scenario, no more than half a day. Should be enough time for word to reach Erroman, and that's about the most I can hope for." That, and to live long enough to command the surviving Kingswords in the final battle.

One step at a time, Black.

"They're closing ranks, General," Middlemarch said, pointing.

"Get to the rear lines, scout. See you at the far end." So saying, he slammed his visor down, drew his sword, and kicked his horse.

They came at the enemy in a classic pinching manoeuvre, splitting the cavalry in half and riding out wide. The flank wouldn't work, of course—the enemy was ready for that—but the Oridians would be forced to turn to meet the charge, exposing their rear to the archers on the bluff.

Rig rode flat against Alger's neck, sword arm cocked and ready, eyes misting in the wind and dust. Ahead, he could see the Oridian ranks break open as the enemy commander general sent his cavalry surging forth. *One column . . . two, three . . .* And they kept coming, too many to count, too many to fight.

Too many. The battle had not yet begun, but it was already over.

The grim reality sank like a stone to the bottom of Rig's

belly. At least half cavalry, the scouts had told him. Rig had guessed it would be more; it was what he would have done. Still, he'd hoped to be wrong. *So much for making it to the final battle.* He'd gambled, as he so often did. But this time, he'd lost.

There, you see, Vel? Eldora doesn't fancy me after all. He'd taken risk after risk in this war; it was bound to catch up with him eventually. Now that it had, he felt strangely at peace with it.

The enemy cavalry was headed straight for them. Rig glanced beside him, buoyed by the sight of his men streaking alongside, lances glinting in the afternoon sun. At least they would die bravely. He'd never had much care for glory, but there was a beauty to their charge that he hoped to carry with him to the afterlife.

He started to point with his sword, to issue a final, futile command, when the crimson wall of horseflesh bearing down on him swerved suddenly. Rig sat back, hauling on Alger's reins and watching in astonishment as the enemy horse peeled away, slowing to a trot at the edge of the field.

What in the Nine Hells? And then Rig saw the banners. Or rather, he didn't: The Oridian cavalry had lowered their standard, and as he watched, a crimson-clad knight separated himself from the others, walking his horse out toward Rig with the golden trident of Oridia dangling at his side. There, in full view of the whole battlefield, he tossed it to the ground. Behind him, his men put up their lances. He was standing them down.

The enemy cavalry was *standing down.*

Rig looked up at the bluff, but the Kingsword horse archers hadn't even moved yet. The other half of Rig's pinching manoeuvre had continued the charge; Kingsword cavalry ploughed into the enemy infantry in a crash of spears and horseflesh. The Oridians had more than enough horses to protect their footmen; there was no reason for the enemy cavalry to stand down. *Unless he's abandoning his comrades, just as the Raven did at Boswyck Valley . . .*

Oridian horns blared, urgently summoning their cavalry to the defence of the infantry, but still the enemy horse did not stir. Rig glanced back at the cavalry commander, met his gaze from across the field. Slowly, deliberately, the crimson knight inclined his head. There was no mistaking it—he *was* surrendering. But why?

Some kind of trap, maybe, even more elaborate than the one they'd been expecting? But no—that made no sense. A moment ago, the enemy had been certain of victory. Now, as Rig watched, their infantry was being overrun by Kingsword cavalry. *This must be how Sadik felt when the Raven stood down at Boswyck.* Surprised. Confused. But the Warlord hadn't hesitated, and Rig didn't dare hesitate now.

He signalled to the horse archers. They poured down the slope en masse, while behind them the longbows loosed their shafts in a high arc to rain down on the rear columns of Oridian infantry. Rig kicked Alger into action, his men following hard at his heels. They broke over the enemy foot in a thundering wave, carving a bloody trench through their middle while the horse archers scoured the rear. Punching through the far side, Rig pivoted, preparing for another pass. The infantry lines had shattered under the Kingsword assault. Half were in full retreat; they would be easy prey now.

Just as Rig was about to order a second charge, the Oridian cavalry commander rode hard across their view. For half a heartbeat, Rig feared he'd been duped after all, but no—the Oridian knight had the golden trident in hand again, upside down in the symbol of surrender, waving it frantically for all to see. The battle slowed, Kingswords and Oridians alike distracted by the spectacle of the crimson knight cantering up and down the lines, brandishing his upside-down flag. Having secured everyone's attention, the knight turned his horse toward Rig and hurled the trident like a spear. It arced through the air to impale the ground barely a stride in front of Alger's hooves.

"General Black!" The crimson knight's voice rang out over the dwindling sounds of battle. "I did not stand my men down to be slaughtered!" He spoke in Oridian, with a highborn accent.

Rig raised a hand, and those Kingswords who had not already put up their weapons did so. A few of the enemy took the opportunity to break and flee, but otherwise the battlefield stood still, as though time itself had been frozen.

Rig crossed the field at a trot, drawing up his horse before the crimson knight. The man was impressive up close: tall and straight-backed, gold filigree on his breastplate and gauntlets tooled to resemble eagle talons. His visor was down, but a pair of keen blue eyes stared out through the slat. "No one attacked your unit," Rig said in Oridian, gesturing at the enemy cavalry. "There they stand, unmolested. These, on the other hand"—he indicated the infantry around them—"continued to fight until a moment ago. What would you have me do?"

Before the other man could answer, one of his comrades rode up and barked something at him, gesturing angrily at the confused knot of soldiers behind them. He wore fancy armour too—a nobleman like the crimson knight, and higher ranking, judging from the golden trident adorning his cape. The commanding officer, Rig guessed. The two men argued—in a heated undertone at first, rising in pitch until the newcomer cried, "You disgrace the Trionate, Corren!"

"The Trionate has disgraced itself."

"You self-righteous—"

"The thing is done. You're free to follow your own conscience, Hictor, as I must follow mine." Raising his voice for the benefit of his men, the crimson knight said formally, "General Black, I hereby offer my surrender, and that of my men. I ask that you grant amnesty for all who seek it. We are in your power."

Rig glanced over the battlefield and realised it was true. Somehow, impossibly, they *were* in his power, an enemy force more than three times the strength of his own. If not for this man, the Kingswords would have been slaughtered. Instead they were victorious, and as an added bonus, they'd just secured several battalions of desperately needed horseflesh. "Not to sound ungrateful," Rig said, eyeing the man called Corren warily, "but *why*?"

"I don't owe you an explanation, General," the crimson knight said coolly. "My officers know why I have done this, and they alone have the right to ask. In any case, now is hardly the time. Do you accept my surrender?"

Luck is not a Holy Virtue, Vel had once told him. At that moment, Rig wasn't so sure.

Dain Cooper appeared, weaving his horse through the

Kingsword ranks to draw up at Rig's side. "Is this what I think it is?" he asked incredulously. Like most of the Kingswords, he didn't speak enough Oridian to follow the exchange.

"Believe it or not," Rig murmured, "it is. Stand by." Switching back to Oridian, he said, "I accept your surrender. Those who lay down their arms will not be harmed. But I can't simply let you go free on Aldenian soil. I am duty-bound to place you under arrest and escort you to Erroman. Do you agree to those terms?"

The crimson knight inclined his head. "But know this: Neither I nor any man under my command shall bear arms against the Trionate, nor betray secrets that may result in the deaths of our countrymen."

"Fair enough," Rig said. To the other officer, the one called Hictor, he said, "And what about you? Like your countryman here, I've seen enough bloodshed for a lifetime. But if you fancy some more, say the word." He rested his hand on the hilt of his sword. Taking the cue, Dain raised his hand, preparing to give a signal to the Kingswords behind him.

The Oridian's face twisted into a snarl of impotent rage. "What choice do I have? Without cavalry, my men are little more than fodder for your horses."

"Glad we worked that out." Turning to Dain, Rig said, "Disarm them. No thieving, no beating."

"Understood."

The Kingswords set to work. In spite of Rig's promise, there were a few scuffles, and one Oridian foot soldier succeeded in getting himself run through resisting disarmament. Fine words notwithstanding, not all of Corren's men, and fewer still of Hictor's, were happy about surrendering to the enemy. But the job got done, and by sunset, they were heading back down the Imperial Road toward Pir, fifteen hundred Kingswords forming a ring around five thousand Oridians on foot. Only Corren was permitted to keep his mount; he rode at Rig's side, a place of honour.

"What you said earlier, about not owing me an explanation." Rig glanced over at the other man. He'd removed his helm, revealing a middle-aged man with hair as black as Rig's, except where it was dusted with silver. Seen from a few paces away, they might have passed for father and son. "You're right, you don't owe me one, but . . ."

A thin smile passed over Corren's face. "But you would hear it anyway."

"If you're willing to tell me."

Corren was silent for long enough that Rig figured he wouldn't answer. Then he said, "Do you know much of our religion, General?"

"Some. I know you worship the Three: Birth, Life, and Death. I know Varad is meant to be the mortal incarnation of Life, and the Priest and the Warlord represent Birth and Death. That's about it."

Corren nodded. "Of the Three, Birth is the most revered, because she alone has the power to create. But something cannot come from nothing, even for a goddess. In order to bestow her gifts, she requires the energy of mortals."

"She needs worshippers, you mean."

"Our devotion is what makes all this possible," he said, gesturing at the fields around him.

"Forgive me, Commander, but what does this have to do with you throwing down your banners?"

"The war began as a holy undertaking, to convert souls to the true religion."

"So they tell me. Except Alden is the fourth country on your list. Your goddess must be very hungry, Commander."

"You misunderstand. The goddess doesn't consume our souls, she transforms them. As a blacksmith moulds molten steel, so the goddess harnesses the raw material of our souls to forge new life, and in so doing, preserves our energy within the sacred cycle of the Three. At the end of my life, the goddess will lie with Death. In return, he will release my energy to her, and through the goddess's power I will be reborn. As a man, perhaps. Or as grass, or as a deer. Do you see?"

Rig didn't see, and he was losing patience. He should have known asking too many questions would only earn him a lecture on religion. *Bloody zealots. They're even worse than the Onnani.*

"This only happens because I'm a believer," Corren went on. "When *your* life is over, General Black, Death will claim you, as he claims us all. But the goddess will not come to him to retrieve your energy, and so you will not be reborn. You will drift for eternity. You will be *nothing*. Lost to the sacred cycle, for your energy won't contribute to new life. A tragedy for you, and for us all. Do you see now? Conversion is not about strengthening the goddess, it's about saving souls. There can be no more righteous quest." Corren looked away. "Or so I believed."

"But you don't believe it anymore."

He sighed. "Saving souls is a righteous quest, but I'm no longer convinced that's what we're doing. The Priest is dead, and the King. Only the Warlord is left, and I do not believe he fights for souls. He fights for his own greed and bloodlust, and I will not be a part of it, even if it means being branded a traitor. As you said earlier, there has been too much death already."

Rig nodded slowly, he understood now. "A hard choice. You have my respect, Commander." Somehow, he doubted that was much consolation.

They rode on in silence, Rig turning the conversation over in his mind. Since learning of the spy in his ranks, he'd lost hours of sleep wondering what could prompt a man to betray his own country. Here, at least, was a possible answer. *Could it be something like that? Someone who legitimately believes he's doing the right thing?*

A cloud of dust down the road interrupted Rig's reverie: a rider moving at speed. Shielding his eyes, Corren said, "One of yours, General?"

"Must be." Rig cantered out ahead, Kerta Middlemarch falling in beside him.

"One of our scouts," she said. "Heading from the border, looks like. This can't be good news."

"No," Rig said grimly, "it can't."

TWENTY-SEVEN

† *Brother, please . . .*
Erik's eyes snapped open. A shower of sparks swirled against stone, sending tongues of flame leaping out from stacked timber.

"No!"

He lunged at the inferno, knowing it was already too late . . .

The clatter of an iron poker hitting the floor jarred Erik from the dream. A serving girl stood by the hearth, eyes wide with terror. "Forgive me, sire!" She dropped into a curtsey. "The fire was cold . . . I thought you would want . . . Forgive me!"

Erik sagged back against the bed, drawing deep, ragged breaths. By the time he opened his eyes again, the serving girl had fled. He stayed where he was for long moments, letting his pulse slow. Then he rolled to his feet and padded across the cold stone floor. The water in the washbasin was cold too; the serving girl had not had a chance to add hot water before he had frightened her off. Just as well—the water was bracing, throwing off the last cobwebs of sleep.

Sleep. Erik smiled wryly at himself in the looking glass. How long had it been since he had truly slept? Judging from the hollowed-out face staring back at him, it had been a long time indeed. He looked down at his bare chest. That too looked like someone else's, someone not nearly as fit. Nothing about the man in the mirror looked as it should.

He shaved. A superficial gesture, but it helped; the face in the looking glass was younger now, not quite so shadowed. Erik tied his hair back and dressed, choosing a particularly splendid doublet. That helped too. But what truly put the steel back in his spine was opening the door to find a familiar figure waiting for him. "Good morning, Alix," he said, and the words were better than any tonic.

Her hazel eyes lit up when she saw him. "You look refreshed. I was worried. The serving girl left in . . . something of a hurry."

"Poor thing. I gave her quite a fright, I think."

Her gaze was sympathetic. "Nightmare?"

"The nightmare is over," he said, squeezing her shoulder. "Whatever comes, we're together again, all of us. I understand more than ever what that's worth."

She laid a hand over his. "Ready?"

"Not remotely," he said with a weary smile, "but I have you to help me."

He headed for the study, Alix's footfalls matching his, her presence a shield at his back. With each step, he felt stronger. His tread grew bolder, his gaze more keenly focused. All along the corridor, servants and attendants paused in their work. Erik felt their eyes on him, sensed the subtle current of hope running between them as they watched their king and his bodyguard stride past.

They turned a corner to find Raibert Green on his way out of the study. "Blessed Farika," he said, his kind face breaking into a smile. "There's a sight to soothe the soul."

"It's good to see you, my friend," Erik said, clasping his arm warmly.

Green held out his arm to Alix next, but she brushed it aside and embraced him. "It's been too long."

Green sighed. "I have much to answer for. To you especially, Lady Alix. I should have realised. I should have—"

"Rubbish," she said. "You couldn't have known. As ever, you did what you thought was right."

Green was not convinced; he looked away, pursing his lips. *Regrets and more regrets*, Erik thought. *None of us is spared.*

Aloud, he said, "We move forward. There is too much ahead to waste time looking back."

Wonderful advice, Your Majesty. You might consider following it yourself. The voice in his head was Tom's; Erik could almost picture his brother standing there, smiling wryly. There was no magic here, only a memory—but in a way that was worse, for unlike the bloodbond, it could never be banished.

They found Liam and Highmount in the study, as expected. Liam was seated behind the desk, but he sprang to his feet when Erik entered. "Sorry," he said, colouring. "We weren't . . . er . . ."

"Weren't expecting me." Erik made a dismissive gesture. "It's fine, brother. It looks good on you." He summoned his most charming smile.

"Not a very comfortable chair," Liam said. "Metaphorically, I mean. Physically, it's tops, obviously. Really nice, er, cushion . . ." He grimaced, glancing skyward. "I'll stop talking now."

Erik laughed. It was as if they had gone back in time and the man before him was the old Liam, the awkward scout who could never quite meet the king's eye. *Here's a fellow I haven't seen in a while*, he started to say—before realising how bitterly ironic that would be coming from him.

Rudi trotted over, sniffing at the newcomer. Erik took an involuntary step back. His last encounter with Liam's dog had nearly cost him a hand. But the wolfhound just wagged his nub and lapped at Erik's fingers in greeting. "Are we friends again?" Erik murmured, scratching his ears. For some reason, that comforted him.

He sat, motioning for the others to do the same. Rudi flopped down at his boots. Alix started to take her customary place in the corner, but Erik stayed her with a gesture. "Take a seat, Captain. I need advisors more than I need bodyguards today."

Alix and Liam exchanged a look of profound relief. Highmount stroked his beard approvingly. Erik pretended not to notice.

"We have had a message from Lord Black this morning," Highmount said. "He had word from the Blacklands yesterday: The garrison in the foothills was overrun a little less than a week ago."

Erik closed his eyes briefly. "So it has begun."

"Afraid so," Liam said.

A breath of despair rippled through Erik, like wind through wheat. If the enemy had invaded the Blacklands, it meant they had crossed through Harram. Again. *If only you hadn't failed in Ost . . .* But he had, spectacularly. Not only had the Harrami king refused to help, Erik's appeals had obviously fallen on deaf ears among the mountain tribes as well, for they had let the enemy pass through their lands a second time. "How many?"

"Five thousand," Liam said. "Rig has ridden out to intercept."

"What about the border?" Alix asked.

"He left as many men as he could," Liam said, "but he didn't dare let the enemy head this way unchallenged."

"Five thousand." Alix frowned. "That's no invasion. It sounds like a trap."

"To me too," Liam said. "But neither of us has anything to tell your brother about tactics. If we smell a trap, you can bet he did too. I'm sure he knows what he's doing."

There was a stretch of silence. Erik could feel their eyes on him. *They look to you, Your Majesty. Don't keep them waiting.* But Erik had no words of wisdom to impart, still less a decision. He settled for a relevant question. "Whom did he leave in command of the fort?"

"Rollin." A bemused expression came over Liam's face. "Meanwhile, he commandeered my second. Promoted him to adjunct commander."

Alix's eyebrows flew up. "Dain Cooper?"

"A shrewd move," Highmount declared, "given our urgent need of Onnani support."

Erik doubted very much that Rig had had politics in mind, but Highmount was right—they needed to contact the Onnani straightaway. That much, at least, was clear to him. "Send a message to First Speaker Kar. Let him know the enemy has crossed the border and a full-scale invasion is imminent. It's now or never. The fleet may not be ready, but they have foot soldiers, and we need them now."

"If I might suggest," Liam put in, "send one to Speaker Syril as well."

"Syril?" Erik frowned; the name meant nothing to him.

"His voice carries weight in the Republicana, especially

with those who've been reluctant to get behind the war effort."
Turning to Highmount, Liam added, "I can help with the draft-
ing, if you'd like. I think I know how to get through to him.
We'll have to be discreet, of course—we don't want to get Kar's
feathers in a ruffle—but I have an idea how we can manage that
too."

Highmount could not have looked more astonished if Liam
had casually announced he could fly.

"It seems as though your time in Onnan has paid divi-
dends, brother," Erik said. "Well done."

The look that crossed Liam's face was somewhere between
pride and pain. "Thanks," he mumbled awkwardly. "That
means a lot, coming from you." He looked like he wanted to
say more, but thought better of it.

"The message from Rig," Alix said. "It came by pigeon?"

Liam nodded. "He sent it just before he rode out. Two days
ago, by the looks of things."

"Meaning he rode into battle yesterday." Her gaze fell to
her lap.

She was right, Erik knew. Even as they sat here talking, her
brother could be lying dead in a field somewhere north of
Boswyck Valley.

"I'm sure he's fine, Allie," Liam said. "Rig knows how to
handle these things."

"He's bought us precious time," Erik added. "All we can do
now is make sure it doesn't go to waste." He said it with all the
conviction he could muster, but it sounded hollow even to him.
Feeble, Your Majesty, said the voice in his head that sounded
like Tom.

They were looking at him again, waiting. "Well," Erik
said. "Let's get those letters off to Onnan."

"I guess you'll want Ambassador Corse in here straightaway?" Liam asked.

Erik looked at him blankly.

"I second that recommendation," Highmount said. "He
would certainly take it ill if we contacted his capital without
informing him."

"Yes," Erik said, "of course. I should have mentioned that."
So why hadn't he?

Highmount nodded and withdrew. Liam, meanwhile, hovered. "Er," he said.

"Yes?"

"I just thought maybe . . . when you're done with the ambassador . . ." He shifted on his feet. "Maybe you might want to join me on the walls? See what we've done with the defences? I mean, there was only so much we could manage, but you should probably have a look. On top of which, I guess it would be a good idea for people to see us together, after . . . you know." He scratched the back of his neck awkwardly.

"That sounds like a very sensible suggestion, Liam." So sensible, indeed, that Erik was horrified he hadn't thought of it himself.

"Good. I'll, um . . . leave you to it, then." He departed, but not before throwing a worried look over his shoulder.

Erik swore under his breath.

"Give it time," Alix said gently. "You'll find your rhythm soon enough."

"Will I?" He closed his eyes, but all he saw was Tom's face.

"Of course," she said, sounding just as feeble as her king.

Erik decided to turn in early that evening, and Alix didn't discourage him. He'd struggled to make it through the day; he needed his rest. In public, he had largely managed to keep the royal mask in place, smiling and nodding as he received the inevitable stream of well-wishers. But in the moments between, when they were alone, he'd sagged in his chair, head cradled in his hands. Liam had spoken of his brother's pain, of the guilt he suffered for what he'd almost done. But it was the doubt that truly crippled him, Alix knew. She told herself it was only natural after what he'd been through, but the truth was, it terrified her. Though Liam had done an admirable job of keeping things running—better than she would have imagined—Alden needed her king, now more than ever.

Such were her thoughts when she nearly collided with a priestess.

"Sorry," she said, steadying herself against the wall. "Had my head down."

"Heavy thoughts," Vel said.

"Heavier than I've ever known."

"Do you wish to discuss it? Perhaps I can help." This in the priestess voice, her dark eyes full of wisdom and empathy.

"Thank you, but I'm not sure I have the energy just now." Anxious to change the subject, she added, "What about you, are you finding your way all right?"

"I am utterly lost, in fact. Figuratively and literally." Vel scowled at the walls, as if they were to blame.

"It's overwhelming, I know. We're down to a skeleton crew at the moment or Arnot would have assigned someone to you."

"I heard. Most of the capital has been evacuated, they tell me. That accounts for the streets being so deserted when we arrived yesterday. I had wondered."

Alix smiled. "Probably not the Erroman you imagined."

"This place . . ." Vel's gaze roamed over the corridor. "It occupies so much of my people's folklore, good and bad. I'm not sure what I expected it to be, but . . ."

"Disappointed?"

"That is hardly the word." Vel reached for one of the windows, fingertips dusting across the etched glass. "I have never been any place like this. The finery, the courtly manners . . ." Her eyes met Alix's briefly before dropping to the floor. "Is this how you grew up? Is this . . . ?"

Alix understood what she was asking. *Is this where he comes from?* "Not quite. Blackhold was never as grand as this, and I didn't spend much time at court growing up. Rig was here more often, as you can imagine."

"I can't, in fact. For someone like me, this world exists only in fables." She was silent for a moment, her gaze abstracted. Then she drew herself up proudly. "Except fables aren't real, least of all those where the handsome prince runs off with the scullery maid. Or a banner lord with an Onnani priestess."

Alix regarded the other woman with a mix of sympathy and respect. "Vel—"

"Don't." She held up a hand. "I knew what I was getting into, and your brother made no promises."

Alix sighed. "There's something you should know. About Rig . . ."

Vel's lips pressed together grimly. She waited.

"We received a message from the front. He rode into battle yesterday. We've had no news, and I . . ." She faltered. The past year had done much to harden her against the fear of her brother falling in battle—or at least, to equip her to put it out of her mind temporarily. But discussing it with Vel somehow stripped away all her defences, perhaps because she was beginning to suspect that this woman loved her brother nearly as much as she did.

Vel drew a breath. Then: "Will you pray with me, sister?"

"I'm not sure even the gods can protect him now."

"It is not their protection we seek, but their blessing. The Holy Virtues do not control our fate, Alix. They help us to make the right choices, and to cope with the consequences. To be our best selves, if you will."

Alix nodded slowly, processing that. "In that case, I will gladly pray with you." If anything happened to Rig, she would need all the help she could get.

She led Vel to the sitting room of her chambers, where they knelt before the hearth. Alix bowed her head and listened to the rise and fall of the priestess's voice, a soothing melody against the gentle crackling of the fire.

Thus did Liam find them. "Oh," he said. "Hi."

"This is Daughter Vel," Alix said, rising. "You remember."

"Right. Well, you should probably hear this too, then."

Alix steadied herself against the hearth.

"Rig's fine. Well . . . not fine, obviously, but alive. That's the good news." Liam paused, shifting on his feet. "I'm afraid there's more."

"The trap?" Alix was amazed how level her voice sounded. She'd known this was coming—they all had—but even so, the confirmation should have turned her guts to water. Instead, she felt a grim sort of resignation.

"The citadel has fallen. The fort too. It was a trap all right, but it looks like Sadik's plan wasn't to weaken the border, just to take Rig out of play."

"Which is exactly what he did." Alix moved mechanically to the table and took up the wine jug, only a slight tremor in her hands betraying the fear that lurked below the surface. "They've crossed the border, then?"

"Twenty thousand strong, the bulk of them making their way up the Imperial Road."

"Well," Alix said. "There it is."

She went to replace the wine jug, but it slipped through numb fingers and smashed, scattering bloody droplets everywhere. A dark red pool spread over the polished stone. Liam knelt to gather up shards of earthenware, but Alix just stood there, transfixed, watching the bloodred stain crawl between the cracks.

TWENTY-EIGHT

✝ "What do we know?" Erik said, stitching his hands on the table before him. He looked calm, decisive, but Alix knew better. Beneath the royal mask, he was as uncertain as ever—which was why he'd balked at Liam's suggestion to convene the council that morning. *I'm not ready for that*, he'd confided to her quietly. So they had compromised on inviting Rona Brown and Raibert Green to join their inner circle.

"We had another pigeon this morning," Liam said, "just after dawn. Rig is heading up the Imperial Road as we speak."

"And the enemy?" Highmount asked.

"Holding position just north of the citadel, waiting to regroup with the forces that attacked the fort. That'll give Rig a healthy head start, on top of which, he reckons he can move at least twice the speed of the enemy."

"That sounds about right," Alix said. "Small force, minimal supply train—he should outpace Sadik easily."

"Meaning what?" Green asked. "How long until he reaches Erroman?"

Erik looked to Alix. As a scout, she'd been trained to estimate such things, but she'd never had to factor in escorting a captured enemy force. "I honestly don't know. If it was a host of Kingswords . . . about a week, if Rig pushes them hard. But it all depends on how cooperative those captured Oridians are. If they refuse to march at speed . . ."

"We'll assume ten days for now," Erik said, "and hope for better. Rig's next message should help us narrow it down."

"What about numbers?" asked Rona Brown. "Do we know how many Kingswords survived the attacks?"

"Not yet," Liam said. "A few survivors from Pir have joined up with Rig, and more are apparently on the way, but no word from the fort."

"I saw those defences," Alix said. "They wouldn't have been able to hold out for long."

"Let us hope they had the sense to retreat," Highmount said. "They can do more good regrouping with us than throwing their lives away guarding a pile of timber."

Alix regarded the chancellor coolly. It irked her more than a little that he, of all people, would presume to second-guess her brother. "If I know Rig, those are precisely the orders he left. He has no delusions of glory. If the cause was hopeless, he wouldn't waste the men."

"Agreed," Erik said, "assuming he had a choice. Does he mention it in the letter?"

Liam shook his head. "That's all we know, I'm afraid."

"Actually," said Highmount, "not quite. There is a new development, Your Majesty, which may change matters profoundly." He paused, keen eyes doing a rapid tour of the table. "Before I continue, I must be assured of your absolute discretion, my lords."

Alix frowned. Rona Brown and Raibert Green shifted in their seats. Even Liam recognised the chancellor's impertinence, cutting an awkward glance at Erik. Highmount would never have spoken so presumptuously before the king's ordeal. "Assurances of that nature are mine to demand, Chancellor," Erik said coolly.

"Forgive me, Your Majesty. A bad habit I acquired during your illness." After a suitably contrite pause, Highmount said, "With your permission, sire?" At a gesture from Erik, he called, "Nevyn, if you please."

The door opened to admit the royal bloodbinder.

An uncomfortable hush descended over the king's study. Nevyn himself looked ill at ease, walking with his head bowed, acutely aware of the eyes tracking him across the room. Erik sat perfectly still, taut as a bowstring.

"Take a seat, Nevyn," Highmount said, "and tell His Majesty what you told me yesterday."

Nevyn lifted his gaze briefly to Erik's, but couldn't seem to hold it. "First, Your Majesty, I wanted to convey my deepest regrets for the ordeal you endured. It was an appalling crime. I cannot tell you how it wounds me that my art would be perverted to such an end." Alix thought he might have glanced briefly at Highmount as he said this last.

Erik gave a stiff nod. "Thank you. And now, you have something to tell me?"

With another uncomfortable glance at Highmount, the bloodbinder said, "I have discovered the secret of the Priest's magic."

Erik flinched, his whole body going rigid. "I see," he said, very softly.

Silence drifted over the table like a dusting of snow. Erik stared somewhere over the bloodbinder's shoulder, face pale, expression unreadable. Alix wanted nothing more than to wrap her hands around Albern Highmount's throat. "Perhaps it would be better if we discussed this in private," she said through gritted teeth.

But Erik shook his head. "It's done now," he said, still in that soft, distant tone. "Proceed."

"I am sure it is clear to all of us the potential this has to change the course of the war—" Highmount began.

"Forgive me," Raibert Green interrupted coldly, "but I don't see how, unless you are suggesting that we commit an unspeakable evil."

"He can't be." Liam turned a horrified gaze on Highmount. "You aren't, are you? Not even you, surely?"

The chancellor's lips pursed with displeasure. "I am not certain what you mean by that, Your Highness, but I assure you that I have only the best interests of the kingdom at heart. An opportunity of undeniable potential has been laid at our feet. We would be fools not to consider it."

"It is not an opportunity," Green said. "It is a matter of conscience. What you are about to propose is an abomination."

"How could you even suggest it, after everything His Majesty has been through?" Rona Brown added.

Highmount brushed them off with a wave, his eyes on the king. "We would be fools to overlook this," he repeated deliberately, as though speaking to a child.

Erik scarcely seemed to hear. His gaze remained abstracted, and when it finally snapped back into focus, it fixed on the bloodbinder. "How?"

"I beg your pardon, sire?"

"How did you discover the secret?"

Nevyn shook his head. "I cannot account for it. I was experimenting—on animals," he added hastily, "when it just . . . happened."

"Explain."

"I wish I could. In truth, I was not attempting anything I had not tried before, and yet for some reason, it worked. I thought it pure chance, but when I tried again I was successful. So I tested the procedure on Egan, the blacksmith, and—"

Erik shuddered violently.

"He volunteered," Nevyn said quietly, dropping his gaze again.

"Continue," Erik whispered.

"I wish I could tell you more, sire. All I know is that it works. Why now, when I have been attempting it for months, I do not know."

"But you could . . . if you wished . . ." Erik couldn't bring himself to say it.

Nevyn nodded miserably. Alix felt sorry for the man. None of this was his fault—he had only done what Highmount asked of him.

"Whom?" Green snapped.

Highmount gave him a disapproving look. "I beg your pardon, Lord Green?"

"Not at all, Chancellor. I would simply like to know *whom* we are proposing to bewitch? Our own soldiers?"

"It would confer upon them an incredible advantage in battle," Highmount said, utterly unrepentant. "But as it happens, that should not be necessary."

It took Alix a moment to work out what he meant; when she did, she felt sick. "The Oridians who surrendered. You want to use them."

"What I *want* is immaterial," Highmount said with mounting impatience. "It is the logical proposition."

"Logical." Raibert Green laughed bitterly and shook his head.

"Enemy soldiers, responsible for the deaths of more than a hundred of the king's men. *Five thousand* enemy soldiers. As thralls, they would be worth twice that, unfettered by fear or pain. Quite simply, they would turn the tide of the war."

"Those men surrendered to the Kingsword banner in good faith," said Rona Brown. "Honour demands—"

"Honour will not save us. It cannot trouble us now."

"When has it ever troubled you, Chancellor?" Green asked in disgust. Turning to Erik, he said, "You cannot seriously be considering this, sire. It's repugnant."

Highmount slammed a fist down on the table. *"Of course it's repugnant, you overgrown child!"* Alix and the others stared, stunned into silence by the sight of the ever-unflappable Albern Highmount shaking with rage. "It is repugnant and unspeakable and every other foul word, and it is the *only way.* Do you think I relish this, any of you?" His gaze raked over them. "Do you imagine that I would suffer such a stain upon my own honour were this not a matter of our very survival? It is our duty to protect this realm, my lords. *Our gods-given duty.* You say it is a matter of conscience, Lord Green. I quite agree. If your conscience allows you to put your personal honour above the well-being of this kingdom, may Destan guard you in his Domain. But you will watch us burn before that, and this land with it."

The silence that followed was deafening. Erik passed a hand over his eyes. "Leave me."

Chairs scraped. Boot heels rang out.

"Not you, Alix."

The door closed noisily. Alix reached for Erik's hand, but he flinched away. "Sorry," she murmured, flushing.

"No, I'm sorry. I'm just . . ."

"I understand."

"No," he said, shuddering, "you don't."

"You're right, I couldn't possibly. But I'm here for you, whatever you need."

"I know, and I'm grateful. The trouble is, I don't know what I need." He slumped down in his chair, hand still shielding his eyes. "I can still hear them, you know."

"Hear what?"

"The voices. Echoes of the words they whispered in my mind while I was . . ." He trailed off.

"You heard voices?"

"At first, in the mountains, it just felt like the wilful part of me. That inner voice that's forever urging one to act impulsively, against one's better judgement." With a faint smile, he added, "You know it well, I think."

"I certainly do," she sighed, "though I'm getting better at ignoring it."

"I assumed it was the stress. Held captive in a foreign land, Qhara and her tribe so alien, so hard to reach . . . I was concerned about it, of course, but I never dreamed . . . And then, in Ost, I had no control at all. The merest thought in my head leapt straight out of my mouth, the merest flicker of emotion became a raging inferno. I've never felt so naked, Alix. As if my mind were stripped bare for all to see."

"I remember," she said quietly. And then she was hearing echoes of her own. Erik's voice in the royal palace at Ost: *Dear gods, Alix, what have I done?*

"It wasn't until we returned to Erroman that the magic truly took hold. I know because I no longer noticed anything amiss at all. Those voices in my head . . . I thought they were my own. Reason. Conscience. *Wisdom.*"

"That's what the bloodbinder wanted you to think. You couldn't have known, Erik."

He didn't seem to hear her anymore, too lost in his nightmare. "Whispering, always whispering. Clawing at me so that I couldn't even sleep. And if my mind started to stray . . . the headaches." He slumped low in his chair, hands gripping the crown of his head. "Until finally, he pulled my strings taut . . ."

"Stop this." Gently, Alix pulled his hands away. "It's over now. You're free."

Haunted eyes met hers. "I will never be free, Alix. How can I trust those inner voices ever again?"

She stared at him helplessly, her heart aching. She was supposed to be his guardian, but how could she protect him from this? She couldn't close a door on his memories or fight the demons that came charging through. Desperate to lash out at something, she singled out the one target she could think of. "Albern *bloody* Highmount," she spat. "Throwing this back in your face without so much as a warning. It's lucky Rig wasn't here or the servants would be sweeping the chancellor's teeth off the floor."

"Poor old Highmount." Erik sighed, shaking off his dark reverie. "We use him poorly sometimes, I think. He truly believes he is doing his duty, and I think it wounds him more than we know—having to play the role of ruthless strategist, then enduring our scorn for it. If I'm honest, it's much easier for me to keep my conscience clean with someone like Highmount around. I don't have to suggest the unthinkable, because I know he'll do it for me."

"I think I know what you mean. I have a similar relationship with a man in my service."

"Your spy," Erik said, nodding. "That reminds me, I have a debt there. Any suggestions?" Bitterly, he added, "I don't believe there is an established etiquette for *I'm sorry I almost had you beheaded.*"

"Don't worry, I'm sure he'll think of something." Having a king in his debt was probably the greatest boon of Saxon's career.

"He's not wrong, you know. Highmount."

Alix blinked in astonishment. "You actually think we should—"

"Of course not. How could I? I've already told you I think it's an abomination, and that was *before* what happened to me." Shaking his head grimly, Erik went on, "But he's not wrong to suggest it. We have so few options . . . it would be irresponsible to dismiss any of them out of hand."

Alix paused, considering the man before her. A year ago, Erik would have refused even to discuss it. Idealistic, principled to a fault, the Erik of a year ago would sooner let his kingdom perish than consider using dark magic. *How he's changed*, she thought. *How we all have.* It was bittersweet, to say the least.

Seeing her expression, his mouth twisted wryly. "You think I've been corrupted?"

"Hardly. Tempered, maybe. You're more pragmatic now."

He sighed. "Pragmatism is not a Holy Virtue."

"But duty is, and maybe Highmount is right. Maybe duty demands that you put being king ahead of being a good man."

Strangely, Erik smiled at that. "I've heard that somewhere before."

"Oh?"

"It was Raibert Green, ironically enough. He said something very similar to me last year. He told me there would come a time when I would have to choose between being a good man and being a good king. It seems that time has come."

Alix regarded him sadly. It seemed to her that the blue eyes were a little darker than they'd once been. *Not bittersweet*, she thought. *Tragic*. And necessary. "What will you do?"

"Convene the council. My views on this haven't changed—*cannot* change—but that only makes it more important that I consult my advisors. My judgement is irretrievably clouded by what happened to me. I need help."

Alix nodded. "Tomorrow, then. I'll inform Highmount straightaway." Rising, she headed for the door.

"There is nothing to discuss, brother," Tom said after Alix had departed.

Erik went rigid. "You shouldn't be here. You're gone."

"Dead, but not gone. Not yet." Tom leaned against the door, arms folded. "Surely you didn't think it would be that easy?"

Erik's breath came in short gasps. He could feel his pulse climbing dangerously; his chest grew painfully tight. "The bloodbinder is dead. The spell is broken."

"Calm yourself, brother." Tom approached the desk, and when Erik looked up he saw genuine concern in his brother's eyes. "It is not the magic. You are free, as Alix told you."

"Then why are you here?"

"You've seen what happens to soldiers who have known too many horrors. This is only battle shock. It will wear off eventually, assuming you live long enough."

The arms of Erik's chair creaked in protest at his clawlike

grip. He forced himself to relax. "You shouldn't be here," he said again.

"Don't be so quick to banish me, Erik. You need me."

"Like I needed you while I was bewitched?"

"I was as bewitched as you," Tom said patiently. "I *am* you, remember? Or at least a part of you."

"The prick, presumably."

Tom laughed. "That's better." Slipping into a chair across from Erik, he said, "Back to business. You don't need the council, Erik. Highmount is right and you know it."

Erik regarded him coldly. "It may come as a surprise to you, but your endorsement is hardly a point in Highmount's favour."

Tom ignored that. "What Alix said is true: You have changed. You broke your word at the parley. Took my head with your own sword. Little by little, you have begun to realise what it takes to be king, and it isn't pretty. This is merely the next step in a necessary progression."

"A necessary progression or a slippery slope?"

Tom shrugged. "Both, perhaps."

"Do you truly believe that?"

"Part of you believes it," Tom said, "or I wouldn't be here."

Erik squeezed his eyes shut. "What they did to me . . . to my twin. I had a *twin*, Tom. We had a brother."

"I'm sorry. I know how badly you wanted that. Even I cannot help but wonder how things might have been different if we'd known him."

"But he was taken from us. Tortured. My *mind* was tortured, harried to the brink of insanity. And now you would have me perpetrate this atrocity on others?"

"You must protect the kingdom at all costs. Difficult as it may be, that is the duty of a king."

"It's evil, Tom."

"Not evil. Merely tragic. Blame the ones who have forced your hand. Blame the Warlord."

"Enough," Erik said, waving the apparition away. "Leave me."

When he opened his eyes, Tom was gone. Except he wasn't truly gone. Erik wondered if he ever would be.

TWENTY-NINE

The council listened in grave silence as Nevyn explained what he'd discovered—as much of an explanation as he could give, at any rate. As before, the bloodbinder maintained that he had no idea why, after months of trying, he had suddenly been successful.

Silence followed this monologue. No one wanted to be the first to break it. Erik waited patiently, fingers knit, gaze trained firmly on the table. Alix wondered if he was afraid of what they might see in his eyes.

In the end, it was Sirin Grey who found the courage first. "From the expressions around this table, it would appear that these tidings are not new for all of us. How long have we known of this?"

"His Majesty, Their Highnesses, Lord Green, and Lady Brown were apprised of the matter yesterday," Highmount said. "I have known for a handful of days, but thought it best to wait until His Majesty had recovered from his ordeal."

In that case, you should have waited a little longer. A similar thought must have occurred to Erik, judging from the bitter twist of his mouth.

"And the discovery itself?" Sirin Grey asked.

"A little over a week ago," Nevyn said. "Eight days, to be precise."

"Meaning it was the day after . . ." She cleared her throat primly. "After the unfortunate events in the courtyard."

"I suppose so." Nevyn's gaze grew thoughtful. "An interesting coincidence."

"One that there will be ample time to ponder," Highmount said, "assuming we reach the right decision here today."

"There will be no decisions reached here today, Chancellor," Erik said coolly. "This council has been convened in an advisory capacity. The decision will be mine alone."

"Gods help you," Raibert Green muttered. He'd worn a scowl through the discussion, though he at least had the good grace to refrain from directing it at Erik. Green was rarely driven to anger, but Alix knew him to be a fiercely principled man, just like his late cousin. *I wonder what Arran Green would have made of all this.* For that matter, she wondered what his successor would think. Rig was a principled man too, but if it came down to a choice between five thousand enemy soldiers and his entire army . . .

"It is difficult to advise," Lady Stonegate said, "without more of the facts. I have a few questions for Nevyn, if I may."

Erik nodded wearily.

"You say you can replicate the procedure with the blacksmith, but he is only one man. Surely it is far more difficult to control five thousand?"

"Numbers appear to be less of a factor than proximity," Nevyn said. "I have found that if one is close enough, a man is frighteningly easy to control. The same goes for two men, or three. I have no reason to believe it would be any different for a hundred or more, provided they share a common set of instructions. However, I have recruited Egan's apprentices for my experiments as well, and from what I can deduce, the farther away a man is, the more concentration it requires to control him, and here numbers *do* enter into it. I had Egan ride all the way out to Calder's Bridge without any noticeable change, but when I sent Dannel and Ramsey out to join him, I had to concentrate just a little bit harder. The difference was subtle, but it was enough to confirm my hypothesis."

"That fits with what we know," Alix said. She glanced at

Erik, but he seemed to be holding up better than yesterday, so she continued, "The Priest needed to be close to control his hordes—that's what made him vulnerable—whereas Dargin was able to reach His Majesty from a great distance."

"Something I don't understand about that," Lord Swiftcurrent put in. "Where did he get the blood?"

Highmount cut him off with a gesture. "That is a tale for another time. Please continue, Nevyn."

"It also matters greatly whether one seeks to control the body or merely the mind. Taking full control over a man's actions as well as his thoughts requires much greater concentration, and so the distance factor becomes even more important."

"We worked that out too," Alix said. "It's why Dargin was moving north when we took him: He was looking to close the distance so he could assume full control. When he did, it demanded so much concentration that he was virtually catatonic." Poor Rodrik, meanwhile, nearby as he was, would scarcely have required a thought.

"Catatonic or no," Nevyn said, "it was an incredible feat, if you will forgive me for saying so. I doubt very much I could replicate anything close to that, at least not without months of practice. Were I to do this, I would need to be in immediate proximity to the forces you wished me to control."

"But you *could* do it?" Lady Stonegate pressed.

"We cannot know for certain until the attempt is made, but . . . yes, I believe I could."

"Now that we have thoroughly discussed the mechanics of the thing," Raibert Green said, "perhaps we could discuss the ethics."

"I don't see what there is to discuss," said Lady Stonegate. "This discovery may be our salvation."

"You have a very different definition of *salvation* than I, my lady," Green returned. "Controlling men against their will, obliging them to fight and die for us—it's immoral."

"It's war, is what it is," said Lord Swiftcurrent. "Come, Green, no one denies this is uncomfortable, but is it really so different from what we're doing now? We have already pressed tens of thousands of Aldenians into mandatory military service."

"Many against their will, one presumes," Lady Stonegate added.

"But not with magic," said Sirin Grey, looking troubled. "This is quite different, surely."

Erik observed the exchange in silence. Alix would have given anything to hear his thoughts, but the royal mask was impenetrable.

"The equivalency of the thing is irrelevant," Highmount said. "The fact of the matter is that we have no choice. We will lose this war, my lords. It is a simple question of mathematics. Lord Black has a force of fifteen hundred with him now. According to his latest letter, no more than a thousand Kingswords survived the attack on the citadel. Assuming the men at the fort fell back and all our men along the border are able to regroup, the maximum size of our armies is ten thousand. The Onnani will never reach us in time. The Kingswords stand alone, at *half* the enemy's strength."

"If that is so," said Norvin Gold, "then even five thousand enemy soldiers will not make up the difference."

"Five thousand *thralls*," Highmount reminded him. "Lord Black himself estimates that every thrall is worth two ordinary soldiers—to say nothing of the psychological impact of the enemy seeing their own turned against them. When the Oridians realise what is happening, they will run."

"You can't know that," Green said.

"What I know, Lord Green, is that this choice decides the war. If we do not do this, Alden *will* fall. And after that Onnan, and then Harram, at a cost of how many thousands of lives? What is so very ethical about allowing this bloodshed to continue?"

"So if our cause is just, we are justified in anything?" Rona Brown shook her head. "An argument like that can be used to rationalise all manner of horrors."

"Indeed," said Green. "No doubt the Priest used the same reasoning to defend his actions. To him, conquest in the name of religion was doing the work of the gods. Are we no better than the Madman of Oridia? Would we truly become the very thing we are fighting against?"

There was a heartbeat of silence. Then everyone started talking at once.

"We can't possibly—"

"The matter is clear—"

"How will history judge—"

Around and around it went, all of it boiling down to the same two positions. *It's wrong. We have no choice.* With each raised voice, Erik looked a little wearier, his gaze a little more detached. Eventually, he held up a hand. "That will do, I think."

The voices died down, but the glaring continued. Many of those relationships would never recover, Alix knew.

"It is clear we will not reach a consensus here," Erik said, "nor did I really expect one. I have listened to your arguments and I will weigh them carefully. Once again, my lords, I thank you for your service."

Each and every one of them looked like they might say more, but then Erik rose, effectively stifling any further discussion. This time, he didn't wait for the lords and ladies to file out of the room; instead he quit it himself. Alix let him go. He needed to be alone.

"What do you think he'll decide?" Liam asked as they made their way down the corridor.

Alix shook her head. The choice was hard enough on its own, but for Erik to have to make it after everything he had gone through . . .

A good man, or a good king?

"He shouldn't have to choose," she murmured.

"He shouldn't," Liam said, "but he does. And soon."

A soft knock drew Erik out of his reverie. Rubbing his eyes, he called, "Come," and was more than a little surprised when the door opened to admit his brother. Liam had not come to see him privately since . . . before.

"Thought you might want some company," Liam said. "But if you'd rather not . . . I mean, I know you've got a lot on your mind."

"Actually, I think a bit of company is just what I need. Can I offer you some wine?"

"No, thanks." Liam settled into a chair across from Erik, the one Tom always used to occupy when he came to his elder brother with some complaint or another. "How are you holding up?"

"I haven't come to a decision, if that's what you mean."

"Can't say I blame you. It's a terrible choice to have to make."

"Terrible choices are a part of war. I daresay victory never comes without them." Erik sighed. "Though perhaps Raibert Green would disagree."

"Easy for him. He isn't king."

"Precisely. I haven't the luxury of following my conscience wherever it may lead."

"Says who?"

"Pardon?"

Liam regarded him with a clear, frank gaze. "What else are you supposed to follow if not your conscience?"

"Duty. Wisdom."

"Well, sure, but those things are subjective, aren't they? It's your conscience that defines what they are."

"I suppose you're right. I suppose the real problem is that my conscience is divided."

"Good man versus good king." Liam nodded. "Allie told me."

"And does she have an answer?"

"You should ask her, maybe."

There was a tone there, Erik thought. He had sensed it more than once over the past few days. Something had changed between the two of them, a distance that hadn't been there before. It was yet another stone on the cairn of Erik's grief.

Now was not the time to confront it, however. "What about you?" Erik asked. "What do you think?"

"I'm flattered you would ask, but the truth is, it doesn't matter a damn what I think, or anyone else. All of us put together don't amount to the man you are."

"Don't be ridiculous—"

"I'm not. Look, there's something I think you need to hear. My whole life, I've looked up to you. Or the idea of you, anyway. Growing up, you were the person I wished I could be." Liam coloured as he spoke, and Erik was painfully aware of how awkward this must be for him—for them both. "It's different now, obviously. You're not just an idea anymore. I've seen you make mistakes. But if anything that's only deepened my respect, because I know the man I'm looking up to is real, with the same fears and doubts as anybody else. These past few weeks, while you were"—his gaze dropped briefly—"while you were unwell, and I was trying to fill your boots . . . it was the hardest thing I've ever done. I don't know anyone who could do what you do, Erik. And none of that changes because of what happened to you. Not if you don't let it. I guess what I'm trying to say is that you should trust yourself. If anyone can find the right thing here, it's you."

"I . . . thank you, Liam." He wanted to say more, to tell his brother how very much it meant to him, but the words fell short, just as they had with Alix the other day.

It was then that her words finally sank in. *You still have family.* More loyal, more loving, than any he had known before. The thought was a light flickering to life inside him, like a candle in a long-dark room. They had done so much to protect him; now it was his turn.

He would not offer his soul, but he would offer his life, and gladly, in return for theirs. His head in exchange for their safety. The Warlord would honour such a bargain, Erik felt sure. He had done so before.

"Thank you, brother," he said again, his voice strong now. "I believe I know what I must do."

Highmount bore the news with icy calm—perhaps because he could not truly have expected his king to decide otherwise. The fact that Erik had even been willing to discuss it was a testament to how deeply his ordeal had undermined his confidence. But he'd been true to himself in the end, and though Alix knew, as they all did, that his decision must surely spell the end of the Kingdom of Alden, she understood him perfectly when he said that a kingdom willing to enslave five thousand men with magic would not be worth saving.

"If I must choose between the body and spirit of this country, then I choose her spirit, for it is eternal and can never be conquered."

Highmount nodded gravely. "As you wish, Your Majesty. We will go to war with such means as we have at our disposal, and what will be will be."

Erik put a hand on his shoulder. "Take heart, old friend. We may yet survive this. Regardless, you have done your duty, and for that the kingdom owes you a great debt. As do I."

Alix's heart flooded—not with fear, as she might have expected, but with relief. For here at last was *Erik*, looking and sounding more like himself than he had in months. His strength was her strength, flowing into her and straightening her spine. *We may yet survive this. By the gods, we're certainly going to fight.*

"I can feel that, you know," Erik said when Highmount had gone. He sat at his desk, writing.

"What?"

"Your eyes on my back." He looked over his shoulder with a smile. "What are you grinning at, Captain? Haven't you heard we're about to be conquered?"

"It's just good to have you back, that's all."

"Not quite," he said, turning back to his writing. "I still have dark paths to travel, I think. But now I have a light." Without turning, he held out a hand, and Alix clasped it.

THIRTY

† R ig entered the study to find his king in full armour, a sight he hadn't seen since the Siege of Erroman. He'd been told to expect a slighter, paler Erik, but he saw none of that. If the king was thinner, it was hidden beneath his armour, and as for his face, he looked as strong and gravely composed as he had on the day Rig had ridden out to the front. "Your Majesty," he said, clasping Erik's arm. "Damned good to see you."

"And you." Smiling, Erik stepped aside to let Rig embrace his sister.

"You made good time," Alix said. "How did you keep those Oridians marching?"

"I didn't. Corren is a proud man—he wouldn't stand for his men slowing me down. Dishonour to the Trionate and so on. I have to say, they march well for a bunch of barely trained peasants."

"A proud man," Erik said, "and yet he surrendered. Why?"

"Long story," Rig said. "Not sure I fully understand it myself. An act of conscience, I suppose you'd call it. He's a good man, I think. Principled."

Erik nodded, exchanging a look with Alix that Rig didn't

fully understand. He knew there'd been talk of mobilising the captured Oridians to some purpose, but he hadn't yet had the details. Seeing his confusion, Erik said, "Your opinion of the enemy commander strengthens my conviction that I made the right decision. I'll explain later." He gestured for Rig to take a seat. "What news of the Warlord?"

"Still in the eastern Greenlands, and apparently in no hurry. Burning and looting at their leisure. We came across a large crowd of refugees on the road with nothing more than the shirts on their backs. The whole town was razed, they told us. Corren confirms he had orders to do as much damage as possible. That was what put him over the edge, he told me. Made up his mind to surrender."

"Sadik is trying to draw us out," Erik said.

Rig nodded. "He has the men to grind us down in a siege, but it would be so much easier to smash us on the open field."

"Coward," Alix growled. "He's all but won, but still he spills the blood of innocents."

"Doesn't bode well for the kind of ruler he'll make, does it?" Rig said darkly.

Erik looked puzzled for a moment, but then his brow cleared. "I had forgotten. With Madan and Varad gone, Sadik rules alone."

"Alone and brutally," Rig said.

Alix squeezed her eyes shut, a flicker of . . . *something* crossing her features. Fear, perhaps? But no—that didn't seem right. Rig made a mental note to ask her about it later.

"Onnan has marched at last," Erik said. "Too late, of course."

"At least they marched. More than we can say for the Harrami."

"Nevertheless, by the time they get here, there will be nothing but ash and rubble."

Not quite, Rig thought. The Red Tower would still stand. Erik would be imprisoned there, and Liam too. Alix, perhaps. Not Rig, though. The Warlord was known to collect the skulls of his most respected foes, and Rig fancied he'd earned that respect, gods help him.

"I suppose you'll want to get up on the walls," Erik said.

"As soon as possible."

"You won't be impressed, I'm afraid. They're still badly damaged from the siege."

Rig flashed a humourless smile. "If you think they're in rough shape, it's a good job you didn't see the fort."

"That reminds me," Erik said, "have you done a final tally of our numbers?"

"Ten thousand, give or take. Rollin acquitted himself well. If there's a medal for swift and orderly retreats, he should definitely receive it."

"Duly noted," Erik said dryly, rising. "Shall we?"

The three of them spent the afternoon touring the walls with the other members of the war council: Liam, Raibert Green, and Rona Brown. Albern Highmount was there too, and formally part of the war council, but the old man's views on military matters were about as much use as Rig's opinions on courtly etiquette. Not that it took an experienced commander general to understand the lay of things. The walls would never hold up against a sustained attack and they all knew it. Sadik knew it too, though that didn't stop him trying to goad the Kingswords into the field.

Erik briefed him on the discussion in the council. Rig wasn't sorry to have missed it. He would have been sorely tempted to side with Highmount. He was no stranger to sacrificing men for the cause; he'd spent the better part of the past year ordering soldiers to lay down their lives. But turning Corren and his men into thralls . . . being part of that would have haunted him for the rest of his days.

It was evening before he finally managed to slip away to find Vel, and the impatience that had been gnawing at him all day gave way to nervousness. It had been over a month since they'd seen each other, but that wasn't the heart of it. No, the real problem was that he had something to tell her that wasn't going to be easy to say. "Get a hold of yourself, Black," he muttered as he made his way toward the guest quarters. *Should have done it a long time ago anyway. No point in putting it off, even if the timing isn't the best.* But all the stern thoughts he could muster weren't enough to keep his pulse from racing as he approached her door. *Look at you. Like a sodding adolescent.* Growling inwardly, he knocked.

He didn't know what he expected from her—tears, perhaps, a frantic embrace, or maybe a swift slap in the face—but he got none of those things. The woman on the other side of the door looked drawn but composed, gesturing politely for him to enter. Caught on the back foot, Rig didn't know what to say.

Vel broached the silence for him. "Welcome back, General. Or perhaps I should say welcome home. Wine?" Without waiting for an answer, she fetched a decanter and poured two glasses. "Crystal," she said, handing him one. "I have never held anything so fine. Heavy and yet delicate, and look how it refracts the light." She twisted the cut crystal in the firelight, demonstrating. Then she brought it to her lips. She had yet to meet his gaze.

"How are you?" Rig asked, wincing inwardly at the banality of the question.

"Well, thank you. It is good to be back on friendly soil."

Rig wanted nothing more than to gather her in his arms, but this strangely withdrawn demeanour held him back. He wasn't sure how he was meant to react. Was he supposed to make the first move, or was this distance a sign of something deeper? *Might as well get the necessary out of the way first*, he decided. "Thank you for what you did for my sister and the Wolves. I know words aren't enough, but—"

"No thanks necessary, General. Your sister is a remarkable individual. And Dain Cooper too. You did well to promote him, I think. Not that my opinion on such matters counts for much."

Rig sighed. "What is this, Vel?"

"What is what?" She took another sip of wine; Rig saw that her hand trembled slightly.

"Do you want me to leave? I wouldn't blame you if you did. I sent you into a terrible situation without so much as a scrap of information. I exploited your feelings and gave you nothing in return. You have every right to hate me, if that's what you feel."

She laughed bitterly. "You are a fool, Riggard Black."

"You've mentioned."

She turned full circle, gesturing at her surroundings. "Beautiful, isn't it? Like nothing I've ever seen. Though perhaps it's not so impressive to you. I imagine your chambers at Blackhold make this look positively shabby."

He frowned. "Before they were ransacked, you mean?"

If she noticed the tone, she ignored it. "I cannot conceive of what it must have been like to grow up amid such wealth."

"Am I supposed to apologise for being highborn? I'm sorry if the trappings of my station offend your republican sensibilities, Daughter."

"On the contrary. I love this glass. I love this table—Harrami, isn't it? I love these tapestries, and this carpet is like walking on a cloud." Her voice grew more vehement as she spoke, and Rig had the distinct impression she was half a heartbeat away from hurling her wineglass into the hearth.

He approached her warily, lifting the glass from her hand before it met a terrible fate. "It's all right. You're supposed to love those things."

"No, I'm not," she said, dark eyes flashing. "There is no point in loving them, because I can't have them."

Ah. Now Rig understood. Reaching out, he brushed her cheek. "Who says?"

"Please. I am not some little girl to be enchanted by stories."

"That's a pity, because I have a story to tell. A little over a week ago, I led a force of fifteen hundred men against five thousand Oridian soldiers. I knew I couldn't win, but I thought I could at least slow them down a little."

"I've heard about the battle. It doesn't—"

"Just listen. I thought I could slow them down, but I was wrong. It turned out that they were mostly cavalry. More than three thousand horses. I looked across that field and saw my death. And then I saw something else. What do you think it was?"

She scowled. "Don't play games. You told me to listen, so I'm listening."

"I saw you, Vel." Rig took her face in his hands. "In those last moments, when I thought my time in this world was done, it was your face I saw. Your voice in my head. I might be a fool, but even I know what that means."

"What does it mean?" she whispered.

"It means that I love you."

She paused. Then: "Don't be ridiculous. You're a banner lord. You have responsibilities, and—"

"In case you haven't noticed, I don't give a fraction of a

damn what other people think, not anymore. I've done more than enough to restore my family's name. It's time to do something for me. Let them call me a hypocrite—they'd be right, and I don't *care*. So what about you, Daughter?" He stroked the hair back from her face. "I've never known you to back down from anything. It would be a shame if you started now."

She gazed up at him mutely. Sensing his opening, Rig leaned in and kissed her. It was soft, lingering, more tender than passionate. The words hadn't been spoken lightly, and he wanted to make sure she knew it.

She pulled away after a moment, and he saw that her face was streaked with tears.

"What's the matter?"

"Damn you, Riggard Black. Damn you for saying this now." She turned away from him, folding her arms tightly across her body. Then she said, "I'm the spy."

Just like that, without any warning. Hurled from her lips out as though propelled by a supreme act of willpower.

Propelled like a fist into Rig's gut. "Impossible," he blurted, a denial as instinctive as raising his shield to ward off a blow.

"I was the one who told Sadik about Whitefish Bridge, and Wraith's falcon. I'm the one who fed him information on your numbers and defences."

Rig's chest felt tight. He couldn't tell if the pressure building inside him was rage or grief, or both. This couldn't be happening. It didn't make sense. "Why would you do that?"

"My brother." Her voice caught on the word. "They have my brother."

"Who? The enemy?"

"He was in Timra when it fell, on a pilgrimage to see the Holy Relics. They threw him in the dungeons along with the rest of the priests."

Rig dimly recalled hearing something about that. The clergy had great influence in Andithyri; Sadik feared they would stir the populace to rebellion. He'd had them rounded up and locked away.

"They rotted there for months," Vel went on. "Then my country declared war. Sadik's inquisitors came for the Onnani prisoners, hoping to find one of value, someone they could use as leverage. And they did. A priest whose sister was close to a top Onnani commander." She paused, shuddering. "They came to me in the night. They had . . ." She faltered, gazing down at her shaking hand, turning it over as though seeing it for the first time. "They showed it to me, this bloody, mangled thing . . . They said that if I didn't help them, they'd send me the rest piece by piece . . ."

Rig could feel his pulse pounding in his temples. Part of him wanted to go to her. Another part wanted to call the guards. He did neither, standing there like a dark, glowering statue.

Vel turned to face him. She wore the most extraordinary expression, fierce and yet pleading, eyes lit with both pride and pain. "I gave him nothing of value after Whitefish Bridge. Once I realised you knew there was a spy, I saw my chance to hurt Sadik even as I helped my brother. I deliberately walked into every snare you set. I knew I was feeding the Warlord misinformation. I *rejoiced* in it. And all the while, I did everything I could to help you. It was Sadik who bade me gather intelligence on the Resistance. I did as he asked. But it was you who reaped the fruits of that reconnaissance, while Sadik got only a pack of lies."

It was true, every word; Rig knew because it was the only way any of it made sense. He'd already remarked to Wright that the spy had done no real damage, and indeed had helped their cause—inadvertently, he'd assumed. Vel had had every opportunity to destroy him, but she hadn't, which was why he'd ruled her out as a suspect. More than that, she'd been the one to give them Wraith and the Resistance. Who'd led Alix to Rodrik, and saved his sister's life.

True, every word. But not good enough. She'd lied to his face. *In his bed.* How could he trust anything that had passed between them?

She saw it in his eyes. "I told myself you could forgive me, that we could get past this somehow. I wanted so badly for that to be true, but deep down I always knew it was a lie. You said it yourself—trust, once lost, can never be rebuilt."

Rig shook his head. He didn't dare speak. He had no idea what might come out.

"I'm sorry," Vel said. "Not for the spying—I did what I had to, to save my brother's life—but for the rest. I knew from the moment I saw you that day on the road . . . Standing there like some kind of wild animal, streaming wet and covered in blood, and yet you spoke with a highborn accent, all wit and easy self-assurance . . ." A smile touched her lips, fleeting and fragile. "But when I found out who you were, I should have left well enough alone. I had all the intelligence I needed from Commander Wright—I need never have put myself in your path. But as you said, I rarely back down from anything." Bitterly, she added, "Perhaps I wear the wrong robes after all. I let Ardin take hold of me, even though Eldora whispered that I was a fool."

Even now, as she spoke of her regret, the fierceness never wavered. Her beauty in the firelight pierced Rig to his soul. It hurt worse than he ever would have thought possible.

All he'd wanted, all he'd dreamed about for weeks on end, was gathering Vel in his arms and telling her that he loved her, spending one last night of passion together before he met his end on the battlefield. He was going to die anyway; maybe it shouldn't have mattered that she was the spy. But it did. In that moment, it mattered more than the ache in his chest, more than the beauty in front of him, more than the stirring of desire he felt even now.

Wordlessly, Rig turned and left the room.

"It's late," Alix said. "You should turn in."

"As should you," Erik replied, his quill scratching across the parchment. Glancing up, he added, "both of you." Liam was slumped in the chair across from him, looking exhausted. "Go ahead, you two—I'll only be a few moments longer."

Nodding, Alix started toward the door. "Coming?" she asked Liam.

"Soon. There's something I wanted to talk to Erik about. You go on."

There was a stretch of silence, awkward enough that Erik looked up from his writing. Alix hovered by the door, gazing at the back of her husband's head with an almost pleading expression. She hesitated a moment longer, then slipped through the door and closed it behind her.

Erik sighed inwardly. Whatever stood between them, it was growing like a cancer. Setting his quill aside, he said, "What is it you wanted to speak about?"

"Hmm?" His brother looked up distractedly.

"A moment ago, you told Alix you wanted to speak with me."

"Oh, right. I was, you know . . . just wondering how you're doing."

"Much better, thank you. I still have some difficulty sleeping." *As do you, from the look of things.*

"How are the nightmares?"

Erik glanced away. As far as he had come, he still was not ready to discuss his nightmares—least of all with Liam, who featured so horribly in all of them. "At least they only plague me in sleep now." For the most part, at least. Tom still dropped round from time to time to remind Erik what a reckless, sentimental decision he'd made in refusing to bloodbind his enemies. But the hallucinations were less frequent now, and he was confident that Tom would soon fade away altogether. Or if not altogether, at least from view; the voice of his self-doubt, Erik suspected, would forever be Tom's.

"Well, if it helps," Liam said, "you look worlds better. Like your old self, really."

Erik grunted sceptically. "And what about you, brother? How have you been sleeping?"

"Not great," Liam admitted, raking his fingers through his ever-dishevelled hair. "Can't stop my thoughts from churning round, you know? Tossing and turning, keeping Allie awake."

"I doubt your tossing and turning is what's keeping Alix awake. She is having troubled thoughts of her own, from the look of her."

"Could be." Liam's gaze fell to his lap.

"Do you want to talk about it?"

"No offence, Erik, but you're the last person I want to talk about it with."

Erik sighed. *Just as I thought.* It had been too much to hope that the three of them could put the past behind them so easily. Just one more way in which he had been naïve.

Choosing his words carefully, Erik said, "The other day you gave me some good advice, brother, and now I'm going to return the favour. I've thought a lot about what you said. It means more to me than you know that you would look up to me, and I can only hope to prove worthy of that regard. But I cannot help thinking that the reason you look up to me so is that you consistently sell yourself short."

Liam groaned as if to say, *Not this again*. He started to interrupt, but Erik held up a hand.

"Let me finish. You say that filling my boots was the hardest thing you've ever done. But I wonder, have you actually reflected on what you accomplished?"

"What did I accomplish?" Liam gestured irritably at the papers on Erik's desk. "I wrote some letters. I had dinner with the Onnani ambassador. I had endless meetings with the council."

"You *governed*. Much of what you did was routine, yes. And some of it was anything but. You began your tenure with what must have been the most difficult decision of your life."

"What, you mean the whole treason thing?"

Erik ignored that. "You made another hard choice, at considerable risk to yourself, in ordering the evacuation of the city—an evacuation that proceeded smoothly due to the confidence the people held in you, and the way you inspired them. And finally"—Erik arched an eyebrow pointedly—"you put up with Albern Highmount for the better part of a month without killing him."

Liam smiled. "That was the toughest part, no question."

Sobering, Erik went on, "You *did* fill my boots, Liam, admirably. For that you have not only my thanks, but my respect. You also have the respect of those around you, though you seem not to be aware of it. The Wolves, especially, are fiercely loyal to you."

"Soldiers," Liam said dismissively.

"Is a soldier's esteem worth less than a courtier's? Rig would have something to say about that, I'll warrant, as would Rona Brown."

Liam flushed fiercely. Erik had touched a nerve, though he was not quite sure how. "I appreciate you saying all this," Liam said, "but it's really not necessary."

"I disagree. I've watched you and Alix over the past few days. I see the way you look at each other."

Liam scowled. "I don't think that's any of your—"

"But it is, Liam, because I've a good idea what lies between you." *Who lies between you*, he might have said. He had done his best to vacate that space a long time ago, but apparently it had not been enough. His ghost lingered, as much a presence for his brother as Tom was for Erik. Both of them had conjured their brothers as the embodiment of their own insecurities. The only difference was that Erik knew his for an illusion. "You and I are not the same," he said, "but that doesn't mean we aren't equals."

"I know that."

Erik shook his head. "Not good enough. Listen to me, Liam. There is nothing standing between you and Alix except your own self-doubt. It is a poison, and you alone can overcome it. If you don't, it will destroy your marriage."

He expected anger. A flare of resentment similar to the one he'd endured that day in the rose garden, when he had told Liam he would stand aside. But Liam just wilted in his chair, dropping his head into his hand. "I love her so much."

"That's the easy part. Now you need to let her love you."

So saying, Erik rose and slipped quietly out of the room, leaving his brother alone with his ghost.

THIRTY-ONE

† "The Brownlands are aflame," Rig said.
   Erik's hands balled into fists on the desk. Alix could almost feel the wave of desperation rolling over him.
"Where are they now?"

"South of the Arrowhead. They're burning every field they come across."

"The breadbasket of Alden," Highmount said gravely. "There will be famine."

"Never mind the fields!" Rona Brown snapped. "They're butchering my people!"

"Just as he did at Raynesford." Rig's eyes burned. He wanted vengeance as badly as Rona.

"If we ride out, it will be just what Sadik wants." Alix knew she was stating the obvious, but someone had to. "He'll crush us in the open field."

"Unless I missed something," Liam said, "he'll crush us behind these walls too. There's no avoiding the crushing."

Highmount *tsk*ed. "The unlikelihood of our success is no reason to race to our doom."

All eyes shifted to Erik. The king's gaze was fixed in the middle distance somewhere, as though staring at something only he could see. After a stretch of silence, his expression hardened. "No. Liam is right. A sliver of a chance is not enough to justify sacrificing thousands of lives. It's not just those he massacres now, but those who will die the slow death of starvation. If we are to be defeated, it will be in defence of the people, not cowering behind these broken walls. Let the people's last memory of the Kingdom of Alden be a proud one. It may help them through the hard times to come."

Or make them all the more bitter. Alix kept the thought to herself.

"Good," Rig said, "now that's settled . . ." Unfurling a map, he swept it across the table. "I propose we make our stand here." He dropped a finger just southeast of Brownhold. "With the Arrowhead and the hills protecting our flanks, Sadik will be forced to meet us head on, and we'll have the advantage in elevation. He'll have to run a gauntlet of archers just to get to our front lines."

"Are you sure?" asked Raibert Green. "What's to stop him bypassing us altogether and taking the Imperial Road straight to Erroman?"

"Not Sadik," Rig said, staring at the map so fiercely that Alix half expected it to burst into flame. "Once he finds out where we are, he won't be able to resist. It's not Erroman he wants, it's total victory. Knowing that Alden's king and her commander general are both alive and in the field will feel like unfinished business."

"If this is going to work," Liam said, "we'll need to get into position before Sadik realises what we're up to."

Rig nodded. "Forced march. We can rest when we get there."

"It's decided then," Erik said. "We march first thing in the morning." Glancing around the table, he added, "If anyone has farewells to make, I suggest you do it now."

Alix had none. Nearly everyone she loved in this world either was in this room or would meet her on the battlefield. The same went for Liam, and probably even Erik. Rig, though, had someone to say good-bye to—or so she thought, but her brother merely snatched his map from the table and stalked off to make his preparations. *Something must have happened with Vel.* The thought saddened her. She doubted the two of them would have had much of a future together, but even so, the timing could hardly be worse. Alix knew only too well what it was like to carry a weight like that into battle.

Dawn came too soon. They assembled in the courtyard: White, Black, Brown, Green, Gold, and Grey. Though Lord Gold was too ancient to fight, he would ride alongside the others, joined by his grandson, Garek. The Greys, meanwhile, were represented as ever by Lady Sirin. In place of her customary silk, however, she wore full armour, probably for the first time since her King's Service. The seconds, Dain and Ide and Pollard, sat behind their respective commanders. Kerta would be waiting for them outside the gates, in command of the scouts. Even Rudi was coming along, since Liam reckoned the wolfhound was "good for at least a throat or two."

Vel was in the courtyard too. Alix was momentarily surprised, until she remembered that the priestess was attached to the Onnani battalion. The older man by her side, Alix presumed, must be Battalion Commander Wright. He'd survived the attack on the fort, acting as Rollin's second to lead the Kingswords in retreat. It must have been a pleasant surprise for him to find his spiritual guide waiting in Erroman. The priestess didn't acknowledge Alix's gaze, or anyone else's for that matter, sitting her horse as rigidly as if she'd been lashed onto it.

"That's everyone then?" Erik asked, twisting in his saddle.

"Everyone," Rig confirmed curtly.

Erik paused, his gaze travelling up the wall of the keep as though in silent farewell. "All right then," he said. "It's time."

It would be two days' hard marching with minimal rest, but Alix was glad of it. The last thing she wanted was more time to contemplate their doom. As it was, the day unfurled like a scribe's scroll, offering memory after memory of all they had gone through to reach this point. *The longest year and a half of my life*, she thought. Indeed, it almost felt as if her whole life had been squeezed into that brief period, and everything that came before but a dream. She scarcely recognised herself as the girl she'd once been. Looking over at the men she loved one by one, she knew that they were different too. Erik was wiser. Liam subtler. Rig had grown so much harder. As for herself, she had learned that her own instincts were both her greatest gift and her most dangerous enemy. She couldn't say if they were better for it, any of them, but one thing was certain: They were warriors all, and if death awaited them on the battlefield, then it was as fitting an end as any.

The sun had begun to set when Liam dropped his horse back to ride alongside her. They hadn't spoken more than a few words since the day before. Long periods of silence had grown frequent between them, but yesterday had been unusually sparse, especially after his talk with Erik. Whatever they had spoken about, Liam was still wrestling with it. All of them, it seemed, had extra baggage to carry into battle.

"How are you holding up?" he asked in an undertone.

"As well as can be expected, I suppose. They say your life flashes before your eyes when you die. I think that might be what's happening to me."

"You're not going to die, Allie," he said, low but vehement. "We're going to have a long and happy life together, you and I. We're going to make babies and grandbabies and die old and loved."

She looked over at him. "Do you really believe that?"

"I have to. I have to believe I'll be given a chance to fix this. To fix us."

Alix reached out and took his hand. "Even if you don't die old, you'll die loved."

"Nobody's dying. We have a plan. It's a good plan."

It *was* a good plan. Just not as good as Sadik's.

Alix knew it the moment she saw the dust swirling ahead of them, the telltale flash of golden hair beneath the helm of an approaching rider. Kerta was pounding up the road from the south, returning from her scouting position a few miles ahead. Rig threw his arm in the air and the column came to a halt.

"He's waiting for us, Your Majesty," Kerta reported once she'd caught her breath. Pointing, she said, "We can see the tents from the top of that rise."

Erik paled. "How is that possible? He was supposed to be south of the Arrowhead!"

"He must have crossed the river," Rona said. "There's a ford not far from where it empties into the lake."

"That puts him between us and the only source of water," Liam said grimly. "We'll have to change course."

Erik swore viciously. "How did the Warlord know we were—?"

"He has excellent spies," Rig said, and there was an extra hint of bitterness there that Alix didn't fully understand.

"Maybe," she said. "Or he just outsmarted us. If his maps are good enough, he would have known the hills north of the Arrowhead were an ideal place for us to sink our spears. We already knew he was trying to goad us into the field—is it so hard to imagine he'd guess the place we would choose?"

"You give him too much credit," Albern Highmount opined.

"No," Rig said, "she's right. He didn't become the Warlord by making compelling speeches." Shaking his head, he added, "I'm sorry, Erik. Of all the moments to let you down—"

"We need solutions, General. What are our options?"

"None but to change course. We need water."

Erik turned to Rona. "Nearest source, Lady Brown?"

"I'm sorry, sire, but aside from the Arrowhead and its river . . ."

"Fork Lake," said a new voice. Sirin Grey walked her courser forward. "On the western border of the Greylands. It's very small, but it should serve."

"How far?" Rig asked.

"A day's ride."

He scratched his beard roughly. "Terrain?"

"Farmlands. Relatively flat, with some sparse stands of trees."

Swearing under his breath, Rig said, "It'll have to do."

They swung west, quitting the Imperial Road and plunging into fields high with winter wheat. Almost immediately, the infantry began falling behind, bogged down by the long grasses and uneven ground. *The Warlord will have planned this too*, Alix thought. *He knew we would spot him and be forced to change course. He knew we would head for water. He's trying to separate the infantry from the cavalry.*

Her theory was confirmed the next morning, when the raiding began.

Enemy archers on horseback began harrying the rear lines. They lacked the grace and skill of Rig's Harrami-trained horse archers, but they succeeded in slowing the march still further, drawing out the column until it was dangerously vulnerable. Liam was obliged to pull the Wolves out of line repeatedly to chase off the raiders. By the time night fell, the column had become so scattered that Rig feared a night raid would end them. He was forced to call a halt, though they were still more than a day's ride from Fork Lake.

"The trap is sprung," Highmount said gravely as the war council sat clustered around the table in Erik's pavilion. "We should have remained behind our walls."

Erik was in no mood for *I-told-you-so*. "And then what, Chancellor? Watch him cut Alden's throat and let her bleed to death? No, we were right to ride out. Our mistake was in underestimating the Warlord's cunning."

"*My* mistake," Rig said, reminding Alix very much of the late Arran Green.

"Can we assume Sadik will continue to march through the night?" Erik asked.

Rig nodded. "He'll be on us by morning."

"So we make our stand here," Rona said, with only the faintest quaver in her voice.

"Or," said Highmount, "we retreat and return to Erroman."

"It pains me to admit it, Your Majesty," said Raibert Green, "but the chancellor may be right. It was a good plan, but now that it is foiled, perhaps the walls are indeed our best option."

"They are our only option," Highmount declared.

Rig's expression darkened. "Stick to your areas of competence, old man." To Erik, he said, "Retreating now is pointless."

"Give me an alternative, then."

"Attack. At dawn."

Highmount snorted. "As bold as a Black," he said, at great peril to his health. Fortunately for him, Rig was too focused on Erik to be bothered with the chancellor.

"It could work," said Alix, "if we strike before Sadik has a chance to organise."

"Won't he anticipate that?" Rona asked. "With due respect, General, it would hardly be an unexpected move coming from you. What if the Warlord is ready for it?"

"He might anticipate it, but that's not the same as being ready. He'll just be coming off the march; he won't have time to organise himself properly, not if we hit him early enough. The only advantage we've got is a few hours' head start. We'd be fools not to use it."

Erik considered for a moment in silence, elbows on the

table, fingers knotted before him. "What are our chances of success?"

"Slim," Rig said bluntly.

"And if we retreat?"

"Slightly less slim," Liam said, "but if we're weighing our options, the difference is a question of pebbles rather than stones. I'd rather fight than run."

"Agreed," said Rig.

"I concur," said Rona Brown.

Erik turned to Raibert Green. "My lord?"

"I am with you whatever you decide, sire. There are no good options here; perhaps the best we can hope for is to die with honour."

Erik's gaze skipped over Highmount—he knew what the chancellor thought—to land on Alix. "That leaves you, Captain. What say you?"

Alix glanced across the table at her brother. He was angry and hurting, enough perhaps to affect his judgement. Rona Brown would side with Liam whatever he said, and Green had admitted that he didn't prefer one option over the other. Erik had similar misgivings about their counsel; Alix could tell by the way he was looking at her. Asking her wasn't symbolic. Her answer could well sway his decision one way or the other.

For a moment, the enormity of it made Alix's head swim. She could feel Albern Highmount's hawkish eyes on her, silently reminding her of his warning months ago: *There will come a time when the memory of this regrettable incident is all that stands between you and another rash decision.* But no—there was nothing rash about this. She was afraid, yes, and angry, but those weren't the things that whispered to her heart in that moment. Instead, the voice she heard was her own, the deepest voice of her blood.

"As bold as a Black," she said with a thin smile.

Erik nodded slowly. "So be it," the king said. "We attack at dawn."

THIRTY-TWO

† A lix moved in a world of shadows. Dark shapes shifted behind a veil of predawn mist, indistinguishable but for small glimpses: a glint of metal, a shining patch of horseflesh, the bone-white gleam of war paint. Spectres of war winking in and out of their phantom realm, or so it seemed to Alix. She gauged the activity around her by sound alone, jingling harnesses and creaking leather and the sound of a sword being loosened in its sheath. No one spoke.

Drawing her own blade, she tested her wrist gingerly and found it stiff and sore. Not yet healed, but what could she do? She would rather die than stand down.

Gradually, the sounds faded. The shifting of shadows slowed. They were ready. Alix glanced over at Erik and found him looking back at her, his expression unreadable in the gloom. "It comes at last," he said. "One way or another, it ends today."

Alix nodded, girding herself against another swell of fear. It had been coming in waves all night, periods of resigned calm punctuated by spasms of terror, almost like the pains of labour. *Steady*, Alix told herself. *It will pass.*

"I had hoped . . ." Erik shook his head. "I thought I would have more time."

"So did I."

"The curse of being mortal, I suppose. We always think we'll get more time."

Alix didn't trust herself to speak; her heart was too full.

Erik sighed, so softly that Alix barely heard. Then, raising his voice, he said, "Battle commanders." Rig, Liam, and Rona Brown brought their horses forward to stand before their king. "Lady Brown, I want no heroics from you. The reserves are our absolute last resort, so choose your moment well."

"Aye, sire."

"Liam, the same goes for you. We stick to the plan."

"Of course."

Erik shook his head. "It won't be easy. Your discipline will be sorely tested, brother."

"I'll be ripped apart in the van," Rig said flatly. "Heavy cavalry or no, that's just what's going to happen. The rearguard needs to stay in the rear or the king is vulnerable."

"I understand," Liam said. "I won't let you down."

Erik's gaze took in each of them in turn. "It has been an honour, my lords. May Olan guide your hearts and Rahl your blades, and should death find you, may you know peace in your Domains."

They bowed their heads and separated, Rig to the van, Liam to the rear, Rona to command the reserves. Erik would command the centre, with Raibert Green, Sirin Grey, and Garek Gold fighting alongside. Alix and her guardsmen would do what they always did: protect the king or die trying.

Erik snapped down the visor of his helm. "For Alden," he said, and he spurred his horse.

It was like watching a storm coming. First the thunder: a distant clash of metal, the cries of horses and men as the armies came together up the field. Then, gradually, Rig's vanguard began to rustle like a forest buffeted by strong winds. Alix watched as the turmoil moved steadily back through the lines until the entire contingent boiled. And then the enemy broke through, the storm crashing over them in full devastating force.

Heavy cavalry pierced the rear lines of the van, shredding

it into ribbons as though a great claw had raked through the ranks. They didn't turn to finish the job; Sadik had vanguard to spare, and they rumbled toward Erik's centre now, bloodied lances gleaming, thousands of hooves sending a great cloud of dust into the sky and obscuring the vanguard.

"Archers!" Erik cried.

From the flanks, the longbows thumped, sending a volley arcing into the sky. A few horses skidded and fell; men screamed and pitched from their saddles. But most of the horde thundered on, undaunted, a terrifying wall of blades and beasts and cruel-tipped spears.

"Lances ready!"

Alix scarcely had time to obey before the Oridian cavalry broke over the pikemen. The first few lines of enemy horse shattered, but there were so many, *so many*, and they were streaking toward her, horses wild-eyed and spattered with gore, riders screaming their war cries and turning her blood to ice. With a feral cry of her own, Alix spurred her horse.

She lost her lance on the first charge, punching it through the breastplate of a passing rider and nearly unseating herself as the weapon was torn from her saddle. She had only a sword now, scant protection against an enemy lance. But she had no more than a heartbeat to think on it; an Oridian rider was bearing down on her, lance aimed at her gut. Alix did the only thing she could, swerving suddenly so that her horse took the brunt of the blow. She dove from the saddle as the mare screamed and went down, jarring the Oridian's lance from his grasp. The knight was thrown off balance and Alix didn't hesitate, lashing out at his horse's hock to sever the tendon. The animal buckled. The knight tried to dive free, but he wasn't fast enough; Alix ran him through from behind.

She whirled to look for Erik. He was still on horseback, Raibert Green at one flank, Pollard at the other. Alix started toward him, but she'd scarcely taken a step before she was intercepted by an enemy foot soldier. He was on her in a heartbeat, polearm swiping at her midsection with enough force to feel the draught. She skidded back on the balls of her feet. He followed the move with a quick jab, but Alix was ready, twisting aside and charging him before he could recover from the swing. Taking her bloodblade two-handed, she stabbed up under his exposed shoulder, the bloodbond guiding the tip of her sword into the joint between cuirass and pauldron. His mail shirt deflected the worst of it, but the pain brought him down to one knee, and that was enough. Alix hacked open his neck. A clean kill, but it came with a price: The impact was brutal on her wrist. Her arm throbbed from thumb to elbow. Already she could hear another wave of cavalry crashing over them, and this time the Kingsword pikes were largely spent, leaving only a thin barrier to protect them from the charge. Between the teeming mass of bodies, she could see thousands of pounds of horseflesh bearing down on her.

Alix stood paralysed, the calm in the eye of the storm. *I'm going to die.* The realisation came to her not in a bolt of panic, but as a cold, dull ache.

The scream of a horse pierced the haze. Alix turned in time to see Erik tumbling from his saddle. For a moment she thought she dreamed: She was back at Boswyck, watching in horror as her king was surrounded . . . But no—Raibert Green was there, shouting for someone. Shouting for her.

All thought fell away. Alix dove between the bodies, making for her king.

Even before he ordered the charge, Liam knew it was too late. He'd done as Erik asked, waited as the enemy trampled its way through the van, slaughtering untold numbers on the first pass. He'd watched the crimson wave break over the Kingsword centre, grinding his teeth as the screams reached his ears. *The rearguard needs to stay in the rear*, Rig had said, *or the king is vulnerable.*

Well and good, but the king was vulnerable *now*. It was Boswyck all over again, and Liam would be damned if he'd play the part of the Raven, sitting idle with the Pack while his brother's army was butchered.

"Bugger this," he growled. "We're going."

"Thank the gods," said Ide.

Liam drew his sword. *"Wolves! With me!"*

He brought them out wide, making for the enemy centre. All he needed was to get enough pressure off the Kingswords for them to regroup. It meant riding under a hail of arrows, for enemy longbowmen had taken up positions along the Kingsword flank, crouched behind tower shields as they let fly volley after volley. Apparently the Warlord didn't give a damn how many of his own men went down under the deluge; he had more than enough to spare.

Liam pushed his horse to a full gallop, offering as difficult a target as he could while he ran the gauntlet. Arrows peppered the grass around him, but he got through unscathed; daring a glance behind him, he saw that the Pack had taken minimal damage. They were moving too fast for anything but a lucky shot to find flesh. Meanwhile, the Kingsword horse archers had peeled off the van and were circling back around the row of tower shields to take the enemy archers from behind. Liam chose to believe that meant Rig was still alive and giving orders from whatever was left of the vanguard.

Behind the melee, the enemy lines were a mess. Sadik hadn't had time to issue orders, so his commanders were making it up as they went along. Not that it mattered—at this point, Sadik could vanish into thin air and it wouldn't make much difference. Tactics were an unnecessary bonus when your army could trample over the enemy like a herd of stampeding bison.

But that didn't mean Liam was going to give up. He'd had a good look and thought he spied a weak spot; veering sharply, he cut in.

Wooden dummies, he told himself, *just like in the yard. That's all they are.*

His bloodblade flashed, biting through flesh and mail, severing limbs and heads and anything else that got in his way. Ide rode close at his side; he could hear her grunting and swearing even above the chaos of battle. The Wolves carved a trench through the soft Oridian flank, broke though the far side, and wheeled to do it all over again. Just a few passes, enough to buy the Kingswords some breathing room, and then he would close up the rear . . .

Liam was turning his horse for a third pass when he saw the White banner go down at the heart of the Kingsword centre.

"No." Allie was with that banner. Erik's banner. If it had fallen . . .

Ide drew up at his side. She'd seen it too. "Can't be," she said. "Can't be."

Liam gripped the reins, numb with horror. The words he'd spoken to Alix the day before came back to him, bitterly vivid. *I have to believe I'll be given a chance to fix this.* "I'm too late," he whispered.

"Not your fault," Ide said. "Your orders—"

She didn't understand. Liam kicked his horse. He rode harder than he ever had in his life, the lines whipping past him in a blur. Dimly, he was aware that the battle had slowed; he didn't dare contemplate what that meant. *Please, Farika*, he prayed, *please don't let me be too late.*

Alix fought raggedly, keeping her foes at bay with sloppy two-handed swings. She could barely hold her sword. She gritted her teeth through the pain, keeping tight to Erik's left flank while Raibert Green covered the right. Pollard had been taken in the back while dragging the king away from his horse; his body lay near that of Erik's destrier, spitted cruelly upon a spear. The column of enemy cavalry that had broken through did not long survive, but the infantry were on them now, bloodred tabards haemorrhaging out of the Oridian centre in an unstanchable deluge.

Alix tried not to think. She swung and she hacked and she pivoted, glancing over her shoulder every few moments to check on Erik. The king fought with grim determination, even though he could not fail to notice how steadily they'd been pushed back. He gave no orders. What orders were there to give?

The bodies were so thick now that Alix couldn't see more than a few feet away. Oridian and Kingsword bled together in a teeming wall of metal and horseflesh. And then suddenly the wall shattered, a massive destrier blasting through like a stone flung from a catapult. Its rider was huge, more powerfully built even than Rig; he gripped a greatsword one-handed and wielded it to devastating effect, scything through flesh and bone as though it were ripe wheat. He wore bloodred armour gilded at the pauldrons and a helm fashioned to resemble the snarling maw of a carrion wolf, the Oridian symbol of death.

Again and again he swung his sword, reaping the bodies around him with little regard for friend or foe.

The Warlord.

The sight of him turned Alix's guts to water. She dove at Erik, started to tell him to run, but it was too late—he'd seen Sadik too, and a strange look came over him. Having a sudden premonition of what he was about to do, Alix reached for him, but he stepped away from her and cried, *"Stop!"*

At first, nothing happened. No one could hear him above the fray. He shouted an order at his flag-bearer, and the man brandished the White banner high.

That got the Warlord's attention. Reining in, Sadik threw a gauntleted fist in the air. Erik did the same, and gradually the fighting subsided. Oridian and Kingsword alike separated and stepped back warily, opening a ring of space at the centre of the merged armies.

"Enough, Sadik!" Erik's voice rang out clearly against a sudden, eerie silence. "Will you hear terms?"

The Warlord walked his huge destrier forward. Alix stepped in front of Erik, but he put a hand on her arm and moved her gently aside. The wolf helm gazed down on them in silence. Then Sadik dipped his head and tore it free. Cold blue eyes stared out from a face hewn from granite, its brutal edges framed by a short-cropped beard as meticulous as that of the late Arran Green. "King Erik White," he said. Looking Alix up and down, he added, "And your troublesome body-guard." He levelled a gauntleted finger at her. "You owe me a bloodbinder, my lady."

"You address me," Erik said, "and me alone."

Sadik snorted softly. "Very well. What terms do you offer?"

"Get down from your horse and let us discuss it." He met the Warlord's gaze unflinchingly, and though he looked small and vulnerable standing before the massive destrier, there was a dignity to his bearing that filled Alix with pride, as even as she felt her heart must burst with grief.

Sadik's mouth curled in amusement, but he complied, stepping down from his warhorse. Still he towered over Erik. "Is that better, Your Majesty? Now, what terms?"

"My head. It's yours if you want it."

"Erik!" Alix seized his elbow. "What are you doing?"

"Protecting the people I love." Gently, he pried her fingers free. "Don't make me have you restrained, Captain."

Sadik regarded the king with narrowed eyes. He was no beast, however beastly his actions; Alix saw a cold intelligence in his gaze that terrified her.

"You know as well as I do," Erik said, "that you will need every man at your disposal to hold the territory you've gained. Accept my terms, and you need not spend even one more soldier today. The Kingswords will stand down. I will give you my life. You will have your total victory."

"And in return?"

"My family goes free. My brother, my sister-in-law. Her brother, if he yet lives. There will be none of your royal purges. The banner lords retain their holdings, provided they swear fealty to you."

"Your Majesty." Sirin Grey appeared at his side. "The Greys will forsake their lands if needs be. The price is too high."

"Far too high," agreed Raibert Green. "We are together in this, if Alden has any meaning at all."

Erik ignored them both, his gaze locked with Sadik's. "Do you accept?"

Alix took his arm again. Let him have her restrained if he dared. "Please, Erik, don't do this. Liam wouldn't want this. I don't want this." Tears brimmed in her eyes, but she would die before she let them fall. She wouldn't give the Warlord the satisfaction.

Erik was breathing hard, but he didn't even glance at her. "Well?"

Sadik bowed his head as if in thought. Then, in a single smooth motion, he yanked a spear from a corpse at his feet and hurled it into the breast of the Kingsword flag-bearer. "There is my answer, Erik White," he said as the young knight sank to his knees, grasping pitifully at the weapon in his chest.

"Make way!" cried a voice, and Vel jostled through the crowd. *Everyone's gathering round now*, Alix thought dully, *to witness the end*. The priestess's robe was spattered with blood, presumably from treating the wounded. She dropped to her knees beside the flag-bearer, but it was hopeless; even Alix could see that.

Erik's face flooded with rage. "This is a game to you, isn't it? You kill for sport!"

Sadik shrugged. "Your offer does not interest me. You are defeated, Your Majesty. It makes no difference to me if I lose a few more men convincing you of that fact. As for your head, it is not your skull that belongs on my mantelpiece."

"No," said a familiar voice, "it's mine."

Rig shoved his way through the ring of soldiers. He looked like he'd been in a bare-knuckled brawl with a grizzly, scratched and bloodied from helm to boots, but he moved with the same powerful stride as always. Somehow, he'd survived the van.

"General Black," Sadik said, and there was such a wistful tone in his voice that it made Alix shiver with dread. "I am pleased to see you whole. It vexed me to think you might have fallen to some anonymous spear."

"I'm tough to kill," Rig said. "Would you like to try your luck?"

Sadik laughed. "Are you challenging me to single combat?"

"Looks like it."

Alix made a small, strangled sound. Everyone had heard the tales. The Warlord had earned his place by defeating his rivals in single combat.

"Now that *is* a tempting offer," Sadik said. "It has been a very long time since anyone dared challenge me."

"Afraid you're rusty?"

The Warlord's expression darkened. "Mind your tongue, or I'll cut it out."

"You're welcome to try," Rig said, unsheathing the greatsword strapped to his back.

Sadik's gauntlets twitched at his sides. His eyes bored into Rig hungrily. *He's going to do it,* Alix thought. *He's going to fight my brother.* The idea brought hope and grief in equal measure.

Then he snorted and said, "You think to goad me as if I were some brash young fool? I have nothing to gain and everything to lose."

Rig's lip curled. "Coward."

"What's it to be, then?" Erik demanded. "Do you truly wish to fight to the last man?"

Sadik started to reply, but was cut off by a commotion behind him. His men were stirring, heads turning, and then a voice cried in Oridian, "We're under attack! They're coming at us from behind!"

Rig frowned. Alix and Erik exchanged a look. Neither Liam nor Rona could have outflanked the entire Oridian army. *Who . . . ?*

Sadik paused for half a heartbeat. Then, without warning, he flicked a blade into his hand and lunged. Alix threw herself in front of Erik just in time to take the Warlord's dagger in her gut. It punched through her armour as though it weren't even there, a pain unlike anything she had ever known. The force of the blow doubled her over, sent her staggering back into Erik.

There was a moment of silence, a single heartbeat that sent a wash of dark blood over Alix's fingers. Then Rig threw himself at the Warlord with an inhuman roar; blades met in a brutal, ringing blow.

Alix's vision swam. She heard Erik's voice in her ear, and Vel's, and she thought she even saw Liam diving toward her, face twisted in anguish.

The battle flared to life. Bodies teemed in every direction. Someone had taken off her cuirass. Vel was leaning on her with both hands, bloodied to the elbows, shouting something Alix couldn't make out.

"Who?" Alix whispered.

"Stand back!" the priestess cried over her shoulder. "I need room!" Then, to Alix: "Hush. Don't try to talk."

"The attack . . . who?" She had to know before she fell into darkness. She *had* to.

Then she heard a sound from her childhood, and she knew: a ram's horn just like the one she'd played with as a girl in Blackhold. Her father had claimed that warhorn in battle long ago, after a skirmish hard-fought against a formidable foe.

The mountain tribes. The men who had captured Erik and Alix in the mountains, who'd brought the King of Alden before their council to plead for his life, and for his kingdom. The tribesmen had turned him away, his pleas falling on deaf ears— or so everyone had thought. But the horns told a different tale, their thick, rasping notes heralding the arrival of an army that had not ridden as one in centuries.

"They came," Alix murmured. "Erik, they came . . ." She clung to that thought as she tumbled down and down into blackness.

It was not over yet. The Harrami had come.

THIRTY-THREE

For a moment Erik stood frozen, a single thought circling his mind like a vulture, over and over: *I've killed her. I've killed her.*

Then another voice spoke. Tom's voice. *Focus*, it said. *The battle is not over. You must focus.*

Erik shook his head to clear it. He stood within a protective ring of his guardsmen, but it was steadily collapsing. All around him, battle raged, the brief lull already a distant memory. He concentrated on the nearest point of clarity in the chaos: Rig and the Warlord. The two of them circled each other like pit dogs, twisting and lunging, their bloodblades ringing off one another in reckless fury. The rest of the men gave them a wide berth. More than a few had stopped to watch, Oridian standing idle beside Kingsword to gawk at the spectacle. Even the priestess, occupied as she was tending to Alix, could not help glancing over every few moments.

Erik started toward the Warlord. He had no qualms about taking him in the back, not after what he had done. But then a familiar voice called his name, and he turned to find Liam fending off two attackers, trying to keep them away from Alix and the priestess. Erik dove in to help, driving one of them back even as he pivoted to face a third. Out of the corner of his eye he saw Raibert Green and Sirin Grey fighting for their lives, surrounded by an ever-tightening ring of crimson. They would be no help. The royal guardsmen were all but spent, every Kingsword locked in combat. Slowly but surely, they were drowning in a sea of Oridians.

The Harrami tribesmen had come, but whatever brief jubilation Erik had felt was long gone. At this rate, he would be dead long before the battle was decided, and Alix and Liam with him.

But not yet.

He closed with his brother's flank. Together they would be a wall shielding Alix. And if they fell, at least they would fall together.

"I've stanched the bleeding," the priestess called from behind them, "but I need to get her out of here or we'll lose her."

She will be lost anyway, Erik thought dully. *We are all lost.* He fought on, regardless.

The Oridian tide swelled. Rig and Sadik were the only faces Erik recognised now. Green had vanished, and Sirin too, swallowed in the melee. Everywhere he looked, all he saw was the enemy . . .

There. A single Kingsword cavalryman, hacking away from atop his destrier. But no, there was another, and another . . . As Erik watched, they seemed to multiply before his eyes, fresh as the dawn, mowing down the enemy foot soldiers with sword and mace and heavy-shod hooves. A moment more of confusion, and then Erik understood: Rona Brown crashed across his view, sword swinging in a blood-stained arc. The reserves had arrived.

Choose your moment well, Erik had told her. And so she had, waiting until every lance and spear was spent before driving her cavalry straight at the enemy's heart. The infantry were weak as lambs, and Rona had brought the slaughter to them.

Strength flooded anew to Erik's limbs. An Oridian rushed at him, half fleeing, half attacking. Planting his feet, Erik braced for his enemy.

Rig fought in a blind fury. He knew nothing else. Fear, pain, the bitter sense of failure—all of it evaporated in the inferno of his rage. Nothing but grief could withstand it, and that grief was a great gaping maw at the core of his being. He filled it with still more rage, until it felt as if his very bone marrow were molten steel.

Sadik met his blows with skill and strength, but Rig was undaunted. Every grunt from his enemy, every inch of ground conceded was a tiny victory, a wisp of oxygen drawn into the furnace of Rig's wrath. He swung again and again, aiming for neck, knees, ribs, his bloodblade seeming weightless as the enchantment bound weapon to man. He kept light on his feet, forcing his enemy to pivot like a bull keeping a wolf at bay with its horns. The Warlord was bigger than he, and older, and his vainglorious plate armour was much heavier. Rig processed all of this as he did the clamour around him, the smell of blood and sweat: He absorbed it without thinking. None of it cluttered his focus, his unwavering concentration on the bloodred demon in his sights.

Sadik's blade cleaved the air, seeking to cave in the side of Rig's skull. Rig ducked under the blow and lashed out with an elbow, taking the Warlord in the chin, but the man didn't even stagger; he hooked Rig with his own elbow and threw him to the ground. Whirling, Sadik took his blade half-hand and drove it like a spear at Rig's breast. It bit deep into the dirt as Rig twitched aside, his boot lashing out at the Warlord's knee to send him stumbling. Rig rolled to his feet and cocked his sword, point levelled at Sadik's throat.

Again he dove in, and again Sadik parried. Over and over, long past the point where Rig should have been too tired to lift his blade. Vaguely, as from a great distance, he could sense things changing around him; a breath of hope stirring, like the gentle ruffling of wind in limp sails. He drew it in, fed it to the furnace. He brought a concussive blow down against Sadik's blade, forcing the Warlord to spin out of the way. Rig had just enough human thought left to recognise the grim set of the other man's jaw. The smug look was gone. Rig had beaten it off his face. He fed that to the furnace too.

Gradually, he became aware that the noise around him was growing. Something had happened. Rig registered it, fought through it. Pivoting, he came at Sadik again. The Warlord shuffled back, sending onlookers scattering. All but one. A familiar figure strode up behind him, raised his sword, and plunged it at the Warlord's shoulder blades. Sadik's armour turned the blow aside, but he twisted instinctively to face the threat, and that was his undoing. Rig rammed the point of his greatsword at the joint between faulds and cuirass, burying it to the hilt.

Sadik pitched to his knees with a howl of rage and pain. Raising his head, he looked up at the man who had tried to stab him. Erik gazed back at him with the impassive expression of one who has had his insides scraped out. Rig knew that face. He wore it now.

"You would sneak up on me like a thief, Erik White?" Sadik roared. "Have you no honour?"

"Not for you," Erik said, and Rig swept the Warlord's head from his shoulders.

Liam knew that if he stopped fighting for even a moment, he would come undone. He watched Erik walk away from him to stab the Warlord in the back. He saw Rig take the monster's head. But Liam didn't pause, seeking out the next foe and the next, killing anything in crimson. The reserves had punched a gaping hole through the enemy's side, relieving the pressure, but the battle was far from over. Liam ducked under the blow of one enemy to come up under another, ramming his sword into the man's chest in a quick in-and-out, whirling in the same motion to drive the pommel of his sword into the face of the man who'd taken a swing at him. He brought his knee up into his enemy's gut, doubling him over and exposing his neck. Liam sliced him open and moved on. Seeing him come for them, a pair of Oridians rushed him together; Liam drew his dagger with his off hand and jammed it under the jaw of one while he turned aside the lunge of another. He was bleeding, he wasn't sure from where, but he didn't care. He finished off his foe and scanned the field for another. He may as well have been a thrall for all the thought he gave to it, too numb even to be appalled by the efficiency of his killing.

So intent was he on bloodshed that it took him a moment to realise someone was calling his name. Rona Brown's horse danced in front of him, blocking his path. "The Harrami have scattered the rearguard! The enemy is vulnerable!"

The words skipped over his consciousness like a smooth stone across water, making only the briefest of ripples. "I have to stay with Allie," he said, turning away.

His gaze fell on Erik. Surrounded by a ring of knights once more, the king was pointing, giving orders Liam couldn't hear. Erik strode purposefully over to Raibert Green, passing Alix as he did so, only a fleeting glance at her prone form betraying his thoughts. A fleeting glance, but packed with so much emotion that it struck Liam like a blow across the face, snapping him out of the red haze. *He feels this as much as you do. But he can't afford to come apart, because he's king.*

He's king, and you're the prince. So get a sodding grip and do your job.

Turning back to Rona, he said, "I need a horse."

Ide had the Pack skirmishing along the edges of the enemy centre, but the moment she spotted Liam riding toward her, she rounded them up and fell in behind him. Rona was right, Liam saw as they veered out wide of the lines—the Oridian rearguard was a mess. The Harrami had them pinned in on three sides, peppering them with arrows in a display of horsemanship like none Liam had ever seen. Their thick, shaggy horses wheeled as if of their own accord, guided by the merest pressure of the riders' knees, leaving the tribesmen to fire their weapons over and over at short range. They were dropping enemy soldiers, but mostly they were causing panic. The Oridians swarmed about like ants. Liam didn't blame them—the Harrami were bloody *terrifying*. Wild and foreign, relentless, dive-bombing over and over like birds of prey. And they were untouchable; the few Oridians foolish enough to get close ended up with a curved blade across their throats as reward.

The Oridian rearguard was breaking apart, many in full flight. They were useless. The van had largely been spent devouring the Kingswords. But the enemy centre was still a threat. Only the first half or so had engaged; the rest remained in reserve, seemingly torn between attacking the Kingsword centre or turning back in relief of the rear. Liam made the choice for them, bringing the Pack in a thundering charge to cut through the centre ranks, splitting them in two. He sent one battle pushing east, the other west, deepening the wedge between the two halves of the enemy. The Harrami read the manoeuvre almost immediately, swooping in behind the Pack and herding the stray lines into the rearguard before closing in around them. Surrounded, the swollen Oridian rearguard had two choices: surrender or die.

That left half the centre and what remained of the shattered van to face the entire Kingsword army, and they would have to do it without the Warlord. Bereft of their commander, they did the only sensible thing: They fled.

"You did it!" Ide cried, drawing up alongside Liam. "It's done! By the gods, it's done!"

It was true, Liam saw. The rearguard had surrendered to the Harrami. Only a few pockets of fighting remained, concentrated at the Kingsword centre. They wouldn't last long, not with Rona commanding a full battalion of fresh cavalry.

A current of joy arced through Liam, brief as lightning. It left behind the sulphurous taste of despair. The battle might be won, but his wife still lay dying in a blood-soaked field.

He looked over at Ide, and she read it in his face. "Alix . . . she all right?"

"No," Liam tried to say, but the word didn't really come out.

"Is she—"

He gave a short shake of his head. "But it's bad."

"She's strong. Come on, you'll see." Without waiting for a reply, Ide kicked her horse.

Strong, Liam told himself as he followed Ide back to the place where Allie lay. *Strongest woman I've ever known.* Stronger than he was, that was certain. But being strong was no bulwark against death. Nor could it protect you from grief. Liam could feel it dragging him down with cold claws, whispering in his ear with a poison tongue.

A cool wind raced up from the south, buffeting him as he rode. Bowing his head against it, Liam prayed.

THIRTY-FOUR

✝ "**Y**ou should try to eat something, brother."
Liam started as if from a dream. He glanced out
the window of the farmhouse and saw that it was still
afternoon; sunlight glinted off Rig's armour as he paced
back and forth in front of the window like a caged beast.

Erik held something out to him. A peach. Had they seen
peach trees when they rode up to the farmhouse? Liam
couldn't recall. He barely remembered anything about that
ride. Alix's face, still and bloodless. Fields of wheat stretching
out like a vast ocean, no shelter in sight. The pounding of the
horses' hooves, and then the pounding on the door, Rig's gruff
voice demanding entry in the name of the king . . .

And then there was only this dark little farmhouse. This
scarred table, these rickety chairs, and *that door*—the silent
sentry barring Liam from the bedchamber where his wife lay
fighting for her life. Erik flitted in and out of his awareness,
and Rig's shadow passed relentlessly by the window, but
Liam's every sense bent toward *that door*, grasping for the
slightest clue about what went on behind it.

"At least take some water," Erik said. Dully, Liam complied.

Time passed. Liam sat numbly, watching the door. Until finally, when he could stand it no longer, he rose and started toward it.

A hand on his arm stopped him. Erik's. "Leave it, Liam. There's nothing you can do in there. The priestess knows her business."

"I need to see her."

"I know, but you must wait." He was so calm. How was he so calm?

"It *can't* wait," Liam said. "It might already be too late. If this is our last . . . if she . . ." He couldn't choke out the words. "I need to tell her—"

"Sit down, brother."

Liam wrenched his arm free, almost grateful for the flash of anger that warmed his skin. At least it was *something*. "That's my wife in there, Erik. My *wife*. Do you understand?" He started to say more, but the look on Erik's face stole the words from his gods-cursed tongue.

"Don't you dare," Erik said softly. "Don't you ever again ask me if I understand."

He sounded so dispassionate as he said it, and yet Liam could sense that his brother was clinging to the tatters of his composure with every scrap of strength he had.

Shame flooded his breast. "Erik—"

"Never mind. Just please, stay here."

Liam gripped his brother's arm. He didn't trust himself to speak, but maybe his eyes said it all, because Erik nodded and returned his grasp warmly. They stood like that for a long time, and when finally they turned back to the door, Liam felt a measure of peace come over him. Not *instead* of the grief and fear, but alongside it, in solidarity. And that was the thing about emotions, wasn't it? You could feel so many incompatible things at once. They didn't replace each other, just crowded together into something strange and maybe beautiful.

It was then, standing beside his brother staring at that door, that Liam figured it out. Erik's love for Alix, and hers for him, didn't come at the expense of their love for Liam. It was there alongside, in solidarity. Their bond was their own, different and wonderful and something to be cherished. Including by him.

If only he'd understood that sooner.

The sun slumped in the sky. Outside, Rig's muted footfalls beat out a steady toll, like the passing of time. Until at last the door opened and the priestess emerged.

The sight of her nearly brought Liam to his knees.

Her sleeves were soaked in blood, her face lined with exhaustion. And when she closed the door softly behind her, Liam was certain that it was over, and all his precious insights had come too late.

Called as if by instinct, Rig burst through the door. He too was brought up short by the sight of the priestess; he stood in the doorway trembling like a child.

"She is out of danger for now," Vel said, and for a moment Liam heard nothing more, clutching at the back of a chair for support. He felt his brother's hand on his arm, steadying him. When the roar in his ears died away, he heard the priestess continuing, ". . . at least a few days. And the stitches will need constant treatment if the wound is not to become septic."

Rig blew out something between an oath and a prayer and plunged back outside, shoving his hands through his hair in a gesture of violent relief.

It took Liam a moment to find his voice. "Can I see her?"

"She sleeps, but yes, you can stay by her bedside."

Erik stepped back, but Liam said, "No, you should come. She'll want you there when she wakes up."

Gratitude flashed through Erik's eyes. He nodded, and they went through the door together.

Alix drifted in and out of sleep. Every time she opened her eyes, she found a different set of faces: Liam and Erik, then Liam and Rig, then Vel . . . Each time she tried to speak, and each time she was gently hushed and left to slip away again. She had no notion of where she was or what had become of the battle, but she knew her loved ones were safe, and that was what mattered. So she slept peacefully, if fitfully, aided no doubt by a concoction of Vel's. And when finally she felt herself climbing back to consciousness, it was Liam's face, and his alone, she found leaning over her.

"Hi," he said, his fingers drifting along her hairline.

"Hi."

She expected a quip, some remark about how long she'd slept, but the customary spark of mischief was nowhere to be seen. Instead, his eyes were the dappled grey of the sea, soft hues of exhaustion and sorrow mingled with something else, something . . . still.

"What happened?"

"It's over. Sadik is dead. The Oridians are on the run."

At first she was confused, but as Liam explained, small details began to come back to her: the sound of the Harrami horn, the brutal clash of steel as Rig fought the Warlord . . . "It really happened," she whispered. "I thought it must have been a dream."

"No dream. Alden is still free, and our allies are mopping up as we speak. The Oridians are caught between the Harrami in the west and the Onnani in the east. Those who don't surrender will run all the way back to Varadast with their tails between their legs."

"And the Kingswords?"

A wave of grief swelled in his eyes. "As bad as Boswyck," he said quietly. "Worse, maybe. But it's over."

He climbed into bed beside her, wrapping her in his warmth. *It's over.* Alix knew that wasn't quite true, but she clung to it all the same, even as she clung to her husband. Outside, dawn was breaking over a free Alden, over the farmhouse filled with the people she loved most. A blessing beyond any she had dared to hope for.

For now, at least, that was enough.

Vel had come to him the night after she'd saved Alix's life. She'd found him sitting alone outside, hunkered down by a fire, honing his greatsword with numb, practiced movements. He'd looked in on his sister briefly, placed a kiss on Allie's forehead and a hand on Liam's shoulder, and then he'd gone out to the yard to be alone, having nothing to offer but the same bittersweet mix of relief and sorrow that already saturated the place. He hadn't known how to react when Vel came to him except to thank her for what she'd done. But she'd brushed that off, putting her arms around him and letting him *take* from her again, offering freely the comfort he so desperately needed but would never ask for. And he'd let her, gods damn him, selfish to the last, basking in the soothing cadence of her voice and the soft touch of her fingers in his hair. He'd needed the priestess and she'd come to him, in spite of everything, and he had no doubt that if he'd needed his lover, she would have been that too. That, more than anything else, was the blade in his guts.

The intervening days had done nothing to dull the guilt, nor the conflicting emotions that still dogged him. Rig knew how he *should* feel, and also how he *did* feel, and the fact that he couldn't reconcile the two drove him to haunt the corridors of the royal palace like a restless spirit.

Thus did Vel find him on the day she came to say good-bye.

"I thought you might be here," she said as she entered the Map Room. Glancing around, she added, "From the moment I first blundered into this room, I knew it must be a favourite of yours. Soldiers do love their maps." She joined him where he stood, gazing up at a centuries-old rendering of the Blacklands. "You are thinking of home," she said. "Missing it, no doubt. It must be very beautiful."

Taking in her travelling clothes, Rig said gruffly, "I suppose you're heading home too?"

She shook her head. "Timra. It will be liberated soon. I must find my brother, if he yet lives. If Sadik uncovered my lies, or learned of my role in rescuing Rodrik . . . But that is unlikely. I choose to believe my brother is still alive and in those dungeons, in which case, I must go to him."

Stay.

Rig wanted so badly to say it, but for once he restrained himself. He would not ask her to wait around while he sorted through the tangle of his heart. It wasn't fair. Besides, he knew instinctively that this was the one thing she would deny him. Her brother commanded her love and loyalty first and foremost, and the gods knew he must deserve it more than Rig.

"You could have told me, Vel."

She looked away, her composure flickering. "I see that now. You cannot know how bitterly I regret it." Sighing, she added, "Ironically, it was my feelings for you that prevented me. You were already unattainable. If I had told you, whatever slim chance I might have had would be lost. I wanted you too much to risk it. So I followed Ardin instead of Eldora. A pattern, it seems."

"For us both."

"But it means rather more for me," she said, wry and bitter. "When I find my brother and return to Onnan, I will relinquish the grey robes. Perhaps they will let me take the red."

He turned to her in dismay. "Don't do that. Vel, that's the most impulsive decision of them all." She opened her mouth to reply, but he cut her off. "You told me once that faith is supposed to be hard. I might not be a priest, but even I know you can't expect to pass every test. You're only human."

Dark eyes met his. As always, Rig felt as though he were swimming in their depths. "Perhaps," she said. "I will think on it."

Rig managed a weak grin. "Besides, if you change orders, what chance do I have? Eldora never fancied me until you came along."

"May she watch over you all the same, General." Standing on her toes, Vel kissed his forehead.

"Good-bye, Daughter, and good luck. I hope you find your brother."

"Thank you."

"Maybe you'll pass through here on your way home?"

But she denied him that too, shaking her head. "Perhaps you should come to Onnan City instead. Every man should see the sea at least once in his life."

"I'd like that," he said roughly.

Rig stared at the door long after she'd gone. Then he lifted his gaze once more to the map of the Blacklands before him, her mountains and pine forests slanting gracefully across the leather. *Blackhold*, it read in a suitably bold hand.

Time to go home, Rig thought. To what life, he could not say.

"Beg your pardon, sire."

Erik turned. A guardsman stood in the doorway of the study. Erik cast about for the man's name but came up empty-handed; virtually every guardsman he knew had fallen on the battlefield, and he had not yet had time to learn all the new faces.

"Visitors for you. They're with the, er . . ." The guardsman glanced behind him. "The *guest* contingent."

"We have rather a lot of those at the moment. Could you be more specific?"

"Harrami, sire." Then, in a whisper, *"Tribesmen."*

Stifling a smile, Erik said, "Please show them in."

It was more than passing strange to watch his two former captors walk through the door of his study. And not just for him; Sakhr was as coiled as a suspicious cat, and Qhara's gaze roamed about the room as though she had never seen anything quite like it. Which, Erik supposed, she hadn't. Certainly there was nothing in their tiny mountain village that would prepare them for the gilt wood and marble of the royal palace of Alden. "Welcome," Erik said in High Harrami, gesturing for them to join him at the window.

Brother and sister crossed the room in long strides. They were every bit as beautiful as he remembered, tall and grace-ful, dark of skin and hair. Only now they were clad in battle armour, impressive scale mail fashioned of horn and boiled leather. The only metal they wore was the curved blades strapped to their slender waists.

Following Erik's glance, Sakhr said, "Do your guards not fear letting armed strangers near their king? Especially those who were once your enemy?"

"You were never my enemy," Erik said. "And now you are allies."

Qhara eyed him shrewdly. "And you are making a point."

Erik smiled. "Perhaps."

The tribeswoman's green-gold gaze travelled the compass of the room once more. "Your bodyguard. She is not here?" Sakhr frowned and said something in their own language, and his sister winced. "Forgive me, I had forgotten. She was wounded in the battle. How does she fare?"

"Well enough," Erik said. "I have given her some much-deserved time off." Gesturing at the cluster of plush chairs, he added, "Please, sit."

The Harrami lowered themselves warily onto the chairs, eyes widening briefly as they sank into the upholstery. Erik recalled only too well what passed for chairs in their culture.

Compared to a tripod of sticks and a saddle of leather, the Andithyrian wingbacks must have seemed ridiculously soft.

"King chairs," Sakhr muttered, not flatteringly.

Qhara had already lost interest in the chairs. She was staring at Erik even more intently than she had done in Harram, when he had felt her eyes on him at every turn. She had stared at him on the battlefield too, as they had exchanged their brief greetings. What fascinated her so, Erik could not guess. He arched a questioning eyebrow, and it was all the invitation she needed. "Is it true?" she said. "Did the Oridians control your mind?"

Sakhr blurted something exasperated. "Forgive my sister. She has no respect."

Qhara scowled. "I have plenty of respect. The more so if the stories are true and he was fighting off the dark witch even while he met with the *pasha*."

Erik hesitated a long moment before replying. He could not allow his composure to slip, a task he still found difficult when discussing his ordeal. He meant what he had said—these people were not enemies—but Alden was weak, and the health of her king was the subject of much speculation at home and abroad. He needed to convey strength and stability, especially in front of foreigners. "It is true that I was under the influence of an enemy bloodbinder," he said carefully.

Qhara was not about to let him off that easily. "Even while you were in Harram?"

"Yes."

"Your words to the *pasha* . . ."

"My own," Erik said firmly. "Though it was difficult for me to speak them. The spell the enemy had cast upon me made it hard to concentrate, and even harder not to become emotional. It was a struggle."

Sakhr grunted. "It did not show. Your words convinced the *pasha* that the time had come to fight the foreign *mustevi* once again, as our ancestors did before us."

"That," Qhara said, "and yet another provocation from the Oridians. They were fools to cross the pass again. Your words resonated even more after that."

"I am glad," Erik said. "And I have not yet had a chance to

formally express my gratitude. Who leads your armies, that I may thank him or her personally?"

"We have no single leader," Sakhr said. "The tribes agreed to plan and fight together, that is all."

"And your tribe? Who led them on the battlefield?"

Qhara laughed. Even the solemn Sakhr looked amused. "You did not know? My sister led our army." He glanced at her, and with unmistakable pride added, "A great honour."

"A punishment," she said wryly, "for my words that day with the *pasha*. Since I spoke for you, Ghous thought it only fitting that I carry the responsibility of seeing through what I had set in motion. I think it amused him."

Erik smiled. It sounded like the old man. "I did not know you were a commander general."

She made a dismissive gesture. "I led our kinsmen this time. The next, it will be someone else."

"Regardless, the Kingdom of Alden owes you a great debt, all of you. If there is any way I can repay you, do not hesitate to ask."

Qhara didn't hesitate. "You can tell Ost to release us. Give back our lands and leave us be."

Erik sighed. "That I cannot do. I have nowhere near enough influence with King Omaïd to treat on your behalf, especially not now. You may be aware that we quarrelled over the fate of the mountain tribes while I was in Ost. It is why the Harrami legions did not respond to my call for aid."

"But the *sukhadan* answered your call," Sakhr said.

"You did, and I am eternally grateful, but . . ."

"But Omaïd will be even more angry with you now," Qhara finished.

"Very probably. Your bravery has shamed him, and my extending you full diplomatic courtesy will not ingratiate me, either."

Qhara hitched a shoulder indifferently. "His friendship has no value. Therefore, it is no loss."

Erik was inclined to agree, though it would not do to say so. "Is there anything else you would have of me? Something within my power to give?"

Qhara and Sakhr exchanged a look. "We will think on this," Qhara said. "It must be discussed with the *pasha* and the Council of Twelve."

"Of course. I will await your reply."

They rose. Sakhr started for the door, but Qhara said, "You go. I have something else to discuss with the king." Her brother arched an eyebrow but took his leave.

Qhara turned back to Erik, and there was a glint of mischief in her green-gold eyes that had not been there before. Glancing over him, she said, "You look better than you did in the mountains, Imperial Erik. Like a proper king. But you grew the beard back. I do not like it."

Erik laughed, rubbing the week's worth of growth on his jaw. "I needed a change. And it's my way of honouring someone." A twinge of pain as he said that, somewhere in the deepest part of him.

Qhara went to the window and gazed out into the rose garden. It had hit its full exuberance these past few days, rows of yellow and white and bloodred crisscrossing over sparkling white gravel. "The roses in my lands are not like this," Qhara said. "They are strong and covered in sharp thorns, but not so beautiful."

"These are strong and sharp too," Erik said, "even if they are beautiful."

"I believe you." She turned and gave him a strange look. "They suit you, I think."

Erik wasn't quite sure what to say to that.

Qhara reached for him. Erik flinched away instinctively—this woman had been his captor, after all—but she only touched his cheek, trailing her fingertips gently through his beard. She grimaced. "You imperials with your face hair." Then, quite without warning, she leaned in and swept a fleeting kiss across his lips.

For a moment, Erik was too astonished to speak. "What was that?"

"The beard. I have always wondered."

He laughed. "And?"

"It is not so bad. Perhaps I will try again sometime."

Sobering, Erik said, "In earnest, Qhara, thank you. I think this makes us officially even."

"No, not even. You owe me, Imperial Erik, and one day I will collect." The words were lightly spoken, but there was a hint of iron in her eyes that signalled something deeper.

Erik inclined his head. "Until then."

It was only after she had gone that Erik remembered she had stayed behind to tell him something. Perhaps, in her own way, she had.

Alix appeared in the doorway. "What was that?" she said, hooking a thumb over her shoulder.

"I honestly have no idea."

"She looked like the cat that found the cream."

"Never mind Qhara—why are you walking about?"

Alix waved him off irritably. "If I stay in bed any longer, I'll go mad."

"Where is your husband? Terribly remiss of him to let you out . . ."

"Taking Rudi for a walk."

"Don't we have people for that sort of thing?"

"To walk Rudi? You want some poor servant to lose an arm?"

"Fair point."

Gingerly, Alix sank into a chair. "Rig says he's off tomorrow."

"I heard."

"I'm worried about him. After so long at war, going home to find Blackhold a shadow of its former self. And now this business with Vel . . ."

"He'll be all right. He'll hurt for a while, but Rig is strong. He'll get past it." *We all will*, he added silently.

A solemn look came over Alix, as if she had heard his thoughts. Hardly surprising; she knew him better than anyone in the world. "You're right," she said. "For the first time in a long time, I believe that."

Erik reached out and took her hand—tentatively at first, mindful of her injured wrist, but she didn't flinch. *It's healing*, he thought. *Slowly, but it's healing.*

Glancing up, he saw that Alix had read his thoughts again. She smiled.

EPILOGUE

† "A tournament," said Albern Highmount, stroking his beard. "An interesting notion, sire."

Erik snorted softly. Highmount had two ways of pronouncing the word *interesting*. The first meant that the chancellor indeed found the idea of interest, the second that he thought it complete rubbish. His inflection just now was decidedly of the second variety. "I know what you're going to say. We can't afford it."

"I believe that is what your brother His Highness would refer to as the understatement of our age. We are quite thoroughly bankrupt, sire."

"We'll work it out. Taxes or some such."

"Taxes," Highmount echoed dubiously.

"The people need something to take their minds off the war. Celebrate our glorious victory, so on and so forth. You know I'm right."

"I do not dispute the sentiment, Your Majesty, it is the state of the royal treasury that concerns me. We are already borrowing heavily from Onnan to purchase Harrami grain."

"You say that as though I didn't sign the documents myself. Don't be such a pessimist, Chancellor. There is always a way."

"I shall make a note of it, Your Majesty," the old man said dryly. "Now, if we may pass to the next item on our agenda?"

Erik's gaze strayed to the window. It was a splendid day outside, and he wanted nothing more than to take a stroll through the rose garden. How was it that the peacetime agenda managed to be even more cumbersome than in wartime?

"Sire?"

"I'm listening," Erik said with only the faintest sigh.

"I will indulge you, sire, and skip to the last item, which is the lynching in Andithyri."

Just like that, Erik's good mood evaporated. "It's confirmed, then?"

"I am afraid so. Two Andithyrian bloodbinders, both hanged by the mob—in full view, they say, of the city guard."

Erik shook his head grimly. "It's started, then. Just as we feared."

"It was all but inevitable after word got out of what happened here."

"I understand the anger against the Oridians, but to murder their own?"

"The Andithyrian bloodbinders did work for Sadik for over two years, however unwillingly. Besides, all bloodbinders carry the stain of what happened in this war. First the Priest and his thrall army, and then the King of Alden . . . The bloodbond is tainted now, as are those who wield it. People fear it as dark magic, and in their fear they do beastly things."

"But the danger has passed." So far as they knew, at any rate. Nevyn believed himself the only bloodbinder alive to have mastered the Priest's secret, and was convinced that would remain the case until he died. As usual, however, he had been damnably vague about the details of his theory.

"That was obviously of little comfort to the mob," Highmount said.

"Perhaps we should release Nevyn from service. He may be in danger. Perhaps it's better if he finds someplace discreet to wait this out."

"And let a man with such power roam free?" Highmount's bushy eyebrow climbed.

"I suppose you're right. Still, we had better put a guard on him. His has become a deadly profession, it seems."

Highmount made a note of it on his ledger. "Just one more thing, Your Majesty . . ."

"Oh no," Erik said, holding up a hand. "That's enough for today. I have barely an hour of sunshine left and I mean to take advantage of it."

"Very well," Highmount said, rising. "I will add the remaining items to tomorrow's agenda."

Erik waited until the door clicked behind the chancellor. Then he said, "You can stop smirking at me like that."

"What?" said a voice behind him. "I'm not smirking."

"Of course you are, and I know why. It's frivolous of me, I'll grant you, but I've simply a very low tolerance for doom and gloom these days."

"No need to explain," Alix said. "I quite approve, actually."

"You approve of me being frivolous?"

"I approve of you taking some time for yourself. The gods know you deserve it."

He glanced over his shoulder. "As do you, so if there is nothing else, you are through for the day, Captain."

There was a time, not so long ago, when Alix would have needed convincing. But she was anxious to get back to Liam, so she just nodded and headed for the door. "See you at breakfast."

"What, you'll miss supper?" Erik asked, all innocence. "Again?" He burst out laughing as the blush flamed across her cheeks. It was cruel to tease her, perhaps, but he couldn't resist. It was just so good to see the two of them basking in each other's company once more.

He took his time strolling through the rose garden, soaking up the fading rays of early summer. Ducks frolicked and flapped in the pond, and a low hum of honeybees droned in the air. If he closed his eyes, Erik could almost pretend that everything was as it had been two years before, and peace truly meant *peace*, instead of merely the beginning of a long and difficult journey back to normalcy. For the kingdom, and for himself.

"A crown for your thoughts, sire," said a rasping voice.

Erik's mouth twisted sourly. Somehow, he was not surprised to find Alix's spy skulking among his roses. "If you wish to have authorised access to the royal gardens, you need only ask."

"And pass up the chance to test my sneaking skills? Besides,

I would not be much use as a spy if my face were known to every man and woman at court."

"That ship has most likely sailed, as the Onnani saying goes. You were paraded before half the city as a traitor."

The spy shrugged. "They will forget me in a few months. I have one of those faces."

"Perhaps," Erik said. "Still, I owe you a debt. You did your best to save my brother from my madness, and in return I nearly took your head. If there is anything I can do to reward your loyalty . . ."

"Someday, perhaps. In the meantime, I thought you might be in the market for a skilled set of eyes and ears, what with Gedonan politics in such disarray. These are dangerous times, and I have strong networks abroad."

Erik frowned. "You are already employed."

"By a great many people, to be sure. And my first loyalty is to my lady of Blackhold. But I presume your interests shall rarely, if ever, diverge."

"You may be sure of that, spy." Now more than ever, that truth was the anchor to which all else in Erik's world was moored.

"In that case, Your Majesty"—the man bowed low—"you may call me Saxon."

"Back early?" Liam said, tossing a book aside as Alix walked through the door.

"What are you . . . ?" She froze in her tracks. "Are you *reading*?"

"That's fantastic, Allie. Try to sound a little more surprised."

"Sorry, it's just . . . I don't think I've ever seen you with a book." She glanced down at the discarded volume. "*An Illustrated History of Harram*?"

"It has pictures," Liam said solemnly.

Laughing, Alix tossed herself into a chair, not even bothering to remove her armour. Rudi came over, nub wagging, for a scratch behind the ears.

"And how's our good king today?" Liam asked.

"Cheeky. He mocked me for being . . . *unavailable* . . . these past few evenings."

Liam winced. "Awkward. Do you suppose people are talking about it?"

"I really don't care," Alix said, and was half surprised to find that she meant it. "If it pleases people to imagine us in our marriage bed, they're welcome to it."

"Someone's in a sprightly mood."

"I had a good day. *We* had a good day. He's doing so much better, Liam. He's even talking about having a tournament, if we can find the coin. Part celebration, part distraction."

Liam hummed thoughtfully, sliding into the oversized chair beside her. "Not a bad idea. People could use some cheer, that's for sure. It might even be a good way to help identify some new recruits for the Wolves."

"Are you worried? About finding new recruits, I mean."

"A little. I'm not keen on filling out our ranks with squires and stableboys, especially now that I've lost so many experienced officers."

"A pity Rona resigned. I wonder why? She seemed to be doing so well. Perhaps she feels she's needed at Brownhold."

"Could be." Liam looked away, fidgeting with his discarded book.

Alix picked it up and thumbed through the pages. "Learn anything interesting?"

She expected a gibe, but Liam's tone was unexpectedly contemplative. "Quite a few things, actually. Did you know the Onnani and Harrami are meant to be distant relatives?"

"I've heard that theory, yes." It was possible, she supposed—it would explain the skin colour, and why neither race could grow beards.

"I think I'd like to see it someday. Harram, I mean. Do you think you'd ever be willing to go back?"

"I'm not sure I would, frankly. But it doesn't much matter anyway—I don't think a member of the royal family could visit Harram anytime soon with things as they are between Erik and Omaïd."

"Onnan, then. Wouldn't you like to see the ocean? They say everyone should see it at least once."

Alix regarded her husband with a bemused smile. "Why the sudden thirst for travel?"

"Not sure," he admitted, shrugging. "I guess it's never

really been an option for me before. Now that the war is over, it feels like we should experience the world a little."

She sighed. "The war might be over, but these are still dangerous times to be abroad. The largest empire on the continent has just collapsed. It's hard to predict what comes next."

"I guess we'll just have to be ready for anything, then, won't we?"

"Yes," Alix said, leaning back into the cradle of her husband's arms. "I suppose we will."

GLOSSARY

THE KINGDOM OF ALDEN
CAPITAL: Erroman

Feudal monarchy, ruled by the Whites since the disintegration of the Erromanian Empire more than four centuries ago. Aldrich the White, claiming descent from the royal bloodline of Erroman, fought a brutal campaign to unite what was left of the empire, founding the Kingdom of Alden and naming it after himself. He awarded his closest ally, Konrad, a banner of green silk. This historic event marked the foundation of the Banner Houses; forever more, Konrad's descendants would be known as the Greens. Since then, only four more banners have been awarded—Black, Grey, Brown, and Gold.

King Erik White
Prince Liam White (commander of the White Wolves)
Prince Tomald White (deceased)
Rodrik White

Riggard Black (banner holder, commander general of the king's armies)
Alix Black (bodyguard to the king)

Raibert Green (banner holder)
Arran Green (deceased)

Alithia Grey (banner holder)
Sirin Grey
Roswald Grey (deceased)

Rona Brown (banner holder, White Wolf)
Aina Brown
Adelbard Brown (deceased)

Norvin Gold (banner holder)

THE TRIONATE OF ORIDIA
CAPITAL: Varadast

Theocracy ruled by a triumvirate, fiercely committed to expansion in the name of religious conversion. The King is said to be a living god (Varad), whose soul is reborn through millennia. When his mortal body dies, Varad's soul passes exactly one year in the heavens before being reincarnated as a newborn baby. It is the Priest, appointed by his peers, who identifies the reincarnated Varad, assembling all male children born on the designated day and subjecting them to various tests until he is certain he has recognised the anointed one. The Warlord earns his place through victory in battle and single combat.

The King, Varad (deceased)
The Priest, Madan (deceased)
The Warlord, Sadik

THE REPUBLIC OF ONNAN
CAPITAL: Onnan City

Democratic republic. Political parties, known as *leagues*, are elected by district, each district being represented by a speaker. The league with the most seats is said to be *in power*, its leader becoming First Speaker. Most speakers are also priests, reflecting the deep religious convictions of Onnani society. However, it is said that the real power lies with the secret societies, most of which were founded as underground revolutionary movements during the time of the empire, when the Onnani were enslaved by the Erromanians. The slave revolt—known in Onnan as the Great Revolution—marked the beginning of the end of the empire.

First Speaker Kar (Worker's Alliance)
Chairman Irtok (Worker's Alliance)
Defence Consul Welin (Worker's Alliance)
Speaker Syril (People's Congress)

THE KINGDOM OF HARRAM
CAPITAL: Ost

Feudal monarchy, ruled by His High Lordship King Omaïd. Protected on all sides by mountains, sea, and arctic, Harram holds itself aloof of affairs on the wider continent of Gedona. While politics are generally stable, Ost has never been able to extend effective control over the mountain tribes, whom it views as savages. Because of its imposing geographical barriers, Harram was the only kingdom never to succumb to Erromanian rule, though it did play an important role in the empire's demise. The mountain tribes are generally credited with dealing the death blow to the empire, uniting for the first (and last) time in history to sack Erroman more than four hundred years ago.

THE KINGDOM OF ANDITHYRI
CAPITAL: Timra

Feudal monarchy, ruled by King Berendt until his execution by the Warlord, now under the stewardship of Governor Arkenn of the Trionate. Andithyrians claim direct descent from the Erromanian nobility. During Erromanian times, the so-called purebloods were easily distinguished by their white hair; when the empire collapsed, this trait became deadly, marking them out for reprisals as chaos gripped the former empire. The imperial race fled in droves, founding their own small country on the southern border of modern-day Alden. To this day, most Andithyri have white hair, though this is slowly changing over time due to intermarriage. Andithyri is the most recent country to fall to the Trionate of Oridia, but rumours have begun to stir of an underground resistance movement.

THE NINE VIRTUES

RAHL (STRENGTH) SYMBOL: the sun. Also associated with power, leadership.

OLAN (COURAGE) SYMBOL: the moon. Also associated with determination.

ELDORA (WISDOM) SYMBOL: the all-seeing eye. Also associated with temperance, experience.

DESTAN (HONOUR) SYMBOL: the ram. Also associated with duty, integrity.

FARIKA (GRACE) SYMBOL: folded hands. Also associated with mercy.

ARDIN (PASSION) SYMBOL: the flame. Also associated with impetuousness, boldness.

HEW (WIT) SYMBOL: the crow. Also associated with guile, cleverness.

GARVIN (EMPATHY) SYMBOL: tears. Also associated with solidarity, generosity.

GILENE (FAITH) SYMBOL: the star. Also associated with devotion, truth.

Erin Lindsey, author of the Bloodbound series, including *The Bloodbound*, *The Bloodforged*, and *The Bloodsworn*, is on a quest to write the perfect summer-vacation novel, with just the right blend of action, heartbreak, and triumph. She lives in Brooklyn with her husband and a pair of half-domesticated cats. Visit her online at erin-lindsey.com, facebook.com/ELTettensor, and twitter .com/ETettensor.

Also from

Erin Lindsey

THE BLOODBOUND
A BLOODBOUND NOVEL

A cunning and impetuous scout, Alix only wishes to serve quietly on the edges of the action. But when the king is betrayed by his own brother and left to die at the hands of attacking Oridian forces, she winds up single-handedly saving her sovereign.

Suddenly, she is head of the king's personal guard, an honor made all the more dubious by the king's exile from his own court. Surrounded by enemies, Alix must help him reclaim his crown, all the while attempting to repel the relentless tide of invaders led by the Priest, most feared of Oridia's lords.

But while Alix's king commands her duty, both he and a fellow scout lay claim to her heart. And when the time comes, she may need to choose between the two men who need her most…

erin-lindsey.com
facebook.com/ELTettensor
twitter.com/ETettensor
penguin.com